Sarah's Song

James W. Mimbs

ThomasMax

TM

Your Publisher
For The 21st Century

Acknowledgments

I especially appreciate the efforts of my coterie of astute readers. These readers include Karen Bair, Barbara Duffey, Bunny Marshall, Sarah Gordon and Joseph Hodge. Among my most acerbic and demanding critics was Daniel Jenkins who, from the comfort of his hammock in Mayaguez, Puerto Rico, pummeled me with questions and (sometimes) legitimate demands for revision. Alas, he was also my primary advocate for pushing the envelope of both excellence and impropriety. Marti Moody spent many hours in painfully perfecting the manuscript. Lee Clevenger, my publisher, has been most helpful in his role as a champion and supporter of first-time novelists, and that includes me.

Sarah's Song

Thanks for your early encouragement!

Fondly, Jim

ISBN-13: 978-0-9914332-7-8
ISBN-10: 0-9914332-7-0

First printing, May, 2015

Cover design by ThomasMax

Published by:

ThomasMax Publishing
P.O. Box 250054
Atlanta, GA 30325
Website: thomasmax.com

For all the Sarahs of the world
whether mute or eloquent
who remain unbowed,
unvanquished

About the Author

James W. Mimbs M.D. is both a psychiatrist and cardiologist who held distinguished academic appointments on medical school faculties in Missouri (Washington University) and Georgia (Mercer University). Although he has published over 125 scientific articles, he has found his previously published poetry as equally exhilarating despite having been hounded and bitten at the heels by James Dickey as an interloper (invited) in Mr. Dickey's creative writing class. Jim's range of vocations from working in a peach canning factory, as a weaver in a woolen mill, a psychiatric aide (while at Emory), and over twenty years as a mechanic and automotive restorer has provided him with a rich and varied exposure to his fellow man and woman in an unusual variety of settings. His long hours with clients in psychotherapy and his efforts to help steer many through their heartaches and headaches have provided him with another unusual vein of observation. *Sarah's Song* is his first novel after many years as a physician and poet.

Escaping the Devil's Dirt

Sarah Sewell awoke before dawn on the first day of June 1976. It was a Saturday morning of mists with a predawn silence not yet interrupted by the calls of crows planning their day and the impatient chirping of wrens. She reasoned that this, the first day of school's summer recess, would be the morning she would have to escape. As she would soon say to her Aunt Sallie, "I was afraid if he caught me, I'd be beaten half to death trying to flee that devil and the dirt he had already put in my body."

To say that the Sewells lived in poverty was to understate the plight of a family that stumbled from week to week in the stifling grasp of a father whose anger was fueled by his alcoholism and in the frigid embrace of a mother who inhaled fear and exhaled indifference. As a third-generation coal miner, Sarah's father was accustomed to the tedium of a life spent five days a week in the mines of West Virginia, a tedium broken only by his liquor-fueled delusions and the false bravado of his rages. Centered above the living room fireplace was a hand-lettered plaque that read: *The Onliest Rules Is My Rules.*

Sarah had been born sixteen years earlier on the wide-planked pine table in this kitchen attended by a toothless midwife and, strangely, Sarah's older brother, Ben. The only doctor in town had been called finally to deliver Sarah from what the midwife had called breech blockage. When Doctor Allison arrived, he turned the infant's head with the forceps he had used for thirty years, delivered her and quickly suctioned the struggling baby. The midwife yelled that Sarah's mother was bleeding, beseeching the doctor to give Sarah's care to Ben who had also witnessed the birth and helped in the bathing of Jacob, who was now one year old. In the middle of this chaos, Mr. Sewell, being a man who did not like the sight of blood and who also was sipping sporadically from a half-pint of bourbon, had quickly left the room, leaned against the rail of the front porch and rolled a cigarette.

Doctor Allison, although almost sixty, had volunteered for a two-year tour in Viet Nam six years earlier, partly out of boredom and partly to escape a divorce that had surprised him. Between the torn bodies he triaged and treated in those jungles and the impoverished patients he treated in the mine-scarred hills of West Virginia, he had seen it all. He was surprised that Sarah survived because his attention at the time had to be devoted primarily to Sarah's mother, whose uterus had prolapsed as she lay bleeding on the table. Doctor Allison knew that the only remote possibility of Mrs. Sewell's survival depended upon his attempting a hysterectomy with only intravenous Valium and a can of ether. Otherwise, she would bleed to death. He tied Mrs. Sewell to the table with strips of a sheet, slipped two pillows under her, laced an intravenous line into her left arm and threatened Mr. Sewell with condemning him as a coward to the community if he did not come inside and hold his wife's legs. He deputized the midwife as his scrub nurse and complimented her for how efficiently she wielded both a speculum and a retractor. In this primitive way, not unlike surgery at the turn of the century, he deftly completed the hysterectomy.

Sarah's father liked to tell the story of how Doctor Allison had snapped off his gloves and said to the midwife, "Just like my first one as a resident except that one took two hours instead of fifteen minutes. Let's thank the Lord and Valium and a touch of ether for keeping her fairly quiet." Of course, Mr. Sewell advertised himself as the hero who had so valiantly and efficiently restrained his wife and made the life-saving surgery possible. Doctor Allison helped Mr. Sewell carry his wife to their car for the thirty-mile trip to the hospital in Petersburg. "She'll need a couple units of blood, transfusions I mean, and to be started on strong antibiotics. They'll probably keep her a few days to check on the bleeding and infection. Anyway, I'll call them and tell them you're on the way. It'll be a lot faster than waiting on some damn ambulance," he concluded as he closed the large medical suitcase he carried for house calls.

Although Doctor Allison was given a cured ham and sack of potatoes, he would be revered forever as an angel of deliverance in the eyes of Mrs. Sewell. This was especially true since her husband soon came to regard her as "a woman as barren as that briar patch by the road and not worthy of none of my attentions," saving his ardor instead for the prostitutes in Petersburg. And so, indeed, Sarah had been born into a cauldron of chaos and dropped into the dirt-poor desperation of a coal mining family in the raw hills of Appalachia. As she would say later, "It weren't all fun but I learnt survival skills in a hurry."

But on this morning of mists and tentative silence, now sixteen years later, Sarah awoke in her room, a room haphazardly added to the back of their tar-paper-and-shingled shack. On Sarah's thirteenth birthday her mother had taken a rare stand for propriety and declared to her husband, "It just ain't fittin' for all three younguns to still be sleepin' in the same room with her comin' into womanhood and all." The room itself was built by her two brothers under the sporadic and drunken supervision of their father and with scraps of lumber taken from a dilapidated house half a mile down the gravel road. The boys laughed as they stuffed newspaper, rags, and old clothes between the clapboard frame and the interior walls made not of sheetrock but of doubled pieces of cardboard from refrigerator boxes.

Ben looked at his sister and said, "When that wind starts to howlin' like a hoot owl, you gone be comin' back to us boys' room, sister." Sarah knew she would never return to that room and wrote her beloved Aunt Sallie, for whom she was named, asking for a lock for her door and a small propane heater, both of which had been refused by her father. She got both before the first frost.

For three years since its completion and though indeed cold in winter and with its tin roof creating a virtual sauna in summer, this room had been Sarah's retreat and her favorite place to read and study if she could not be in the nearby woods or beside the creek bordering their two acres. Ben, six years older than Sarah, had no aptitude for school and failed the seventh grade. Halfway through his second mostly futile attempt at grade seven, he had been removed by their father for what was termed reasons of family hardship. Of course, their father had a plan, which was to move Ben next door to a small adjoining ten-acre vegetable farm that had been left to the family by a recently deceased uncle.

Ben was joined a month later by a mule, three hogs, four laying hens, and a rooster. It was this farm and Mrs. Sewell's canning of vegetables along with the daily eggs that sustained the family, especially through the hard winters. Jacob, only a year older than Sarah, and Sarah both enjoyed school and were dutifully placed on the school bus each morning by their mother despite the objections of their father who saw any academic endeavor as an excuse to avoid work on the family farm. They excelled, especially in high school, each recognized as the best student in his or her respective grade in the county high school fifteen miles away. Sarah found more than an escape in school. She found a universe of discovery and especially liked writing essays about American history and unnecessarily long book reports for her English classes. In addition to her assignments, she would also read at least a book each week from a library bus that came weekly to the school from Petersburg. Although she and Jacob were required to help Ben with the hard labor of the vegetable farm both after school and on some weekends, she relished her nights of quiet reading in this, her very own room.

And it was in this same bedroom on a certain Saturday night in early May, one month after her sixteenth birthday, that Sarah lay in her bed reading by the light of an old goose-neck lamp when she heard a rustling outside her locked door and then watched silently as the door knob turned. A single loud thump from a boot dislodged the sliding steel lock, tearing it from the wooden doorframe. Her father, whose acrid breath wreaked of liquor and whose unwashed body smelled like a sour towel, took three quick strides toward her bed and leaned toward her face. Before he spoke, she noticed the peculiar odor of an after-shave lotion. And she knew that this was something he used only when visiting one of the prostitutes in Petersburg.

"My little princess, so sweet and pretty, is gittin' her a little learnin' is she?" he asked.

"Daddy, don't mess with me."

"Princess, I don't want no trouble out of you and no screamin' for your momma, or I'll have to hurt you both."

"Daddy, I'm beggin' you not to do something you'll regret."

"Regret, hell. I been takin' care of you for nigh on sixteen years, watchin' you ripen right under my nose, even built you this here private room when you was startin' to blossom. And now it's time we christened you into womanhood. I might've been drinkin' tonight in town but I gots plenty of spunk in me and your momma don't want none of it. She's just about as dried up as a old prune. Instead of visitin' Louella earlier, I saved myself for you, little precious."

She pushed him away twice, scratched his face and neck, but finally he placed his big paw of a hand against her throat long enough that his face became gray and hazy instead of the blood-red it really was. The bare bulb in her lamp seemed to emit an eerie glow, quickly becoming indistinct, almost disappearing. She had fainted once before and she knew this was how it felt. He loosened his grip. Sarah relented and turned toward the wall, avoiding his eyes and his breath. She grabbed each side of her mattress, burying her nails in the soft ticking. She tried to relax her lower body, to let it be somewhere else. It was then she noticed one of the first sounds of the spring that had arrived earlier that year than anyone could remember. The repetitive thrumming of newly emerged frogs after a week of warm days and the recent rains seemed to fill the night. Their cadence was soothing, an elegy for the hell she was enduring as though the night and its shadows, its soft sounds, its secretive creatures, were already weeping for her.

"Now that's my girl. Just relax with it. I always knowed you was gone be good just by the way you'd cut yo' eyes at folks, 'specially boys," her father said.

Sarah drifted, even dreamily seeing herself as transported by these sounds of the night, as though all the world had ceased its ineluctable rotation and that she, like the small ceramic ballerina that pirouetted about the top of her Aunt Sallie's old German music box, was lost too in dance. That despite the slapping sound of the grunting mass leaning over her, she was at least in her soul untouchable and safe, turning about some static axis as though nothing else in the world existed except her imagined dance and the dance of the pirouetting ballerina, now as one. Drifting in the solitude she remembered when she would visit her Aunt Sallie for several weeks each summer, she thought of the song that wafted from the old music box. And then, she began to hum this song, the rhythm of "The Dance of the Sugar Plum Fairy," lost still in this land of dreamy unreality for how could this be happening to her, now or ever, this night, any night.

When suddenly her father groaned, arched his back and thrust with all his force into her, she was shocked from her dream. She screamed, reclaimed her body and pulled herself free from him. She gagged, turned her head and vomited onto the planked floor.

"Damn you was good, but now you tryin' to ruin it for me," he said and drew back his hand but did not slap her.

In five minutes it was over but of course it would never be over. The next morning, Sarah burned the stained sheet in the woods. She did not cry. She made a plan. She did not bother to replace the lock on her door because she did not think her father would return again, that he had gotten what he had come for. On Monday, she returned to school where she removed two small paring knives from the school lunchroom when no one was looking. At home, she sat with her family for meals, never looking at her father. She answered the questions her mother and brothers asked in a terse manner. She told them that this last month of the school year was critical because of her final exams. And then she would excuse herself immediately after their meals, retreating to the now spoiled sanctuary of her room. Of course, everyone knew. How would they not have heard the thunderous clap of her father's boot on the door to her room that night? But everyone was complicit in the denial of her violation.

Two weeks later, again on a Saturday night, she watched as that same door handle turned slowly and she knew then that she was wrong, that she had underestimated her father's deranged ardor. She did not speak and perhaps in the dimmed light he thought she was asleep. Lying in bed, she waited for him to remove his pants and underwear which he let fall slowly to the floor as though this, the seductive dance of a buffoon, might make him more attractive. He then removed his denim shirt and in his now clumsy exuberance ripped a button from one sleeve. Sarah lay calmly in bed beneath her blanket, gripping a paring knife tightly in each hand. She breathed slowly as Jacob had taught her in the woods while hunting squirrels. Breathe calmly, she remembered, breathe calmly, then exhale slowly before you squeeze the trigger.

As he leaned toward her, she pushed herself up so that she was suddenly standing at the head of her bed. She made two swift, sweeping thrusts. She drove the first knife into his left forearm as he reached for her, and almost simultaneously pierced the meat of his right shoulder with the second knife with such force that her body torqued from the bed. Now, standing next to him, she twisted each blade, exhaling with a cool and satisfying determination.

"Hello, Daddy," she said as his scream ripped through the still cool late spring night.

"Good God, girl, you have done cut your Daddy," he yelled as he stood naked except for his undershirt that was wet with his expectant sweat and yellowed beneath the hair of his armpits.

"If you don't get your clothes and get out of here this instant, I will cut you on your face where everybody can see it. And it won't be a scratch you can lie about like last time, but a nice long cut" Sarah said, looking down at her father who was bending to gather his clothes.

"Look here at this bloody shirt I'm puttin' on fast as I can, girl. You ain't no princess, you a bitch from hell's what you are."

"I am five feet, nine inches tall, taller than Jacob and almost as tall as Ben. I am strong from working on the farm and I am also smart. Nobody will ever do to me again what you did when you defiled me. Now if you don't get on out, I promise I'll try to kill you even if I burn in hell."

A week later, when Sarah completed the last day of the tenth grade, having made all A's except for a B in chemistry, she returned home from school. In her room, her bag (an old Purina seed bag) was already packed and hidden under her bed. The bag contained a plain black winter dress and a summer gingham dress, a pair of men's Red Camel overhauls that she wore when working on the farm, three sets of undergarments, the tortoise comb her mother had given her for her thirteenth birthday, a small compact and mirror from Aunt Sallie, six strips of beef jerky, a loaf of bread, two canteens of water, six Milky Way candy bars, and a worn paperback copy of "Jane Eyre." The next morning before daybreak, the morning of mists and silence about which we speak, she heated a pan of water on top of her propane heater and bathed from the tin basin in her room. She then placed four sealed envelopes on her bed.

Dear Jacob,
You are cursed to be a son in this family
but there is nothing you can do about that.
What you can do is use that good brain
and work your way through college
or go to a vocational school to get a trade
because you deserve a better life than this.
It could be, Jacob, that I may never
see you again because I aim to start
a new life for myself and I hope also
to regain some self respect for myself,
But I want you to always remember
that I love you and will pray for you.
Your loving sister,
Sarah

* * * * *

Dear Ben,
You are a good potato farmer
and that's likely all you will ever be.
I have gotten strong working for you
but you sure gave Jacob and me a hard time.
You have your daddy's meanness and
our momma's meekness, and that makes
for a very bad combination. Perhaps
you can find yourself a good woman
who can maybe tolerate you
and then you can try to make
a life of your own someday.
Your sister,
Sarah

* * * * *

My dear pitiful Momma,
I am sorry your life has turned out to be
such a sad tale, such a lost life, but I guess
that is what God or somebody dealt you,
like a bad hand of cards, I mean.
My hope for you is that you
will someday stand up for yourself
like you stood up for me that time
you got them to build me my room.
But that didn't work out very well
and I think you know why.
With a little love and a lot of sadness I leave you,
Sarah

* * * * *

Dear Daddy,
If you come after me or send anyone after me,
you will regret it. I can prove what you did
to me as I am carrying it inside me.
I hope you burn in hell for the way
you have treated me, my momma,
and Ben and Jacob. You are truly
the most vile and soulless scum
the devil ever let loose on this earth
if you aren't the devil your own self.
Remember just one thing beginning today:
I will find a way to avenge the evil
you have cast upon me, believe me I will.
Not your princess (or anybody else's),
Sarah

Sarah Speaks of Safety and Solace

Now I don't think I'm special just because my daddy raped me. And everybody knows that in that hollow where I have grown up—so wide you couldn't holler across it—that kind of thing likely happened more than people knew, or at least would admit. The reason a girl couldn't talk about it was that she would get a thrashing from the old man, and her brothers too if she had any, that she wouldn't forget. That was on top of already being defiled. So it didn't get talked about. "Grin and bear it" was what I heard one of the older girls at school say to her best friend when it happened to her. When I walked out of my little room into the mists beginning to lift from that valley even before the sun had burnt them off, I knew one thing for sure. I knew that I wasn't never going back to that hellhole. I might leave my goodbye notes but I was gone. Gone forever.

You might say I had two things in my mind. One was to escape clean and free, and the other thing was to make something of myself if I could just get a few lucky breaks. It was just that simple. I knew that if I could make it to my Aunt Sallie's house, and I figured I could walk the six miles in two hours, that I'd be safe. For one thing, Daddy would be sleeping late after his Friday-night drunk, and Momma and Jacob knew to leave me alone in the mornings if we weren't going to have to work on the farm. And I thought my note to Daddy would scare him just enough, I mean by making him think I was pregnant. That way, he wouldn't get the boys and come after me. Of course, gettin' the old '62 Ford Galaxie cranked was another thing in my favor because you never knew about it — would it or wouldn't it, crank I mean.

So I walked with my old seed bag, which got heavier by the mile, until I got to the rutted driveway that snaked its way to Aunt Sallie's dogtrot house. I don't know why it's called that except if it was summer and the screen doors was open at both ends of the middle hallway then her old dog could trot down it without hardly even breaking stride. When I could see the corner of the front porch, I could also see the curl of smoke from her small kitchen chimney and I knew she was cooking a late breakfast. As backwoods as we all was, she was the only person who still cooked on a old green and white porcelain wood-fed stove. She said that slow cooking, like with her wood-burning stove, caused the seasoning to seep into the vegetables better and the gravy get in the meat better. At the same time I'm straining with my old bag, her ancient hound Bingo either heard or smelled me. He started in whooping up a storm as he pawed open the screen door and ran toward me.

"Come here to me, Bingo. You don't see me much but let's see if you smell a relation," I said as I showed him the back of my hand. And for the first time I felt free, free of the sin that had been visited on me but mainly free of fear. Because I knew that what my daddy had done to me I'd never let happen again. But more than that, I knew that if he tracked me down and I had to, as mad and hurt as I was, I would kill him. So now I had to figure out what to do about this hatred in my heart, not to mention how I also despised my momma for her cowardice and even had pretty hard feelings for both my brothers. Like they say on TV and the radio, they were accessories to the crime visited on me by being silent. I'm talkin' about that next morning at the breakfast table when there was stone silence except for the hum of my hatred and humiliation. This was louder in my ears than that chorus of frogs I had turned into that soothing song from Aunt Sallie's music box.

Aunt Sallie came out on the porch and called my name, so I put down my old seed bag and ran to her as fast as I could. Despite her bony arms and long, spidery fingers, it was an embrace I'll never forget. "Well child, you've growed another three inches since last summer. I reckon them tall genes come from your daddy," she said, her voice like a God-send to my ears.

I didn't want to speak. I just wanted her to keep on holding me. And come to think of it, it was the first time I had touched another human being since that night my daddy had his way with me. Somehow, she sensed my need for being comforted. Not only did she keep holding me tight but she patted my back, almost like you do a baby's to console it or to help it go to sleep. And all this came from Aunt Sallie who hadn't had any children at all. She made no secret that she regarded most men as one step above trash and was her own self sworn to what she called "my own brand of flowering freedom." Among my teachers and my classmates' mommas, I had never known any woman who could live so alone and be so independent. She didn't need nobody for nothing.

"Well, come on in Sarah and tell me about that worthless scoundrel of a brother of mine and your momma and the boys too. And, first of all, what in God's name are you doing walkin' with a big old seed sack when you always come each summer delivered up in that old piece-of-shit Ford?"

"I'm on the run I guess you could say. So if you get a phone call from the folks, deny that I'm here. And if I could have a little of that breakfast I smell, smells like you're frying country ham, we'll settle down and I'll take the whole day to tell you what has happened to me and why I'm escaping that hellhole."

I guess I could describe that day as one of the best of my life. I told her first about the situation — all right, what I mean is being raped by my own daddy and then him meaning to do it again when I cut him. She wanted to know if I could be pregnant and I told her no, that I had gotten my period two days ago. I told her about the notes I left and that I would never go back, and that the only vague remorse I felt was leaving Jacob. But then he hadn't been much of a brother to me when it really counted. We went on a long walk in the late afternoon and lay down on a little bed of moss next to the creek. Once, when things got real quiet, she reached over and held my hand and when she did, I started bawling like a baby.

And I thought that this must be what heaven is like if there is one. On the one hand, I was free but still captured by the memory of what had happened to me. But on the other hand, here I was, nestled up against the warmth of Aunt Sallie, the wood smoke in her shirt and the hint of that pink powder on her neck. I must have cried for twenty minutes because I just couldn't stop. It was enough to wet the whole top of her red-and-green flannel shirt, the kind she wore year round whether it was hot or cold. She didn't say a word the whole time, but just let me snuggle up next to her.

After I settled down, I told her how at school I had looked at different towns on maps where I might escape to, and that I had decided on Hamilton Hills up in Pennsylvania. The place was big enough to get lost in, even a young teenage girl, but not so big as to be scary. I liked the sound of Hamilton Hills because of how it rolled off my tongue and I just hoped it would be a friendly place. I knew I wasn't about to go to some old big city and be swallowed alive. And I told her how I had read in the library about the different churches and my plan to see if one of the preachers knew somebody who might take me in for the summer or at least find me a place to live while I got a job.

The best way to describe our day together is that I felt joined to her not at the hip like people say sometimes but joined at the heart. I mean even before what happened to me that night at home, I really didn't have anyone to talk to. My girl friends were all from families just like mine, making it from week to week. They was usually put to work at home except when they went to school and, even worse, likely would end up married to some old worthless boy like Ben who would treat them more like a slave than a wife. A life of hell in that hollow and it went on forever and ever, all but hopeless. But more than that, I thought how sweet it would've been if only my own momma had ever in her life just once listened to me or talked to me in some serious way. Somehow, as bad as everything still was, I had some glimmer of hope. I might be defiled but I was alive. I had always been a fighter and my day for revenge would still come.

Aunt Sallie asked about school, how had I done in my courses. I told her that Jacob and I both made the best grades in our two classes and that I loved my reading, literature as the teachers liked to call it, more than anything else. I told her too how I had started playing basketball, had a real knack for it, shooting and rebounding, and that I had also won the 100 yard dash and the 220 over all the girls in school. But the school was too poor to have a track team. So we 'bout covered it all, you could say. After Aunt Sallie made up my little single bed in what she called the guest bedroom that was about as big as a closet, it seemed like she didn't want the day to be over.

"Sarah, come sit by me for a few minutes before I show you my new blankets and shawls. What I mainly want to say to you is that hatred and revenge will eat you up if you let them. They're like twin snakes in your heart feeding off each other. Now I don't blame you for wanting to right the wrong your daddy did, for getting revenge any way you can. He stole something sacred from you that can't never be given back. But try not to let it control how you feel about other men and boys. In my case, I've never had no use for them. I truly believe I was born that way, was a tomboy growing up, never had a date or wanted one. I got kissed by a girl in gym class when I was a senior in high school, sort of liked it, but decided right then that I'm gone make it by myself and I have. But I don't need much and I git plenty of lovin' from Bingo, sometimes more than I need. But what I'm trying to say is that you are nothing like me. You're tall, pretty, loveliest locks of hair I've ever seen. Why, how many girls with coal-black hair and sky-blue eyes do you even know? But even more important is your brain, girl. Between that and your gumption, you can make something of yourself. You know how persimmon tastes, how it gives you bad breath and leaves a bitter aftertaste. Well, don't be breathin' no persimmon breath on everybody the rest of your life because you're hurtin'. You're still grievin' for yourself but whether you heal or not is gone be up to you."

"Aunt Sallie, you know how I've always respected you and how my two weeks with you every summer, they was the highlight of my summers. I've always looked up to you because you're like that old Frank Sinatra song on the radio called 'I Did it My Way,' and you sure have done it all your way. Today has had some of everything. We've laughed and cried, held and been held, but just having you listen to me was the best thing of all. And as bad as things have been, I think it's probably the best day of my life."

"Well, honey, let's lighten up before we go to bed and let me show you my handiwork. You know I spend all winter gettin' ready for the summer craft fairs, July Fourth, Labor Day and all. I still use my old Singer sewing machine and now I got a heavy-duty new one too. What I want to do is get a weaving loom and one of them real fast sewing machines from Italy, then I'd sure be ready to roll. I got them books with pictures and patterns of blankets from the old days, like back in the eighteen and nineteen hundreds. I used a bunch of new colors and patterns this year but, truth be told, I can almost sell out with my repeat customers because them blankets, they's so much in demand," Aunt

Sallie said with pride. "And when you leaves in the morning with Mr. Malpass who I called earlier, you ain't gone be carrying no Purina sack, girl. Your stuff will be in my big old leather suitcase and I'm giving you two thin quilts and two shawls to carry so you can sell them for some seed money if you need to while you're looking for a job."

Because she hated driving except when she had to, Aunt Sallie had arranged for her neighbor, Mr. Malpass, to drive me all the way to Hamilton Hills. My only condition when I talked to him was that he let me out somewhere about half way to Hamilton Hills because I had it in my head that, before Mr. Malpass, I was goin' to hitchhike the whole way. It was sort of like my own version of a freedom march, but just me marchin' though. I slept like a rock until I heard a mockingbird singing her songs not long after daybreak. Aunt Sallie, already dressed, had already started her cooking fire in the old stove. After breakfast, we heard Mr. Malpass's truck in the front yard and we all trundled out to meet him, me loaded down with Aunt Sallie's leather suitcase that had all my things and the shawls too. And Aunt Sallie was right behind me carrying the blankets all bundled up tight.

She kissed me goodbye with tears in her eyes and said, "You can always come on back here if you needs a haven to retreat to, Sarah. You know you've always had a big place in my heart 'cause you the closest thing I got to a daughter. Now don't sell them blankets too cheap 'cause I been gettin' around two hundred dollars for them. Collector's items they all say, and I have to concede they the best I've ever seen my own self even at the big craft fairs. And listen here, I stayed up late making this banana pudding so be sure you eat it before this afternoon or it'll be spoilt." Unknown to me until later, she had also wrapped her precious German music box with the little fairy queen ballerina inside one of the shawls with a note attached to it that read: It saved you once and it might save you again.

Finding a New Home

Sarah asked Mr. Malpass to take her only as far as Elkins so that she could hitchhike the final hundred miles. He reminded her that Aunt Sallie had paid him to make the entire trip to Hamilton Hills but she said no. "When I was planning my escape from home, I just somehow wanted to make my own way and hitch a ride if the driver looked safe," she told him. Deposited near Elkins, she finished the last of the banana pudding and waited for three hours before a farmer in a faded GMC pickup stopped and offered her a ride. He said he was going only as far as a rural intersection near Phillipi and that would leave her four miles from town, but she decided to take a chance. As she watched the old GMC pickup disappear over the ridge, she soon realized she had made a mistake. She saw only three cars during the next four hours.

None slowed except for an old Jeep with two laughing teenage boys who blew their horn, threw a beer can out of their window, and yelled, "Suck on that, you big old country girl." Sitting beside her old leather bag and bundled quilts, she looked at the darkening sky that signaled the likelihood of rain. She walked back up the road where she had seen an old abandoned barn. She spent a sleepless night among the vestiges of cows and horses, their smells still permeating the old wet straw, and awakening throughout the night to the frightening sprints of scampering rats above her head.

At daybreak, she had a breakfast of beef jerky and bread, then washed her face with water from the last of the canteens. She walked back to the crossroads bemoaning the additional weight of the two blankets. During the next five hours, she counted seven cars and two trucks that passed her without slowing. She was hot and tired, dirty and demoralized. Around one o'clock, a miracle appeared in the form of a Buick station wagon and a family of four.

The mother leaned from the passenger window and said, "Where are you going, honey? You certainly do look worn out." Sarah told her that she had been waiting for hours for a ride and was going to Hamilton Hills in Pennsylvania. She was ecstatic when she heard the woman say, "Well, aren't you the lucky vagabond. We're on the way to Pittsburgh for a week's vacation. So we're driving up through Fairmont and Morgantown, then up I-79. We'll be close to Hamilton Hills, just a short detour off the interstate, and would be happy to deliver you there safely. I would say we just might be the answer to your prayers if you're the praying type."

"Oh, happy day. I'm willing to be whatever you want me to be if you folks could give me a ride. I'm almost at the end of my rope," Sarah shouted.

As they approached Hamilton Hills, Sarah pulled her list of churches from her pocket and asked that she be driven to the Baptist Church on Pine Street. She did not know the word "parsonage," but Aunt Sallie had told her that the minister or priest would probably be living next door to the church, especially if the church should happen to be a Baptist church. As Sarah was saying goodbye and now exhausted from the journey of the past two days, she decided to give one of Aunt Sallie's quilts to the family. The mother refused politely only to have her whining daughter burst into tears. So Sarah bid them farewell and insisted the whimpering little girl at least accept one of the red and purple shawls.

Sarah knocked on the door of a stately white clapboard house next door to the First Baptist Church and was immediately greeted by a tall, sneering older woman who looked like the human version of an ostrich. Sarah asked for Pastor James Smathers, whose name appeared on the church bulletin board in the front courtyard of the church.

"Child, this is not the Baptist parsonage and why do you need to see him anyway?" the tall woman asked as she peered over her rimless glasses and down along the entire length of her long beaked nose.

"I have business with a man of God who might be disposed to welcome me," Sarah said.

"Well, you look like you need to conduct some business with a bathtub instead of with the Lord, young lady."

"Yes ma'am, it's true I'm in the middle of a trying ordeal. I reckon I must smell like the back end of a mule because I've been on the road for two days now, but still and just the same, I'm needing to see the preacher," Sarah reiterated as she looked into the wide foyer lined with old portraits in gilt frames.

"We get your kind coming through all along, especially in summer, but usually not at the very end of the day. They're usually looking for a meal, meaningless work, or a handout of some kind. Sometimes they're surveying the place, probably looking to steal something that wouldn't be missed until the next day. As for Pastor Smathers, he is away for a summer retreat, recharging his batteries as he says. So you probably won't need to be hanging around here for much longer."

"Ma'am, if you could just direct me to the next church here on my list, I won't be bothering you anymore. It says it's the Saint Michael's Episcopal Church on Cedar Street."

Sarah listened carefully, licked the tip of her pencil and wrote the sequence of street names, so foreign to her, then looked at the woman and said, "I'll be moving along now. I sure do appreciate the directions and I'm sorry for your trouble."

She received no response except for the pursed lips and rolling eyes of the woman who dismissed her, saying, "Run along now, miss, and do seek some ablutions, if you will. I'll give Reverend Reid a call to forewarn him you'll be arriving imminently."

As Sarah approached the Episcopal Church anchored elegantly on the crest of a hill, the setting sun on the far side of the church illuminated the old stained glass windows so that each resembled a kaleidoscope of dizzying and abstract colors. She considered this a good omen and said out loud, "Heaven help me, but I bet this is going to be my rainbow, that's what these pretty windows are signifying to me. Now I've just got to see what's at the end of my rainbow."

Walking toward the front door of the church, she saw a tall man motion to her from the adjacent two-story brick house. "Over here, young lady," the resonant voice boomed.

Sarah placed her old leather bag and the bundle of quilts on the ground, reached for her tortoise comb, and removed the ribbon that tied her hair into a ponytail. She paused long enough to smooth her matted hair before proceeding to the front porch where Reverend Alfonse Reid stood. As she approached him, she said, "I know I'm not exactly presentable but at least I'm not a wayward pregnant girl and I'm definitely not looking for charity of any kind. I am in a little bit of a quandary about exactly where I'm going and where I can stay tonight. Being on the road for several days without much sleep hasn't been much fun, but I'll take that to the situation at home I'm running away from. If you can point me in the direction of somewhere I could get cleaned up and have a restful night, I would be most appreciative to you, sir. And, sir, I can do almost any kind of physical work to earn my night's keep."

"Well, that's quite a little speech, and what kind of work do you do? By the way, I am Reverend Alfonse Reid, associated obviously with the church next door. And whom do I have the pleasure of greeting at the end of this rather warm summer day?"

"Thank you, sir, for not sending me immediately along like that other lady while ago did making me feel like some tramp. I am Miss Sarah Sewell, and these callused hands have done it all — work I mean. I've farmed, tended animals, plowed, even cut wood, but I never missed a day of school and made my A grades, well except for a B in that chemistry course. And beneath this matted hair as dirty as a horse's mane is a good head that thinks straight. Show me the job, any job, and I'll get 'er done right for you, no complainin'."

Sarah was invited to come in for a visit by the minister and his childless wife who offered her a cup of tea that she declined in favor of a glass of water. Mrs. Reid then took her on a brief tour of their house, commenting on photographs of her husband at various civic functions. As they entered the den, Mrs. Reid said, "We always make our home open to a stranger in need, especially a young lady, until we can help her find her way. But in your case, I think a good bath would be the order of the day. You look exhausted, child, and I don't know what's in that big old antique bag on the front porch but the patina of the leather is just beautiful. So, let me get you a blouse and some slacks to change into when you finish your bath."

When Sarah saw the bathroom, she exclaimed, "Lord, running water and a toilet too. I'm sure gone smell good in a little while." She bent then to examine the bar of soap, smelled it and added, "Maybe I'm already in heaven."

From the sweat-stained stench of her matted hair materialized the lustrous black tresses that her mother had claimed to be part of their heritage from a Native American grandmother along with their high cheekbones and the rich deep amber tint of their skin. From her father, she had inherited both her height and her strong shoulders and arms that were sculpted too by the long hours of work on Ben's farm. And yet, her hands, though somewhat calloused from working on the farm, were long and delicate like those of a concert pianist but also perfect for dribbling a basketball. She wasn't certain whether her unusual blue eyes came from her father or her mother.

She remembered that Aunt Sallie had once said, "Why, Sarah, eyes like yours are as rare as a blue diamond I saw once in a fancy jewelry store in Petersburg. The man who owned the jewelry store said it was five carats and he hadn't ever had a diamond that expensive, for the mayor's wife on their anniversary he said. He said it was cut like a emerald so you could better see its depth. And when I looked at it, that diamond, I knew what he meant. It was the same blue as a spring I seen once at a salt mine. So, I'd say your eyes look more like that deep blue on your momma's side instead of that blue of the Sewells. You just don't see them so crystal clear, like you can see through to your soul some people say."

And from the dirt-beaded lines of her neck, unwashed during her journey under the smoldering June sun, evolved the erect and elegant profile of a young woman who could pass in another century, another country, as perhaps an Elizabethan lady of privilege. As Sarah stood naked before the full-length mirror mounted on the door of the bathroom, she turned from side to side, touched her breasts, traced the muscles of her arms and legs with a finger, and turned finally to see the tightly sculpted shelf of her hips. She spoke to this image, an image at once breathtaking and frightening because this was the first time she had seen all of herself, "Well, aren't we something sweet to behold, Miss Sarah Sewell."

She entered the kitchen where she heard Reverend Reid and his wife talking and smelled the makings of dinner. "I'm sorry but I don't have no makeup, never have worn any to be truthful because we just didn't have no money for luxuries. Sometimes we didn't even have money for essentials and victuals."

"Why, Sarah, you're a different person and those old blue slacks look better on you than me but your height makes them about two inches too short, I'd say. I suppose we'll simply call them Capri pants, honey. But how beautiful you are, transformed before our eyes," Mrs. Reid said as she reached for a table to steady herself.

"I can't thank you folks enough for takin' me in. At my house, we had an outhouse and the only runnin' water was the cold water we finally got. I would heat water and bathe at my little basin in my room but sometimes I would sneak a sponge bath at school where they did have hot water. Oh what a pleasure that was. That's one reason I went out for the basketball team, I mean when I found out about those hot showers after practice. I have to tell you both though that I still have what I call the devil's dirt on me or in me," Sarah said as she suddenly flushed and tears slipped silently from her eyes.

There was a calm, almost serene silence in the kitchen as Reverend Reid left the room and his wife reached for Sarah's hand. Though Sarah was almost four inches taller, she nestled her head against the warm neck of Mrs. Reid, crying more audibly until her chest began to shudder with sobs like she had felt with her Aunt Sallie. An arthritic but firm and comforting hand slipped beneath her hair and held the back of her head as Sarah murmured, "I just cain't tell it now; don't know if I can ever tell it all, ma'am." Suspended between the raw memories of the last few weeks and now this semblance of sanity, she felt both liberated and still imprisoned, a new almost-woman and a sad and bewildered still-child who cherished the strength of such an embrace.

"Oh, I'm so ashamed for exposin' myself this way to strangers. I guess I'm just exhausted from my walkin' and travelin'. But the other side of it is how free I feel now that I have escaped my daddy's version of hell, if you'll excuse the term. He was such a tyrant, yelling and cursing us every day, only to get worse when he drank on weekends. And that's part of the reason I knew I had to escape or my soul would have decayed to nothing. If you can just put up with me until we can find a place for me to stay, I'll get a job, any kind, and make both of you proud of me. When I say I can do any kind of work, I really do mean it."

"We don't have a rule against expressing feelings in this house,"

Reverend Reid said as he walked back into the kitchen. "And now, Ms. Sarah Sewell, come join us at the table. Prayer is how we start and end our day and celebrate our gifts, whether the breaking of bread or the clothes on our backs, not to mention it may help you with your healing as well although we don't know yet what prompted you to leave your home. Heavenly Father, what is this day but a day of supreme celebration. We come before you now not questioning this God-sent child, this young woman, whom we are pleased to nourish and cherish. She will have much to learn, as will we. Lead us upon this path by your compass and compassion. In Christ's name we pray, Amen."

"Thank you, both of you. I knowed I was takin' a chance by runnin' away from home, if you can call it a home. And I hope that you can help me get placed with some family like I said earlier. I can't say I'm exactly God-fearin' because we didn't go to church much, only had that church of the Jehovah's Witness folks in our little mining town of three hundred poor folks. But I am God-listening. I mean I have a ear for what I call the songs of nature, the birds, the cicadas, the frogs, even the trees that moan when they're caught in the howlin' hard winds of winter. That's where my Lord lives, right in those raw songs of nature. One of my brothers, Jacob, he could hear the same songs, the same language. They've been alive for me since I was a little girl, soulful sounds that excite me and comfort me. And as for here and now, right now, I feel like what I've got is a new start, a gift I couldn't ever have even dreamed of."

"Sarah, we like what we see and hear of you already although someone could say that we don't really know you, but one has a feel for a person who's honest, genuine, or like I say to my parishioners, authentic. So, we will go forth from here and it may be that you can make your home here with us instead of temporarily. Martha and I were talking about that when you walked in for dinner."

"Sir, I don't deserve this."

"You deserve whatever you will work for. And maybe together we will turn the hourglass of time upside down and reset your clock from simply surviving to enjoying the gifts of life. And speaking of sand, we'll also have to work on getting every last particle of what you call the devil's dirt out of your system. Now I'm hungry, so ladies let's enjoy this meal."

The Naiveté of a Young Woman

Sarah Sewell, born into poverty, potatoes, and coal in a pine and tar paper shack, now found herself in the embrace of this childless couple who saw her as a late-life answer to their prayers. Reverend Reid, as she would forever call him, introduced Sarah to the congregation of Saint Michael's as "an exchange student from Appalachia" which sounded certainly more convincing than anything she could think of. As a prominent member of society and the shepherd of arguably the town's most affluent parishioners, he could easily steer her into a new way of living that while initially both foreign and frightening, could change her life forever.

During the second week of her stay, he arranged for her to work at the local McDonalds. As he said, "One of our first goals for you is for you to meet people and to hear their manner of speech, the tones and inflections. Sarah, you've got to admit that there's a little rawness to your use of the English language. You drop the endings from some of your verbs, use 'ain't' and some other slang, and then there is that flat sound you tend to give vowels. I'm not criticizing you because you grew up with it. I just want you to listen, to keep your ear open to the music of language, just as you say you like to listen to what you call the music of nature."

At the end of her first month at McDonalds, she made a deal with Reverend Reid whereby each would pay half the cost of a small television for her room. As usual, she had a plan. She set her alarm for six in the morning and spent several hours before work listening to the cadence and enunciation of the various Pittsburgh announcers.

Although Mrs. Reid enjoyed sitcoms and variety shows, Sarah would retreat to her room in the evening to watch nature programs and interviews. She took seriously what Reverend Reid had said to her about improving her speech.

As the summer progressed and before school was to open in September, Sarah was taken to the high school counselor by Reverend Reid for an interview and testing. She had attended a rural school where the superintendent hired teachers who were notorious for enforcing discipline, rather than encouraging education. This was because students drifted in and out of class at the whims of families who disdained learning and championed manual labor. Sarah's brother, Ben, who had repeated the seventh grade and was removed from school at fourteen, was an example of a family flaunting state laws for what was perceived as the imperative of survival. Despite her impoverished background, Sarah tested 124 on the Stanford Binet IQ profile and could read at an eleventh-grade level. With a sly wink from Reverend Reid and a knowing glance from the principal, it was agreed that she could enter the eleventh grade.

In many ways this conceit, this arrival of Sarah as someone who would become someone else (emerging from the savagery of a childhood she would reveal to only three people in her life, not out of shame as much as from a recalcitrant pride and a determination to vanquish from both body and soul those years of deprivation and abuse), this conceit mirrored the conceit of Hamilton Hills itself. Like so many towns nestled in the southwestern corner of Pennsylvania, the fate of these towns was entwined with the fortunes and fates of the nearby cities. As the market for coal waned or expanded, as steel was needed or not, so would these small towns either thrive or die.

Hamilton Hills was reviled at times by many of its citizens precisely because its fortunes had been so dependent upon the now declining foundries of the nearby cities, most prominently in and around Pittsburgh, and the coal mines to the south and east in West Virginia. And yet this small town of almost ten thousand was celebrated for its beauty in a verdant valley of firs, chestnuts and maples that had been spared the rapacious saws of the early twentieth-century foresters. Ironically, Hamilton Hills had re-invented itself in the image of a quaint, supposedly pre-Revolutionary village, now advertised by the chamber of commerce as having been founded in

1770. This image was more fancied than real, because any reputable historian would or could have revealed the genetic bones of this town for what they truly were. This town had been nothing more than a stagecoach stopover, a watering trough for rogue horse thieves, malodorous mule traders, and mercury-crazed fur tanners. Most of whom were destined for the wilds of Missouri and Iowa and lands farther west. Those lands that were then neither charted, named, nor peopled, at least by squatters of proper European blood. Thus, Hamilton Hills had actually waffled into existence not in 1770 but around 1840, when it assumed its more sophisticated name based upon its matriculation from Hamilton's Crossing (the stagecoach stopover) to Hamilton Hills proper. All the rest was a ruse, a deft sleight of hand by some savvy and prescient businessmen gathered around a table at the chamber of commerce during the depression of the 1930s.

Not unlike her new town, Sarah, though birthed on a hand-hewn kitchen table to a family of failures, was determined to be reborn, recast as a young woman who would not have her dreams denied or fractured. After a faltering start in the eleventh grade and surviving the ridicule of her accent, not to mention her gait ("that girl walks like she knows how to plow a mule"), she quickly learned the rules of this new culture. Her height, because she had grown another two inches over the summer and was now almost five feet, eleven inches, and her agility were noticed immediately by the coaches in her physical education class. Although she had played a year of basketball at her former high school, she was essentially self-taught and knew few of the fundamentals.

A few months later, Sarah told her two new girlfriends, Toni and Meredith, how she remembered those first few weeks: "I'd have to say that from the day I walked into Hamilton Hills High, I felt like a duck out of water. For one thing, I was taller than most of you girls and a lot of the boys because I had grown another two inches over the summer. And I guess, to keep it physical, my broad shoulders and my strong arms and thighs also set me apart. Like a lot of us girls, I wasn't really ashamed of my breasts but I spent more time hiding them, like with a loose shirt or a sweater, than a few of the racier girls did showing them off. But don't let anyone tell you it's fun to go to a new school of any kind in the eleventh grade. The stares and whispers are one thing. But even when someone would come up to me to say hello, I didn't know if they were testing me, teasing me, or just saying hello for heaven's sake.

But beyond physical stuff, where the ox got gored as my momma would say, was that I didn't sound like you two or anybody else. I mean I sounded normal to me, but that wasn't the vibrations I got from most of them and even the two of you at times."

She continued, "Yeah, sure, I had watched TV and I listened at McDonalds to how the others talked, especially when they put me on the drive-through, and I had improved a lot. Like Reverend Reid would keep reminding me, I had gotten better at putting proper endings on my words, especially all those verbs. My 'ises' and 'ares' didn't get as mixed up, meaning my subjects and verbs were getting along much better, thank you. And I had mostly gotten rid of the 'ain'ts' although I still hear that word used a lot by others. The thing that stood out, though, was that flatness or twang to my hillbilly accent. So at first, I was quiet, even bordering on shy, until I decided after about two months, 'To hell with them, especially the smart asses, I'm just going to be me.' That's when I started saying anything I wanted to, mountain accent or not."

"Oh, and like all of us girls, we're always wondering what the boys are thinking. I remember how it stung when that Chapman boy said I walked in long strides like I knew how to plow a mule, which sounded sort of weird because Hamilton Hills probably hasn't seen a mule in twenty or thirty years. So, how would he know? But I think most of the boys just didn't know how to take me at five-feet-eleven especially with my broad shoulders and big hands. They didn't know whether to flirt or fight. And all I was trying to do was just blend in. I didn't have much money for clothes like you two, although the Reids would have bought me anything I wanted or asked for. But I wanted to earn my way, buy my own clothes, which is why I still work at McDonalds on weekends. Well, I do have to admit that being discovered by Coach Hodge in physical education class and being quickly sent from the usual physical education class to the basketball team, all of that sort of opened the doors to everything else. From a black sheep out of hillbilly country to Cinderella in the city, you might say, and the rest is history, girls. But I don't have to tell you two how it was. You saw me when I'm sure I looked lost and bewildered, like when I first started school. And beyond basketball, what truly saved me, made me feel like I belonged here was you, my two new soul sisters."

By November, she had been taught the fundamentals as a forward on the basketball team. She loved the rhythm and flow of the plays and quickly moved to first team after being a substitute for six weeks. She had always been coordinated and had an uncanny strength acquired in part from the work demanded of her by Ben on the family farm. She would glide down the court with her black ponytail swishing and, accelerating with her long stride, she would quickly separate from whoever attempted to guard her. Although stronger than anyone on the team, her musculature rippled under the glow of her smooth, amber-toned skin rather than appearing sinewy and stark.

As the Hamilton Hills Terriers streaked toward a winning season and a possible berth in the regional finals, an opposing coach had commented to Sarah's coach that there was a fluid grace that masked her strength and rebounding ability. He said that she reminded him of Secretariat, the beautiful triple-crown winner. Of course, this was spread across school and at the next game, a small group of rowdy boys in the stands were chanting, "Sexy terrier, sexy terrier, she's our Secretariat, woof, woof, woof." It caught on fast and she was catapulted into that sacred society of high-school celebrity. After the statewide tournament in December, she was selected second team All-state as a forward but remained humble even with such an accolade. She continued to work weekends at McDonalds, because she liked to earn her money for clothes and movies instead of depending upon the Reids.

She did not date. But when she was called "butch" once in the school cafeteria, she decided to form a friendship with a shy, nearsighted Italian boy who weighed 230 pounds but was only 5 feet, 10 inches tall. Worse still (in the eyes of his fellow students), he also stuttered. Sarah saw him, as she said to one of her girlfriends, as "a sweet teddy bear I'll take on as a project." Indeed, with his rotund face, wide mouth of bad teeth, and dark-framed thick glasses, Joe Santorone looked comical, almost like a crudely carved pumpkin. His saving graces were that he played center on the football team, quite competently because of his mass, and excelled in English. Sarah told Mrs. Reid that she considered him to be "my cover date because of everything that went on at home, and I'm simply not comfortable dating yet." The beauty of the arranged consort was that both benefited socially but they remained more like brother and sister than boyfriend and girlfriend.

She knew that she was neither "butch," nor sexually unawakened. But she also knew that she bore a secret and the scars of that secret. Her rape at the hands of her father would sometimes slap her in the face while doing something as mundane as eating an ice cream cone or brushing her hair. More often, usually late at night when in bed, her secret would wash ashore without warning like a barnacled old beam whose bluntness and sharpened edges bled tears onto her pillow. She remembered every detail of that night but especially how the fat slab of her father's belly would slap rhythmically against her abdomen. Sometimes when she would remember how he had startled her with his climax, she would begin to hyperventilate and sweat would sweep across her entire body. And then she would feel she might faint until she reflected upon where she now lived and what she had escaped. There were many nights that she would reach to her bedside table, wind the small brass key of Aunt Sallie's music box and listen to the soothing strains of "The Dance of the Sugar Plum Fairy." This would calm her and she then could sleep.

Sarah's primary delight in high school, besides sports and the comforting warmth of her new home with the Reids, was derived from her friendships with these two best girlfriends, Meredith Wilson and Toni Alligheri. They were known as the "Three Musketeers" because of their camaraderie and the mirth they plied in the hallways of Hamilton Hills High. They looked nothing alike: Sarah, tall, that amber tint of her skin, dark hair and those luminous blue eyes; Meredith, a petite five feet five inches, blond, chiseled features, and what was whispered among the boys as a "Greek goddess body"; and finally Toni who was somewhat pear shaped, stocky, had close cropped hair dyed a sort of burnished red with orange highlights and then there were those penetrating cinnamon eyes.

While Sarah was somewhat reserved and unimpressed by her emerging popularity, Meredith confessed bluntly to them both that she was "a man-eater, or rather a boy-devourer, because they are all so juvenile and I love to tease them, watch them dance to whatever tidbit I toss out to them." Meredith was notorious for sometimes telling three different boys that she would agree to a date on Friday night simply so that she could deny and deflate the two she then eliminated later that day. Yet, to be seen with her was such a badge of celebrity that they (the boys) kept coming for punishment. Toni by contrast was Catholic and a member of a small group of girls in school who advertised their commitment to what they called "sustained virginity as our gift to Jesus Christ and to our future husbands." Meredith disavowed any such vow of chastity.

They did have one thing in common which bound them more than anything else: a caustic sense of humor and a dedication to "acting out our parts in this theatre of the absurd." This was a term that Meredith brought to the group. Her father taught drama and European history at nearby Carleton College, and he had passed many a tome to his daughter since she was thirteen ("old enough to let literature blow your mind, sweetie," he had said at the time). Along with her rather adventurous spirit, Meredith drove a red Mustang GT convertible with a bench seat that usually meant Toni was in the middle and Sarah anchored the door. Toni, despite her demure façade, was not merely antic-prone but could be dangerously disruptive. She was famous for inserting herself into the graces of anyone who could grant her access to the school's intercom system. And finally this had become a daily school tradition so that there was a fifteen-minute session for students at one o'clock to share current events and advertise social and sporting events.

Toni's breathless sightings of UFOs and early class dismissals announced over the intercom were not nearly as celebrated as when she rather formally stated ("now this is very serious, my fellow students and faculty members" came the introduction over the intercom) that two unmarried faculty who were known to despise each other had "not only buried the hatchet but after eight months of quietly dating have become engaged." She concluded, "Let us all, fellow students and faculty, wherever you may be at this moment, stand and applaud Miss Appleton and Mr. Hathaway." Although, yes, this had occurred on April first, Toni was nevertheless given a one-day vacation (otherwise known as a suspension) for this prank that was deemed so personal as to border on defamation, especially when the two allegedly betrothed disliked each other more than ever. And so the eleventh grade passed far more rewardingly than Reverend Reid and Mrs. Reid or Sarah herself might have anticipated.

Throughout the eleventh and twelfth grades, Sarah and her friends continued a friendship that would last for many years. In addition to starring on the basketball team as a senior, she was celebrated also as the softball pitcher with the most wins in one season in the history of

Hamilton Hills High. Because of her height, Coach Hodge switched her to the 440 and 880-yard runs in track. With her thighs and stamina, she lost only two races all season and finished third in both at the statewide Class A finals. In the spring of her senior year, she was voted both "Most Athletic" and "Best All-Around Student." To say that Reverend Reid and Mrs. Reid were delighted with how their commitment to her had reflected also upon them would have been an understatement.

But all was not well with Sarah. In her job at McDonalds, she had met someone in January whom she later described to Toni and Meredith as "handsome in an unusual way, debonair I guess you'd say. Anyway, I just sort of melt whenever I see him." This sounded dangerous to both Toni and Meredith. She did not mention that this mysterious man was twenty-eight and had only one leg and no job. Nor had she told anyone that he had borrowed eight hundred dollars from her over a period of several months, a sum that represented half of her savings from working two years at McDonalds. When she confessed to them a week later that by shifting her work hours she had been dating him on Saturdays after work for almost four months, Meredith and Toni were incredulous.

"We suspected that you were dating someone and that you would tell us when you were ready but we feel almost betrayed by your silence, girl," Toni said. "And one more thing, what do Reverend Reid and his wife say or have you deceived them as well?"

"One reason I'm telling you now is that I had it out with them last night, to the extent that I may have to come stay with one of you for awhile."

"Well, what exactly did you tell them?" Meredith asked.

"This is very hard for me but what I told them was that I have decided to delay going to college because I may want to make a life with this man, with Sam, I mean. And to do that I'll have to go to work which means that one thing I've always thought about is cosmetology and opening a beauty salon."

"Have you lost your mind, Sarah? You mean you're going to throw your ambitions and dreams into the gutter for some greaser you know nothing about? Why he's probably some wino who's running from the law. He probably has more skeletons in his closet than you'll ever know. Are you absolutely crazy?" Toni screamed at her.

"About him, Sam, yes, I have to say that I am crazy, crazy in love.

I've never felt anything like this. It's even like God sent him to me as a special gift, just like Reverend and Mrs. Reid said I was for them. The only thing I can tell the two of you is that I have experienced things you don't know about, not just hard labor on my brother's farm and not just being ignored by an illiterate, beaten-down momma, but outright horror. I feel like now the most special man on earth is rescuing me. He's not perfect. In fact, when you meet him, you'll see that it's not about surfaces or looks. He touches me in a way that is so true and exciting that I can hardly go to sleep at night. That's what makes me know it's right."

Toni turned abruptly and put her hands on Sarah's shoulders, shook her, and said, "There is something, maybe a lot, you aren't telling us, sister. I agree with Meredith that nothing about this makes any sense at all. Here you don't date at all for a year and a half and then, then you fall for some jerk we've never met. But what hurts even more is how you hid it from us, like we aren't the biggest part of your life or at least we thought we were. I can only wonder how betrayed Reverend and Mrs. Reid must feel. I'm not trying to guilt-trip you, I'm just giving you a heartfelt reaction. You know Meredith and I love you. We're all three so different but the strongest bond we had or have is always being honest with one another. Are you listening to me?" Toni asked.

Sarah sat on a nearby bench and hid her face behind the picket fence of her strong hands and long fingers, sobbing. When finally she could speak, still between stuttering sobs, she said, "Then I might as well tell you the rest of it. When I came here to Hamilton Hills, I felt like I'd been delivered up from hell. And to find myself a home like the Reids gave me was truly a miracle. But what I came from, well, that's a story I've never told you or the Reids. Suffice it to say that my older brother, Ben, treated Jacob, who was my younger brother, and me almost like animals working on his farm. And he could get away with it because my daddy permitted it, actually thought it was amusing at times. But the real trouble was with him, my daddy I mean. There was constant tension and raging anger toward all of us that only got worse when he had been drinking. What you don't know and what I've lived with is not only my daddy being that way to all of us but a month before I came here he broke into my room and raped me, then tried to do it again. I thought many times about telling Momma Reid about it but I just never could. I've finally sort of sealed it away but it's like one of those old secrets that suddenly, out of the blue, will raise its nasty head, I mean the memory of it. And this is the first time that I've told anyone besides my Aunt Sallie."

"Sarah, why haven't you told us before now? You know you can trust us with your soul and even now, our lips are sealed forever," Toni said, still standing in front of her.

"Well, there's a little more to it. You know how, like you said, I didn't want to date even when the two of you would try to fix me up. I think that was all a reaction to what I went through. But then Sam shows up at the drive-through at McDonalds one cold night in January, smiling with those beautiful teeth that may be his strong suit, and I was just captivated. I didn't want the Reverend and Momma Reid to know. For one thing he had an old jalopy and didn't have a job, not to mention he had just moved here. But, well, well the other thing is I gave in to him several months ago and now I think I'm pregnant."

"Oh my God in heaven," Meredith screamed. "Let's just all commit suicide then. I can't believe what I'm hearing. Are you out of your fucking mind, girl? And did you say p-r-e-g-n-a-n-t as in meaning that you are going to have a baby when we're barely out of the cradles ourselves? Well, we'll just find you a doctor right quick who can get us out of this jam," Meredith screamed at her.

"At least now the two of you, who've always sort of treated my chastity vow as a little joke, can see the logic of it even if you don't see the moral side of it," Toni said calmly.

"I know we can beat it like a dead horse, but something tells me to have this baby. Sam noticed my breasts changing some and we talked about it. I'm not sure how committed he is, but he says he loves me more than anyone he's ever known. So, we are going to marry, and it's set for the day after graduation," Sarah concluded.

"Well aren't we just one happy fucking family. Here you are, graduating third in our class, voted "Most Athletic" and even "Best All-Around Student." We all three have committed to staying here in town to attend Carleton the first two years, and now you bolt on us. You opt for 'Little Miss Homemaker,' or shall we say 'Miss Teenage Mom?' But I'm not saying any more right now or I'll lose it. I'll call you both later, but, Sarah, I want you to think about your options. Mainly there are two. You can marry this guy, have his baby, and ruin your life. Or, you sit down and realize that what you think is love is nothing more than a reaction to your father's abuse. And the terrifying irony of it is that in not talking about your father's abuse, whatever you see in this Sam character is probably the same thing with a veil over it. By the way, how old is this Sam?" Meredith asked.

"Oh Sam, he's twenty-eight and has already lived quite a life," Sarah said proudly.

"Well I'm sure he has, you idiot. It's sort of like you're out of the frying pan, meaning your father's lap, into the fire, meaning the backseat of this rogue's broken-down car. Sarah, to be so smart and so careful about people, I think you've lost your mind. I'm so furious that I'm leaving this minute, but I'll call you both later," Meredith said as she sauntered away.

The day after Sarah Sewell graduated with honors from Hamilton Hills High School, she was married to Samuel Ezekiel Braxton. Or rather, it might be more precise to say that Sarah met Samuel Braxton not at the altar with Reverend Reid officiating, but at the metal desk of the local justice of the peace. There was no best man. Toni was forbidden by her parents to attend the ceremony or to even visit Sarah for a month for what they called a cooling-off period. Meredith, dressed in black as though for a funeral, reluctantly accompanied Sarah and wept throughout the brief ceremony.

When they stepped from the courthouse, Meredith turned to Sarah and said, "I am so sorry for you, for all of us, but I will not abandon you ever." She then turned to Samuel Braxton and said, "Mister Braxley or whoever you are, I think you are nothing more than a psychopath and a seducer of a beautiful but bewildered teenage girl. But I will tell you one thing, and that is that you won't separate us from Sarah. I do hope you burn in hell for what you are doing to all of us though." Samuel Braxton laughed, lit a cigarette, took his young bride by the arm and hobbled away.

From Almost Doomed to Finding a New Freedom

Sarah settled into a pattern of working five days a week from early morning until two-thirty in the afternoon at Betty's Beauty Parlor, a four-block walk from the trailer she and Sam rented in the Hidden Valley Trailer Park. Then, at three o'clock, she arrived at McDonalds for the second shift until eleven. Her only respite was a Sunday afternoon with Meredith and Toni, who were enrolled that summer as first year students at Carleton College. As his contribution to the marriage, "Stump" (which he preferred to Sam) had purchased another car, a used yellow Pinto that already had a necklace of rust around each wheel well but also had a sophisticated speaker system and eight-track stereo tape player. His mornings were spent supposedly searching for job opportunities. After taking Sarah to her afternoon shift at McDonalds, he would drive to one of two favorite billiard parlors where he specialized in eight ball with secondary interests in beer guzzling and small bets on just about any sporting event.

Sarah surprisingly still received some support from Reverend and Mrs. Reid. She visited them in early July for the first time since their June schism (over the marriage), ostensibly to talk to Mrs. Reid about her morning sickness and medical care. This casual visit evolved into a confrontation when Reverend Reid returned home earlier than expected. He was unusually irate and disturbed about her marriage, an arrangement that he did not and would not ever accept.

"Sarah, you may not know it but Martha and I have prayed about your situation daily. You, above all others, know that we came to see you as a daughter and championed all of your explorations, whether sports, class trips, anything. You and Martha will be shocked to hear that I no longer think prayer is the answer. I think that you came to us several years ago as a young girl trying to escape the devil. If I remember correctly you said, 'I still have some of the devil's dirt on me or in me.' And frankly, I think by marrying this Braxton fellow, from all I hear around town, you have found the devil again," Reverend Reid concluded.

"Please, I'm fighting as hard as I can to keep it and myself together. I'm working my fingers to their bones all day and half the night. I may be tall and strong in both body and spirit, but I'm still only eighteen and human, not to mention pregnant on top of that."

"Honey, I'm not here to cause you more heartache. But what I want to do, beyond prayer, is cut a deal with you. Let us say, a deal between our church and you with God being our mediator. In exchange for the church supporting your medical needs during your pregnancy and the care of your newborn child, you will agree to come to church on Sunday mornings. It's your only day off work but my motive is to keep you in touch with us and with the church members, many of whom truly care about you, even love you. Why, you were a local heroine with your prowess on the basketball court and on the softball diamond not to mention running track too. I guess it's the only time a young lady dominated the sports pages in our little town that I can remember. One other thing, I have to admit that I'm having someone look into the history and background of this husband of yours whether you like it or not."

Sarah agreed with Reverend Reid's proposal, and he leaned down to hug her neck as she sat on the sofa next to Mrs. Reid. Even at five feet, eleven inches and four months pregnant, Sarah, at least the hidden little girl in her, would always confide in Reverend and Mrs. Reid and find solace and warmth in their embrace as she did now. At Lot 27 of the Hidden Valley Trailer Park, though, she had begun to face the realities of her pregnancy, but at least her morning sickness was abating. The onerous weight of two jobs and her profligate husband's alcoholism added to her miseries. Yet her pattern was one of predictability and she was esteemed as one of McDonalds favorite employees. Despite the fateful encounter with the man who had become her husband, she was still assigned the drive-through window because customers asked for her, wanted to see her, to speak to her. Pregnancy seemed to become her. She still wore her coal black hair in a ponytail and her winning smile never failed her. If anything, the burnt amber tint of her skin was more radiant and the depth of her blue eyes as beguiling and luminous as ever. She watched her weight carefully and thanks to Reverend and Mrs. Reid visited her obstetrician each month.

But her greatest joy was arriving at seven-thirty each morning at Betty's Beauty Parlor. She enjoyed the repartee and simply having women, who comprised about ninety percent of their customers, to talk with and learn from. Betty and her business partner, Amanda, as well as their customers learned quickly however that her marriage to Sam Braxton was not a subject for discussion. Betty gave her the freedom to move quickly up what she called "the ladder of beautification." Although Sarah initially only washed and prepped their clients, she was soon permitted to cut hair, beginning with some of the men. They liked her and asked for her at their next appointment. As Betty said, "It's like dealing cards, you either have it or you don't, and I can tell within ten minutes after a woman picks up those scissors whether she's got it or not. And you've got it. Probably a little too fast at times, so slow it down so they think they're getting their money's worth." She graduated soon to styling some of the younger, more adventurous women and learned the fine points of tinting and dyeing from Amanda who, though in her late fifties, was regarded as having the skills of an artist.

At home, all was not well. Sarah told Meredith and Toni that she had accepted Sam Braxton's alcoholism as a given. "I don't know which one of you said back in May that underneath Sam's veil was probably someone about like my daddy. Well, in the past few months, that veil has been lifted and I realize how impetuous, if that's the word, I was to get so involved so fast. Maybe the word is just 'stupid'."

"Does he ever attack you or yell at you?" Meredith asked.

"Well, several times when he's been really drunk, I have to admit he has pushed me around in the kitchen wanting me to fix him a midnight snack when I stagger in exhausted from my night shift. There are so many nights, a lot of them he doesn't come home, when I'm so tired I crawl in bed and play Aunt Sallie's music box two or three times until I fall asleep. That beautiful German music box with my little ballerina on top dancing her heart out has been my dearest companion these last few years. It just stills my soul when I feel like I can't go on anymore," Sarah responded.

"You know that we've tried to understand why you did what you did and we've tried to be supportive, especially since you're coming close to having this child. But, honey, if he's done it once, he'll do it again," Toni chimed in.

"We have seen a change in you in the last few weeks, Sarah, and that worries us. You said the other day, something like 'marriage is not only not all moonlight and magnolias but it's more like sundown and sadness.' We didn't press you on that, but we wondered if you were getting depressed or just more realistic about this guy and what you've gotten yourself into," Meredith seconded.

"It's true that if I take a cold, hard look at our marriage that he gives almost nothing to it no matter how dashing and romantic I thought he was or still do think at times. If I'm really honest, I have to admit he's been living off me since that first night in January when he rolled through McDonalds. To imagine that was only seven months ago just blows my mind. I've never told either of you that I loaned him eight hundred dollars during those first two months," Sarah replied.

"Jesus Christ, girl, you're up to your ass in alligators. So you better be trying to find a way out of the swamp," Toni teased.

Several weeks later, on a hot afternoon in late August, Sarah arrived at Lot 27 of Hidden Valley Trailer Park to find a new black Lincoln Mark V coupe idling in what would have been Sam's parking space. She thought it strange that the driver, a tall, balding man around forty, would waste gas by idling the car especially with his window down on a hot day. She asked him if he were lost and could she help him.

He flipped his cigarette to the ground, spit out the window, and said, "Lady, I don't know if you're that little, or not so little now, pumped-up girlfriend of his, but I'm lookin' for Sam Braxton and I believe this here is his trailer, ain't it?"

Sarah, shocked by his presence not to mention his manner said, "Well, sir I don't think that I have to answer that."

"Look, sister, you may have one in the hangar there though you're not much more than a baby girl your own self, and you may pull that high-and-mighty routine on me, but I ain't here to waste no words with you. Let me just start over by saying you lookin' pretty good to be in your condition, honey. But I'm here because I got a problem with Sam Braxton who I'm gone go ahead and assume is your husband. So you just give him a simple message. You tell him that Mr. Gagglione, who'd be my employer in Pittsburgh, has a extra add-on charge when somebody don't pay his debts on time. I been lookin' for him for two days to no avail and I knowed you come home like clockwork at 2:45 in the afternoon. But that motherfucker husband of yours ain't got no schedule a'tall. That's all for now, honey. Real simple. But I'd say you'd better give him my message or it could get a little dicey for everbody around here, including you."

Sarah did not respond but ran into the trailer and locked the flimsy door behind her. She knew intimidation when she saw and heard it and, thinking about how her father could elicit fear by merely pointing his finger at any of the children, she began to sweat, first her head, then arms and abdomen as her heart pounded like a rabbit running scared. When she noticed a rhythmic humming in her ears, she knew to put her head between her knees though at five months into her pregnancy, this was harder to do. She immediately dialed Reverend Reid's office at the church. "Oh, Reverend Reid, I'm so glad you answered," she exclaimed.

"Sarah, is something wrong? Your voice is not right, so tell me what's bothering you."

"Just let me talk, I need to. But just hearing your voice is a relief in itself. You remember those panics I used to have sometimes when I first moved in with you and Momma Reid. Well, they were mostly about suddenly remembering something my daddy had done, I mean to me or the boys or even momma. Well, I haven't had one of those attacks in over a year. But I just did and my heart was beating so fast I thought I might die or hurt the baby."

"Sarah, I'll be right over because I can be there in five minutes. And there's something important I need to talk to you about, I mean really important."

"Well, I hate to bother you when you're working but come on and although I never do it, I think I'll call McDonalds and tell them I'm sick and can't come in at three. They can staff the drive-through with one of the new girls."

She greeted Reverend Reid by saying, "I know you've never been in this trailer but at least I keep it clean and neat. I'm already feeling better. I was sure I was going to faint and I do still feel a little nauseated," Sarah said. She told him about the black Lincoln and the bald, uncouth enforcer driving it. She also told him about her suspicion that, despite her foolish generosity, Sam had continued to ask her for more money and had never found a real job except several temporary ones that paid by the hour.

Sarah was tearful when she looked at Reverend Reid and said, "You know, despite going to church and listening to your sermons, I have to admit that I just don't have your level of faith. What I do believe in is hard work. The excitement of what I am learning at Betty's and even my simple work at McDonalds keeps me going. I thrive on it. Except for talking to Toni and Meredith, I really haven't shared my misgivings about my marriage and how distraught I am about Sam with nobody. But what I can tell you is that there are many nights that my little music box sings me to sleep. You remember how much I depended on it to calm me down when I first moved in with you and Momma Reid."

Reverend Reid did not seem surprised. He seemed to relax, to breathe calmly as he moved to sit next to Sarah on the couch and put his hand gently on her knee. "Sarah, I do cherish our relationship so much that I have tried my best to accept your decision to marry this man. However, you know that I have never trusted him and you know that I had told you I was having his past looked into by a lawyer friend in Pittsburgh. Well, that turned up nothing until someone in Ohio called recently. To cut to the chase, I have to admit that after I received the bad news earlier this week, I've been wrestling with myself about how to deliver such disastrous news to you. Now, especially with this visit you received this afternoon, I don't have any qualms or hesitation. In fact I'm concerned enough that I think we should call the sheriff and have that scoundrel arrested immediately."

Worse than her fear of the man in the Lincoln, worse than her humiliation sitting there with the man who had saved her life in so many ways and had given her a new life, was learning the history of the real Sam. Samuel "Stump" Braxton's formal name was indeed Samuel Ezekiel Braxton. He was thirty-three, not twenty-eight as he had told her. He had been dishonorably discharged from the U.S. Army following a tour in Viet Nam where he was called "Stoned Sam" because of his commerce in marijuana and hashish. He was also under indictment in Ohio for both failure to pay child support and a concealed weapons charge. His employment history was erratic and inconsequential except for a job he had with a railroad. While the name, Samuel Ezekiel, may have been derived from his father's random placing of a finger upon several chapters of the Old Testament (according to "Stump" himself), Sarah's husband had quite another story about his beloved nickname.

In fact, he could tell a long, convoluted and gory story of how his leg had been nearly severed and then infected after stepping into a booby trap in Viet Nam although he preferred to tell this story after either a six-pack of Schlitz or a half-pint of Jack Daniels. Stump's version was that as a platoon leader while leading a heroic mission in the deep jungles of Viet Nam, he had slipped into a bamboo-laced pit and impaled himself. After being rescued, his wounds were so horrific that he became septic and almost died resulting in amputation of his leg. For his bravery and loss of limb, he had received a bronze star and a purple heart and was discharged later because of his disability. Thus, Stump delighted in using his nickname as a sort of nom de guerre and would tell this tale to anyone who would listen.

While the truth unearthed by Reverend Reid and his lawyer friend was that both the stump and nickname were derived from a brief career Mr. Braxton had as a brakeman for the Northern Ohio and Pennsylvania Railroad. He had in fact been fired by the railroad in 1974 for "excessive alcohol imbibing leading to a careless accident at a switching station resulting in amputation of the right leg above the knee," according to court records that Reverend Reid's sources had discovered. Having lost not only his job but also his medical insurance and being ineligible for VA benefits, he had stumbled about on crutches for several months. Finally, he had purchased his prosthetic leg from a wholesaler in slightly used condition, meaning that it was a demonstrator. It was constructed of a cheaper grade of plastic and fit imperfectly. With each step, a sound emanated from it that resembled the ceremonious squashing of a large roach, a sharp crackle followed by a prolonged, mushy decrescendo. Stump found this amusing, while others found it either distracting or simply disgusting. Court records also revealed the indictment for failure to pay child support and that he had been married at least twice before his current marriage to Sarah.

Samuel ("Stump") Braxton was neither injured warrior nor gentleman but had been most recently a debit insurance salesman for Jefferson Life and Assurance for the four months before he drove out of Akron, Ohio and cruised into Sarah's life as she leaned out the serving window of McDonalds one cold night in early January. Sarah, a determined, gutsy, and gifted senior in high school was nevertheless both naïve and gullible as most seventeen-year-olds would be. Because of her distorted view of romance and her miscalculated indiscretion, she had decided to marry this man so that her child would at least have a father at birth. She should have known that his motives were less than noble when he borrowed the initial two hundred dollars from her after they had dated for only two weeks. Such blindness was the consequence of a young girl's myopic infatuation with a slick scoundrel on the scam.

"I simply can't believe all of this story any more than I can believe what a fool I've been. If there's such a sordid mess as this, why couldn't your lawyer friend find out about it earlier?" Sarah asked.

"My dear, for the simple reason that our Sam Braxton has several aliases like many con artists do. The way they finally got to the bottom of it was through two social security numbers and then finding the military records. So I say let's get the sheriff involved immediately," Reverend concluded.

"I understand completely, but it's my life and my mistake to ever believed anything he said. I know you have my best interests at heart but I want the chance to at least question him tonight when he comes home, assuming he does. In the last month or so, he's often away for several days and nights. I tolerate it because it's more peaceful here without him and then of course he's always begging for money when he's here. I'm just curious to see how he'll react and then we'll do what we need to tomorrow," Sarah begged Reverend Reid who reluctantly agreed.

Sarah confronted Sam with the information from Reverend Reid that night. She was met with an apologetic and repentant Stump who concocted the alibi that all of the information was inaccurate and that he had grown up on a farm in Iowa, that "The Rev" (as he called him) was guilty of having investigated the wrong Samuel Braxton. He reminded her of the honorable discharge certificate from the army, the bronze plaque for salesman of the year from Jefferson Life, and what about the actual bronze star and purple heart he always carried, he challenged her, almost irate. And yes, although he did have all of these, Sarah knew they were very likely forgeries and the result of a visit to an army-navy store. They argued for an hour until he encouraged her to "slip into our bed of ecstasy." Exhausted, she did just that.

When Sarah, still exhausted, stirred from her sleep around six o'clock the next morning, she found that Sam Braxton had stealthily fled from the trailer during the night with only the clothes from his chair. The yellow, rusted Pinto was no longer in the driveway. There was no note. He had simply vanished, vaporized into the night in a fashion not dissimilar from how he had arrived in Hamilton Hills and inexplicably captured Sarah's heart as she leaned from the serving window at McDonalds. And so it appeared that Samuel ("Stump") Braxton had again cast off the uncomfortable raiment of imminent fatherhood and the choking collar of marriage.

Although Sarah reported him to the sheriff as missing when he had not been seen by noon that day, no one was surprised. In fact, Meredith summed up the reaction of most of Sarah's friends when she said, "Actually, honey, I'm relieved. When you signed on with him, you basically signed up for a life of misery. I won't get into that 'out of the frying pan into the fire' thing again, but you grew up with an abusive, alcoholic father, and proceeded later to fall in love with the same damn thing. Our psyches may play tricks on us, girl, but accidents don't just happen. So I'd say, everything considered, you've just gotten free again, about like that so-called freedom march to Hamilton Hills you told Toni and me about when you escaped your father."

In most ways Sarah agreed. She hated being cast as a pawn in Sam Braxton's latest game but once more, just as she had done when she left the hills of West Virginia, she made a plan. She appeared again at the courthouse but this time it was to reclaim her maiden name. "If I'm going to have this little girl I saw on the ultrasound last week and rear her by myself, then I want her to have my name," she told Reverend and Mrs. Reid who offered again their home to her but she refused. She told them she was eighteen, too young to be a mother but if that was God's will, so be it. She explained that she actually enjoyed her work at the beauty salon where she had graduated from doing wash-and-prep to cutting and styling. Her popularity from her high school days also followed her to her new job at Betty's Beauty Parlor.

As a woman who had chaired the high school's PTA said to her friends, "With those long fingers she's as fast and facile with scissors as she was nimble and graceful on that basketball court." But beyond that, what most heartened her friends was her renewed spirit and determination. She did capitulate to the demand of Reverend and Mrs. Reid that to be a healthy expectant mother she should work five days a week at the salon and only three nights at McDonalds so that she would have her weekends free.

On December twentieth, Meagan Evangeline Sewell was born. Over the next two days of her hospitalization, Sarah and Meagan were attended by a rotating trove of Episcopalians and men and women in the community who had come to know her both at church, at the beauty salon, and through her illustrious exploits in high school. Reverend Reid, with an eye on the future and a finger on the pulse of her emerging popularity, had arranged for the rental of a small suite in a strip mall where he confided to Sarah three weeks before her delivery that she would soon become the owner of her first business funded by a loan from him and his wife. She named it "Sarah's Beautification Salon," assuring its appeal to as diverse an audience as possible. During the early afternoon of Meagan's birth, Reverend Reid had a small brochure printed that announced both the birth of Meagan Evangeline Sewell and, effective January fifteenth, the opening of Sarah's new salon. These brochures were given to each person who visited Sarah and Meagan in the hospital. Reverend Reid knew not only how to manage a church but also how to sell an idea, always with that engaging gleam in his eye accompanied by that sly and mischievous wink he was known for.

Sarah Opens a New Salon

The reporter from the Hamilton Hills Herald had agreed to meet Sarah at her new salon a week before its grand opening. It was a cold day and he was a smart ass. "Morning, Miss Sewell or is it Mrs. Sewell? I'm Roland Arnold from *The Herald* and for some reason I've been assigned to do what we call a human-interest story about you and this new salon of yours. Frankly, I think that Episcopalian minister is a close personal friend of our editor and it's a blatant promo, but I know who the boss is."

"Mr. Arnold, I'm so happy you're here to interview me because I'm going to need all the help I can get. Let me say that I tend to favor Ms. Sarah Sewell instead of Miss or Mrs. Sewell. They're just a little old-fashioned I'm afraid," Sarah responded to her handsome guest.

"Oh, I didn't know we had a budding feminist here," he retorted.

"Well, we're about ten or fifteen years beyond ripping off bras and marching in the streets. While it's true that I'm a mother, I'm definitely not married. So Miss or Mrs. doesn't quite fit but Ms. feels about right. But let's get on with your questions."

"Yes, indeed we shall and in full disclosure I want you to know that I was second in my class in journalism at Penn so if I use any words you don't know, simply ask me to clarify my verbiage. First, let me finish setting up my tape recorder. And now, why don't we recapitulate those halcyon days when your prowess on the basketball court was the talk of our quaint village because that could be formulated into a bit of background for our article, Ms. Sewell," he said with a strong and sardonic emphasis upon the 'Ms'."

"Mr. Arnold, I meant to ask you whether you would like coffee, hot tea, or hot chocolate as we get started? I've got a new coffee maker and a hot plate at this little bar that I'm setting up for my customers. Just an extra enhancement for my beauty salon, if you'll excuse my big word," Sarah said smiling.

"Well, well, splendid, and I'll have hot tea with lemon and no sugar. And I see you move even now, despite your recent pregnancy, with the grace if not guile of the tigress you were on that basketball court," he said as he watched Sarah walk to the small antique table she had found in a consignment shop and converted into what she called her bar. Of course, she was watching his eyes in the mirror that covered the wall.

"So, why don't we have a little background music for my background story," Sarah said as she tuned the radio to the local soft-rock station. "So much has happened to me in the last six months that what I did in high school sports has sprinted out of my memory faster than I ever toughed out a 440-yard run. You know how athletes always answer your kind of question by talking about team spirit, or being united in some common journey, or pursuit of excellence, all that kind of thing. Well, I've got a totally different take on it. I grew up among poor coal mine workers in West Virginia and on a farm that mainly grew potatoes, greens, and corn with a few hogs and chickens thrown in for color. This was all before I moved after the tenth grade to our quaint village as you call it. But my attitude is that a person can accomplish almost anything he or she wants to if they will work hard enough. If you don't reach for the golden ring, nobody's going to boost you up to grab it."

Sarah sipped her tea. "When I was younger, I called it 'gumption.' That's a funny word if you think about it because it's sort of a combination of up, jump, and motion. I learned it from my old Aunt Sallie, a hard-working woman who lived in the country, never married or even wanted to. But she didn't lack for nothing because she was up with the chickens in the morning and hunting with the owls at night. And so, I'm sitting here with you as a still poor, teenage mother with only a high school diploma about to open a new beauty parlor, but I don't ever call it that. I only use the term beauty salon or just plain salon although I know that can mean different things. You, and what a handsome sport coat that is, you have a college degree in journalism as you said and probably are wondering how soon you can be moving along to the Philadelphia Inquirer. So, let's make a deal. I'll answer any question, give you some good material, and you write something exciting instead of a pitying piece about some poor hairdresser opening a shop on the south side, also known as the wrong side, of our town," Sarah concluded.

"That sounds like a balanced equation to me and notwithstanding our facile jousting, may I simply call you Sarah now that we've gotten the protocol established?"

"Yes, Roland, you may," Sarah responded as she reached over and patted his knee. "But I do wish you would start speaking English, plain English I mean, because one thing I don't have in my shop is a dictionary. I do have two at home though."

"Right, right, madam. Now, my next question for you is to ask what was your greatest moment on the basketball court and, secondly, have you ever heard of Ayn Rand?"

"The first question is easy. That would be in the state finals this past winter when I scored thirty-nine points, had twelve rebounds, and ten assists. They call that a 'triple double' and I always wondered why they didn't add 'whammy' on top of that. That's a joke, Arnold, so give me a little smile at least. Yes, I was in one of those so-called zones. I hit fifteen field goals from all over the court, the other points were from foul shots, and it was sort of like a magic arc when the ball would leave my hands. I didn't have to look it in because that ball was destined to swish from the final second it rolled off my fingertips. Well, we lost the game in overtime as you know, but we were ecstatic because, aside from having been given no chance at all, each of us had played her best game ever. Now what was the second question?"

"This is good stuff and the second part was whether you have read any of Ayn Rand's work, especially *Atlas Shrugged* or any of her essays? The reason I ask that is not to display my erudition but because this 'gumption' philosophy, this emphasis on the individual, sounds like her."

"No, I don't know her from Adam, or let's say Eve in this case. But despite what you may think about me, the truth is that I enjoy reading almost more than anything, and have since the ninth grade even though our little school had to borrow books. Recently, a friend gave me this book called *My Life* by Golda Meir. I didn't care about all the politics, and I'm too young to understand all the trouble and struggles the Jews have had for centuries, but wow, what a strong woman. She never gave up on anything she believed in or wanted to do. The other book I read not long ago was a novel by Walker Percy that my friend Meredith gave me. Well, actually, her father's a professor at Carleton and he's always passing books along to her. That one was called *Lancelot*. Oh, I loved how it got so tense between the characters except it didn't end too well. Actually, the fires of hell fueled by Lance's jealousy erupted but I won't ruin it for you because you may want to read it. And if you do want to know one of the secrets of my life, it is that I left home in West Virginia with an old dog-eared paperback copy of *Jane Eyre* and I read it or parts of it every six months. There's something so gutsy, so brave and defiant about Jane and at the same time something so romantic about her whole story. But I'm not much of a romantic myself because I'm more of a nuts-and-bolts woman. Sort of like when I first arrived here and told Reverend Reid to give me a chance and show me a job, any job, and I'd get it done and mostly I have. Well, we're way off track."

"I am going to bring you a copy of one of the Ayn Rand books because she can be somewhat extreme but she captures the essence of what seems to be your guiding philosophy. Now, you alluded to your impoverished beginnings in West Virginia, so would you care to elaborate?"

"No," Sarah answered.

"Quite a succinct response, I dare say. Why so definitive in your desire to seal it, hermetically, one might say? Is there pain embedded in those memories?"

"No question about that, Roland. I always say that I'm real honest with myself and with my closest friends about those days, but that is a place I have forever moved away from. It's a place both on this earth and in my heart that reeks of pain and desperation. The only thing I've got to show for those years are the scars and scabs that almost anyone from there carries. But I tell you what I'll do. If you ever want to write about the most down-trodden, desperate poverty you'll ever see, I'll tell you where to go to find it. The only thing would be that you could never, and I mean never, mention me or anything about me. I literally disappeared from there, vowed to never go back, and I don't want to be found."

"Understood and I may actually want to do precisely that in the spring. Here we are mired in a recession, stratospheric interest rates, humiliated in Iran, and are very likely going to elect a millionaire Republican President from Hollywood in a year. It might be interesting to contrast his emergence with the still rabid and recalcitrant poverty of your people in rural West Virginia. Might even be something that would catch the eye of the Philadelphia Inquirer you joked about. But getting back to us, to you. Why a new salon, what are its chances for success and why located here?"

"Let me get each of us another cup of tea because it's a treat I've discovered this winter for myself, warms my bones when they're creaking from cold. I always thought hot tea was something only rich folks would drink. When I made certain choices, for example to marry my daughter's daddy, I drastically changed where I thought I was going with my life. That original path would have been to go to college, not for sports even though I was recruited, but to become a teacher. Of course Meagan who is my almost one-month-old daughter changed all that. And it seems strange but the only other work I had always had in mind was to have a salon, be a stylist. I don't know why except perhaps I've always loved doing my own hair and maybe because my momma hated hers, called it the bane of her existence. You have to have at least six months of training or apprenticeship as it's called to get your license in this state, and I couldn't have had better teachers than Miss Betty and Miss Amanda. But I've always wanted to be my own boss and that is another way of saying I don't want a boss besides my own self. Reverend Reid has always been my savior along with his wife and he loaned me the money to set up my shop."

"You mean venture because I assume it's a business first and a social scene secondly. Which brings me to my next question. Who will be your assistant and how were you so fortunate to discover an old barbershop?"

"Well, although I'm not very religious, the Lord brought me this old barbershop through Reverend Reid who heard about it closing several months ago. If I had to buy those chairs over there, I would go broke before I even opened the salon. The nice thing is that it's over two miles from Betty's beauty shop and yet is still not so far from my little trailer. And there's nothing I like more than fixing up a place. While both men and women will be welcomed, the vast majority of my customers will probably be women. That's why you see this new light blue paint, compliments of the men's Bible class at St. Michael's, and also why I have these silk flower arrangements I got on sale at Pier 1. The furniture is from prowling around antique shops looking for bargains. Back to your question, my assistant is going to be a young woman who took courses at our tech school, highly recommended by her teachers and hungry, if you know what I mean. But here I am sounding like a forty-year-old matron of a fancy salon. It will take hard work and long hours but that is what I specialize in, hard work I mean."

"Sarah, we've covered a lot of ground but what strategies do you have for managing your maternal responsibilities while embarking upon this entrepreneurial quest?"

"I guess you mean how am I going to be a momma while trying to make the salon a success. For the first few months, Mrs. Reid has enlisted the help of a small group of young mothers in the church, Saint Michael's Episcopal Church that is, who don't have day jobs. In a way, they will be my daycare center. They're already helping me because, honestly, what does an eighteen-year-old know about being a momma? Not much, Arnold, but I'm learning."

Arnold leaned back in his chair, pulled an already packed pipe from the pocket of his wool blazer and seemed, in some profound professorial manner, to be contemplating the future of all mankind, before he asked, "Although our educational heritages are quite different, would you be so disposed as to having dinner with me some evening, Sarah?"

Sarah seemed surprised but finally leaned forward, again patted his knee and, smiling, said, "Arnold, you're a handsome young man, obviously smart as a whip, but I suspect we don't have a lot in common. There's another thing. I've got three full-time jobs on my hands and they would be this business, my daughter, and, last but not least, myself. Me spelled s-u-r-v-i-v-a-l and I aim to show them I am one of the fittest if you get my drift. I hope someday, if you are still around, you will interview me when I'm a success story with the finest salon in town. I am serious when I say that I will only accept making something of myself that people will envy. And I don't mean money necessarily. What I mean is that I will pour my heart and soul, and hands I might add, into this effort. And I have never accepted failing at even the most trying times of my short life."

"Well spoken again and I don't doubt that you will succeed. Nevertheless, I plan to drop off one of Ayn Rand's books and perhaps we can at least have a glass of wine one evening and discuss it," Arnold said as he stood and moved to embrace her.

"You've pushed me to be honest and clear and I couldn't have had a better interviewer," Sarah said as she extended her hand toward his chest to shake hands, stopping him in mid-stride before he could reach her.

"Well, yes, indeed and now off we go," Arnold said as he turned gracefully on the heel of his highly polished loafer.

Two days later, Sarah unfolded her copy of *The Hamilton Hills Herald* and read the lead article on the first page of the community news.

SARAH SEWELL: SUCCESS FROM SORROW

By Roland Arnold

She may have been born a coal miner's daughter as the country song goes but she finds herself now on the cusp of success with her imminent opening of Sarah's Beautification Salon. We know her as the most phenomenal female forward to ever play for the Terriers. Indeed, on her shoulders our Terriers fought their way into the Class A finals and came within three points of being Class A Champions. Along the way, she graduated as "Best All-Around Student" and "Most Athletic" from HHH, our fine high school. Not bad for a tall, gangly eleventh grader (at that time) coming out of the hills and hollows of West Virginia.

Ms. Sewell attributes much of her determination and success both in school and on the court, not to mention the softball diamond and track, to her patron, Reverend Ambrose Reid. An imposing figure himself, Reverend Reid and his church, St. Michael's Episcopal, are both spiritual stalwarts of our community. And it was he who brought Sarah Sewell to us as an exchange student from Appalachia. From interviews with her friends, we know that Sarah grew up in the throes of abject poverty surviving on potatoes, pumpkins, and poultry from the small family farm. But you won't hear much about her early life from her.

Ms. Sewell's decision to open her new salon in the Midway Mall is the result of a lifelong interest in styling and of her embarking upon a new life as a mother to a young daughter. "If you don't reach for the golden ring, nobody's going to boost you up to grab it," she says. Her determination to succeed was evident early in her life when she taught herself to read in an almost illiterate family. To this day, her exploration of contemporary literature is just one more intriguing facet of this multifaceted young woman and now owner of a new business.

At times spunky and saucy, Sarah sprinkles her comments with a combination of down-home wisdom and new-age philosophy. Her guiding principle is that "a person can accomplish almost anything if she will work relentlessly." With some help from friends, she has converted an older four-chair barbershop into a robin's-egg-blue salon with inviting seating, reclaimed antiques, and elegant floral arrangements. Another interesting touch is a small bar where customers may get hot tea, chocolate, or coffee along with homemade cookies.

Sarah says her objective is to start small, give superb, individualized service to her customers, and to provide a social venue for lively discussions. She apprenticed with another local beautician prior to opening her new salon. Although she welcomes both men and women ("I've had excellent training both cutting, tinting, and styling"), she anticipates the women of Hamilton Hills will comprise the majority of her clients. Ms. Sewell will be joined initially by Miss Cathy Eubanks, a graduate of Valley Technical College, who will facilitate a smooth cascade of appointments and has also received excellent training in the arts of styling. The salon will be named Sarah's Beautification Salon and opens on January 15th with appointments available from 8 AM to 5 PM. At noon on Friday, January 19th, there will be a formal ribbon cutting that will be attended by many of Sarah's friends and supporters. Hot refreshments from the attractive bar, another novel concept for a beauty salon, will be provided.

Life at the Beauty Salon

Diapers, diapers, and more diapers. Those first two years of Meagan's life were a delicate balance with Sarah on the tight rope as she worked tirelessly between managing a fledgling business while also learning how to be a mother. Not that she didn't have the support of Mrs. Reid and her "Mother's Brigade" as they came to call themselves. Before she would open the salon each morning, she would awaken her daughter, feed her, and one of the brigade would arrive to take Meagan first to Mrs. Reid for the morning and then to a rotating member of the brigade for the afternoon. Most of these women lived across what was jokingly called the cosmopolitan divide, meaning Reading Avenue that divided the have-nots living in the southern sector of town from the more affluent families residing in the northern sector. Only a few miles separated the salon from Meagan's surrogate mothers making it convenient for Sarah to take an hour at lunch and spend that time with Meagan at one of the ladies' homes with the added attraction that she could see how they lived and decorated their homes and spent their money.

By joining Sarah at the opening of the salon, Cathy Eubanks had proven to be both a talented beautician and a good friend. Twenty-three, unencumbered by boyfriends or family, proud of her associate degree in business from Valley Tech with a secondary specialty as a licensed beautician, she was a perfect fit for Sarah and the salon. She was tall, as thin as a model stepping from the pages of *Elle*, and wore her long blond tresses straightened in what she called an "Annie Hall" style. Almost the antithesis of wide-shouldered Sarah with her long black ponytail, Cathy had a narrow face with a small nose and thin eyebrows. Her florid smile dominated her face and she advertised this smile with various bright shades of lipstick or gloss.

As Sarah said to Charlotte, their newest assistant who joined them a year after opening, "There are times I look at Cathy's face and just imagine different flowers in full bloom. When I mentioned that to one of our customers, she brought in a book of paintings by a woman artist named Georgia O'Keefe and all of us in the salon including Cathy would hoot and holler each time we turned a page to a new painting. We loved her colors and it was like the flowers were magnified so you could see their internal secrets, like you were a bee living down inside the flower. One of the girls said the flowers Ms. O'Keefe painted were very sexual and graphic, even seductive, and like you could almost smell them but I couldn't quite see all that."

The salon was an unexpected success from the first week and Sarah always wondered how much her interview with Roland Arnold and his subsequent article in the newspaper had helped. She also joked about their interview, how he had tried to impress her with his encyclopedic vocabulary and how he had promised her a book but had never contacted her because she thought she had intimidated him. Six months after the opening, Cathy was working almost independently in a second chair and a year later, they had hired Charlotte to do the shampoos, setups, and drying. After Meagan turned three, Sarah would take her to daycare following their morning breakfast and hour together. And then at three in the afternoon, Meagan would be driven to the salon where she had her private corner of the shop with her desk, crayons, children books and puzzles. She had her mother's thick black hair, her grandmother's small, pursed lips, and those same luminous blue-diamond eyes that had trickled down through the family and, in Meagan's case, were always curiously scanning the room when she wasn't absorbed in one of her books. She also had Sarah's large hands and long fingers for her age but she had, unlike her mother, a small, petite body that already resembled that of a budding gymnast.

Meagan became everyone's pet, meaning that the salon's customers lavished her not with gifts that were forbidden but with questions and little stories that she relished. She could play quietly, solve her puzzles, or engage in almost-adult repartee, because she was always around a diverse group of adults who were primarily women. By the time she entered the first grade at the Montessori school (Reverend Reid's idea), most of Sarah's patrons jokingly said that

Meagan already had the equivalent of a primary school education. While obviously an exaggeration, she had been reading since she was five but more importantly she had been immersed in a sea of garrulous and entertaining if not sometimes gossipy women for years. And she loved it. If there was one compelling thing about her it was her curiosity. She would cut those blue eyes toward Sarah when someone would be telling her a story, as though to say, "Momma, can I believe all this?"

"Time, oh God where does it go or, as they say, *tempus fugits*," Sarah said to Cathy one late afternoon when their last client and Charlotte had left. She continued, "When you work the way all of us at the salon work, well, the days flow into weeks and months and suddenly you are swept away on the waves of time. I mean it's so fast that it seems you're caught up in a story where the characters are so quickly changing that while you can see them in all their triumphs and weaknesses, divorces and deaths, you lose sight of yourself and your role in the stories. Sure, you see how fate or God or happenstance conspire to toss people around in this storm, but you start thinking you're immune to those same wild winds."

Cathy reached into the refrigerator, grabbed a Michelob and said, "Girl, you've got to remember we're still young and got all of our lives before us. I do sometimes worry that you get caught up in our ladies' troubles. And by that I mean you may feel too responsible for them like it's your job to fix whatever's wrong. They mainly want somebody to just listen. I let them lay it out there like morsels on a tray, tasty tidbits that are usually as much gossip as they are confessions. But I will say that whatever goes on in this town, you usually hear it here first. I just ain't gone be the one who tries to fix everything they throw at me and you don't need to try to either."

"I'm not sure when I began to change, becoming more of a business person and a little less of a mother but I have. I give Meagan what I think is necessary but I let her learn the hard way what life is all about. Giving her a long leash is the best way to put it. Of course, I'm sure how I grew up, our extreme poverty, a momma mostly missing in action, not to mention that gorilla of an abusive father I had. Well, they all combined to exact some toll and to make me think Meagan should be her own explorer, plotting her own path while knowing I'm there to support her."

"Honey, you know that the way I grew up means I'm all for learning on your own. As far as being a mother, why we all marvel at how you pull it off. At the same time, this old ship here couldn't stay on course without you at the helm," Cathy replied.

"Cathy, as social as I am, as understanding as I try to be with our ladies and all their worries, sob stories, and catastrophes, sometimes I think I don't give enough attention to those right around me. That would be Meagan, you and Charlotte."

"Well, you're talking to a girl who grew up in an orphanage. It's not even like when so many girls or boys with a single-mom parent don't ever know who their daddy is. Hell, I don't know who my momma is or was. She might even be dead for all I know, because I've never had no contact at all with her. So in that orphanage and in my whole life of hard knocks, it's been fighting for survival. I could tell you some stories about cat fights among us girls and dirty tricks late at night in that place that would curl every hair on your head without you even gettin' a old-fashioned permanent."

"You've never said much about your early years and why you were placed in the orphanage so I've never pushed you. While my upbringing was bad enough with one idiot brother, a milk-toast mother and as I said a gorilla of a father, well at least I had something to call home. And I did have one brother, Jacob, who I was close to. He watched out for me at school until I didn't need him because I started growing faster than all the girls and a lot of the boys. Then, when I decided to leave home to escape a nasty situation, I just never looked back. But I can't even imagine living in an orphanage."

"Let me tell you, even though this one was run by the Catholic Church, you don't want to imagine it. What I'm saying is that on the surface it looks fine. You got the Jesus flag flying, the bells tolling, and us girls chanting little Bible verses and Hail Marys. You got a bed about the size of a cot and you got three awful meals. We had two pairs of shoes, one for school and working, and the second for church only. But what you also got is a holy terror of a Mother Superior who saw the nuns as her children and sometimes lovers and us children as her slaves. We didn't do the laundry just for our own selves and the nuns but we took in laundry and ironing from outside so they could make money off our backs. Like you know how we spent Saturdays? I'll tell you. We were washing and ironing in a moldy old basement from 7 a.m. until 5 p.m. with a fifteen-minute break for a bologna sandwich for lunch. Them old bitch lieutenants, the Mother's favorite nuns I mean, wouldn't even give us but two bathroom breaks even if you was on your monthly. Sister Myrtle would say, 'Paying the Lord back for his blessings, girls,' and I say excuse me while I grab one last beer and if I could kick her ass even now I would."

Cathy continued, "I didn't end up there until I'd been bounced around agency placements until I was eleven. What I and all us girls learned in a hurry was where the power was and how you had to make alliances, a word a young nun taught me. It was cutthroat and ruthless. And how the so-called Lord's blessings got divided-up and doled-out was purely on who you knowed and whose ass you kissed. And sex, well once you hit thirteen or fourteen, swappin' sex was like dealin' cigarettes in a prison or insane asylum. Sex was just one big trading game, favor for favor. And I ain't pleading innocent but me and my two best buddies made one of them alliances with a young nun who wasn't really in the game. So we pretty much stayed above the fights and ambushes. It was sort of like one of them shows on TV about how the people in English castles live. Like you've got a big old turkey dinner playing out upstairs and downstairs you've got petty grievances, illicit sex, and you're eating leftovers half the time. It ain't nothing but jungle warfare, just ruthless shit you wouldn't believe. But, stop me before I say too much!"

"Honey, I never imagined anything like that really existed. Of course I don't know anything about the Catholic Church except reruns of that ridiculous television show about that flying nun. And I do remember Reverend Reid would talk to me sometimes about how some of the Episcopalian church rules and rites were from the Catholic Church but he didn't emphasize that stuff. He would also preach from the Bible in a modern way, said that the words were not nearly as important as one's intentions. He always said that all you had to do was remember the golden rule and you'd do fine. You know, Meagan and I have sort of drifted away from them and the church. But, anyway, if you ever want to talk about it, I'm here and not much scares me or even shocks me anymore. I hope that doesn't mean we're growing old before our time."

Cathy shrugged her shoulders, sighed, then said, "Just like you escaped when you was sixteen and you've never told me why. Well, the law where the orphanage was said you got adulthood at seventeen. So when I hit seventeen, a week later my ass was kissin' all of them goodbye. It was rough makin' it on my own and being a night clerk at a Seven-Eleven. Later, I was waitressing at Waffle House on the four to midnight shift because lots of the students at Carleton came in drunk and you'd get better tips. That's when I started wearing loud, or as you say vivid, lipstick. I'd put some kind of a smile on them, drunk or not. Several years later I finally got my GED and then wound up at Valley Tech. And now look at me: a great job, my first good car, you as a boss and good friend to boot. I never had it so good."

"Cathy, I've never heard you lay it out there like that. I read this poem one time about a woman who lived with another woman, they were lesbians I'm guessing, and the poem was about how the writer never had realized her friend liked to whistle little tunes and even classical music. I mean until she stopped the chatter in her head and being so focused on herself day in and day out, and actually listened to her friend or lover or whatever they had, she just hadn't realized there was this music around the house all day long. And so I mean I'm trying to say that I appreciate you speaking your mind."

"Listen, Sarah, if they's one thing me and you have always had, that thing would be honesty and I mean since day one. You opened this shop and gave me a chance straight out of school. We're not much different in age, but I'll always see you as my boss and, in some strange way, a little like a momma. You've taught me how the business side works and you've spotted me an advance early on a few times when I couldn't quite make the rent. You've taught me how to listen and talk to our fussy, self-centered girls and our old, blue-haired buzzard ladies too. They's an art to it. Don't think I don't know how rough around the edges I was when I waltzed in here and maybe still am a little bit."

"I appreciate that and take it as a compliment, Cathy. But when I hear you speak so clearly, eloquently I'd even say, I wonder if we could be closer friends. Because the truth is we really do learn from each other. It's not as one-sided as you suggest."

"I hear you, girl, and in some ways it's funny we haven't talked quite like this until now. But you know I'm pretty much a loner when I leave here. I've got a couple of girlfriends and an old fart who treats me to a movie and a meal once a month, always curious if he can get in my pants and me not remotely interested in him. That kind of simple life is about enough for me. You don't care about it, but I'm more in love with my television and old movies than any old reprobate. But let's get back to us. The way I see it is that we work together all day long. Your life with Meagan and your friends is full enough. That don't mean I cain't still love you like, well if not a momma then the big sister I didn't have neither, and you are big, you know. You ain't going to deny that are you?"

Sarah laughed, then became tearful as she reached out to Cathy, took her by the arm and pulled her close, folding her arms around her. "You know, Cathy, there's a sweet way I love you, because you've got no airs about you, no pretenses," she said.

"Well, I don't quite know how to take that because I hardly ever get any hugs," Cathy replied.

"Then let's say there are two things we'll work on or maybe three things. Two are for you. Namely, we'll work on your English some like Reverend Reid drilled into me and number two is you, Meagan and I will practice sharing a good hug twice a week because she loves you too, always talks about your clothes, your mod jeans, your Western shirts, your jewelry, and is crazy about some of your Western boots. And the third thing is for me. And that is for you to remind me to listen when you whistle. By that I mean paying more attention to your opinions, what you say, and also what direction this business should take. Is that a deal?"

"That's a deal, fair and square. Now I've had about enough of this intimacy business for a while. I say let's boogie on home. Plus, you've got to pick Meagan up and get her rested up for little-tot soccer tomorrow."

In Sarah's Words

One thing we, Meagan and I, did not have to worry about was that ex-husband of mine. I've never heard one peep from Sam Braxton because, among other things, I'm sure he wants no part of paying child support. It's almost like he never existed or it's like when you wake up from a dream and aren't clear about whether you are still in the dream or you're living it out in your real life. I've always wondered why Meagan has never shown much curiosity about her father, but that's one of those things that could come when she is older. My guess is that I rarely talk about him, even in reminiscing, not that there's anything much to reminisce about except me falling in love with a scoundrel. The other thing is that Meagan and I spend most of our time with women friends. I do encourage her to spend the night with her girlfriends so that she can get a taste of what being around a father is like. And at school she has some good male teachers and coaches. Of course, Reverend Reid loves her like a granddaughter. That first year in business was pretty rough financially, but since then we really don't have to worry about money. Not that it's been rags to riches but the salon is so successful that we're sort of the envy of the beauticians in town.

Montessori has been perfect for Meagan, once again proving that Reverend Reid was right. The way the teachers let them move ahead at their own paces has been a boon for Meagan. Probably the most amazing thing is how she loves reading, one little book after another, but really anything she can get her hands on. I vaguely remember how it was for me in the ninth grade when that traveling library from

Petersburg started coming to our little school. And later after I would read to my baby girl at night, I always looked forward to my own quiet time in bed with a book. What I loved then and now was a book with some history in it, but I also like just plain old fiction because with my day-in and day-out work, I get more than my dose of reality.

I'm not sure what sort of genes Meagan got from her daddy but I see some of his expressions on her face, even her manner of gesturing if those things can come from genes. And she definitely has his compact, tight, muscular body. Her school was too small to have soccer but the new city leagues for different age groups are all the rage. When she's not on the soccer field, she's flying off the bars and flipping over the mats at gymnastics classes like a circus acrobat. Smiling always smiling, teasing and being teased, that's my Meagan. She's also sort of a friend to everyone in her classes regardless of that Reading Avenue cosmopolitan divide. It's like all of her gifts combine to make her one of the most popular girls in her grade.

So, here we are toward the end of middle school and now that Meagan is about to bloom into puberty, I'm not certain what we will discover. One thing I've had to enlist the girls at work, Cathy and Charlotte, to help me with is keeping her reined-in at times. It's like she grew up around adults, spent so much time at the salon, and probably heard more about all the local news and gossip than I would have preferred. Because of how she was always listening to the stories and escapades of our customers, she's a little like a grownup in a girl's body. I have to admit that makes her a little different from most of the twelve- and thirteen-year-olds.

I won't say that Meagan's curiosity hasn't also been tainted by a mild touch of arrogance. Or I guess maybe I should call it just plain stubbornness. I remember when she arrived home after school last year in the seventh grade and sheepishly said she had been suspended for two days. That's a perfect example of her being a little arrogant coupled with her slightly stubborn streak. I'll never forget our exchange that day because I wrote it down in my diary and I can tell you just how it went.

She came home, a little sheepish, and said, "Well, Momma, I admit maybe I said something a little too strong. And what I said was, well I just told my girlfriends what I had heard Cathy Eubanks say one time at the shop. You might not have known I was listening."

"And Meagan, do I have to pry it out of you or do you want to protect your sweet momma from something terrible?"

"No, Momma, I will tell you the same thing that I said to Emi, Shirley, and Ava. We were talking about how things are not fair sometimes. So I told them when Miss Cathy was talking at the salon about things being unfair, and she just laid it out there. She said, 'A woman's got to be a real bitch to survive in a man's world.' And then I told my three friends that I'm going to be a really serious bitch when I grow up. One thing I've already learned is a loser comes in last, well next to last, because a whiner is dead last."

"Meagan, that's no way for a young lady to talk whether you accidentally overheard Cathy or anyone else use those words or say anything remotely like that."

"Well, that's not all. Someone must have squealed on me because fifteen minutes later I was called to the principal's office. There she sat, Miss Stembridge, her glasses half way down her nose and her lips as tight as chicken's lips. But I will say that her old gray, lined face had a fresh rosy luster like that old lady Sammons who always has her appointment with you on Fridays. You know how she wears so much rouge that she looks like a clown. But Miss Stembridge was hot, breathing fire."

"Go ahead and get to the end of it, please. Why couldn't you talk her out of a suspension, even if you had said something so uncouth that I'm ashamed of you?"

"It didn't get better. It got worse. So, she proceeded to lecture me about how the smarter girls in my class were supposed to be role models and that included me, I guess. And that was followed by another lecture about what she called civility, whatever that is, and also ladyhood. Well, I couldn't resist the chance to tell her that I didn't think 'ladyhood' was a real word. I just couldn't bite my tongue in time. At that point a one-day suspension became a two-day suspension. When she stood up behind her desk with both hands on it and leaned toward me, I actually was afraid she might explode. She was red as a beet, about like a female dragon spewing fire. It was truly scary. I asked to be excused after I told her I had learned a valuable lesson about curse words. She was still standing when I tiptoed out of her office with a little line of sweat running down between my eyes. Momma, a lot of what I've learned has been from you and being around the ladies that come to the salon. But I am sorry."

"Honey, you are all I've got in this world besides this salon and I'm not expecting any great rewards in the next world if there is one. But to get ahead, you're going to have to use your brain as well as your looks along with a touch of humility, being humble. You flash that smile, bat those pretty blue eyes, and you think that you can captivate just about anybody. And you can. On top of that, you're already changing into a grown woman. If anything, you're going to be even more alluring, so learn your lessons now."

"Well, I didn't mean a bitch like the way people, boys especially, mean that word. I meant it like scheming or flirting or doing what's necessary to get what you want. I can't imagine how you made such a success story of your life. There you were, a teenage mom saddled with me and with no money and no college education. And now look at you. I don't think it's an accident at all. I think you made a plan and you were so driven and determined, you've never even thought of failing. Listen, it's not just that I love you, Mom, it's that I really respect what you pulled off."

"But let's get back to you, Meagan. Do you think I don't know what you meant? Of course I do, but you can't say it that way. For one thing, the girls go home and tell their mothers and they are our best customers. Our survival depends on them. So you see, everything is linked to how people see you. They don't usually care what's in you, what's in your heart or your head, but what they notice is your appearance and what you say and do. Do you remember when you would choose one of those Breck Shampoo girls from a magazine when you were younger and show her to me and make up a story about the two of you. This is the same thing. It's all about surfaces, my darling girl. Beyond that, though, is your heart and the few people you can trust to reveal that to, the same people who love you and will always love you. Now give me a hug, you sweet, devilish angel."

So now I look around my salon at the end of the day. All four chairs are always busy and in a month another Valley Tech graduate will join our little working sorority of beauticians. I have a daughter in the fresh bloom of puberty. One who is popular, and seeks out extra assignments for extra credit from her teachers. Maybe she's going to be my next Jane Eyre, we'll see. And here I am at thirty-one more successful in my business than I would have ever dreamed. My customers are mostly now from the rich side of town. Unknown to them, if I have someone come in who lives in south town, Cathy and I and now Charlotte quietly will give them reduced rates. Like Cathy says, "Don't ever forget where you came from, girl." On the home front, the trailer Meagan and I endured through two hard winters was history after that year we opened, and now we're in a small, comfortable brick ranch that I keep re-decorating just for fun.

Just the other day, Cathy asked me what kind of pleasure was I getting from my "private life" as she called it. I answered that I didn't know, that I had not slowed down enough to think about such a simple question. All of that is another way of saying that I've become even more of a workaholic including Saturdays, while saving my nights and Sundays for my daughter. I still try to see my two old girlfriends, Toni and Meredith, one Saturday night each month. Toni has followed the predictable path she mapped out in high school. She finished college with a degree in education and is teaching third grade here in Hamilton Hills. She preserved her virginity as a gift for her husband, Edward, like she vowed to do in high school. They now have a boy eight and a girl who is six. Nice house, car and minivan, country club, the whole ball of wax is what she has. In many ways, except for having a child, or two in her case, we don't have a lot in common but we love each other.

Meredith, now there's a trip, and she is the complete opposite of Toni. It's always about beautiful clothes, her latest conquest, and some reckless adventure. On top of all that, she can afford whatever she wants, because she's in pharmaceutical sales ("Just call me what I am, namely a drug rep," she says). She has worked her way up the ladder of McElhenney Pharmaceuticals to be regional manager for all of the southern half of Pennsylvania. Three years ago, she was married to the Vice President of the company for fourteen months before leaving him and confessing to Toni and me that "marriage is another form of prison and I hated every minute of it, because it's like that saying in New Hampshire, 'Live Free or Die.' I'll tell you right now that I'm not going to die for any man." I always worry that Meredith's wild spirit will get her in trouble.

Of course when she blows into town from Pittsburgh or Philadelphia, she's dressed to kill but still acts just like her same old self. Meagan dotes on her, listens to her travel and cruise ship stories, and is fascinated with her clothes, her shoes and handbags, not to mention her jewelry. She's sweet to always bring Meagan a silk scarf or something. One time she brought her a French scarf made by a company named Givenchy, a word I never could pronounce, and another time, some kind of Prada purse that cost six hundred dollars if you can believe that. I mean her things are just like you see in the magazines. Whatever she has used three or four times and is tired of is what she brings Meagan. I suppose it is the same thing with the men that come and go in her life. Once she is tired of one, she simply tosses him away even if they are just out of the wrapper, almost new. She has a favorite saying that goes "I take no prisoners, suffer no fools, and never look back." Toni shudders when she hears this and says, "I'll pray for you, sister."

When the question of men in my life comes up, I have to confess that I've probably given up on them. I did date a nice instructor from Carleton College about a year ago. It sort of dragged on for four months, even went to bed with him twice at his house which I never admitted even to Toni or Meredith. Until one morning I woke up with Meagan snuggled up against me, a rarity now, and listened to the songs of birds filtering in the window and I thought, "This is all I need out of life." More than that was admitting to myself that there was no real chemistry with Max and really never had been. So I told him and he was shocked, wanted to know how he could change. Well, of course, at our ages, and because we're pretty much hardened into who we are, neither one of us is going to change very much, so he disappeared.

There are times when I wonder whether I'm not becoming more like Aunt Sallie every year as I get a little older. It's like those black holes they've discovered out there in the universe, but I don't really feel anything like that in my life. I mean that if I am supposed to be missing something critical or special in my life, I don't know what it is. Living without a man seems comfortable, probably easier than putting up with one when most of them still act like big old grown-up boys, especially from all the stories I hear at the salon. Being self-sufficient like Aunt Sallie and not dependent on anyone is more of a blessing than a curse. It's true that I'm not as isolated as she was and with Meagan at home, there's never a dull moment.

And when I think of the family I left behind in West Virginia, the only one I ever miss or am curious about is Jacob and whether he escaped that hellhole or not. The taste for revenge toward my daddy lasted only for a few months, and I would guess that poor old dumb Ben would have spilled the beans about that night of terror. And if he did, then my sorry, old daddy would've had to live with the shame, not me. Although he was half-drunk that second time he came in on me, I would guess that the next morning he had to get both his shoulder and arm sewn up by Doctor Allison, because I gave those paring knives a good stab and twist. A pound of flesh and his soul as payback for his sin would be about right, or at least a good down payment for violating me. Sometimes people ask me about my life before coming here and if I miss my family. I always say no and that's the truth. I have this fear that if I wrote them or went back or told even Jacob where I am, nothing good would come out of it. I'm afraid that opening old wounds might backfire on me. So I just keep that painful part of my life as a closed chapter. I'm afraid to even get in touch with Aunt Sallie because she might get mad at my old reprobate daddy and spill the beans.

So, yes, I stand here in the salon sometimes in the late afternoon when everyone has left, and I wonder about two things. One is how I, and Meagan along on the ride with me, have been so blessed or why fate has smiled so bountifully on this poor old sister. Of course, I don't really think it's just the Lord's blessings or because I've got Reverend and Mrs. Reid praying for us. Surely I don't think fate is always fair or predictable. I think it's more that I simply grab fate by the throat, shake the hell out of her and let her know what direction I want to go. But my half of the bargain is that old mother fate knows I'm willing to work like a maniac to make good things happen. So, the other thing I wonder about is what changes are ahead for Meagan and me. Or, as someone jokingly told me that the old blind man said, "I can't see around the next corner but I feel like we're almost there."

The Summer of Change

Tumultuous would be the best way to describe the summer of 1992. Having been in business for thirteen years and with a clientele now almost exclusively women of whom ninety percent lived north of the proverbial cosmopolitan divide, Sarah had been considering relocating for several years. One Monday morning she walked into the salon and said, "Girls, I was in Wal-Mart yesterday morning when the store was deserted, my favorite time to go, and I was scanning the greeting cards, which is a little hobby of mine. You know how some of the cards are funny, some ridiculous or silly, and a few are really clever. So I found this one card that had a quote like 'Change is the most important word in the world,' and I thought well, why not?"

Living in the same rented small brick ranch for the past thirteen years, she and Meagan were known for their frugality. Sarah's clothes usually came from Nellie's Nearly New. This was a shop of consignments where the more affluent women of town dropped off their almost-new old clothes that could be bought for twenty cents on the dollar. Meagan, having watched her mother devise sophisticated ensembles from Nellie's clothes, also enjoyed creating colorful and coordinated outfits following her raids on T J Maxx and Ross ("Hit them at the right time and you can score a mother lode," she always says). Sarah's other hobby was reading many of the interior design magazines. She would then explore the antique shops for bargains and every few years redecorate their small house. Later, she would donate her older furniture to Salvation Army. All of this meant simply that Sarah had saved most of her earnings for these thirteen years.

In April, a real estate broker whose wife was a long-time patron approached Sarah with information that a larger space in a small complex of four shops on Sycamore Drive (north of Reading Avenue of course) would be vacated by July. Relocating the salon would not be easy. New chairs would need to be purchased, the plumbing would require upgrading for the necessary new lavatories, and of course installation of the requisite wall mirrors would be required. But this new space, beyond the generous size, had another attraction for Sarah. Namely, a large adjoining paneled sitting room already existed. The refreshment bar that had been an afterthought when she opened her salon thirteen years ago had proven immensely popular and had given her an initial edge over the other beauty salons. Sarah now envisioned the paneled room as not only a lounge for refreshments but also for displays of art and pottery. It would also provide a larger venue for display of the hair and cosmetic products for which the profit was considerable.

Sarah was anything but impulsive. She discussed the possibility with "my girls" as she called her staff after swearing them to secrecy. She talked with Reverend and Mrs. Reid, several bankers, and also the local representatives of two mortgage companies. Her accountant, who had encouraged her to invest in the stock market after the 1987 crash, reminded her of the healthy profits in this portfolio as well. But to complicate matters, the same real estate broker had also mentioned a particularly beautiful Victorian cottage on two acres located only a mile from the commercial space. And the hook was that the elderly woman who had restored the home was moving to an assisted living complex because of medical problems and was eager to sell this charming cottage. Sarah initially said no but relented when the elderly woman invited her and Meagan for two o'clock tea one Saturday afternoon.

"Now Meagan, when we walk in here to meet Mrs. Willingham and see the house, just be your polite little-lady self. I have no idea what it will look like inside or how she decorates, but from riding by here we know it's stunning outside and I hear she put oodles of money into it two years ago, had the best contractor in town."

"Mom, when have you ever had to tell me about manners. Yeah, I'm just thirteen but unless I'm fooling around with my girlfriends, I can be sweet as sugar. I'm excited enough about you maybe moving the salon, so if anything, I don't want us to go overboard on this house if it costs too much. My friends kid me about our little rented ranch house, but that doesn't faze me. I learned from you long time ago that it's not what kind or how much stuff you have, it's who you are that counts."

"All right, honey, you're on a roll. Now before I ring this doorbell, just one more thing. And that is, don't appear too impressed, like we're salivating at the chance to get it."

"Look, I'm not as naïve as you think. I've seen you wheeling and dealing for those old antiques and even for clothes at Nellie's. I know how you work it."

For two hours, Mrs. Willingham pointed out the hand-hewn cabinets, the eight-inch stepped molding, the heart pine floors, and the beautifully crafted fretwork and lattice of the porches. When finally they approached the front door to leave, Mrs. Willingham said, "Do me the honor of sitting with me in the parlor for a few more minutes." She then explained that her three-room apartment at Wild Woods Retirement Villas would require her to dispose of most of her antiques and family heirlooms.

Mrs. Willingham, despite her osteoporosis and stooped shoulders, straightened herself, looked at Sarah and Meagan calmly, and said, "I don't know what you know about me but I am a person of comfortable means because of my deceased husband's investments and that is how I could afford the restoration of this house. The great irony of which is that I have no heirs. What has that to do with the price of tea in China, you ask. Well, nothing would please me more than for the two of you to acquire my home. Sarah, everyone knows your success story and your work ethic. Miss Meagan, you're making a name for yourself in soccer and as a gymnast in those junior tournaments we all read about. One other thing to which I have already alluded is that the furniture is going to have to be disposed of in some appropriate fashion. So let me talk with Paul before he formally lists the house. I am going to tell him that I wish to make a mutually favorable arrangement for you to purchase my cottage and the antiques. In a strange turn of fate, I will have created for you this folly as they called it in the days of old when you restored an unusual home."

"Oh, Mrs. Willingham, I'm sure this is going to be too expensive for us to start negotiating," Sarah said as she stood and touched Meagan on the elbow.

"Nonsense. I've decided what I want to do. And the other benefit to me is that if you do move in, I will feel that part of me will still reside here. My legacy will be my largesse, if you will. I am presuming you will have me over on the occasional Saturday or Sunday afternoon for tea. Now, off with you both, so that I may proceed to call Paul. I've known him since he was a wee tot and he will ascribe to my desire to accomplish this. Let me kiss your forehead, Miss Meagan. It will bring you good luck."

Sarah, rarely shaken, never noticeably perturbed, almost stumbled down the steps of the front porch, as she grabbed the banister and said to Meagan, "Well, what do you think?"

"Mom, I'm totally blown away. I don't mean by what she said at the end, that's all up to you, her, and that broker. And it's still likely to be too pricey for us no matter how much she wants us to have it. But what I'm blown away about is how beautiful it is, just breathtaking. I don't know anything about carpentry but I've never seen such glorious detail. I mean it's sort of like a perfect doll house but so livable and not stuffy at all."

"Well, I agree. I'm dumbfounded. I have no idea what she means about pricing and even throwing in the antiques. We'll just have to see, but don't get your hopes up too high. And the business purchase, relocating the salon, is the crucial deal to get done."

On the first day of July, 1992, Sarah Sewell signed the closing statements relating to two properties: a 3,000 square foot business at 140 Sycamore Drive and a 3,200 square foot home at 108 Elm Street with the proviso that the owner could remain for two more weeks after closing. The Willingham cottage had four bedrooms and three baths and was "cottage" in name only. The grand dame stated that she "would gravitate to her new villa on July fifteenth" so that Sarah and Meagan could accomplish their move before school began in late August. Preparations for work on the new salon were to begin the first week of July and would require two months.

On July fourth, following the downtown parade, a delayed celebration at the old salon was co-hosted by Toni and Meredith. One can easily assume the motif but one would have underestimated the copious flow of champagne, beer, and punch not to mention the veritable cornucopia of deli cheeses and exotic fruits, all compliments of Meredith and McElhenney Pharmaceuticals. By sunset, a number of inebriated celebrants found it necessary to call taxis, and Meagan, having been permitted "only two small glasses" of champagne had foolishly exceeded her limit and was paying the price. Only Sarah, who had never tasted an alcoholic beverage and had no desire to, was able to watch the frivolities with a sort of detached bemusement while chatting with her friends and customers. She seemed as elated and ebullient as she had ever been in her life except when Meagan was born and perhaps when she scored thirty-nine points in the state basketball finals.

Across town at Saint Michael's Episcopal Church and parsonage, all was not well, or certainly not celebratory. Reverend Reid, although having built this ministry from a fledgling and divisive base into the third largest church in Hamilton Hills, was summoned for an interview by the bishop and standing committee of the church. It was assumed that this meeting, a mere formality, was to discuss whether the diocese once more would make an exception for him because of the local congregation's repeated advocacy for his retention. Sarah was surprised when Alfred Robson, the oldest deacon in their church, called her and asked if she would visit him to discuss Reverend Reid's reappointment.

"Sarah, you know I've been in our church for forty years and you know how I've always been the supreme supporter of Alfonse since the day he walked through the front door of our church. If he wanted a new fellowship hall, I marshaled the forces, twisted the arms and by God we got it. And I think you and I know him better than anyone except for perhaps his wife. This is strictly confidential and I'm only going to share it with you. What I have here is a leaked tape recording of the proceedings when Alfonse met with Bishop Smithson and his committee. I'll play you a few parts of it but mainly I'm going to summarize it for you."

"Mr. Robson, I want to first ask you why you selected me as the person to hear this tape or your summary. You know I'm not, can't be, objective about him at all. He has my heart. And he's saved my soul, heart, and life so many times, I practically worship the ground he stands on," Sarah said, her voice cracking.

"I know all that, Sarah. But I also know you have good common sense and run a successful business. You may feel with your heart but you think and manage with your head. So, may I proceed?"

"Yes, sir, go ahead. I simply cannot imagine that Reverend Reid has done anything wrong, though."

"Well, Sarah, at the Bishop's meeting, Alfonse was told that a sworn and corroborated statement from a woman in our congregation had made specific charges of certain sexual improprieties. But almost as bad, the statement included a statement that the woman was irrevocably in love with him. Alfonse, who as you and I know, is not known to capitulate to even the most problematic circumstances or disconcerting odds, told the bishop's committee that he wanted to read the corroboration of the allegations. He was told that this separate document from a friend of the woman's had been misplaced. And that's when he hit the roof. He proceeded to label the several charges as malicious rumor but then informed the committee and the bishop that they were consorting with forces of darkness by accepting half-truths at best, and engaging in nothing short of a modern day version of a Salem hunt for witches. He then reviewed succinctly his history with us. Well, let me play that part of the tape for you."

"I am dismayed that you men of the cloth would be so gullible and naïve. Do you not know that I injected God and the pride of the Episcopal Church back into a congregation that was splintered and spiritually spent with more members going out the front door than coming in when I arrive there twenty years ago? Would any member including you, Bishop Smithson, care to comment upon my tireless efforts as well as the glowing annual reports from the congregation requesting my reassignment?" Reverend Reid's words filled the room until Mr. Robson stopped the tape.

"Sarah, my guess is that Alfonse was met with faces of stone because there is a long pause on the tape, a deafening silence, until Bishop Smithson tells Rector Reid, as he formally addressed him, that their intentions were to keep him in what they called their collegial ministry if possible. Then the Bishop threatened him that if he continued to profess his innocence and to challenge their authority, the committee would be left scant room for negotiation. All of which was another long-winded way of telling him that he could either retire short of the usual thirty years with reduced benefits, or accept a new assignment to a small church in Hopkens, Maine, of all places. It pretty much ended there with Alfonse telling them he would pray for them as well as himself and for them to do whatever they wanted to destroy his life," Mr. Robson concluded.

"All I can say is that it all seems so out of character for him. I know we're all human and vulnerable, that no one's above temptation. But I'm still shocked beyond all belief. I confess that I've noticed he and Mrs. Reid haven't seemed as close during the last year. But, Mr. Robson, what do you want from me? Why have you asked me to listen to this with you instead of the other deacons?" Sarah asked.

"Sarah, there are certain rumors that Alfonse's sly wink has evolved into something of a wandering eye. I won't mention her name, but a recently divorced, attractive woman of the church was said to have dragged her languorous and depressed self into his office for counseling. And it was said that some eight weeks later, a revived and vivacious woman seemed to have emerged from one of her last sessions with a smile on her face and let's say Reverend Reid's soul nestled in her lap."

"Well, I'm not very interested in gossip although I have to deal with it every day in my work along with so many stories that it would curl your hair to hear them. So, let me ask again, what do you want from me," Sarah repeated.

"Sarah, I am an old man. You and I are probably closer to Alfonse than anyone in this community. In fact, besides reviving our church, he will tell anyone that he regards you as his ultimate gift to Hamilton Hills. He truly loves you, respects you and your accomplishments more than you'll ever know. I want you to go with me and we'll take this tape and talk to him, just feel him out on where we go from here and how he wants the church to proceed. Will you do that for me?" Mr. Robson asked as he reached for Sarah's hand.

"This will be the hardest thing I've ever done. Even divorcing my so-called husband before Meagan was born was easier. But for you and for both of them, Reverend Reid and Momma Reid, I will do it. Now pass me that box of Kleenex before I explode," Sarah said as she began to sob.

On July sixteenth, Reverend Alfonse Reid preached his last sermon. Sitting on the front row were Mrs. Reid, Sarah, Meagan, and Cathy Eubanks (in full Western regalia). Behind them were all of the officers and deacons of the church. And behind them seated separately were the Stephen Ministers who were all dressed in black in protest of his leaving. The church was filled, the hymns rattled the rafters and the sermon caught everyone off guard. It was expected that Reverend Reid would simply review the history of how he almost single-handedly resuscitated their dormant hearts and fractured spirits, breathing life again into their faltering church twenty years ago. But what he had in mind was far different.

"Good morning, my brothers and sisters, and welcome to the last message I will deliver here. Our beginning, do you remember it? It was as though the threadbare runner down the center isle then was a metaphor for the trampled spirits of our congregation. There were cracks in five of our beautiful stained glass windows. And when I first arrived, I was shocked by the scaling paint exposing the wooden foundations, and the old hand-hewn and band-sawn boards that hinted of our history here. So I asked you then whether we wished to survive as a congregation and rise like Lazarus to assume again the prominence in our town that we deserved. You, all of you sitting here, know what your hard work has delivered to us and to this community. From the first group of men who scraped these old boards, primed them, and painted them a white so brilliant the church was radiant, almost a mirror to the sun, the moon. From those painters to the women who removed the stained glass windows themselves, drove them to Lancaster, and spent three days while that young couple just graduated from the Academy of Fine Arts restored them, section by section. From all of these efforts twenty years ago to where we sit today in these new pews under these three Baccarat chandeliers, I cannot tell you what joy it brings to my heart every day. My wife and I are leaving this gift of God and of your labors, but we are leaving it in the best of hands, your hands.

"So now let me change the pace a bit. Printed in your program is one of my favorite poems, 'The Road Less Traveled,' by Robert Frost that I want us to read together silently." And then Reverend Reid said, "I have chosen verses from 'Lamentations' as our Bible reading today, and not without a certain ambivalence I must concede, because Mrs. Reid and I truly lament our leaving this church, this community, and most of all you, our dear friends. You know that 'Lamentations' is sometimes called the book of funeral songs and with good reason. The people of Jerusalem have suffered defeat, destruction, starvation, and death. And in some ways, I can identify with them because of the defeat and soul-searching I have experienced in these past few weeks. But when you dig deep into this morass of suffering depicted in

'Lamentations,' you find a glimmer of hope. Or, as that old spiritual suggests, 'be not dismayed whatever betide, God will take care of you.' Here then are verses twenty-two through twenty-six:

Because of the Lord's great love
we are not consumed,
for his compassions never fail.
They are new every morning;
great is your faithfulness.
I say to myself, The Lord is my portion;
therefore I will wait for him
The Lord is good to those
whose hope is in him,
to the one who seeks him;
It is good to wait quietly
for the salvation of the Lord."

He then put away his notes and spoke extemporaneously of how each of them, like the traveler in Frost's poem, would repeatedly in life be confronted by hard decisions they would have to make. And of how the triumvirate of faith, hope, and charity provides another road map. He seemed to falter, to hesitate, but gathered himself after an interminable pause and said, "But whatever you do, whatever path you choose, put your whole heart into it. Strike out with passion, with fire in your heart. You then will be true to yourself. You will have chosen as a warrior instead of having made the choice of a coward. And when you are true to yourself, when you are authentic, you will be good with your God no matter how anyone else may judge you."

Reverend Reid stepped back from the pulpit, sipped from a glass of water, and swayed slightly before he resumed: "Some of you may remember an old musical standard entitled *What Is This Thing Called Love* and there are even jazz versions of it. My first love is my God and this church and that indirectly means all of you. My second love is my wife sitting here and supporting me day after day. There is, for all of us, a third love, a dangerous love, a serpent with two heads. One head is venomous, lethal and destructive and like that of a viper, we recognize it immediately. But it is the bite of the other head like that of the coral snake that is more subtle, more seductive, and ultimately more intoxicating. We float upon the cloud of its euphoria, its rapture, until we see that it too can be lethal if we let it, and then we fall back to earth. As you go through life, beware of the beauty, the allure of serpents, and especially of that secretive and toxic head that lures you into its lair of deceit and death of the soul. And by the way, we do not handle snakes in this sanctuary," he concluded. There was a smattering of chuckles but also there was a vague sense of floating anxiety among the worshippers, because they sensed he was trying to tell them something but couldn't quite say it.

"Now, Lamentations, what has that to do with my message today? While my wife, Martha, and I may lament our leaving, it is in fact that time. We have grown together as a church and as individuals. I've never liked that trite term, 'growth experience,' so I will rephrase it to say that we, both together and as individuals, have had an exciting and rewarding experience of maturation. I look at your faces even now, and in my heart are joy, celebration, and hope. That is why I chose these verses. As that first verse read, 'Because of the Lord's great love we are not consumed,' but I would add to that the love we share as mere mortals also helps us survive our daily trials and temptations."

He then did something he had never done in his twenty-year tenure. He opened his hymnal and said, "I don't think I have ever sung a solo in my life so this will be my gift to all of you. I've chosen this hymn because it alludes to the beauty of nature and that between each of us, we sometimes must help one another in bearing the burdens of the heart. I would add that however you see God or nature, it sometimes helps to be able to turn to something greater than yourself even if you're not certain it's always there. I give you now from my heart the first and last stanzas of *How Great Thou Art*."

And then it was over. Reverend Reid and Mrs. Reid stood at the altar as everyone in the congregation came forward except for an attractive woman who appeared to be crying and a gentleman new to the congregation, both of whom remained briefly in the back of the church before quickly departing, speaking to no one. Men with their handkerchiefs in hand, women with small embroidered squares or tissues, children and young adults unabashedly crying, enjoying their tears, celebrating their freedom. Everyone waited patiently to embrace both of them. Someone, probably the music director, had retreated to the library, retrieved a disc, and was playing Beethoven's *Moonlight*

Sonata over the church's sound system. As the long procession neared its end, the children's choir suddenly appeared behind Reverend Reid and Mrs. Reid. A small girl with a missing front tooth but a felicitous smile stepped forward and said with a slight lisp, "Reverend Reid, we have a little present for you. Are you ready? Now here we go." And this choir of veritable if not virtual angels sang all five verses of "Jesus Loves Me." Then they shouted in unison, "And we will love you too, forever." Spontaneous applause swept across the church as Reverend Reid reached for his own handkerchief. Mrs. Reid squeezed his arm and whispered, "And I too will love you forever no matter what may come of us."

Sarah's Success Awakens Hamilton Hills

Their lives changed. But she, Sarah, did not change as she continued to center her life about her work and a certain heartfelt devotion to her "other family" as she called her customers and her bevy of beauticians. Meagan was now caught in the cauldron of adolescence and was changing every month. Moving into the Victorian cottage was like migrating from the barren steppes of Russia to the gilded palaces of Saint Petersburg. They had walked out of a two-bedroom, one bath brick ranch into a two-story Victorian home with elegantly crafted fretwork and fine antiques. It was another step in the freedom march Sarah began years ago, yet another symbol of her liberation. A lifetime of labor, from farm to serving window at McDonalds to salon along with the dreams of a girl hitchhiking out of the hills of West Virginia had led to this.

Reaction within the community to the opening of Sarah's Salon of Elegance ranged from admiration to envy. Something that happened to Meagan is one example of the kind of envy easily provoked in a small town. From the time Meagan entered Hamilton Hills High, she was something of a celebrity. Her success on both the soccer field and as a star gymnast on the city's junior teams was well known. Although a late bloomer, which delighted her gymnast coach, she suddenly exploded into puberty over the summer and within six months grew four inches. But she retained her muscular, tightly sculpted, and buff body, and at five-feet-four, it was obvious that she had not inherited her mother's statuesque and powerful presence. She was one of the first girls in school to adopt a sort of casual style of dress preferring slacks or jeans and shirts to skirts, blouses, and dresses. In fact when she and two of her girlfriends entered the ninth grade, they started something of a fad in their rather conservative high school that led to a debate among parents and faculty about dress code. This debate was resolved quickly by adopting a policy of "tolerance for style while emphasizing hygiene and fitness." No one knew what that meant but the controversy about young women wearing more comfortable attire was nothing more than a tempest in a teapot never brought to boil.

Two weeks after entering Hamilton Hills High, one of several jealous girls confronted her at school with the comment, "Well, Meagan, you won your battle to dress like a boy and now we are all pressured to do the same because the junior and senior boys say they want all of us girls to loosen up and wear more casual outfits."

Meagan hardly slowed down as she walked down the hall except to look over her shoulder and say, "Oh you do anything you want, but your fancy little daytime debutante outfit doesn't look so comfortable to me."

Known as the leader of a clique referred to as "The Country Club Quartet," the other girl yelled, "Well, Meagan, you've come a long way for a girl whose mother is nothing but a hairdresser and whose father disappeared before you were even born. I guess because she's got a new beautician shop and you moved out of the projects to the north side where most of us have always lived, you think you're hot shit."

This stopped Meagan in her tracks and as she wheeled and turned toward her adversary, her best friend grabbed at her arm, "Let it go, Meagan, because Terry's always been known as a spoiled brat who stirs up trouble then tries to become the victim."

"Let it go, hell. That's a direct insult to my mother," Meagan said as she jerked herself free and ran to confront the tall, tanned girl who was impeccably dressed with gold bracelets dangling on both wrists.

"Let me tell you something to your face, you fancy little bitch," Meagan said. "You'll never know how proud I am of my mother. She may not have a college degree but that's because she suddenly had a family to care for at a very young age. That would be me. And we may not be in your daddy's country club, but I assure you we don't want to be in it."

"You mean if you could get in it, don't you, Meagan. Because you might see how the other half lives. You know, golf tournaments, shuffleboard and badminton, socials, formal dances with live music, even croquet on some Sunday afternoons."

"All of which is one big bullshit waste of time. While you are whiling and whistling away your hours because you're so bored, my mom has built a successful business. And do you know how we waste our spare time, what little there is of it? By reading, broadening our horizons."

"Oh, now aren't we the young intellectual?" Meagan's adversary responded.

"But I've got just one more thing to say to you even though I don't know your name. That one more thing is that you need to get down off your high horse and jerk that silver spoon out of your mouth. This town has a lot of fathers and grandfathers who pulled rebar and turned kettles in the steel mills and others who worked for the coal companies. They were the guts and backbone of what this town became. And a lot of the mothers worked out at the sewing and fabric factories. It's not your kind that made this town at all. So, sass your ass in your little Ralph Lauren dress and Hilfiger loafers on down the hall, but learn some manners, honey."

The small group of girls now gathered around Meagan and her accuser clapped loudly, shouting, "Go, girl, it's about time Terry's bluff got called."

The other reaction to the Sewell success story was not only one of admiration but one of shock and surprise. Except for her accountant, Sarah's financial success had been under the town's radar. When it became known that she had purchased the new building for her business without financing, she began to get calls from banks, insurance companies, the two small stock brokerages in town, and others who proposed various schemes for investing her money. The local newspaper published a story about her new business and featured parts of her interview from thirteen years earlier with Roland Arnold who had long ago departed not for Philadelphia but for Hollywood where he was enjoying a successful career as a writer for sitcoms according to a blurb at the article's conclusion.

Sarah was also interviewed a week later by Dr. Bella Newbridge, who was a new associate professor of women's studies at Carleton University. After fifty years as a four-year college, Carleton had received university status with its vastly expanded programs of graduate studies and a new school of nursing. The three interviews with Dr. Newbridge each lasted several hours, but for Sarah they were both fun and stimulating. A month after the interviews, a four page article entitled "Women Business Owners in Hamilton Hills: A Feminist Perspective" was published in the *Carleton Hype It Chronicle* or "CHIC" as the students called it. The students cherished it because of its controversial articles and it came to be sponsored by the university. Dr. Newbridge profiled four women in the community: Sarah, who was chosen because of the recent opening of her new salon, a pediatrician who had established a successful stand-alone practice, the owner of a small but highly acclaimed and expensive restaurant, and a "former barmaid" as she called herself who had opened her own bar on a hilltop overlook along with an adjoining Starbucks after an unexpected inheritance. The histories of these four women were so improbable and finely written by Dr. Newbridge that they were compelling reading for everyone in the community. Two of the women (Sarah and the "the barmaid" Stella) were extraordinary rags-to-riches studies of survival and triumph over poverty and neglect as children. The pediatrician was from an old, wealthy Hamilton Hills family but had worked her way through college. She was the first woman in town to create an independent medical practice, not to mention she had recently hired two additional pediatricians (who were men) to join her office. The restaurant owner had distinguished herself early in her career by being admitted to a French culinary school notorious for graduating men and rarely admitting women.

These profiles were both provocative and entertaining. But Dr. Newbridge's observations that were subsequently published in *The Hamilton Hills Herald* truly stirred the hornet's nest of controversy. She documented the difficulties these women encountered in financing their ventures (all four), in finding insurance coverage (the bar owner), in obtaining business permits (the restaurant owner and the bar owner), in being countersued by the business of her male competitors (the pediatrician), in getting lines of credit for operating expenses (all four), and even in getting a permit for a new sewer connection (Sarah). While the litany of obstacles these four entrepreneurs encountered was even longer, it was a subsequent section Dr. Newbridge entitled "Provocations and Questions for Hamilton Hills" that captured the attention of everyone.

One would have thought Martin Luther had risen from the dead to nail his ninety-five theses once again on the door of the Wittenburg Church. But in this case, Dr. Bella Newbridge did not have to nail anything to any door because *The Hamilton Hills Herald* did it for her with a front-page headline that read, “Bella’s Below-the-Belt Blasts.” This large-font headline condescendingly emphasized the first name of another feminist many had heard of while telegraphing “*The Herald’s* editorial intolerance” at the same time. When of course this was precisely (and joyously) the over-reaction Dr. Newbridge had if not hoped for, at least had entertained as a sublime fantasy. Ruffle a few feathers and every voice on the roster of roosters (that is, the all-male editorial board of *The Herald*) was in high and strident form.

But, first, the “Provocations” from Dr. Newbridge as they were delineated on the front page of *The Herald*:

1. Why are there no women on any of the three local banks’ boards of directors?
2. Why are only men in supervisory positions in eight of nine departments at the county courthouse?
3. Why are no women (not to mention minorities) sitting on the city council of eight members?
4. Why are women granted only one afternoon for play at the country club golf course by the all-male board?
5. Why is Doctor Elizabeth Gunderson, our featured pediatrician, the only female physician on the hospital board?
6. Why is the local MLS real estate board populated only by men?
7. Why is the Episcopalian Church the only church in this community to permit women to serve as deacons, elders, or officers of the church?
8. Why are gay women (and men!) encouraged to stay underground in this community?
9. Why are there no women who function as head coaches on any of the schools’ sports teams (including women’s basketball)?
10. And, finally, should not all women in Hamilton Hills and Greenleaf County be insulted by what happened to our four champions depicted in this article?

Controversy is a polite if not pusillanimous word for the fusillade of letters, incriminations, rebuttals, hate mail, and condemnations that were soon pouring into the editorial office of *The Herald*. One letter accused Dr. Newbridge of being a "Machiavellian, male-bating, male-hating radical feminist for stirring up trouble that will surely get her fired if I have anything to do with it." Another letter included the rant that "The author's views and intentions are not those of a feminist but those of a fascist!" In another under-handed insult, an anonymous writer noted, "While Socrates described himself as 'a gadfly to the state,' at least his gender orientation was clear (as opposed to that of Dr. Newbridge who often dresses like a man)."

One of the more ridiculously facile responses was from F. Harold Aldridge III, the President of the Evergreen First National Bank. This was the largest local bank and also the bank most of the elderly women and widows of Hamilton Hills entrusted with their life savings. Mr. Aldridge wrote: "As the bank of choice of both young and elderly women in this community, we have been considering for two years the appointment of a female director with the only problem being that she, the applicant, would need a grasp of mathematics and risk management which are generally not the strong suits of women. We would anticipate concluding this search within the next twelve months and if such a qualified little lady could be found, we would consider adding this fortunate person to our board."

Doctor Newbridge's "Provocations," introduced to the streets, salons, churches, and private residencies of this small, mostly white, conservative town a level of chaos and rancor not seen since the wild stagecoach and fight-prone days of Hamilton's Crossing in the mid-nineteenth century. As one old-timer who frequented the local billiard parlor and heard about the articles and letters to the editor, put it: "All this ruckus reminds me of when we was camping out one time and Lawson Lafayette and me throwed a big old live rat snake into a circle of Girl Scouts who was having a group sing. You talk about getting a reaction, well, I never heard so much squealing and hollering in my life even to this very day." Worse, this provincial explosion of vim and vinegar, of polarized and polarizing opinions, rippled all the way to Philadelphia where both the *Philadelphia Inquirer* and WFIL-TV picked up the story line and played it for all it was worth. Their interviews with Dr. Newbridge stirred yet another round of public debate.

The most biting comment of the professor during her interview by WFIL-TV was when she concluded rhetorically with, "What in common do the Catholic Church, Playboy Incorporated, the Pennsylvania statehouse, and most other institutions in our state share? The answer is a simple one. The answer is that they are all male hierarchies dominated by and for the advancement of their agendas. And the remedy is, I might add, equally simple. Women, young and old, exercise your vote, because we are now a majority! And I would also add that we should close our pocketbooks unless businesses and institutions give us some skin in the game. By that I mean we should be treated as partners and not as slaves to whatever they are purveyors of. It's like we drew a line in the sand in the sixties but forgot what it meant. Well, it is time to wake up and live the dream instead of placidly and impotently dreaming about what might have been."

And a funny thing happened on the way to the forum. The sedate town of Hamilton Hills, nestled so comfortably in its verdant valley with a mind-set of the nineteen fifties, appointed what was called a community action committee of twelve women and ten men tasked with producing within sixty days a roadmap for action. The men were from the Chamber of Commerce while various civic and religious groups nominated a group of thirty women. All except two were younger than forty. Dr. Newbridge was considered "too polarizing" and it was requested that she not be on the committee. However, she and Meredith's father at Carleton University interviewed the entire group of nominated women to make certain that the twelve "feminist finalists," as they were called initially, represented the informed and aggressive posture needed for the task. And so it was that what began as interviews with Sarah Sewell, Doctor Elizabeth Gunderson, Stella Shineholtz (of Stella's Bar and the adjacent Starbucks), and Ellen Smithson (of the Etoile Verde restaurant) resulted in a cataclysmic call to action for the women of Hamilton Hills and Greenleaf County. When it became known several months later that Bella and Stella were spending more time together, this was treated with muted if not feigned respect by most men and as a topic of celebration among many (but not all) of the town's women.

Jason and His Mother

The new salon was a roaring success, so much so that the four beauticians alternated working full schedules on Saturdays because of the salon's popularity. The one thing Sarah knew before relocating the shop was that the women of Hamilton Hills, except for the relatively small number in the country club, had nowhere in town to socialize, to call their own. And beyond being finely coiffed, she knew they liked to talk, yes to perhaps exchange a few dollops of salacious gossip, to serve a few spicy anecdotes from the past, and "to network" as some of the younger professional women would say. But an equal priority, she thought, was for her "other family" to simply be seen and share their dilemmas while seeking advice in a town of now almost fifteen thousand with only one therapist who was a woman. Yes, there was another therapist, a middle-aged psychologist who had relocated from Indianapolis, but it was widely known that he often interrupted his clients with his narcissistic diatribes. While these rants seemed to entertain him, they offered his clients a paucity of insights. At least they "got in touch with their feelings" as he suggested because they usually left their sessions flushed, frustrated, and mad.

Because the arts den of the new salon was slow to generate much interest or involvement, Sarah decided to align the salon with the art classes in drawing, painting, and sculpture held at the local studio for amateur artists. This strategy was fruitful and led to rotating exhibits of crafts, paintings, and photographs. After she initiated a "First

Wednesday" lecture at 7 p.m., the art department at Carleton University became involved and provided many of the guest speakers. In addition to the faculty's participation in the lectures and roundtable discussions, the graduate students discovered a new venue for their exhibitions as well. Despite all the glamour of the arts den, Cathy Eubanks (who called herself the "sanity stylist" because of her home-spun witticisms) would often remind Sarah that, "We still got to remember why we're here and that's because we need to make these women feel good about their selves, even the old silver hairs. And you and me, Charlotte and Hilda, got to always remember where we came from and that wasn't much. Getting too big for our britches just ain't, I mean isn't, an option."

The brouhaha, not to mention the bravado of the warring factions, about Doctor Newbridge's "Provocations," although now a number of months in the past, had been another catalyst generating interest in the new salon because of the interview with Sarah. The community action committee had been surprisingly effective in provoking meaningful discussion and debate as well as implementing a number of changes in the local businesses. During an entire week before Christmas, all of the merchants agreed that any purchase by a woman would be coded with a "W". On January fifteenth, a long article in *The Herald* revealed that the "W" purchases accounted for seventy-two percent of all purchases (liquor stores were exempted at the request of the Baptist women's circle). This startling fact and the analysis by the service and business sector caught the attention of everyone. Doctor Newbridge was catapulted from her perceived public persona of villain to that of victor. *The Herald* graced her with a new interview because the public knew that it was her analysis and conclusions not to mention the personal vignettes of the four women that had fractured the somnolent façade of this town famous for its beauty but infamous for its mid-twentieth century attitudes. To augment their standing in the community, not to mention their chances for re-election, the mayor and city council requested that the chair of the business school at Carleton University provide a monthly report on the town's progress with implementing the recommendations of the community action committee.

In the midst of this awakening, many things in Hamilton Hills remained as they had been for the past one hundred and fifty years, meaning essentially unchanged. The have-mores continued to have more and the have-nots were tucked away south of Reading Avenue as hopeless as ever. After relocating her salon to the north side, Sarah had noticed from the beginning a new influx of customers who lived in this more affluent section of town. Among these new clients, Amanda Aldridge fancied herself as residing at the rarefied upper edge of the have-mores of Hamilton Hills. Being married to F. Harold Aldridge III, the president of the largest local bank, guaranteed her a prestigious perch atop that highest social stratum, but the ultimate justification of her elite status, again in her mind, was that she was descended from the Harrimans of the Main Line of Philadelphia. Although she never tired of speaking of her lineage and the elegant homes (not to mention genealogic trees) posited on the Main Line, most who heard this thought the Main Line was a bus or subway route. None of this resonated very well with most of Sarah's customers, but Mrs. Aldridge's exaggerations and her abrasive remarks did provide entertainment for both Sarah's customers and the other stylists. "The Mrs. Aldridge" would have her driver deliver her to the salon in her black Lincoln Town Car, and would often arrive in pink or chartreuse cashmere ensembles that included Gucci patent leather slippers and purses. She typically requested a three o'clock appointment because as she said, "Most certainly I am required by F. Harold to be refreshingly beautiful when he arrives home from our bank."

She also made it quite clear that she preferred "Mrs." to "Ms." and had once berated Cathy Eubanks, saying, "Miss Eubanks, it's 'Mrs.' for me because of my marriage to the most elegant man in town, not to mention his considerable assets." To which Cathy Eubanks said, "Well, 'Mrs.' it is but you can kiss the bottom of my Western boot, honey." Sarah had quickly intervened, telling Mrs. Aldridge that Cathy was having an unusually trying day.

When Mrs. Aldridge departed, Sarah's stylists always had several ribald riffs for what the "F" in F. Harold represented although the debate usually came down to "fubar," "flake head," or far worse. Of course, Mr. Aldridge had acquired an unfortunate notoriety for having written what was considered the most fatuous and condescending of all the letters to *The Herald*'s editor following the article about the "Newbridge Provocations." The other reason Amanda Aldridge favored a 3 p.m. appointment was, as she said, "Well, I do need to spend some time with my son, Jason, because the evenings are always so committed to social engagements for F. Harold, myself, and the leaders of the community."

Providing time for the son who accompanied her on almost all of the weekly visits struck Sarah's patrons and staff as bizarre if not cruel. After Jason, the son, had dutifully opened the door to the salon for his mother, she rarely spoke to him again during her two-hour appointment. Jason, just beginning his sprint into puberty, not unlike the late-blooming Meagan, was still rather shy, and seemed eager for the attention he invariably received from Sarah or the other stylists. Indeed, as an only child, he relished this nourishment and would spend several other afternoons each week after school at the salon, unknown to his mother of course. Sarah had a strict rule that Meagan, as she grew older, was not permitted at the salon until thirty minutes before closing when she would arrive to help sweep, clean mirrors ("it's either perfect or not, my darling"), and do the laundry ("let's use the soap with the scent of spring since it's been snowing and gray all week and you know how the ladies get moody in winter"). Jason and Meagan, star-crossed lovers that they were to become, would meet each other at times and when they did, Jason seemed intimidated, uncertain of how to take this bon vivant.

The triple curse of growing up as an only child, as the son of the wealthiest man in town, and as the son who was always looking backward and analyzing his many mistakes as his mother called them, was a curse worse than that of Cassandra. At least according to Greek mythology, Cassandra could see what was coming, could predict every event of the future whether war, pestilence, romance, or death, though her curse was that no one would believe her prophecies. For Jason, spending day after day with a mother who tolerated him at best and despised him at worst, there was little to prophesy except the strange quiet of solitude, of afternoons and evenings in his room alone either reading or watching television while his parents wined and dined the town's power brokers. He was not encouraged to have friends visit like most of the other kids. And why? Well, his parents were too busy to be bothered, or it just wasn't a good day for it, or maybe tomorrow. Within that solitary existence, he learned to hate himself because something (someone?) was obviously missing. Let us call it some remote possibility of intimacy or a parent who genuinely cared about him. He also learned to love himself because he was all he had and he knew it. The nature of this love centered around himself seemed destined to turn upon itself, to devour the very disturbed heart from which it sprang.

Whenever Jason would venture out to try to involve himself in the normal activities of thirteen- and fourteen-year-olds, something would invariably go wrong. On his first Boy Scout camping trip, Al Salter, a notorious bully, pointed a finger in Jason's chest and said, "My momma says you were born with a silver spoon in one side of your mouth and a steel nipple in the other side."

"What's that supposed to mean, mister high-flying Eagle Scout?" Jason asked.

"It means your daddy's a rich prick who takes advantage of poor people and that your momma's an aloof, prissy princess who's got no feelings or regards for anybody in town unless there's a reason she wants something from them." Salter countered.

Jason swung without thinking, his fist smashing into Al Salter's nose with such force that the fracturing cartilage and broken bone sounded like a walnut being cracked, slowly, methodically, sickeningly. Al Salter staggered three steps backward before falling over an ice cooler and screaming for Old Man Poston who had served as Scoutmaster of Troop 64 for twenty-five years.

"Good God, somebody find him a cloth or a tee shirt. He's bleeding like a stuck pig," Scoutmaster Poston screamed.

"He can have my shirt, its soft," Jason said apologetically. "I guess I just exploded because he's always smarting off or bullying the nerds and scrawny guys. I've seen it at school plenty of times."

"Boy, don't you go near him, Jason Aldridge. You're in enough trouble already. If I could, I'd give you the thrashing your daddy probably don't ever give you," Mr. Poston shouted.

The following Monday when Jason walked into his ninth grade homeroom, looking down at the floor, expecting a new challenge from one of the lieutenants in Al Salter's entourage, he heard instead applause which grew louder and louder until finally Peanut Sanders, the shortest boy in the ninth grade, unable to contain his glee shouted, "You did it, Jason. You did what half of us have wanted to do for two years. You took him down." The crackling adolescent voices of the majority of boys began a chant of "whoop, whoop, whoop, hooray, dude," repeating it for two more cycles until Ms. Burton, one of the younger and more liberal teachers, said, "All right class, I've let you have your morning high. Now, class, please settle down before you get me fired for being too tolerant. From the back of the room came one final cheer, "Whoop, whoop, hooray, we love you too because you're the best, Ms. Burton."

Jason treaded along the usually schizoid path of early adolescence, being one day on top of the world and the next day mired in the inexplicable morass of feeling betrayed and misunderstood by everyone he knew. Most of the other kids bragged about their confrontations with parents, but Jason remained the dutiful son at home, marching to his father's cadence and his mother's condescension. Always handsome and athletic, he found in the ninth grade the perfect outlet for his still unexpressed anger: the tennis and golf teams. His father had encouraged him at a young age to adopt those sports and had paid for expensive camps and private lessons at the country club for Jason since he was ten years old. But it was not until he began to lift weights earlier in the eighth grade that he became a stronger and more effective player in both tennis and golf. For Christmas that year, Jason's father added a small gymnasium to their garage and of course it was equipped with the most expensive Nautilus weight and exercise machines.

As usual, his father's interests in his son were important primarily should they cast favorable lights upon the family name. The father held a ridiculously formal presentation of the key to the small gym by inviting the directors of the bank and select friends (not Jason's) and informing Jason that "I'm expecting big things from you not only eventually in our bank but with your talent and the investments I've already made in you since you were ten years old, we want you to become a killer on the court and a threat at every tournament. I think if we get you bulked up a bit more since you've finally started to get your growth spurt and with some continued private coaching you won't fail me or my management team here from the bank, son." Jason's rather weak response was, "I'll certainly do my best, sir."

And now in the ninth grade, he was suddenly five-feet-ten instead of five-feet-five and still growing. Not only was he, as they say in baseball, a natural, but he came to be fiercely competitive. He cherished a topspin forehand down the line almost as much as he did the fifteen minutes spent with a favorite magazine hidden under his mattress. Golf came more slowly but, unlike most thirteen- and fourteen-year-olds, he had “the patience of Job, the stamina of Samson and a swing as sweet as Arnold’s when he was a young player I’d watch over at Latrobe and the other country clubs around Pittsburgh,” according to Coach McGill.

Jason came to expect nothing from his mother and little more from his father except summer jobs far more challenging than those of his peers for he was being groomed to someday assume control of the Evergreen First National Bank and its three branches. He was, however, accorded the benefits of money and privilege. His mother purchased his wardrobe from Macy’s and Brooks Brothers on her shopping trips to Pittsburgh and Philadelphia. His father, forever trying to shape Jason into his own image, insisted that he attend both tennis and golf camps for six weeks each summer. As his father said, “Your summer work here at the bank is important but you can separate yourself from the masses not simply by your clothes or your manners but by becoming proficient in sports they can’t afford. You know, a little envy among your teenage buddies might be a good thing, not to mention giving you an edge with the girls, son.”

Meagan Navigates the Social Maze of High School

At the same time, Meagan's life throughout high school was "a bowl of cherries, picked fresh, washed, and fed to you by your adoring mother," as Emily, her closest friend would tease her because she, like everyone else including Sarah's customers, knew how close this mother and daughter were. They could be seen walking together hand in hand in the late afternoon and although Meagan began to date as a junior in high school, she and her mother would at times go to the movies together. In the early years of high school, Sarah impressed upon Meagan the importance of excelling in her studies.

"You've got a head start on most of your classmates because we've both always liked to read, almost like it's our favorite hobby. So you're a step up the ladder already. And it comes so easy for you. If there's one thing I want to see, it's my baby girl marching over that stage collecting her college degree no matter what you decide to major in. Yes, our salon has been wildly successful but I've always regretted that I couldn't ever go to college. And it shows. If you think about all the ladies who come to the salon, there's just a difference when you've been to college. I don't care how much somebody may read or study at home, it just doesn't show up the same. And I know that's true for me also no matter how much I try to improve myself. In a way, because I never had a chance to go, I want you to go for both of us. That's my dream, honey."

From the day Meagan entered the ninth grade at Hamilton Hills

High, she easily aced course after course. She and her best friend, Emily, had excelled on the city's junior gymnastic teams having twice taken their teams to the state finals in their age groups. Meagan, though arriving a bit late to the puberty party, eased from five-feet-two to five-feet-five during the ninth grade. She was famous for her squats and pull-ups in the gym and used her "thunder thighs" as the boys called them for both speed and durability on the soccer field. As a forward she made the varsity team while still a ninth grader. Her focus and ferocity reminded Coach Hodge, now in his twenty-seventh year of coaching, of another Sewell, albeit one who was almost six feet and could handle a basketball as a magician might. Her high cheek bones, butterscotch skin and thick raven-black ponytail, not to mention those blue-diamond eyes mined from her mother, also caused Coach Hodge to say, "You know, she looks for all the world like another Sarah except with a smaller circus acrobat's body. I've seen some second-generation boys and girls on our teams over the years but she takes the cake for the best look-alike. And, as different as they are, we're just blessed to have had them both."

In the tenth grade, Meagan was elected vice president of her class. Beyond her athletic prowess and her participation in the drama club, it was her disarming wit in the drama of daily teenage life that endeared her to her fellow students. She and Emily, newly nicknamed 'Emi' along with another friend, Heather, not only studied together after school or after their practices but had sleepovers several times each month. But it was their junior year that arrived with the biggest changes. Both Meagan and Emi, because of their popularity and wit, won places on the eight-girl cheerleader squad although these positions were usually awarded only to seniors. Of course, their flair for daring acrobatics and fearless flights from small trampolines they carried to the games provided another incentive for the judges to choose them. Their penchant for sartorial incorrectness, like their gymnastics, was also taken to another level. What had begun several years earlier when they wore slacks and shirts to school and got away with it was ramped up to jeans and either sleeveless shirts in summer or tight sweaters in winter in the first half of their junior year. Later, on a cold and boring Saturday night sleepover with Heather, they decided that they would wear black, full-body leotards with loose fitting boy's black shirts tied in front to school on Monday. So, off to Wal-Mart they went that

Sunday afternoon for what they jokingly called their fittings. It was agreed that they would wear loose skirts over these ensembles to disguise their arrivals, meet at their lockers, and quickly discard the skirts in the restroom.

Their grand entrance at 8:15 a.m. as a threesome into their homeroom the next day generated a firestorm of attention. The fourteen boys howled their approval like alpha wolves in heat, some even making bumping noises under their desks. The seven other girls in class seemed astonished at the audacity of the trio. One shouted, "Oh my God in heaven, Lucifer has sent down his black angels to take us all straight to hell." Ms. Stokely, generally regarded by the students as strict but fair, locked her gaze on them like a falcon spiraling down toward a scampering squirrel. Squinting at them, she said, "Girls, a costume party is not what this school is about. It's about getting an education and not distracting half the student population by exercising your freedom of expression."

Meagan, as though she had rehearsed her lines which were in fact spontaneous, retorted, "Ms. Stokely, we honestly think we are within the dress code and we've definitely got the hygiene part covered because we all three showered this very morning."

"But you all three look like you've dressed as black witches or ladies of the night for Halloween or, and I guess this will please you, as ballerinas in the 'Black Swan' ballet if you know what I mean. The real problem, though, is you're simply too provocative. Don't you boys agree?" Ms. Stokely asked. This rhetorical question prompted another chorus of raucous catcalls, hallelujahs, and several horse-like whinnies. One boy said, "Even if I promise not to look too hard, I already know I'm not going to sleep much tonight. Oh, such sweet dreams as I've never had before."

"Please, class, that's enough," Ms. Stokely said in her most authoritarian manner that strangely was appreciated and obeyed by the students. "Now I think I will ask the three of you to report to the assistant principal's office until we can resolve this issue. I really do think you've pushed the envelope a bit too far this time."

Meagan, Emi, and Heather, who were yet to take their seats, said, "Yes, ma'am," and sauntered out of the room. Ms. Stokely called for assistance with monitoring her class and accompanied them. A compromise after the ensuing conference was reached. Leotards with a

V-neck not more than one inch below the collar bone could be worn but only under a skirt and not above the top of the kneecap. Home they went, our three budding feminist heroines, and back to school they came an hour later having slightly cracked one more glass ceiling. And hence was born another new fad at HHH that came to be called "the m-e-h-be" for the first letter of each of their first names and a "be" thrown in to suggest their power. Of course, the intended pun on "maybe," because of the still provocative look of leotards under rather short skirts, was lost on no one, especially the testosterone-primed roving masses of the opposite sex.

There were two other major changes for her during her junior year. One was almost liberating and the other became almost an incarceration. The liberating event was simple, easy to explain, fun to experience. Because Meagan's birthday was at the end of December, Sarah had made a special appeal to the principal of her first elementary school to permit her daughter to enroll while she was still only five. This explained in part her delayed vault into puberty in the ninth grade. But it also meant that she had her "sweet sixteen" birthday in December of her junior year, an event celebrated discreetly at home with a dinner cooked by Sarah, Cathy Eubanks, Emi, and Heather. The surprise that was carefully scripted by Sarah awaited Meagan in the garage. Meagan screamed when she saw the emerald green Ford GT Mustang convertible with a large red bow taped to the windshield. Although three years old, the Mustang was like new and its tan leather interior also smelled new. Having driven Sarah's eight-year-old Honda Accord for a year on her learner's license, Meagan and the party popped the top, piled in, turned up the radio, and took a thirty-minute drive despite the near freezing temperature in the dark of a winter's night. When they returned, Sarah recorded the joyous event with photographs of the smiling, celebratory group, and said, "Now smile, honey, because you remind me of Meredith when she had a red Mustang that we would cruise the countryside. Oh, those were the days!"

The other occurrence that seemed inconsequential at the time but bordered on being an incarceration was an assignment Meagan had in her world literature and world history classes while the class was studying religions of the world. Each student was assigned a term paper of fifteen to twenty pages, the longest of the year, with the topic being a religion of choice. Meagan chose Buddhism, because she found its emphasis upon one's actions, not to mention one's inaction during meditation, as perplexing and something entirely new. She told Sarah that she assumed Buddha was either the Asian version of their Episcopalian God or at least a messiah or prophet resembling Jesus. After Reverend Reid had been separated from Saint Michael's, Sarah and Meagan along with about forty percent of the congregation had abandoned the church during the ensuing six months. Their tie to the church, as was true for many of the parishioners, had always been through the revered Reverend Reid. But it seemed that he had vanished into a strange anonymity and rarely communicated with anyone after his departure. The rumor, according to the same deacon who had received the leaked tape of the bishop's proceedings about Reverend Reid, was that he had separated from his wife and spent his days in silence writing a memoir while delivering blistering sermons on the decay of morality and civility in the western world to the small congregation of his church on the coast of Maine.

So, how did a relatively simple assignment capture Meagan's attention for two months to the exclusion of most of her activities except for being a cheerleader at the winter basketball games? For some reason she took her task seriously and, finding a paucity of books at either the school or public library, she would drive each afternoon to Carleton University to read various essays and books on Buddhism. After several weeks of getting to know one of the student librarians, she was permitted to take home three texts at a time.

Sarah questioned her about this obsession, asking, "What is it that has captured you the way this foreign religion has? I mean is it because it's exotic or weird or because you like those sayings of Buddha you quote to me? For the life of me, it seems like you've gone overboard, jumped into a sea of secrets that are swallowing you. You need to remember you're sixteen and this should be the time of your life. You haven't even had a date for the movies in six weeks and that old boisterous Mustang mainly gets fired up to go out to the library at Carleton. I guess it's got the streets memorized so you don't even have to steer it."

"Oh, Mom, it's hard to explain. I don't pretend to really understand it at all and in many ways it's more like some kind of philosophy, not really a formal religion with some reigning macho god. I'd always thought Buddha was the same as the God we heard about in church. To be honest, I never thought you were very religious. And now we never go to church since Reverend Reid left. A lot of the books I bring home, the heavies I call them, writers like Suzuki, are so dense I can't make any sense of them at all. Trying to read them is like when I'm doing my exercises on the high and low bars in gymnastics. The high bar is like most of the stuff that's too distant or complicated to even see clearly and the low bar is like having my nose rubbed in the Buddhism mud so I can't even breathe it's so suffocating. But then you run into something less complicated like this little book called *Zen and the Art of Archery*, and you think well, maybe I get it after all. Or, there's this teacher named Watts who writes these really readable essays and books and I even got hold of some tapes of his older shows on PBS. Oh, wow, they were just great. And maybe the best of all the essays are those by an English guy named Robert Allen who used to teach in Thailand. He just digests all that heavy shit and puts it out there in simple, understandable terms and little vignettes."

"But where is all this going, Meagan? I'm not worried about you. I just don't want you to get obsessed with some weird religion or to sign up with some guru like the Beatles did," Sarah said as she cleared the dishes from dinner.

"Don't worry. I've been writing for several weeks already and not just making notes for my term paper. It does count as our entire grade for both courses for the eight week period in world lit and history so I want it to be the finest paper I've ever written. And Ms. Jacobs said she is going to enter the two best papers in a statewide contest sponsored by the Interfaith Council of Pennsylvania, whatever that is. So, chill out, I'll be done with it all by the end of March," Meagan exclaimed as she came up behind her mother at the kitchen sink, enveloped her in her arms and said, "You'll never know how much I love you. I've got one momma, as I said when I was little, who's better than anybody's mom and dad combined."

By the end of the eleventh grade, Meagan was one of three juniors from her class of one hundred and forty-seven initiated early into the National Honor Society. Her essay, entitled "Behold Buddhism: An Episcopalian's View From The Pew," won the statewide award for all high school juniors and seniors. While the topic of Buddhism alone, no matter how elegantly written, would probably never have caught the eye of the Interfaith Council's judges, Meagan's shrewd contrast of the enigmas of Buddhism to her exaggerated Christian orientation indeed captured the attention of the Council and catapulted her essay to the top of the heap over two thousand entries. Meagan's award was celebrated at her school's final convocation that May. But the reason she remained so popular was illustrated by her acceptance when she said, "Well, dudes, we beat out all the big-city brains, but the reason I won this is because I've got great teachers and my fellow students are always asking hard questions that make us all think. So I say, let's head out to the lake for a picnic and some real Zen fun and games. I love you all."

During the summer before her senior year, Meagan worked at the local CVS drugstore because Sarah thought she should learn about the discipline of work and the joy of having a little more spending money. She entered her senior year with high expectations. She and Emi had tired of the rituals and relentless pace of practice for the small group of gymnasts and, by the end of their junior year, informed their coaches that they were leaving the gymnastics team and would only play on the soccer team as seniors. This was met with both dismay and pressure from peers, the principal, and the coaches to change their minds. They held firm, were unwavering. As Emi said in a meeting between their parents and the coaches, "Meagan and I are pretty good for high school gymnasts, but we both know we'll be marginal at best in college, never great. And all of you forget one thing and that is besides studying and participating in two sports, we rarely have time or the freedom to just enjoy school and being seventeen. I mean, Jesus, it's like we're professional jocks. So, yeah, you can say we're letting the school down, guilt-trip us, but we say we've given you three good years and one more coming up for soccer. Not to mention that Meagan is definitely going to receive scholarship offers for soccer even if I don't. Believe us when we say we've spent many a night discussing it and we've decided." Meagan added that they were starting an after-school yoga club twice a week as a gesture of their appreciation to their coaches. She added that the yoga class would be open not only to students but to the community as well.

Of course, the biggest question for all of the seniors was where each would apply for college. During the late summer, Meagan, Emi, and Heather took a one-week driving tour and visited the four colleges they were strongly considering. These were Penn State, University of

Pennsylvania, Carnegie Mellon, and Bryn Mawr. Among themselves, they discussed that each had a chance of being accepted at one or two of the four while recognizing that Bryn Mawr accepted small classes and was as hard as Swarthmore to get into. The driving tour, planned with their parents and the assistance of the school counselor, was of course the high point of the summer. No partying, no visiting sororities, simply getting a feel for each campus and meeting several professors at each college that the counselor had arranged. Although they had been considering going as a threesome to Penn, they returned home with decidedly different views and opinions.

Heather, whose parents were both physicians, said she strongly favored Penn because she was considering a career in the health field and possibly medical school. Emi said she was drawn to Penn State because she enjoyed the sciences and her computer classes far more than her friends. Meagan knew only that she wanted to major in something related to liberal arts with a strong interest in English, writing, or art history. Meagan told Emi and Heather that she was captivated by the atmosphere at Bryn Mawr, by the several students she met, by the architecture and beauty of the grounds, and unexpectedly by the prospect of attending a woman's college. Perhaps it was spending hours at her mother's salon in the company of women or because she relished her closest friendships with her girlfriends more than her movie dates and parties "with guys who aren't very serious and are very silly." They all agreed to keep open minds until they would formally apply in December.

Despite Hamilton Hills High being a relatively conservative high school in a town that retained many of its small-town traits (even after the "Newbridge Provocations"), like most high schools it had the usual liberal though surreptitious use of drugs and alcohol. At parties, especially at the home of parents who were away, the most common theme was alcohol with the wrestling team (and their dates) specializing in keg parties. There was a much smaller subset who liked bourbon and vodka but they were often the first to fight or simply pass out. The drug culture seemed to segment itself along lines of identity.

It was well known that a number of the jocks, especially on the football and wrestling teams, secretly took steroids because testing was not rigidly enforced. If they didn't have a contact, they could find one easily at the two commercial gyms in town. The "speed freaks" as

Meagan called them were split between a sort of quasi-intellectual group and, again, the football jocks with the drug of choice being Adderal that was ground and then snorted. Cocaine and heroin were available on the street but rarely used. And finally, second only to alcohol in popularity was weed, preferably pure and not laced with PCP or other drugs. The "downers" were the most peculiar subset comprised of disgruntled, antisocial students who dressed differently, favored dark clothes, spoke in short monosyllabic sentences, and were pleased to be called "the mals" for malcontents.

None of this would be important as anything but social commentary except for one little secret that Meagan and Emi kept even from Heather and their other friends. Before Meagan began dating Jason Aldridge in the late fall of their senior year, she dated for several months someone she met at a keg party who spent hours playing action games on his computer, worked at an electronics repair shop, and read rather juvenile science fiction. He was by almost any definition a true nerd.

Even Emi questioned Meagan about why she would have any interest in someone with whom she had almost nothing in common. Meagan's only comment was, "I like to see how his mind works. He's just so concrete and logical about everything. If I mention some novel I've read, he wants to know about the author's private life, could care less about what I think about the book. Well, one other thing is he wanted to, as he said, 'expand my consciousness and world view' which I thought was pretty weird. So, sure, although you and I have resisted weed, he had this really heavy stuff like almost trip weed we smoked on our second date."

"Jesus, girl, it's been around since the ninth grade but we've always been so dedicated to sports and grades, we resisted it. I hope you didn't get laid when we both have said we would rather wait until we really care about the guy but I have to admit I'm about ready," Emi said, as she put a finger to her temple like a pistol.

"No, Emi, you can get pretty spaced out but you don't lose control of everything. I mean this guy, yes it's Terry Samuels, is a sweet sort of innocent kid, totally harmless. You know he's in that little group of sort of outcasts, but what I like about him is he's very honest, no pretenses. But, look, I'm not even sexually attracted to him."

Meagan stumbled along in this casual relationship that was more a curiosity than anything. When she and Emi began to laugh privately at some of her boyfriend's efforts to be amusing or his fumbling, inept romantic embraces and timid kisses, she realized that it was unfair to continue dating him because he was becoming an amusement that she actually felt guilty about. What she, and later Emi, did enjoy was smoking a joint together although they relegated their mild transgressions to weekends and never smoked while at each other's homes. Although dating had not been a priority for either Meagan or Emi because of their busy schedules and sports, they both agreed that having given up gymnastics meant they should begin to look at some of the more interesting possibilities roaming the halls and sports fields.

The Imaginable Romance of Jason and Meagan

Jason cruised along this same high school path, looking all the while toward escaping his forlorn existence without friends for the freedom of college. For his seventeenth birthday in late October, Jason also became the only high school senior at Hamilton Hills High ever to receive a new Corvette convertible. His reputation as a somewhat aloof loner in perfectly polished loafers and expensive, creased shirts and slacks was humanized a bit by the Corvette. While he was handsome, leopard-like on the tennis court, a relentless stalker on the golf course, and always near the top of his class, he was widely perceived as a whiner and something of a spoiled jerk. Although the black Corvette could have been the proverbial nail in the coffin for Jason and his precarious status among his peers, it served instead as a sort of social lubricant. Boys challenged him to drag races that he had the good sense to let them win on occasion. Girls leaned into the red leather-swathed interior and, seemingly intoxicated by the aroma, offered sweet kisses for a quick ride. One particular cheerleader, Meagan Sewell of course, who was not only petite and cute, but smart enough to have been inducted into the National Honor Society as a junior (her mother's genes again), soon came to occupy the passenger's seat of the black Corvette to the exclusion of everyone else.

Although they had known one another from Jason accompanying his mother to the salon, Jason's obsession with sports and Meagan's popularity and dual sports meant they only occasionally saw one another. A "hello" in the hallway was about it. On this certain afternoon in late October when Jason was parking near the gymnasium, Meagan was about to get into her Mustang. The last breath of an Indian summer didn't blow them into each other but when he saw her, it prompted Jason to say, "Well, Meagan, instead of mounting that Mustang, let me take you for a quick jaunt in my Vette. I'll be careful, I promise." As they drove toward the small lake near the city limits, Meagan's ponytail tossed in the wind and Jason asked, "Aren't you cold in those soccer shorts and jersey?" Before she could answer, he added, "But I'll say one thing, you have the perfect body to advertise any athletic outfit."

"Jason Aldridge, I always wondered if you were a big flirt, a womanizer, although I've never heard that said about you. In fact, I've heard the opposite, that you rarely date and may be a holy terror in tennis and on the golf course, but are shy at parties or dances."

"True on all accounts, Meagan. And I'm not trying to impress you with this car but I do think it's pretty cool. But I admit that I don't date much. One reason is that I'm so obsessed with tennis and golf, not to mention my studies. And as for you, I remember when I would see you at your mom's salon. You were always in high gear, chatting it up, so sure of yourself. Frankly I was rather intimidated but I know I shouldn't admit it."

"On the contrary, Jason. It makes me think there may be more to you than the control freak everyone thinks you are. I mean I'm not telling you something you don't hear whispered every day. Hey, I'm complimenting you for being honest."

"Well, thanks. I'm going to take that as an invitation to call you for a date this weekend. That is, unless you think it would freak out Miss Sarah, because she and Ms. Eubanks used to actually treat me like a real person when I would come there with my mother. I respect them so much that I would never want them upset about anything I did. If you and I should become friends, I may level with you about why I would escape to her salon in the afternoons. To give you a little hint, I'll say it was like visiting an oasis instead of being stranded alone in a desert. But enough, I hope you'll answer when I call."

Driving home, Meagan was surprised by her reaction to their drive and to Jason. Instead of the stiff, over-dressed rich kid he appeared to be at school, he seemed to genuinely want to talk, to share something of his life. As Meagan said to Emi that night, "You know, he seemed like he could be a sweet kid. I don't mean a wuss, far from it. But like under that macho cover and all that badass bravado on the tennis court and golf course is a little boy's undiscovered heart. Yeah, I'll admit one nobody has seen, much less touched, but what I detected was a whiff of vulnerability."

Listening to her best friend on the phone, Emi said, "Easy does it, girl. It's probably true that no one really knows him. I mean his best friend is, well, himself. Sure, he's consumed by sports and making all A grades from what I hear. But you just remember that Alcoholics Anonymous prayer. I think it says, take every day one day at a time. Don't get in over your head, girl."

The improbable became the inevitable. Meagan Sewell, the daughter of a single teenage mother who struggled initially to survive with two jobs and an infant met the potentially wealthiest young bachelor in Hamilton Hills, went for a brief ride in a Corvette convertible and fell in love. But the inverse was equally true. Jason Aldridge, pampered, pompous, and almost peacock-pretty met a gregarious young woman who offered him the promise of social acceptance by his peers who generally ignored him or disliked him.

Emi was the first to recognize it and call it like it was when she said to Meagan, "You know despite having anything he wants, he really is like a shy little bird in a cage that is covered by his parents with a cloth each night. I mean like how he's known to retreat to his room after school or practices, mainly because he has no true friends. And you sort of flip the cover off that cage and show him how to navigate the real world. Everyone sees what's happening to him, a kind of softening. He smiles now at people instead of either looking away or through them. You may save him yet, girl."

Jason, this gifted child of leisure, had learned from his father to suffer no fools, and from his mother that most of humanity was a pool of fools. Lectured by his father and ignored by his mother, Jason once confided to Meagan that, "A lot of times I feel like that Tin Man in 'The Wizard of Oz,' like I have everything but a heart. I don't even know how to describe it, just sort of a dead feeling except when I'm around you."

Meagan, almost incredulous, would look at Jason a long time, then say, "My baby, we're so young at seventeen to have found our love, which sounds trite but maybe I'm here to help you find that smothered heart. My mom and I didn't have much money for a long time, but what she always provided was the warmth of her smile, the constancy of her love, and her gentle touch or caress. I can smell her right now when, as a child, she would bend over me in bed every night and kiss me, and I mean every night. And the first thing I would see every morning when she woke me up were those beautiful blue eyes, so clear, so deep. Seeing them was like a little glimpse of God or maybe even heaven if there is one. One time, she said that her Aunt Sallie told her that her eyes looked like blue diamonds. I didn't think there was any such thing as a blue diamond, but I looked it up and they do exist, but are rarely discovered. One found in Africa is so big that it's in a museum. It's supposed to be worth millions."

"Meagan, I think maybe I just present only an image, that's my father's favorite subject, this image of self-assurance and maybe it's why I'm so relentless on the tennis court or golf course. I feel like if I beat them bad enough, they'll respect me, maybe even fear me in some way."

"Yes, Jason, but they won't like you. You may win your tennis match or golf tournament, but it's never enough. Because in a way when you demolish an opponent, you're probably just striking back at how controlling your dad is and how self-centered your mother is. To make it worse, you must know that a lot of the guys still say you are not only spoiled but that you're ruthless. Like you're your own worst enemy. You wonder why you don't have any close friends but you set it up that way."

"So why the fuck should I care?"

"Jason, that's precisely the point. You learned the wrong lessons from your father and your mother, learned that you don't have to care about the feelings of others. It's like one time I laughingly said something about the colors of Aileen Allen's blouse and skirt not matching or even fitting well. She said back to me, 'Meagan, your mom works her butt off to provide for you and gets you almost anything you want, but my daddy's a drunk, has been all his life, and ends up with part-time jobs at best. My mom struggles to put food on our table and most all of my clothes come from Goodwill. All I've really got is my name. So I'm sorry if you think my clothes are not matched or don't always fit perfectly. All of us including my sisters and me are barely making it week to week.' Jason, I've never been so embarrassed in my life as I was at that moment. I learned a lesson that I'll never forget. Later, I took her a box of special Godiva chocolates, a new sweater I bought with my money, and a letter I truly wrote from my heart asking her to forgive me. She was gracious but that kind of pain, the pain I inflicted, doesn't go away easily."

"I was starting to think you were lecturing me like you know who does, but I do get your point. I don't know if I can change or not, or if I want to, really."

"We'll see, honey. It won't be overnight. You might even come to resent me for loving you but I hope not."

After they started seriously dating in mid-December of their senior year, they spent most weekends with each other at sporting events and parties. They had two major disagreements. Meagan continued to want her weekend weed, something she handled with ease and used primarily to relax, to chill out as she said. But Jason, who did not smoke or drink much less consider sharing a joint with his new girlfriend, resented her lackadaisical attitude. Meagan's taste for marijuana was always a point of contention.

The other assault upon their relationship was Meagan's change of heart about college. Initially, applying in December, they both had been accepted (as they were notified in February) at Penn State. Jason, who was also considering Yale and University of Pennsylvania, specifically Wharton because of its strong business school, was delighted that they would both be together at Penn State. In fact, he had come to see Meagan as not only his lover but also his advocate, and in many ways his teacher of social skills.

The last six months of their senior year in high school were, for Meagan and Jason, the times of their lives. They reveled in the mirrored popularity they brought one another among their friends, and their personalities seemed to perfectly balance each other with Jason's stoic, programmed approach to life being modulated by Meagan's jubilant, carefree manner. They obviously loved each other, and everyone at school, except for a few of Meagan's jealous friends, thought they were the perfect pair. They celebrated their first complete sexual encounter one weekend at Jason's house when his parents were on a banking junket to Philadelphia and were surprised at how easily the mystery of it all was so soon discoverable. In truth, Jason's visit to Penn State the summer before his senior year had provided a brief introduction to the mysteries of sex, compliments of a graduate student from Montreal.

Jason was shocked when Meagan told him in March that she had been accepted at Bryn Mawr. She had thought this unlikely because her SAT score in math was only 580. But on the back of her award-winning essay on Buddhism, the strength of her soccer legs, her 770 in verbal, her early acceptance in the National Honor Society, and being a class officer and cheerleader, she was admitted into the small and select freshman class of approximately three hundred. Meagan was sympathetic but not apologetic as she broke the news while they were parked in Jason's car. "Listen, Jason, one thing that won't change is how much I love you. We're both going to be studying really hard during the week anyway. And on weekends, we'll only be a short drive away. Yes, I'm doing this for me, because I had an almost spiritual attachment to that place the second I stepped onto that beautiful campus last summer. I really hate to use this word but it was a sort of Zen moment in my life. I haven't gotten far with my daily meditation, which I don't talk about even with Emi, so I can't really explain it to you. Yes, maybe I'm being selfish but I have to do this."

Jason seemed to freeze momentarily, then sighed and gripped his steering wheel with both hands. Finally he turned, looked at her and exhaled, appearing almost like a balloon deflating but his eyes were those of a petulant child. "Right, Meagan, well at least I know where I stand and what your priorities are. I've had another woman in my life whose needs and desires always trumped mine. You know who that is? I'll give you a little hint. She's married to my father. You remember one time I told you how your mother's salon was an emotional oasis in my life. You remember that? Well, I've put the same kind of trust in you these last five months, and it feels really good. Hell, it's the only thing I've ever really felt. But now, I don't know. You're changing on me, Meagan."

"Oh sweet baby, I haven't changed at all. I've given you my heart and in a symbolic way my body. You occupy my mind constantly. I dream of ways to keep bringing you out of your shell, and it's been beautiful to watch your emergence. Just ask anyone. Now, come on, let's go to your house while your parents are still away. I want us to make love like never before. And let me tell you one thing, Jason Aldridge, I'll never leave you, so don't even consider pulling out on me now."

This love affair between Meagan and Jason, this classic high school romance, bloomed into the late spring of their senior year, when Jason's parents became more concerned that he might be compromised into marrying (or worse yet, getting pregnant) a young woman of dubious provenance who certainly did not deserve Jason's intense adulation even if she was scintillatingly witty, winsome, and smart. Two days before his son's high school graduation, F. Harold Aldridge III sat Jason down in the mahogany-paneled library of their home. He told Jason that he would attend the University of Pennsylvania and Wharton instead of Penn State. As his father put it, "Actually, I am telling you that you must start early by enrolling for summer semester or I'll basically disown you and you will have to get loans for your education. Your mother and I have been concerned for some time about the deviating path your life has been taking this last year of school with that Sewell girl. I visited with the Dean at Penn last week and since you had a stellar application and had been accepted earlier, he said they had no problem admitting you, even at this late date. Of course, he knew of my generous contribution recently to the new computer lab at the Wharton School of Business. That little beneficence will also help pave your path for acceptance to graduate school there if you go for your M.B.A., which I fully expect you to do. Like it or not, you need to plan to join me at the bank so that we will have an orderly process of succession. And Jason, remember that I do all of this for you, son."

And so it was that the ecstasy and expectations of their senior year crashed around them the day before their graduation. At home, Mr. and Mrs. Aldridge raised high their tumblers of Chivas Regal. In some ways, Jason, though never admitting it to Meagan, suspected that fate (in the form of his father) had intervened conveniently, for he too had harbored reservations about compromising his education and his goals for a gift so mundane as love and companionship. There was something about Jason that made many people slightly uncomfortable, uncertain whether he could be trusted. In fact, it was commonly known that when he engaged a far weaker opponent on the tennis court, he seemed to enjoy humiliating him. He would stuff forehand volleys down his hapless opponent's throat, winning sets 6-0, 6-0 instead of gamely permitting his young opponent an occasional whiff of victory. And yet no one, including the coaches, called his bluff for F. Harold Aldridge was also the chairperson of the Greenleaf Board of Education.

When he was about to leave Meagan for the university and having garaged the additional bribe from his father of a new Harley Davidson motorcycle, Jason felt somehow relieved. He thought that his prematurely cynical view of life was in part a gift of his father's machinations. And he felt that it was not only justified but that it provided him with a rationale for jettisoning Meagan. Meagan, of course, was the only person except for Sylvia he had ever truly cared about or trusted. Now, he only had to worry about himself, his pleasure, and preparing himself for a life of predestined success. In their last week before Jason left Hamilton Hills, their love came to be recast, mostly by Jason, as an affair of convenience. Meagan, spiraling out of control, seemed lost, in limbo.

On one of their last dates, Meagan, stoned and angered, said, "Jason, I don't know if the black widow spider, that would be me, or the praying mantis otherwise known as you, will win this one. I'm just going to ride it out until we know. Yeah, I hate what you're doing, what you've done to us, but I'm still not letting you go completely. Because you see there's one little technicality you and your family overlooked. Do you know what it is, Jason? Jesus, sometimes your silence drives me stark raving mad. Anyway, it's very simple, honey. I love you and it kills me that you don't care, that you would throw all this away merely because I'm an inconvenience or a social step backwards. Who gives a shit? You didn't feel that way when we were first dating. Like you said to me then, 'I never had a reason to smile in the morning until you came into my life.' And it was true. Except for your sports and grades, that misery so apparent to everyone was never hidden by your phony smile and your wise cracks. You know all this but you cannot admit it. It's like you have to ask your adoring mother when you can go to the bathroom and then your father for forgiveness when you jerk off. Well, Jason, I hope you are happy with your newly found freedom."

Jason, staring out the window of his Corvette, all but ignoring the pain of Meagan and without looking at her, said simply, "Don't be so melodramatic, Meagan. You should know by now that we are toast. I'm taking you home so you can lick your own wounds because I've got packing to do."

Meagan Meets Her Demons

Jason left for the University of Pennsylvania and Wharton two weeks after graduation to enroll for the summer semester with the blessing of his parents but without a benediction from his girlfriend, whom he neither called nor visited the last several days before his departure. They had argued once more when Meagan arrived at the Aldridge residence barefoot, stoned, drunk, and shouting for Jason to "come down here and face me like the man you aren't but the coward you are." Jason did not grant Meagan an audience, but he did call Sarah to come for her daughter because Jason's father was threatening to have her arrested. The next morning Jason departed for the furnished condominium his father had purchased ostensibly for his bank directors to attend seminars in Philadelphia.

"From the land of entitlement to the lap of luxury," his father said as he gave Jason not a hug but a single slap on the back as he walked out the front door. "And remember, son, the whole town and I are expecting great things from you. It's time to hang up the jock and buckle down to business with Wharton waiting in the wings and your ticket already punched." Mrs. Aldridge waved goodbye to her only son from an upstairs window, still attired in her monogrammed silk robe.

Several weeks later at the Sewell residence at 108 Elm Street it was 8:15 a.m. and yet another hot summer morning. Meagan, who was already late for her minimum wage job at CVS, looked at herself in the hallway mirror and murmured, "Another rough night, girl." Sarah who had left for the salon earlier had noticed that her daughter was staying out later and assumed she was again dating Terry Samuels. When they were arguing about Jason, she had said, "No man is going to ruin my life because only I have that power." Sarah had tried to reason with her by saying, "Honey, we've all had it happen to us. Why, I even married a scoundrel. But the thing to remember is just don't let it keep you down." Meagan merely laughed, but then said, "Not even you understand it, Mom, because if I could get away with it, I'd kill the bastard."

The long months of summer dragged on day after day, not unlike the ponderous and languid flow of molten steel in the few remaining small foundries near Pittsburgh. Meagan staggered along aimlessly, her only energy coming from the anger that fueled her late-night debaucheries as she careened from one boyfriend to another, sometimes forgetting their names. She found these so-called dates necessary because she was now smoking several joints a day. She had also started doing "shooters" with a student at Carleton whom she would date on Saturday nights. By early August, she had jettisoned her best friends, Emi and Heather, and a week later lost her job at CVS because not only was she repeatedly late but also was told, "In your position as a cashier, you have failed to meet our standards. It's only because your mother is so highly respected in our community that we don't spell that out, or worse than that, have you detained for questioning." In other words, as a cashier she had made herself several small loans.

Meagan covered well. She told her mother that yes, she had lost weight but it was intentional. And she said that while she may have been late for work, the real problem was her manager who continued to ask her for a date, despite her rebuffing him. She said that she preferred not to disrupt the married manager's life by filing a formal complaint. The other ruse, far more serious, was her developing sinusitis despite a rather wet and rainy summer with the lowest pollen counts in several years. When she stopped by Sarah's salon one afternoon in late August to borrow twenty dollars, she encountered someone a bit more worldly than Sarah. Cathy Eubanks had been around a number of proverbial blocks more than a few times. Although she had talked to Sarah about her several years as a waitress, she had not elaborated about a year she had spent on the streets of Philadelphia when she had been addicted to cocaine.

When Meagan walked out of the salon, Cathy put her scissors down, asked sweet old lady Scott to excuse her for a few minutes and whispered to Sarah, "I want to see you in the arts den right now."

Sarah, who was cleaning a lavatory, glanced up at the mirror, saw Cathy's consternation, and followed her into the den where they were alone.

"Sit down, sweetie, we need to talk and I'll make it fast," Cathy said as she popped the knuckles of her right hand. "And I ain't going to be talking about some walk in the park because you've got a big problem"

"Cathy, I hope you haven't been recruited by someone and are leaving me. I need you not only as my most reliable stylist but as my sounding board and I'll do whatever it takes to keep you," Sarah said.

"Look here, your sounding board is about to sound off. You know, you've worked so hard since you opened this place that you're actually a little out of touch with the stuff that goes down in our town. You go home and read one of them books, go to a movie, or meet your two high school girlfriends for a glass of wine since you've loosened up a little in the last year. But look, here's the deal. Meagan's strung out. I don't know what this bullshit about sinus trouble is. But one thing I do know is runny nose, circles under eyes, a little jittery shake, that fast nonchalant speech, losing weight and losing her job, dating around like a cockroach on the move at night, and borrowing money. Well, add all that up and what you get is a distraught little girl who's almost for sure hooked on cocaine. I've seen it enough to be able to sniff it out pretty easily if you'll excuse the pun, honey."

"Cathy, I am totally shocked. You sound like you know what you're talking about . . . and maybe it's been right under my nose. Now there I go too, but I am just oblivious to something like that. I know she hasn't been her usual self. Always on the move in that Mustang, late to work, won't confide in me, not to mention she's alienated Emi, Heather, and most of her girlfriends. And I've never heard the names of half the boys that call our house, like it's a new one every week."

"Hon, I got to go back to Mrs. Scott. I don't want her to die in that chair waiting for me. But word to the wise, the sooner you confront her, the better. This ain't no joking matter. The longer she's strung out, the worser it'll get. Trust me, this is one thing I know more about than most people."

The next morning Sarah remained at home until Meagan came downstairs, which was after ten o'clock. She asked her mother if she had not gone to work because she was ill. Sarah, with a tad of subterfuge, suggested that the two of them take the day to drive around Carleton University, see what was fashionable, and do some clothes shopping at the mall for Meagan's collegiate wardrobe. Meagan agreed reluctantly but then took over an hour showering and dressing instead of the usual ten minutes. As they were driving around the campus, Sarah asked if she were still as excited about Bryn Mawr as she had been earlier in the summer.

"I'm not going to Bryn Mawr or anywhere else this fall, Mom. I simply need some time to find myself. It's not just Jason, it's that I've been really depressed but I didn't want to bother you with it. I mean I know how much you love me, but you're just so driven by your work it seems we've drifted apart."

Sarah pulled to the curb and began to weep, something Meagan had never seen in her life. "Mom, I didn't mean to hurt your feelings. I've only seen tears in your eyes two or three times in my life, but I didn't mean to insult you in any way."

Sarah turned to Meagan, reached out and held her trembling hand. "Oh, my child, my hope, my beautiful young woman, I'm crying for you more than for myself. I've seen you fall apart this summer and to be more blunt about it, Cathy Eubanks thinks you're not just smoking marijuana, you're hooked on cocaine."

"Well, that low-class, slutty bitch. She probably would know what cocaine is because I've always thought that cowgirl, that skinny western dyke, had either done it all or seen it all. I've never understood why you value her so much, her opinions and her jive talk. And she speaks like she just stepped out of the white-trash housing projects. Why do you keep her? Is it some kind of pity thing, Mom?"

"Meagan, this is about you. It's not about Cathy, not Jason, not me, not even whoever last night's date was. I also called Mr. McIntyre at CVS and it's clear he tolerated a lot of your bad-girl act for longer than any average manager would have. I think you lied about him to me and he was gentleman enough to refrain from telling me all the reasons he had for firing you. So, we've got a real problem and it's way over my head. Yesterday, I got on the phone and there is a good therapist on the faculty here at Carleton, a woman psychologist. Are you willing to see her? Yes or no, Meagan?"

"Well, I still don't think I need to go for just smoking an occasional joint but I could talk to her about why I've been depressed. I don't think it's only the Jason saga. So, yeah, maybe it would be worthwhile. And you can forget that crap about cocaine. Cathy Eubanks just wants to keep her head up your ass to endear herself so you'll give her another raise."

"Meagan, I'll have you know that Cathy doesn't have an evil bone in her body. She does speak her mind and I've always respected her for that. And you know I've never heard you be so bitter and your language so foul. You're not the same vivacious young woman who graduated almost three months ago and was so excited to be accepted to the hardest college you applied to. Frankly, I don't know who you are right now."

At the conclusion of Meagan's two-hour interview with Doctor Helen Murray at Carleton the following day, Sarah received a call from the psychologist while Meagan was still in her office. Sarah was told that yes, drugs and alcohol were involved, but that equally if not more worrisome was Meagan's depression. And in fact she was considered a danger to herself because of her relating concrete and specific scenarios for suicide. Dr. Murray said she was legally bound to refer Meagan to a clinic in Pittsburgh where a psychiatrist with whom she was associated had admission privileges. She said that Meagan had agreed to go rather than be committed. Sarah, though stunned by this sudden revelation, left work and packed a bag for Meagan and drove her from the psychologist's office to the clinic in Pittsburgh that afternoon. After the interview in the admissions office, Sarah was told that hospital policy would restrict her visits to Saturday afternoons for the first two weeks and even that was permitted only with the patient's consent.

What was to be a two-week evaluation and treatment stretched into a twenty-eight day hospitalization because Meagan's detoxification from cocaine, not to mention detectable levels of amphetamines and valium, consumed the first two weeks. Sarah was not permitted to visit until the end of the month. When Sarah arrived for the discharge conference, Meagan and the treatment team informed her that her daughter would be placed on mandated outpatient care and would live at an Episcopal-owned recovery and residential center in Pittsburgh. But there was good news, and that was that she would be employed at a local CVS because Mr. McIntyre had given her a favorable review and recommendation based upon her first two months of work and, of course, her intelligence and social skills.

For Sarah, the next three months were the most difficult of her life since she had been abandoned as an eighteen-year-old pregnant young woman. Her telephone conversations with Meagan were tense and terse. The rapport of almost eighteen years had seemed to evaporate during the summer. Sarah made an appointment with the psychiatrist and asked if Meagan might be schizophrenic. She was told no but he mentioned that the treatment team had not precluded the possibility that Meagan was bipolar. As Christmas approached, Sarah called Meagan, begging her to return home for a week's visit if CVS would permit it, but Meagan said no.

Sarah, still working as hard as ever, talked to Toni and Meredith, listened to Cathy Eubanks, and even called Emi at Penn State and Jason at Wharton before deciding to drive to Pittsburgh and try to convince her daughter to come home for Christmas. On Sunday, December twenty-third, with a gentle dusting of snow beginning, she drove to Meagan's apartment. When no one answered her knock, she remained overnight in the lobby and the next morning met with the manager.

"Yes, Ms. Sewell, we know who you are because Meagan has talked about you, always favorably, I would add. But I'm astonished that you don't know that she moved out two days ago. No furniture to move, just her two suitcases, said she'd had a good experience at CVS, even got a raise after only a month on the job. She did leave a letter for you because I suspect she thought you might come for her, it being the holidays and all."

Sitting in her car, alone, in a parking lot not dusted but covered in four inches of snow, the sky still gray and threatening, Sarah slowly opened the envelope addressed to Ms. Sarah Sewell, My Special Confidant.

December 22, 1996
Dear Momma,

I open, salutations as they say, with the old-fashioned way of addressing you. I guess I haven't called you that in ten years but I mean it as a term of endearment. I've probably caught you at a bad time because I was almost certain you would drive up here to try and convince me to come home for the holidays. And you did or you wouldn't be reading this!!! I did get in touch with Emi whom I swore to secrecy. I told her to call you Christmas Eve and tell you I felt great but

I simply wanted to be alone for a while longer. So, where are we?

Well, first of all, I love you with all my heart so that hasn't changed and never will (more of those exclamation marks)!!! At least you can drive home feeling good about us if still a little disconcerted about me. I don't want to drag this out but what I've experienced in the last six months is like a lifetime of misery, ecstasy (not the drug!), and self-examination. When I piece it all together, the psychological parts of the puzzle, I guess I could be bipolar but I think it's just garden-variety depression. And yes, I tossed a few drugs into the mix including cocaine, but I hope that part is behind me.

The future, ah the future. Thank God you gave me this reliable Mustang for my birthday. I have saved most of my CVS salary because the church apartments were free (another vestige of Reverend Reid's divine intervention???). So all I spent money on was food, gas, and a rare movie. Yeah, I've been sort of a hermit but at least I stayed out of trouble. I am basically going to be out of touch for a while longer. I don't know if I'll end up in Central Park like Holden Caulfield or head to Florida where Jimmy Buffett is giving a concert on New Year's Eve in Miami. I remember how you loved that book about Jane Eyre. So, to get a feminist in the mix, maybe like her I've just got to keep working at it until I find the "true me."

Never doubt my love for you. And tell Cathy Eubanks the same because I think my denial about being on the drugs drove my ferocious verbal attack on her. Actually, I admire how she overcame her demons and detractors. Except for you, no one works harder. I think you do have to concede that she's still a little rough around the edges. I told Emi that my destination is not totally clear but my determination is. I suspect I will go to Florida and I promise to call you every few weeks when I get settled. Do you remember that beautiful final sermon of Reverend Reid's? You know he alluded to something like a "growth experience" except he called it something else I think. Anyway, let's just envision this as a growth experience to reset my psychological gyroscope and awaken my heart that you have protected and nourished all my life.

Much Love, Mom, and
Merry Christmas too,
Meagan

Bright Lights, Big City

Three days before Christmas, Meagan left Pittsburgh determined to make it to Miami Beach by the third day. She stopped only twice, once in Atlanta and once in Daytona Beach, Florida. She had never been to a real beach if you discount the gray and black stone beach of the lake outside Hamilton Hills. This was a small lake where teenagers would park and make out or, in rare instances, actually experience the thrill of awkward and contorted sex in the back seat of a car. In both Atlanta and Daytona Beach, she stayed in a Motel 6. This was to save money and also because she couldn't get the trite country and western jingle about Motel 6 that she had heard on television out of her mind. To be frugal, she ate fruits and cottage cheese, although she kept a bag of Oreos in her car for emergencies.

It was Meagan's intention to stay sober, to stay straight and to live, as her mother had suggested, "on the straight and narrow." Sarah meant she wanted her daughter to act responsibly, to tread a predictable path, to not become distracted by rabbit trails, as Sarah called them, that could lead to trouble. Meagan was pleased with her interval of drug and sexual abstinence in the fall while living at the Episcopal-supported apartments. She had worked hard in her job as cashier at the CVS in Pittsburgh, and would often volunteer to work a double shift if someone failed to report to work. Her intention was to stay busy and avoid situations for abusing herself or being abused. While she did not regard her life the past few months as particularly austere or monastic, she did think of it as rather boring and certainly lacking in adventure.

Meagan got a job at a CVS in Miami Beach during her first week because of her prior managers' excellent recommendations. Miami Beach and its neighbors had survived its cocaine-fed debauchery of the seventies and its commercial decline of the early eighties. Its rejuvenation of resort and commercial real estate, though tentative and sputtering for a few years, was finally in full swing. And not only was it the safe haven and new home to a second generation of Cuban immigrants, but it was fast becoming a playground of the rich and famous, and just behind them were the chichi *poseurs* of fashion and the *faux* famous. Bright lights and big city indeed it was, and for Meagan it was a decidedly different cup of tea from a small town in Pennsylvania and even the staid environs of Pittsburgh.

She was enthralled with the vibrant dance of the beach and its younger, hip population. Because apartments had become so expensive in Miami Beach, she could only afford a small apartment on the mainland. The lights at night, the resort hotels, and the old resuscitated Art Deco buildings created a fantasy that was like stepping into a new world or a novel set in some exotic locale. After three months of leading the same kind of monotonous life to which she had become accustomed in Pittsburgh, she began to visit the swimming pool and clubhouse at her modest apartment complex. And it was here she met and became friends with three women who lived two doors down from her. This led to a ritual of Friday nights of club carousing as they called it "because only skanky girls go bar hopping," Lola, the leader of the group, said.

Although Meagan convinced herself that several glasses of sangria or house wine or perhaps an evening-ending white Russian were relatively harmless, she realized her Friday nights were once again exposing her to something she had come to see as risky behavior, namely her drinking. She rationalized it in two ways. One, she felt she deserved a Friday night of celebration after forty hours or more on her feet as a cashier in the checkout line at CVS. Or as she thought of if, forty hours of standing, smiling and greeting silver- and gray-haired grand dames who either deliberately tried to belittle and embarrass her or delighted in some one-line supercilious comment about her admittedly cheap wardrobe. But even worse were the sniveling, balding old men whose shirts were decorated with half that morning's breakfast not to mention dribbled paths along one side of the zipper of their Bermuda shorts. But it was their eyes following the curvature of her breasts with the precision of a cruise missile that especially irritated her. And the second modulating buffer was that her stretched financial situation meant she was limited in how much she could spend on anything, including drinks. The problem was that after several months, she received a three hundred dollar raise. And soon the Friday nights became Saturday nights as well.

Lola and the girls loved having her along for the ride. Lola laughingly said to Meagan, "Come on, girl, you're in better shape than any of us. I mean nobody misses that sweet ass and that sweet little upper deck. All you really need is a visit to the Victoria's Secret shop to really blow the boys' eyes out. And it's not just your petite body, because you see how they react to those dynamite blue eyes framed by that glossy black mane of hair. Well, sweetness, you've got the whole package. And you'd think we'd be jealous but we aren't. For one thing you're funny too. So we love hanging with you, a man-magnet, because you bring them in and we sift them out. One stud ass for each of us is just about right. Sweetness, you're not only the main attraction but our ticket too."

Meagan knew that she had always been popular in school and in the previous summer of her drugged rampage, she could still command the adulation of that new set of addled friends. But she also knew that hiding just behind the frivolity of each Friday night smash, was the danger of something else she did not fully understand but definitely did not want to experience again. The danger she intuitively sensed was that she would slide back into the embrace of alcohol and the asphyxiating grip of depression. It was as though her rational mind was busily informing her of the pitfalls of her renewed recklessness, while her compulsion to live life full and foolishly ripped the reins of sanity from her frontal cortex. So it was that the Friday night flings that began in late April matured into the occasional weekend-long drunk by June.

The July fourth parade was on a Saturday and such a spectacle as she had never seen. The spectrum ran from a wheelchair brigade sponsored by AARP to a leather and thong-themed Gay Pride contingent. Her partying with Lola and "the bad girls" as they called themselves lasted until 3 a.m. the next Sunday morning. When she awoke, miraculously in her own apartment, she saw someone she did not know in bed next to her. He was handsome, in his mid-forties, and naked. He was still sleeping but the hand draped across her body was noteworthy for a certain elegantly woven gold wedding band. On the chair next to him were a white silk jacket, a light blue linen shirt, and navy slacks. The problem for Meagan was that she remembered neither meeting him nor his name though his snoring had a pleasant sonorous tenor quality. She walked unsteadily around the bed, removed his billfold, and determined that Eduardo M. Lopez from Boca Raton was sharing her bed. Still naked, she immediately became aware of two physical sensations: a sort of heavy aching of her upper arms which she saw carried the early flush of bruising, and then there was also a stinging sensation of her buttocks. In the mirror of her bathroom, while standing on the commode, she could see five broken circles of tooth marks toward the center of her buttocks. She returned to her bed and observed Eduardo Lopez peacefully asleep. She wanted to pummel his face, to rip his eyeballs from their sockets and, finally, to call his wife to come for him. Instead she slipped on her terrycloth robe, quietly opened the door of her apartment, went two doors down, and rang the doorbell.

"Meagan, what the hell are you doing? It's eight in the morning and we've been zonked out. Lola's asleep and Marie is shacked up with that idiot stock boy from Kroger. Who'd you end up with? Was it the handsome rich dude you met late or that teenage, tattooed zombie who kept hanging around stoned out of his mind? Sometimes I think I'm the only half-sane one around here," Annette said.

"Sorry, sorry, just let me in fast, I'm desperate. I'll tell you what happened and it's not pretty. Frankly, there is a lot of last night I don't remember at all," Meagan replied, tugging at the belt of her robe. "Thank you oh so much for coming to the door. I've got a real dilemma because this guy, I guess it's the rich handsome one, is over there asleep in my bed. When I woke up, I had no idea who he was but there's more to it than that. I'm sure we had sex but he sort of roughed me up."

"Meagan, what do you mean? Are you injured? And if he's some sort of psychopath, we need to get the cops over here, pronto," Annette said as she put her arm around Meagan's shoulders and pulled her closer.

"Well, I don't want a big stink and I don't want to involve any of you. You know how they would want to question everyone about last night's activities. And I'm not really hurt except for maybe my pride,"

Meagan hedged, because she knew any details she provided Annette would be the hottest gossip around the complex by sundown.

"I understand you don't really want any trouble and it would be embarrassing. Why don't you just call your apartment, explain to him that you don't know who he is and what he is doing there, especially since he's married and all," Annette said.

"Great idea, perfect. I'll just kind of allude to his misbehavior. Then I'll tell him I'm at my real boyfriend's apartment and he says he is going to take the bull by the horns if not by the balls. And he's the type who may just kill you, I'll tell him. I guess that should shake him up a little. I'll give him five minutes to clear out and warn him never to call or contact me unless he wants a lawsuit. That should really get his ass in gear," Meagan said, smiling, vaguely triumphant though still in pain.

The phone rang ten times without an answer. She reasoned that he thought he should not answer at all, so she waited several minutes and called again. On the eighth ring, Eduardo Lopez answered, his voice gravelly but his articulation quite precise as he said, "Good morning, the residence of Miss Sewell who is currently unavailable. Goodbye now."

Meagan interrupted him before he could hang up, saying, "Eduardo, Meagan Sewell here and I'm furious. I'm calling from my boyfriend's apartment. I don't know what liberties you took with me last night but I'm very sore in more than one place. I've looked at your driver's license. If your married ass isn't out of my apartment in three minutes, you'll have a police escort and probably a nice set of bracelets to boot. Now, if my boyfriend beats them to the apartment, you just might be dead when the police arrive. Never, I mean never, call me. The clock's ticking, you shit."

Annette and Meagan watched the stairs from behind a curtain. It was these stairs that echoed with the frantic steps of a handsome Latino man dressed in navy slacks and a blue shirt. He carried his socks and a white jacket in his left hand, the soles of his black alligator loafers barely grazing the cement steps. He paused once, looked backwards, left and right, then quickly descended the last flight of stairs.

Meagan turned to Annette and jokingly said, "Well if I get pregnant, between the two of us, that baby will have the thickest, blackest hair this side of a coal mine at midnight. Just kidding you, because I'm on the pill like everyone else. But listen, we didn't wake up anyone here and you saved my skin. The less said the better, Annette, and I owe you one big time."

"Get out of here, you funny girl, and get some sleep. Your eyes are red as a monkey's ass and your breath's not the sweetest. Sorry the night didn't turn out so well. I thought I was the designated driver and therefore the loser, but with all that went on, I'd say I'm the winner. Poor Marie. When she doesn't score, she always calls this Kroger kid to come over. Even his fingernails are dirty," Annette said as she hugged Meagan at the door.

After going back to her apartment and collapsing into bed, Meagan awoke six hours later to three faces, all belonging to her. One face was more of a façade, a party face, in that her mindless partying was, once again, an accelerating spiral into abusive sex, alcohol, and marijuana. This face Meagan recognized from last summer. The other two faces were waiting for Meagan as she, still somewhat drunk, staggered into her bathroom later that afternoon. These two faces materialized when she washed her face and stared into the mirror. The simple face, the mere physical reflection, was by now familiar. Her eyes were bloodshot and each had a perfect black ellipsoid bag underneath it. Her hair, smelling of cigarettes and cigar smoke, compliments of Eduardo, was also tangled and matted with something sticky. But it was her mouth that disturbed her the most. She might be able to crack a funny joke at a club but she could not now force herself to smile. It was as though her mouth and her lips were made of congealing cement. And she had not noticed until now the three linear scratches on the left side of her neck.

And so it was that Meagan recognized also a third face. This face, sort of metaphorically hidden behind the simple physical reflection, was the face of what she had come to call "The Big D," her code for the creeping tentacles of depression. She braced herself by holding the corners of the lavatory as she began to cry . . . not tears of shame or pain but of utter despair that felt to her as though they were coming from a hollow metallic box in the middle of her chest that would never be depleted, emptied. She sobbed for ten minutes then sank to the floor, her back against the cool tile of the wall, crying still, her face contorted, the salty taste of terror in her mouth, saying to no one, "Oh, I am so sad, so sad," repeating it over and over as though it might be the mantra of someone at a wake, her own wake. Finally, she pulled herself up by a towel rack, stepped into the tub and ran the water as hot as she could tolerate it and poured a cup of scented bath salts into her bath.

She hoped that somehow the hot water and bath salts might calm the pain of her buttocks, and leech this sorrow of her entire soul, this ineffable pain of her depression now returned, from her bones. That God would help her squeeze it, drop by drop, through the tiny pores of her skin. As if by magic she might arise healed or at least with the pain ameliorated. She lay with her body submerged for almost an hour, drifting, everything slowed, almost stopped except the sure and steady cadence of her breath that soothed her. After shampooing her hair and bathing, she watched the water drain from the tub, managed to get to her knees and knelt there for several minutes, then slowly stood so that she would not faint because she knew she was dehydrated. She dried herself, noticing that her arms and buttocks were more painful than when she had awakened. She put on her robe and went into the kitchen, picked up the phone and dialed a familiar number. She said, "Momma, I need to come home."

Sarah offered to come for her or to wire her money to fly to Pittsburgh, but Meagan declined. She asked her daughter if she was still taking her antidepressant and was told no, that she couldn't afford it and the drinks so she had stopped her Wellbutrin two months ago. Sarah had the presence of mind to ask if Meagan was suicidal. "Depressed, yes, because I've been feeling myself slipping back into it and sleeping poorly unless, you know, I am really stoned. But I know when I'm really way down, can hardly get up in the morning, and I'm not that desperate, Mom. The other thing I've noticed is how colors aren't very bright, they just gray out, and at work I have to force myself to smile. But not suicidal, no, and I would tell you, not to scare you but for my own sake."

They decided that Meagan would resign at the end of work on Monday for health reasons and on Tuesday, she would terminate her lease that she had already satisfied for the required six months. Then she would clean her apartment and pack for her trip on Wednesday. "Oh, and I'll fix the girls a pot-luck dinner Tuesday night with all my left-over food because they've been very good to me. And I know, no drinking."

Meagan's trip home was uneventful and when she arrived in front of their Victorian cottage with the roses and tea olive blooming, she could see Sarah's form in the window of the living room. And then, Sarah was running toward her idling car. "Get out of that car, my sweet baby, you're home and you're safe. Like my poor, old Aunt Sallie would say to me, 'This is your safe haven for all your life.' But in this case, it's our safe haven and heaven for both of us. We'll unpack later, honey," Sarah said as she embraced Meagan and almost carried her on the side of her hip like she would a two-year-old.

The next morning, they called the clinic in Pittsburgh and it was agreed that Meagan should come for admission immediately. Although admission on a Saturday was unusual, there was a concern that she would need initial treatment in an alcohol detoxification unit. When Sarah accompanied her, it was agreed that she would visit only on Saturdays but Meagan would call with updates on Tuesdays and Thursdays. As Sarah was leaving, Meagan buried her face in her mother's neck and latched her arms around her. "Momma, you saved me before I was born when it would have been far easier for you to let me or whatever I was go, float away into the black universe. And you keep saving me. I know I've been a disappointment to you but I promise you are going to see a new me in several months. You are my heart. No more crying now, so get out of here."

A Slow Recovery at the Agape Clinic

Meagan thought her stay at the Agape Clinic would be brief. She knew she had to complete her withdrawal from alcohol, but she had done that before. At least she was free of the specter of withdrawal from cocaine, an experience the previous fall that had been wrenching. She also knew that she had responded rather quickly to the Wellbutrin her psychiatrist had started that October, and until now had not been depressed except for the last month in Miami. Thus, she reasoned that a week or two for detoxification and a week to treat her depression would lead to her soaring back into the salubrious and comforting arms of her mother by the end of July.

But soar she did not. No sweet bird of youth, renewed vigor, rekindled spirit or flight to health. No, none of those but something more akin to a buzzard's dance was taking place within her body. Her psyche and her already faltering castle of sanity and sobriety were the prey, the carrion upon which this buzzard pranced and picked its way, in random and strange struts, mindless of the sanctity of Meagan's mind, body, or heart. A routine schedule of detoxification was interrupted by her lack of appetite and refusal to eat.

"Dr. Schwartz, I'm not faking this, and I'm not refusing to eat because I'm obstinate. It's just that I feel completely deflated, washed out as an old dishtowel. I can hardly drag myself out of bed each morning and it doesn't feel like simply depression. I know what that feels like. There's no question that I'm depressed, but it seems there is something physically wrong with me," Meagan said as she lay in bed barely able to lift her head.

"Meagan, you and I came to not only understand one another last fall but also to trust each other. But you've got me in a quandary. We're successfully winding you out of alcohol withdrawal after ten days, but something's not kosher here. And I've held off putting you back on Wellbutrin, which worked so well, until we're totally clear of detox. But you've got me stumped and I wonder if you're not playing some kind of game with me," Dr. Schwartz said querulously.

"Look, I've hardly got the energy to try and smile at you each morning on your rounds, much less concoct some mysterious anorexia bullshit. I'm on your side if you remember, since I'm the one who has lost ten pounds in these last few weeks," Meagan pleaded.

Two days later on morning rounds, Dr. Schwarz failed to notice but a third-year medical student accompanying him asked, after they left her room, why Meagan's eyes had such a yellow tint. They returned to her room and Dr. Schwartz in front of both the student and the nurse exclaimed, "Christ, Meagan, your eyes tell us you're about to be as jaundiced as a pumpkin, something I had not noticed until now. I don't know if you've got hepatitis or what. Are you certain you weren't doing any intravenous drugs, heroin, speed, or anything else? I've got to know," he said as he proceeded to examine her abdomen to see if she had an enlarged liver.

"And Jesus Christ right back to you, Dr. Isaac Schwartz. I'm the one who has been telling you for a week that I feel like I've been run over by a truck. And hell no, I didn't shoot-up any drugs. I've never done that and I don't even know how. And this time, not even a little snort of cocaine like I was using last time. Anyway, you know my drug screen was clean except for the marijuana. So, how do we get to the bottom of this?" Meagan asked.

"I'll immediately get infectious disease and gastroenterology consultants, and I'll go ahead and get liver enzymes and a full chemistry profile stat so they will have those available when they see you later today. I'm just hoping you've got a simple hepatitis and not hepatitis B or hepatitis C from some of your recent sexual liaisons. I do believe you when you say you haven't been shooting up. That's why, when you get out of here, I don't want any more unprotected sex unless you are in a long-term relationship. Oh, let's say thanks to our student here, Steve Hollisman, for having a keen eye and a bloodhound's nose for trouble, not to mention teaching his attending physician to be a bit more observant," Dr. Schwartz concluded, winking at Mr. Hollisman whose face was faintly flushed.

Meagan was transferred the next day to University Hospital after she was diagnosed not with hepatitis from a typical viral infection but with mild liver failure probably related to mononucleosis. As Meagan said to Sarah when she visited, "Wouldn't you know that I would get what they call the kissing disease a little late in life when I mainly wanted a quick tumble in bed and hold the kisses, please. I guess I got mono from my last fling with that Latino lover in Miami. Just kidding, Momma. So don't look so distressed. That's the only time I've felt like making a joke in the last two weeks."

Of course Sarah, nonplussed, scolded her once precocious, now jaded daughter. "Now, Meagan, you clean up your mouth and your act. It's like that time you smarted off to Miss Bertie Stembridge, your principal, and almost caused her to have a stroke. And did cause me to stroke out when I had to explain your two-day suspension to Cathy Eubanks, the other girls at the salon, and some of our more curious customers. I don't want my baby girl back, too late for that, but I do want you to get well soon. Then, we'll get you in college and hopefully you will settle down."

Meagan's hospital course was difficult and a roller coaster of complications. Two weeks of treatment for the mild liver failure was complicated by an unexplained anemia and, a week later, a gastrointestinal bleed that fortunately stopped after two days. Finally, medically stable, but even more depressed because of the stress of her illnesses, she returned in early August to the Agape Clinic. Her depression did not respond to the Wellbutrin begun at University Hospital or to two other antidepressants. Although she had gradually begun to eat after her jaundice remitted before her return to Agape, her weight had fallen another seven pounds. Dr. Schwartz would question her each morning, and it was clear that her sleep was disturbed. She had minimal interest in anything, nothing was funny including movies starring Peter Sellers that she loved, and communicating with Sarah by phone or at the time of her visits came to be something Meagan dreaded.

Her favorite activity was sleeping during the day and writing in her journal and pacing in the hallway at night. Dr. Schwartz called Sarah and asked her to attend a meeting of Meagan's full treatment team. On this first day of September with a first hint of fall in the air, each team member contributed to the prevailing view that Meagan was truly in trouble. Her weight had drifted down another five pounds, she refused any activities when she could be aroused at all, and ate or drank almost nothing except for cranberry juice and forced Ensure. Worse still, she had experienced three episodes of urinary incontinence at night while in bed.

And more telling than any of this was when she awoke one morning in a small pool of urine, went to the bathroom, changed into her gym clothes, and then cut her wrist with a safety razor she had pried open. As she watched the purplish blood flow into the lavatory, she realized she had successfully lacerated a large vein but not the fountain of bright arterial blood she had hoped to liberate as, in her mind, she too would then be liberated from the confines and torture of her lingering depression. She staunched the bleeding with a towel, ran into the hall and yelled, "I can't even succeed in committing suicide, that's how far down I've fallen."

Dr. Schwartz opened the team meeting by saying, "We are all here, including Meagan and her mother, to discuss how serious this situation is. There are two very old terms in psychiatry we don't use anymore. Those terms are morbid depression and profound melancholia. Meagan's course and our inability to pull her out of her depression have given new meaning to these two antiquated terms. As we all know, one of our best LPN nurses became so despondent over Meagan that she requested a transfer to another unit. We have tried multiple antidepressants and other drugs over almost two months with no real benefit. But she is a fighter and we will not give up. We've never given up. And so we are here to discuss the delicate issue of electro-convulsive shock treatment. Sarah and Meagan, you may hear some of us use the term 'ECT' which is the same thing. The staff knows that we use this modality only when everything else has failed. Many other hospitals use it in the modern way with a smaller number of treatments and with the impulse going to only one side of the head. That way, we avoid many of the impaired memory issues, and we find that the patient will either respond rather quickly or not at all. Now, I want opinions from all of you."

"Over my dead body," Sarah objected as she stood to address the group. "I've heard the horror stories. They end up with a destroyed memory while walking around like a zombie. I even saw that movie with Jack Nicholson in it called 'One Flew Over the Cuckoo's Nest,' and that tells you all you need to know about shock treatments. Some people say you even lose your whole personality. So nobody's going to put that machine and those paddles on my daughter's head. Outside of work, I don't take many steadfast stands, but this is one tiger's tail I won't let go of until I've slung him back into the jungle. No, no, and hell no."

Dr. Schwartz thanked Sarah, asked for the opinions of the other staff and finally asked Meagan for her opinion. She reiterated her desperation, saying, "I feel like I'm wasting away, like I'm at the bottom of a well. It's not that I can't see any light, it's that I don't have the energy or motivation to even look for that light. And you don't know how embarrassing it is to lose control of your bladder. I've tried praying, I've meditated every day focused on a picture of a golden Buddha. I've even called Jason and Emi at different times to see if they could cheer me up. Nothing works and it's a mystery to me why all I get from the antidepressants is a grab bag of side effects. So I'm ready to try anything. And as long as I'm the patient and competent, Momma, I can make the final decision."

Dr. Schwartz explained that the procedure would be done under anesthesia and with an electrode to only one side of the head to decrease the possibility of temporary memory loss. He also said that some of the myths about the side effects of ECT were from thirty or forty years earlier when no anesthesia was used, when the induced seizures sometimes led to repeated seizures, and when the number of treatments often exceeded thirty or forty. After considerable debate, the team agreed to a trial of five to eight treatments over the next several weeks. Sarah acquiesced, even reluctantly agreed, and Dr. Schwartz gave her three articles written from a layperson's point of view to take home.

Meagan improved dramatically after the sixth ECT treatment. She was also placed on an experimental antidepressant along with a low dose of Zyprexa, an antipsychotic, and also a third mood-stabilizing drug, Depakote. She began to eat, gain weight, participate in group-sessions and lead the morning yoga group. In the tradition of her mother, she resumed her favorite pastime, reading. She read short stories because she did notice that her memory for recent events was somewhat distorted and diminished and that tracking the events, the timelines, of short stories seemed easier than when she tried to read one of the novels Sarah had brought her. So she became friends with the characters of Alice Munro's short stories, marveling at how easily she was pulled into their dilemmas. It seemed that Munro's characters were visited by the vagaries of fate in which their inner thoughts, unspoken desires, their utter humanness conspired to bring their hopes and fantasies crashing down around their mundane lives. Emi, hearing of Meagan's new interest in short stories, sent her an old copy of J.D. Salinger's stories. Meagan laughed and cried as she reread *A Good Day for Bananafish*, one of the Salinger stories she had read in tenth grade English. This was one of the first times she had reacted emotionally to anything in several months.

Meagan not only greeted each day now with a smile and sun salute, she broached the issue of her discharge from Agape on Dr. Schwartz's Monday morning rounds in now the first week of October. He said that the treatment team had discussed it the week before but, as a test of sorts, wanted it to be initiated by her suggestion. Her medical insurance obtained through Sarah's policy at the salon had refused to reimburse her stay for the past three weeks, resulting in a bill for Sarah that already totaled almost twelve thousand dollars. The following Wednesday, the team, Sarah, and Meagan met to map a plan for her discharge on Friday. They also decided that Meagan should keep her appointments with Dr. Murray, the psychologist at Carleton University. Meagan was told also that she would be expected to attend AA meetings on a regular basis.

"Free at last, Momma," she said to Sarah as they were driving home that Friday afternoon. "I don't know when I've felt such helplessness as I did these last several months. But if it taught me one thing, it is that you do sometimes need the help of others. I think you've been so independent all your life, I guess since that morning you left home before dawn to find a new life, that you can't really understand what I mean."

"Well, honey, that's not entirely true. I'll admit on the surface it looks that way. But if I hadn't had Aunt Sallie to run to and then Reverend Reid and Momma Reid to nest with, and later Meredith and Toni in high school, there's no way I would have survived. Even that marriage, being pregnant with you, working two jobs, still I would call on my girlfriends and play Aunt Sallie's music box at night to lull me to sleep. Sometimes I think if I hadn't had my little ballerina perched up there twirling around and the music of that 'Dance of the Sugar Plum Fairy,' well, I might have never survived. I don't have to tell you how attached I've become to Cathy Eubanks in some strange way. Like we don't associate with each other socially and she laughs at how books are so important and fun for you and me. And yet, I truly depend upon her as an anchor with me to keep the salon successful. I admit I've never had a crisis in my life like you've just had, physically and emotionally, with the liver trouble and that depression. But you've pulled yourself up, honey. You did it."

"Thanks, Momma, but I don't know how much credit I can take. I will let you in on a little secret. Besides the medicines and the ECT, along with sweet old Dr. Schwartz and the nurses, I've been doing a little of my own therapy. I kept my favorite book about Buddhism and a book of the Buddha's sayings by my bed the whole time, read it almost every night except when I was bonkers and couldn't concentrate at all. But the other thing I did almost every day during the whole time was to meditate and write in my journal. I admit sometimes I would fall asleep and I hate that Zyprexa. During this terrible time, I never quit the meditating. And now, it's something I look forward to every day. I don't expect you to understand it really. I mean there is this Buddhist saying, 'If you do not find it in yourself, where will you go to look for it?' I use that saying to provoke myself to work on my healing."

Sarah interrupted to ask, "Is that one of those mantra things you used to talk about when you wrote the paper that got you that statewide award in high school?"

"No, Momma, a mantra is more like a word or several words at most. It's something you can say or think while meditating, but I don't do that. I mean, Jesus, the object is not to think, but to try and clear your mind of all the chattering, the little thoughts and emotions skittering around like bumble bees. They call it monkey mind and what you're trying to do is shut it down. But the irony of it is that you've got to un-try, un-will yourself to give it up, and then you may make some progress. I do it now twice a day for thirty minutes in the morning and an hour each evening."

"Honey, I'm not sure I followed all that. It's just not totally logical.

I'm more like a navigator or a brick mason. One thing leads to the next thing and you've got to plan and know where you want to go with that ship or that brick wall. Or, you'll soon find yourself off course or with a wall that nature's going to push down. But that's just me, the way I see the world," Sarah smiled as she slowed and pulled Meagan over close to her.

"I love you, Momma, and I'm so happy to be home. In the morning, I want to tell you about a scheme I've cooked up to get my life back on track. I figure if you took an unusual path to success, I can too," Meagan said as she patted Sarah's thigh.

The next morning before Sarah left for work, Meagan awoke early and at breakfast excitedly revealed her plans which involved getting formal training in meditation and yoga at the New Visions Institute, a well-known school of holistic health with a decidedly Buddhist orientation. To help convince Sarah of her intentions, she also had found that she could take introductory courses at night at the University of Colorado. Since both were in Boulder, she reasoned that she could easily coordinate her classes. Meagan explained that in the last three weeks of her hospitalization, she had researched in great detail the Institute and thought that path combined with at least an associates degree emphasizing psychology courses would give her a springboard for returning to Hamilton Hills to open what she called a "holistic health club for women." She intended to use Sarah's clientele for recruiting customers as well as Carleton University for attracting participants with the emphasis being meditation and yoga.

Sarah argued that there were at least two or three problems with her scheme. "First of all, honey, it probably won't fly in this town because it's just so conservative and you know it. Secondly, you always hear about people on drugs or alcohol, how they go to AA, and then they want to be the therapists. But most of that is just a combination of their own helplessness and crusading. The third thing is how much this whole fantasy will cost because if I'm going to foot the bill, I'd rather you get a real skill and a real job. I mean do something like this new computer stuff or even like Meredith, try to get on with a drug company. She's made more money than all of us put together, and has a blast doing it, I might add. So I'm running off to the salon now and we'll talk more tonight."

A New Vision, a New Adventure

Meagan was adamant about her ambitions for the holistic health club. Sarah understood the seriousness of her daughter's planning when Meagan showed her a daily log of her research and telephone calls made during her stay at the Agape Clinic. Sarah finally agreed to accompany her on a visit to the New Visions Institute and to talk with an adviser at the University of Colorado. They flew from Pittsburgh to Denver, rented a car, and drove to Boulder the following Thursday. Meagan was told she could enroll in a two-month course beginning the first of November at New Visions and that she could monitor the last half-semester of psychology 101 and sociology 101 at the University for alternative students. Sarah was persuaded more by her daughter's passion than by reason and arranged for her to rent a small studio apartment on the same visit. Her only condition was that Meagan should attend AA meetings, something she readily agreed to do. On the flight home, Meagan said, "Well, Momma, at least you won't have a career CVS cashier on your hands. I can't tell you how excited I am and I'm going to make you proud of me."

Sarah, sipping a glass of wine on the flight home, a suggestion Cathy Eubanks had made some time ago, looked at her daughter, frowned and said, "It's strange how in the last year, you've reverted to calling me 'Momma' instead of 'Mom.' Are you aware of that? I mean I hope it's not some kind of new way of being dependent, because I don't want you to be my little girl. I want you to take fate by the throat and be your own, independent woman."

"And don't think I don't know that simply by the example you've set all my life. You don't think that Dr. Newbridge chose to profile you for no reason. She chose you because the whole community respects you. Which is all I intend to do, gain your respect, I mean. As for that 'Momma' business, I just like the way it rolls off my tongue. It feels genuine like when I called you from Miami so desperate is when I think I started using it again. I don't think it's juvenile at all but more like a term of endearment."

"Lord, girl, you can go on about something. All I want is for this new adventure to work although it seems pretty extreme to me. If I didn't believe in you and in your intelligence, I wouldn't consider supporting it. And, hey, that was clever of you to send your essay on Buddhism along with your introductory letters to both the University admissions and the New Visions board before you were even out of the hospital. And calling your former CVS managers to have them send letters of recommendation was another small stroke of genius. At least New Visions and the University knew how hard you would be willing to work despite skipping out on college. And of course they knew how smart you are with those test scores to even get in Bryn Mawr."

On October twenty-seventh, Meagan arrived in Boulder with two large bags containing her clothes and linens, and a trunk filled with books and two small Steif bears that Emi had sent her while recuperating at the Agape Clinic. In the several days before her classes began on November first, she decorated her studio apartment and met two of her neighbors, one of whom volunteered that she was a recovering alcoholic who attended Alcoholics Anonymous. Meagan admitted her own challenges with drugs and alcohol, and she and her new friend, Margaret, agreed to attend AA together the following day. Having gotten a loan from Sarah for her school and living expenses, Meagan was determined to live frugally. Along with the bed, desk, and two chairs she purchased at the Salvation Army Store, she also got a microwave and a small refrigerator.

That Sunday night before her Monday classes, she called Sarah. "Momma, I know there have been times in the last several years that I've shut you out of my life. I don't want to ever do that again," Meagan said, her voice cracking with emotion.

"Meagan, we've had our ups and downs but I've tried to understand that's part of your growing up. I didn't have the luxury of smelling the roses as my dear old Aunt Sallie used to say. I absolutely don't approve of your drugging days and I've reminded you before that you may have your daddy's alcohol gene. Otherwise, honey, I'm in your corner all the way."

"Oh, Momma, I'm so excited. It's the first time that I've had a clear vision of something I want to accomplish. I don't care how hard I have to study, just bring it on. Two of my next-door neighbors came over and one of them goes to AA. We've already been to a meeting together and we'll reinforce how important our abstinence is for us, especially since she's also a student here. Anyway, I'm not going to call everyday, but always on Fridays I do want us to talk. Love you so much, Mom."

"You too, honey. We, I mean all the ladies at the salon, are so proud of you. I meant to tell you that Cathy Eubanks went out and bought you a Colorado cap with the buffalo mascot embroidered on it. I'll send it to you soon. Night now."

The rigors of the curriculum at New Visions Institute were daunting and required an almost monastic dedication on Meagan's part. As part of the introductory meditation seminar, students were expected to be at the Ashram Center at 7:30 a.m. Since New Visions was four miles from downtown Boulder and Meagan's apartment, she had to change buses twice requiring her to awake at six every morning. The morning didactic session of almost two hours was followed by an additional one-hour session at one o'clock. Interspersed were classes in yoga and the history of Buddhism. When Meagan arrived home at 4 p.m., she would prepare a meal of Progresso soup and a salad, then walk the five blocks to her two audited night classes in psychology and sociology at the university. Although she would receive only a notation of audit, she purchased the texts for the two classes, again taking her new adventure seriously.

Weekends for Meagan were not for the weak of heart or spirit. Saturdays were spent studying because her weekdays were consumed by classes. Her only social activity was a Saturday night supper with Margaret and her roommate. The three of them invited two other students who also lived in their building. One was from Sri Lanka and the other from Mexico. Margaret and her roommate specialized in various types of spaghetti. Yazmeen prepared exotic curry dishes, and Maria, of course, knew all of her mother's Mexican dishes. Meagan knew she would have to use the kitchen of one of her neighbors and as her inaugural supper approached, she called Sarah in panic. Although Meagan had no interest in cooking, Sarah convinced her to try her recipe for fettuccine Alfredo. The result was a rather thick, overly concentrated mass of noodles. Maria said, "Let's eat the garlic toast and just nibble around the edges of the fettuccine before using what's left as a new doorstop." Everyone at the table laughed and looked forward to Meagan's next effort that she said would be a special beef stroganoff.

In this fashion, Meagan established an almost ritualistic way of life while also attending AA meetings at the University on Monday, Wednesday, Saturday, and Sunday. She was astonished at the number of students who had already admitted that they were addicted to alcohol or drugs. Surprisingly, a number of faculty also attended and talked freely about the struggles they had experienced with substance abuse. Although approached for a date by different men, she demurred, saying she simply had to devote herself full-time to her studies. One secret she kept from everyone including her mother was that she had been talking to Jason since he had found her through Emi and called her at the Agape Clinic. Their telephone conversations were primarily about their experiences in school and danced around the issue of their long but broken romance. She could not decide if this were merely some melancholic attachment to her fascination if not fantasy of saving Jason, or was even more simply a way he had of "stringing you along, over and over, the same old thing, and it's all about him," as Meredith had said in the past. Meagan did know that his voice still sang to her in some bizarre fashion if only because of its almost palpable undertone of loneliness.

So, what she really did not know was whether she cared for him out of pity or truly missed the passion they had shared. During his last call, they had agreed to meet in Hamilton Hills for Christmas although his visits to his parents had tapered off during the past year. After almost two months, the holiday break was suddenly upon her. Although the university classes for fall semester ended in mid-December, the New Visions Institute recessed only from December 23 until December 31. Meagan could hardly wait to return to her room in her Victorian cottage, to see Sarah after almost two months and, yes, to once again reunite with Jason.

On Christmas eve, Meagan arrived at the Pittsburgh airport and was greeted by three of Santa's red-capped elves: Sarah, Meredith, and

Emi. Escaping the carnival chaos of the airport, Meagan asked why Sarah had not taken the exit for Highway 87 to Hamilton Hills. She was informed that a small surprise lunch awaited them on the thirtieth floor of the new all-glass Providence Building. Indeed, McIlhenney Pharmaceuticals had leased five floors for their executive office space, and Meredith wanted to show the entire group her new suite following her recent promotion to Vice President and Director of Sales for Pennsylvania and Ohio. After their tour of the offices, the frolicsome quartet retreated to Meredith's suite for a catered lunch and a holiday demonstration of her sound system by the unlikely mix of Bing Crosby, Elvis, U 2, B.B. King, and Buddy Guy. As Meredith said, "Since I'm the host and these are my new digs, I decided I had two votes while you girls got three. Well, I have a new lover who has introduced me to the blues, so you girls have got to grin and bear it." Meagan became the designated driver as Meredith, Emi, and Sarah split two bottles of champagne though Sarah never exceeded her maximum of two glasses. The ride home was a raucous rendition of Christmas carols along with certain delectable nuggets of gossip from the salon.

After Christmas day at home, Meagan agreed to go with Jason the following Friday night to the now established and esteemed Etoile Verde restaurant. Jason, ever the perfect gentleman, brought a dozen roses for Sarah when he arrived for Meagan. He complimented her on her décor and decorations and reminded Sarah of his indebtedness to her for, as he said, "giving me a semblance of a home when I was a boy and young teenager."

As they were leaving, Jason turned to Sarah and in a rare earnest moment said, "I could apologize for how Meagan and I parted over two years ago. But I won't. Instead, I will say quite honestly to you that Meagan was and is the love of my life. It may sound stupid or sophomoric, but I mean it. I have no idea what the future holds for us, especially now that Meagan is really on her feet and has a new vision of who she is and where she's going. But I will always be attached to both of you more than anyone else in my life."

Sarah was astounded at his candor, if he could be believed, but restrained her response. "Jason, you are going to be a success no matter what comes along because you have lots of different talents. Meagan too has many talents but is only now getting a toe-hold on her ambitions. How you two resolve your friendship is purely your business. I just hope you respect each other's feelings. That's all I want."

Their dinner at Etoile Verde was one of the calmest evenings they had ever spent together. Jason told her about Wharton, how difficult the courses were and that his narrowly circumscribed life had left little room for dating although he mentioned two brief romances including one with an artist from Philadelphia. He spoke primarily about how separated he felt from Hamilton Hills, from his earlier obsession with tennis and golf, and how he rarely visited his parents. He admitted finally that only she knew from the phone calls that he had no intention of returning to his father's bank. "I would rather end up on the streets selling magazines and hot dogs than be forever chained to them no matter what the rewards might be. When I think about how they have controlled and dictated my life, I get really angry and it was all done with such detachment. I think my sort of robotic rigidity and all the trouble I had relating to people in high school, well, it's from growing up in that house. That's why I rarely see them."

Meagan listened patiently as Jason discussed his antipathy for both his parents and Hamilton Hills. She noticed a slight tremor and how sweat would suddenly appear on his upper lip and at his hairline. Something she had never noticed before was how he would sigh deeply every few minutes. Meagan asked if he was under any unusual pressure and he said no. Leaving the restaurant, Jason locked his arm in Meagan's and said, "I love being around you, having you listen to my travails because I really don't have anyone to talk to. But I was also thinking that we might want to celebrate by spending the night at the Marriott if only for old times sake."

Meagan was surprised at his audacity and said, "Jason, that's ridiculous and really sort of presumptuous. I can never thank you enough for tracking me down while I was at the Agape Clinic and the two books you sent me were so thoughtful. You can't imagine how down I was and how your calls helped lift me. Although we've gotten closer talking on the phone, it's not going to be like the old days, not yet anyway. I want us to see each other spring break. That will give us time to digest tonight when you've been such a sweet friend. I'm really trying to get my act together. I'll always love you and if we sort things out, maybe you can come out to Colorado and we'll have an Easter honeymoon."

Before Jason said good night, he pulled a newspaper article from his pocket and said, "Oh, Meagan, I forgot to give you this article my mother found in last Sunday's *Philadelphia Inquirer* in the arts section. I just scanned it but it's about a woman named Sarah Evangeline Sewell who lived in West Virginia. Here, you see this picture of her and her loom and then the color pictures of some of her blankets. It seems she was famous for her blankets and their intricate patterns and even had a dealer in the Philadelphia area. Mother was impressed by the fact that she had your last name and the first name of your mom and your middle name. Anyway, give it to your mom. I guess it could be that aunt of yours you've talked about."

Sarah was shocked when Meagan gave her the article that night. They read it together as Sarah cried softly and said, "Oh, honey, of course it is Aunt Sallie. Who else could it be? She's a lot older in the picture but then I haven't seen her in I guess almost twenty-five years. But look at her standing by that loom she had always wanted, so proud, so strong. She was a force unto herself. And I knew she was good but can you believe some of her early blankets are selling for five thousand dollars? Well, we'll just frame this and put it in the living room. And to think old lady Aldridge happened to see it in the Philadelphia paper. I guess she's good for something after all. Of course, don't quote me to your sometime boyfriend."

The next day as Sarah was driving Meagan to the airport, Meagan told her about her date with Jason and how she had handled his suggestion. But Meagan was far more excited about her new adventure and turning her life around. "I haven't been more enthusiastic about anything in years than my yoga, meditation, and Buddhist history classes. Momma, it's like I felt when I started gymnastics and I could feel how perfectly it fit my body. But now this seems to fit my mind in the same way. Every day I awaken to what feels like a new experience, I mean the way I'm energized by both what I'm learning and my own practice of meditation and yoga."

"Well, honey, I haven't seen you so high, so invigorated, since you fell in love with Jason, not that I was ever very much in favor of that relationship. But you were on a mission then and it seems you are now. Since you've been here, I see it in your face, in your color, and in your speech. I do want you to keep thinking about how you will use this. As we discussed on our trip to Colorado, starting a business, especially something new to Hamilton Hills, is not going to be a sweet dream. Instead, it's going to be hard work. And the other thing is that you must never forget that you may have a little of your father in you. By that I mean you need to be sure you don't slide back into drugs or drinking."

"I do know that, Mom. I keep a journal every night and I think about these things. As far as the drugs and drinking, I really have no desire for them. It's not just AA that I go to. The fact is that until an alcoholic wants to change and has a new view about how to live, nothing will ever change. I mean everything I'm learning and doing precludes drinking and drugging. It may seem naïve but I don't see them as much of a threat anymore. Meaning I don't have any desire to go back. And as long as I stay on my antidepressant, I don't live in fear of what I call 'The Big D' anymore."

Meagan returned to Boulder to resume her New Visions classes since they recessed for only a week during the holidays. She also became a full-time student at the University of Colorado. In addition to taking two core courses, she enrolled in a basic physiology course as an elective. Her afternoons four days each week were spent at the New Visions Institute where she continued her studies of yoga, meditation, and a new course in the history of Eastern religions. The Institute had long espoused a multi-disciplinary approach to all of its courses so that she was exposed to a number of faculty members within each of her three courses.

Sarah would talk with her at lunch on Fridays but in early March, she could not reach Meagan. She worried that the stress of taking what amounted to almost a double load of courses might be causing Meagan to regress, to be slipping back into the grasp of the depression that haunted her. Finally, on Sunday afternoon at five o'clock, Meagan answered her call.

"Meagan, I've been worried sick for two days. I can't believe you would ignore me and be so thoughtless. Yes, I know you're under the gun, school-wise I mean, but anyway what's happening out there?" Sarah pleaded.

"Mom, Momma, my angel, I'm so sorry. To cut to the chase, I'm fine, never been better. I did a two-day retreat sponsored by the Institute. It was all about different approaches to meditation like sitting, walking, all types," Meagan said excitedly. "Our teacher was a wonderful woman from California. She was not only really helpful in our individual sessions, but she was really funny. We were so in awe of her that at first we were afraid to laugh. Then she said, 'Do we have real people here or some little Zen robots? So I'm encouraging you to loosen up. Neither laughing nor crying is forbidden, folks.' After that, it was serious stuff but with a lighter mood. Most people cried at the end of the weekend when we were hugging and saying goodbye."

"Meagan, I don't want you to ever do that to me, torture me like that again. I was sure you had stopped taking your medication and the pressure of trying to do too much, taking so many courses, had overwhelmed you. So at least, you're alive and well. But for the life of me, I don't know why you didn't tell me what you were going to do."

"I know, I know. During the week I was working furiously on my core courses and that hard physiology elective so I wouldn't be behind. I knew I wasn't going to have a chance to study over the weekend except for tonight. And the other reason I couldn't call during the retreat was because it's called a silent retreat. No talking to anyone all weekend. Just do your various meditation exercises, help with the chores of cleaning and cooking of course, but otherwise shut out the world's noise. Just listen to yourself, see what comes to you. There were fifteen of us. And while I'm a little spaced out, I would say it was one of the greatest experiences of my life."

"Fine, honey. It all sounds a little weird to me. I can't imagine going two days without talking, especially when you're around people. Can you see Cathy Eubanks and me having a silent salon day, no talking, just cutting and styling? Why, I'd have thirty insane women on my hands by the end of the day."

"Don't be ridiculous, Momma. But it is pretty funny to think about it. Maybe I'll bring it up in my Zen history class. You know, like a radical Zen approach to hair styling. See what they say. Instead of that crap about what is the sound of one hand clapping, it would be what is the sound of four scissors snipping. Anyway, all here is well. I've stopped that Zyprexa and Depakote with Dr. Murray's blessings and I am still going to AA as promised. You know how much I hated the way that Zyprexa made me feel, like I wasn't me. I know that sounds crazy but it's true. I'm seeing the University psychologist every other week and I really like him. On occasion, he and I have a telephone conference with Dr. Murray. She's so aware of my history that I want to keep her in the loop. I'm staying on the antidepressant and despite the course load, I'm actually enjoying the stress if you can believe that, Mom."

"Well, break a leg as they say, meaning the opposite of course. Like keep on keeping on may be better. I miss you and want you to come home on your mid-semester break. We'll talk about that later."

"Yes, I assumed you did. And don't say 'break a leg' even in jest, because a girl slipped in the snow outside my apartment last week and did break her leg. She's fine now and since I was the first one to her, I called 911 and stayed with her until we got to the hospital. Well, bye for now."

Leaving Colorado to Open the Greenleaf Health Spa

Spring break for both Meagan and Jason was in mid-April since Easter fell on the third Sunday. Although they had planned to meet in Colorado, Meagan insisted they both return home to Hamilton Hills. She was reluctant to have Jason staying for a weekend in her small apartment when she was uncertain whether they would mesh as a couple. Meagan was also eager to see Sarah because her bouts with depression and her periodic unraveling had actually brought the two of them closer together. If there was one place she knew was always welcoming and safe, it was at the home she and her mother so loved.

After dinner with Sarah, Meredith, Tina, and Cathy on her first evening back in her hometown, Meagan was glad later that night to have time for just her mother and herself. Meagan discussed the seriousness of her intention to return to Hamilton Hills and open a meditation and yoga center that summer. "Momma, this is not some whim or fly-by-night fantasy. I've been planning it for months. I know you would prefer I get my degree at Colorado or even back here at Carleton, but my heart is truly in this. As I've said before, I'm excited to wake up each morning, and I enjoy what I learn at New Visions Institute far more than the courses at the university. I've definitely learned the fundamentals to be able to teach yoga and meditation although I'm the first to admit that you continue to grow with both the longer you practice. From the beginning when I would read those different books and essays as I was writing that paper in the eleventh grade, I knew it wouldn't be easy."

"Honey, as you know, I have some reservations about whether this town will welcome a business like that. I agree that the students and faculty at Carleton might be an audience, but I'm not sure if even the younger women who come to the salon will be interested. And what you've got to realize is that it would be a business and not a hobby. You would have to run it like a business and that means a studio, utilities, insurance, all the overhead you haven't thought about," Sarah said.

"But I have thought about all of that. I met with two different women in Boulder, each of whom has a studio. I mean one is a woman's health club and the other is a yoga center. I talked to them about exactly what you said. I factored in rent, liability and personal insurance, utilities, advertising, getting endorsements, and anything else I could think of. And I drew up a business plan, modest as it is," Meagan said excitedly.

"I must say that I'm impressed. You know people see me as a workaholic and it all started when I was determined to make a go of that first little salon that Cathy and I opened. Lord, those first few years were stressful, but we made it and then it really bloomed and ballooned into what I have now. So, if I were to loan you start-up money, I would want it to be exactly that. I mean it would be a loan, not a gift. And I would suggest that however modest your studio is, it should be located in a nice section of town. I know these ladies and I can tell you they want a safe place. The other thing they like is for it to be tastefully decorated. And don't get so hung up on that Buddha stuff. Most of the people don't know what it is, don't care, or they think it is some Communist religion. Give it some sort of Christian slant as well, something that the common man and woman can identify with. And they don't want to see a bunch of Buddha statues and candles. For God's sake, promise me you'll never be burning any incense either. It's a dead giveaway for a cheap shop. I really believe that your main attraction should be the yoga and maybe have a class or two of that Pilates, that exercise type of yoga on television, because remember some of our ladies carry quite a few extra pounds."

"Momma, I agree with almost everything you've said. I'll put my heart and soul into it. Ultimately, I know it has to pay for itself. So, when Jason arrives tomorrow, I'm going to sort of scour the town for a place that would accommodate a large studio."

"Why do you need Jason involved? I know you talk to him at times and you've seen him occasionally, but do you really think he has your interests at heart? It's like Meredith reminds you all along when she says that Jason is all about Jason. Actually, she's not that charitable. She thinks he's a spoiled, selfish, damaged piece of goods, but she would say it in four letter words I'm sure."

"Well, I promised him I would go out with him at spring break. And to be honest, he was going to come to Colorado, but I didn't want to be stuck with him there."

Meagan was surprised to see Jason arrive the next day to take her to lunch and again he brought a beautiful bouquet of flowers for her and another dozen roses that they both delivered to Sarah at her salon. They spent the day riding around after talking first to two realty companies. That evening, they went again to their favorite restaurant, Etoile Verde, and Meagan seemed comforted by Jason's gentleness and his interest in her opening the studio. He offered to take her the next day to discuss a loan with an officer at the bank but she declined. Later, she agreed to spend the night with him at a nearby Marriott Courtyard after calling Sarah to say she would see her for lunch the next day. And so it was that once more these high school sweethearts fell together, embracing the futility of a love that perhaps only one of them truly believed in. The next morning, Jason drove Meagan home and announced that he was returning to Philadelphia. He hinted that he did not want to see or confront his parents about his decision, unknown to anyone except Meagan, that when he graduated after the coming fall semester, he would not be returning to work at his father's bank. As he said, "Anywhere at least five hundred miles away would be nice."

As Meagan got out of his Corvette, she leaned in to kiss him goodbye. "Jason, as much as I loved you and, as you know from last night, still do in some way, I absolutely don't understand you. You just seem to operate in a way different from most of us. Sort of like when a politician reads a short, prepared statement and you know he doesn't believe a damn word of it. You know why it sounds that way? Because his heart just isn't in it," Meagan said, as she began to cry.

"Meagan, no more lectures, no more stories about the Tin Man and becoming more human. It's just that I've got a lot going on and to be honest, I'm dating someone at Wharton. She has lots of money, lots of smarts, and eyes more beautiful than yours if you can believe that. But

I'll stay in touch because last night was really fine, really special," Jason said as he jerked away from her hand on his arm.

As she watched him drive away, Meagan's tears turned to laughter when she saw the new personalized license plate she had not noticed before. "Well I'll be damned, 'LOANER,' if that's not a bitch." She mused to herself whether it was a pun for the loner he was, a slap at his father's pecuniary obsessions, or a rather bizarre insinuation that the Corvette convertible, still immaculate, was not his. "Maybe I should never see him again like Meredith and Momma say to me every chance they get. Still, there is something about him that I feel so connected to. But maybe it's just some stupid notion that I can reach the desolation he harbors," Meagan said to the blue sky of April.

After completing her studies at the university in mid-May with three A's, Meagan and Sarah agreed that the lease Sarah had arranged for the new fitness center at the end of April was a perfect arrangement. The building was a former furniture store with large open areas, carpeted floors, and still-functioning restrooms. Meagan's worst problem was not so much saying goodbye to her girlfriends at her apartment as separating herself from both faculty and fellow students at the New Visions Institute. The nature of her studies there had not only engaged her mind and body but her soul as well. She had never experienced such an empathic group of people, all with common visions and a supreme dedication to their Zen studies, as she had with her peers at the Institute.

But break away she did. The month of June was the most frenzied thirty days she had ever spent. Although Sarah had started the plans for the limited renovation needed for the spa, Meagan was consumed with the details of final construction, orchestrating publicity, printing brochures, arranging for two part-time Carleton University students to assist her with classes, and decorating. Sarah helped her with obtaining insurance and setting up communications and on-site Wi-Fi services.

Toward the end of June, Meagan complained to Sarah, saying, "Well, Mom, I don't know if I would rather have a baby or birth this spa. Despite all you had warned me, I never for a moment imagined it would be so complicated. And I have to say, if it doesn't fly, my greatest fear is that I'll be another embarrassment for you not to mention that I've mortgaged my life away."

"Meagan, honey, look at it this way. When I opened my first salon,

I had no money, no credibility, and no customers. What I did have was a squalling one-month old infant at home, a drafty trailer, an over-due gas bill, and a wild-eyed and desperate employee staring me in the face. So, baby girl, just compare the support you're getting from me and the girls at the salon and from the community with my dire circumstances over twenty years ago. I'd say you're sitting in the catbird's seat. As far as succeeding, with your energy and dedication, you've got my vote. Hey, I really mean it when I say that I wouldn't have loaned you the money if I didn't believe in you and that you'll make a success of it."

Meagan's studio opened that July. She named it Greenleaf Health Spa after polling all of Sarah's clients for a week to determine which of three names they preferred. 'Yin and Yang Yoga' garnered only eight of the 170 votes. 'Sewell's Relaxation Salon' received twenty-three votes along with several comments that it seemed too closely related to the name of Sarah's salon. The other factor in favor of naming it the Greenleaf Health Spa was that it seemed so generic that Meagan could easily expand her menu of programs of exercise and wellness.

Fame follows fortune and in this case, *The Hamilton Hills Herald* interviewed both Sarah and Meagan about the history and success of the Sewells in their community. Although there were several challenging questions about why Meagan as an honor graduate had elected to turn down her scholarship to Bryn Mawr, she handled them well. "For some of us, an alternative path to work and hopefully to success takes a more adventurous path. In my case, I truly wanted to live in South Florida, to sample the romance of the place. I never relished the rigors of academic work even when it came easily for me. I think the other deciding factor is when I won that statewide essay contest as a junior at HHH. It wasn't the winning so much as it was the research I did at Carleton University and being turned on by that. I also want to remind everyone that my friend, Emi, and I started a yoga club over three years ago when we were still in high school. We had a large group, though mostly girls our age and women from the community. Emi and I would have the Wednesday afternoon session at Carleton after we had been doing the classes for three months. Those sessions were well attended by both men and women, and especially by the faculty and students at Carleton. I do have to admit there was a brilliant assistant professor in history and he was not only the most experienced but also a great teacher for all of us. Even though Emi and I were supposed to lead the groups, he knew far more about yoga than either of us. So we simply let him teach us as well."

The highly favorable newspaper article that followed included a front-page photograph of the ribbon cutting at the grand opening, as well as remarks by the President of Carleton University who had been recruited by Meredith's father. Meagan had printed brochures that were distributed at her mother's salon and mailed to students and faculty at Carleton. Instead of languishing for six months or longer as a fledging business on the margin of acceptability for a small town, the Greenleaf Health Spa rivaled the success of Sarah's salon from the day it opened. Meagan had decided to live with her mother until she could determine how problematic or successful her spa would be. After a month, the primary change she made was to hire the woman's assistant basketball coach at Carleton (now a woman!) to help with evening classes. There were two big surprises. One was the number of middle-aged women who had no experience or exposure to yoga, but eagerly signed up for yoga classes. And the other was the number of working men and women who preferred to attend one of the two relaxation yoga classes at five and six o'clock in the late afternoon. But a group of younger women and a few men were interested in morning yoga, with more aggressive and active postures, at the 7 a.m. and 8:30 a.m. sessions. Although the Carleton coach, especially during the summer, was a major asset and superb teacher for the evening classes, Meagan found her days started at six and ended at nine each night. She decided to close Saturday afternoon and Sunday, providing her with a respite of sorts when she was not balancing her books.

She thrived and the adulation of her students ("clients" and "fellow explorers" she called them) resulted in a glow to her skin and a gleam in her eye no one had seen since high school. Her athletic build, her agility and flexibility, resembled how she had looked during her halcyon days as a star gymnast and soccer forward. Although she had stopped attending AA meetings except on weekends in June, she resumed seeing Dr. Murray every two weeks. In her classes she would emphasize too the "distraction" (as she termed it) of alcohol, drugs, and smoking. Sometimes she would read short passages from her favorite essays on Buddhism and at other times she would read a few verses from the Old Testament or Psalms.

One Saturday night at dinner, during the last summery month of

August, Meagan said to Sarah, “Mom, yes Mom again, I’ve never been happier, more content. I agree it was a rocky road these past several years, but here we are. I have to admit to you that I saw Jason again when he was here earlier this month, but I think I am finally strong enough to try to end that with him when he visits later this fall. There is no way I or anyone can penetrate his armor, and I’ve probably been a fool to try. Sometimes I think I don’t want to give him up simply because he was my first lover. Like it meant so much to me, and I wanted to preserve something if not sacred at least special about that. But I’m ready to think about dating someone else, and I don’t mean like when I was so wild that summer after graduation. But having someone interesting to talk to, to be with, would be nice.”

“Meagan, in many ways you were a gift from God for me. Maybe your father’s life never amounted to anything, none of us will ever know. But one thing, perhaps the only thing, was that he and I brought you into this world. And now you’re creating your own place in this world. You are forever my sweet love. But one more thing for you to think about, now that your spa is jumping, is maybe finding yourself a little house of your own. You don’t want to be married to your old mother you know.”

A Perfect Day for a Motorcycle Ride

Sarah and Meredith had begged Meagan to stop seeing Jason, but she always responded with some nebulous comment like, "Each day brings a mystery that only I can solve for myself." She simply could not let him go, or perhaps she could not relinquish her notion of saving him from himself. Jason rarely gave her any reason to believe in their resurrection as a couple. He actually went out of his way to distance himself by not calling or writing her unless he was returning to Hamilton Hills. Or worse, when they would make love, and then he would tell her he was dating someone else. Many, especially Meredith, saw him as cold and manipulative and as contributing to what for Meagan had been, until the last year, almost two years of living on the raw edge of drugs, dares, and depression. Sarah truly believed that with the success of her spa, Meagan would be strong enough to resist Jason's casual entreaties. Indeed, Meagan had said as much and seemed now to mean it.

Having almost completed his course work in only three years without a break, Jason was now in his final semester at Wharton. After he interviewed with three firms that had home offices in Boston, he was virtually certain he would not return to his hometown. Meagan and Jason had last seen each other in August when he had hinted to Meagan that he would never return. And it was after this visit that Meagan told Sarah it was finally time that she stop seeing Jason. Still, Jason called one Wednesday in early October and said he was visiting the next day because his classes on Thursday and Friday had been cancelled. Meagan agreed to see him. As she said, "Jason we keep bouncing off each other like those old cars we saw at that demolition derby in high school. But something has come up that we do need to talk about. It may even bring us closer together." They agreed to meet Thursday afternoon for a ride in the countryside.

The afternoon air of that early fall day was permeated with the smell of the early blooming camellias, almost as intoxicating as the jasmine in spring. It was that last whisper of warmth before the hard winter with its sleet and snow that would once more savage the rolling hills of southwestern Pennsylvania. In short, it was a perfect day for a motorcycle ride on the Harley that Jason kept garaged at his parents' house. Jason had never before permitted Meagan to ride without a helmet. As she started to reach for the rider's helmet he kept strapped to the back of the soft-tail seat, he said, "Forget it for once if you want to, Meagan, because you're always begging me to let you ride, as you say, sans helmet."

"Oh, baby, that's fine. I'll let my freak flag fly as the old seventy's song said about the long hairs on bikes. But first, let me tie my hair into a ponytail or I'll never get the tangles out," Meagan said as she leaned forward and kissed Jason quickly on the cheek then slowly eased her tongue around the inner radius of his ear. She whispered, "You know how I love doing things differently, you naughty boy. Meagan mounted the bike behind him, leaned into him so he could feel her warmth and slipped both hands slowly up his thighs. "I love you, Jason, even if you hate me for it. I swore to my Mom that I was not going to see you again after your August visit, but something has changed," she yelled and then leaned forward and bit him, almost too hard, on the small space behind his neck.

"Meagan, I want you to be the one who is deciding to make this a little more daring, I mean without a helmet. You got it?" Jason said as he blipped the throttle.

"Quiet, my little college whiz kid. Now, put on your helmet and let's roll if you're the cool biker you like to portray. When we get to Smoky Joe's, I'll let you in on a riveting little secret over a beer and ribs. A little secret that for better or worse is going to change my life and your life forever," Meagan shouted as Jason prepared to launch the Harley into traffic.

When Jason heard Meagan suggesting her secret involved both of them, he gasped and momentarily froze. For it seemed to confirm his greatest fear. While it was true his classes had been cancelled, it was also true that Jason wanted to see Meagan because of a phone call he had received on Tuesday from an old tennis buddy from high school who worked as a lab technician at the local hospital.

Jason was shocked when his former teammate had called and said, "Listen, old buddy, this is Allen Wilson and I've got some serious news for you. Today I performed a urine test that was positive for pregnancy and the name on the slip was Meagan Sewell. You know she's always been sort of a wild thing, and I don't want her to try to hang this shit on you. Hell, I personally know three guys who've slept with her, and there were others that summer after high school when she was strung out on cocaine. Anyway, I'm just giving you a head's up, a word of caution, man. And I'm not saying a damn thing to anyone else because I could lose my job. You know how tough they've gotten about confidentiality and all that bullshit. Anyway, stay cool, dude."

Jason had said nothing to anyone but he remembered his last fling with Meagan which had been approximately two months ago and he also knew that she had been straight, no drugs, for the last year. But more than that, he knew that Meagan still loved him despite his antics and that since she had returned from Miami, she had had no other lovers. If there was one thing no one could question it was her loyalty. There were no other men. Allen Wilson's words, burned into his memory, presented a rare occasion when Jason feared he had suddenly lost control of his life, his fate that he wanted to remain uncontaminated by anyone's desires, needs, or expectations except for his own. And that included Meagan Sewell.

Finally he accelerated and they both seemed to settle into the guttural rumble and lazy lope of that perfectly orchestrated four-cylinder Harley. Ironically, this was the same metallic blue Harley that Jason had received as a high school graduation gift from his parents for renouncing his love and devotion to Meagan. The same parents for whom his disdain bordered on hatred despite his father doting upon him. This was a sentiment he hid from his family by telling them he was too busy studying to visit them except on the holidays and on the rare visit to see Meagan. Although he had always confided in Meagan, he could be equally dismissive of her as when he had left for college and told her, "Smoking weed, being so free-spirited, you're just a little too wild for me. Despite our closeness and all you've done for me, I can't let you control my life or wreck my ambitions. Sometimes, I see you as an unguided missile."

But the unguided missile this day was Jason's Harley. Rounding a curve, they crashed just before a busy intersection, sending him into a circular spin and the unsuspecting Meagan tumbling across the cement until her head made a sickening crunch into a nearby tree. Meagan's fifteen minutes of unwanted fame in the darkening light of that fall day was signaled by a cacophony of horns, muffled curses of rush-hour commuters, and, finally, the wail of sirens. How the accident had happened and who was to blame would be a source of both conversation and consternation at many dinner tables that night. Some said that Meagan had neither fallen nor jumped from Jason's motorcycle but had simply slipped away because her spirit was too carefree, too wild to be contained by this earth. That despite the recent success of her new spa, she was always teasing fate and testing limits.

The facts of that fateful day were recorded by Deputy Ellison's report. It began: Meagan M. Sewell, a nineteen year old Caucasian female fell from a Harley Davidson motorcycle traveling an estimated 40 miles per hour (in a 45 mph zone) while not wearing a helmet. Said female appeared to have tumbled along the pavement and made contact head-first with a large Bradford pear tree (circumference approximately 18 inches), thus receiving multiple facial injuries and a blowout fracture of the skull revealing copious brain tissue. Subject also appeared to suffer multiple abrasions and probable fracture of left arm and left leg (coroner report to follow). Although receiving immediate attention from Jason A. Aldridge, the driver of the motorcycle, and within five minutes a number of EMT staff, subject stopped breathing almost immediately according to driver Aldridge. However, the official time of death was recorded at the Greenleaf County Hospital emergency department as 6:14 p.m. (instead of 5:30 p.m., the approximate time of her cranial encounter with the tree).

Deputy Ellison's statement obtained from the driver of the motorcycle revealed: Jason A. Aldridge, 20-year-old Caucasian male, was noted to be the operator of a blue Harley Davidson motorcycle (PA license 27152) and while he was somewhat addled from having laid-down said motorcycle (in bikers parlance), he was able to give a coherent assessment of factors relating to accident. Further, Aldridge was the only available witness thought to be present at the precise time of the accident as no other passing drivers or sidewalk observers were available to give statements. It should be noted that Mr. Aldridge was wearing a licensed Bell helmet (per state law) and had sustained only abrasions to left elbow and forearm, a severely swollen left wrist, as well as torn slacks and moderately severe burn-type abrasions to left knee, lower leg and ankle. Aldridge stated that un-helmeted passenger (Ms. Sewell) had pulled at his left arm while screaming that a dog was crossing right to left in front of motorcycle causing driver to suddenly turn to left, sliding on pavement and ejecting said passenger while operator remained with motorcycle. Although operator sustained injuries as noted above, he attended to passenger without regard to his potential injuries. Of note, subject operator was subsequently transported to Greenleaf Hospital ED for blood samples for substance abuse evaluation to which he readily consented and for evaluation of injuries. In addition, operator of vehicle stated he had requested that deceased passenger wear a helmet, but she had refused.

The first call Sarah received was from the scene of the accident when Officer Ellison called around 6:00 p.m. She screamed, "You must be mistaken. Meagan rarely rode but she never rode with him without a helmet. That's just not her. And I know she hasn't been on any drugs for a least a year. But I'm on the way right now." Officer Ellison told her that she would not be allowed access to the accident scene and that Meagan was already en route to the Greenleaf County Hospital emergency department and probably was already there.

Before grabbing her car keys, Sarah called Cathy Eubanks, gave her the disastrous news and told her to call Toni and anyone the two of them could think of. Arriving at the door to the hospital, she left her car running and ran inside where she was grabbed by a nurse. "Don't try to stop me. I want to see my baby girl, even if she's taking her last breath. Out of my way or I'll knock you down," Sarah said, towering over the short and stocky nurse.

She ran to the ED room where a number of doctors and personnel were hurrying in and out, and where it was obvious a resuscitation code was being called off after it was unsuccessful. She tried to break into the tumult surrounding the code but was restrained by two surgeons. One, Doctor Allen Montgomery, tried to calm her. "Ms. Sewell, I'm Doctor Montgomery, the neurosurgeon, and I know who you are, everyone does. I want you to listen to me for sixty seconds if you will.

We've done everything possible to save your daughter. Even though she arrived with a severe head injury and was unresponsive, we performed CPR for twenty minutes, much longer than usual, when there were no vital signs either here or in the ambulance. So, rest assured we didn't give up easily. I've told them to get the room organized. Then, I will let you go in to see her."

Sarah, though rarely at a loss for words, was stunned and speechless. Finally she said, "Doctor, I feel like I'm on another planet, that this can't be happening to me. I don't care how bad it is, her injuries, but I still want to see her because...."

Before she could finish, Toni and Cathy ran to her from the hallway. "Sarah, honey, we're here," Toni screamed as though she might be a block away. "You've got us now so we'll just hold on to each other until we know how Meagan will make it through this," Cathy echoed.

Sarah, almost as tall as Doctor Montgomery, was pulled into the embrace of both of her friends and began to sob. Between sobs in monosyllables she stuttered, "Not gone get through it. It's over now. She's dead." Toni wanted the three of them to kneel in prayer but Sarah stiffened and managed to say, "Not now, Toni, but we'll need it later, all of us."

When Doctor Montgomery and a nurse escorted the three of them to a private waiting room, they were met by Father Flaherty, her other stylists and six others. One of the six was dressed immaculately in a black Chanel suit and wore gold-toned heels and a rather flamboyant large gold-link necklace. Sarah was shocked to see Mrs. Aldridge and merely nodded to her. But Mrs. Aldridge strode forward and extended her hand formally. "Sarah, my husband and I are here to check on Jason, who will be fine. We will be taking him home soon. Harold thought it unseemly for him or Jason to see you yet. Actually, our lawyer said the less communication we have, the better. But I wanted to provide my condolences anyway, because I have known you for quite a while and there is a fondness there," she concluded.

Sarah was aghast and it was one of the few times anyone had seen her blush, not with embarrassment but with rising rage. Cathy Eubanks saw what was happening, slipped between them and whispered to Sarah, "Let me handle this." She turned to Mrs. Aldridge and said, "I would say we thank you for your kindness but frankly it stinks to high heaven. You ain't getting no academy award for some stilted speech. The best thing for you to do is turn on them Goddamn golden heels and go back to your two men. As for your lawyer, he can go fuck himself if you'll excuse the French." Sarah grabbed at Cathy's arm but she turned even on Sarah and said, "Don't, don't mess with me right now. I'm escorting her out as fast as I can." But when she turned, Mrs. F. Harold Aldridge was scurrying down the hall, her heels clicking on the tiles like the synchronized hoof beats of a fleeing deer.

As promised, Doctor Montgomery permitted Sarah, Toni, Cathy, and Father Flaherty to spend a few minutes in the room with Meagan before the coroner and undertaker arrived. Sarah shuddered when she saw Meagan's head wrapped in bandages and gauze but the right side of her face was visible. Her right arm was crossed on the sheet that covered her. She kissed Meagan's cheek as she held her cool, lifeless hand but then asked the nurse if she could see and feel part of Meagan's beautiful, thick ponytail and the nurse said yes, then left the room.

Without any idea of what she was doing, Sarah, still holding Meagan's hand, sank to the floor sobbing. Cathy knelt on one side of her and Toni on the other; they embraced her as Doctor Montgomery left the room. Father Flaherty stood by the door, his head bowed. Finally, Sarah said to her two friends, "I just don't know what to do, having her torn from me with no warning. It feels so cruel and her just beginning to truly discover herself. And the spa, she just couldn't believe how people picked up on her energy. She loved it so much. Oh God, her life was just opening up for her."

Toni interrupted her, "Oh my sweet girl, we know and we'll always be with you. Do you remember what Meredith said when you got married? She said nothing can ever separate the three of us. But I wonder if now you would like me to say a little prayer?"

"Toni, Cathy, I feel you, your warmth even though Meagan's hand is so cold. But Toni, I'm going to try to say a prayer myself, something real simple and right now. So, God, if you are there and I hope you are, somehow take my baby's precious soul. Even if we don't know for sure about heaven, just let her walk in a field of flowers or be moss by the creek behind our house. And let her presence be felt at that Institute she cherished. They seemed to care about her and gave her new hope. And she was so kind to her classmates, loved the poor kids more than rich.

That should count for something. So, God, I'm releasing her hand and her soul is already traveling to you or out into the universe. Keep her safe. Keep her smiling. And always remind her how much I love her, how much we all do." As the four of them left the room, Sarah whispered to Cathy, "What I really wanted to do was see those deep and placid blue eyes one last time, but I was afraid to."

Coach McGill who had coached Meagan in soccer and Jason on the tennis team acknowledged the sentiments of many in the community, calling her "one of the fastest forwards in soccer we ever had and the true spirit of our team, because everyone fed off her energy." But he didn't stop there, also saying, "Jason's father may be part of the backbone of this town, but his only son is a self-centered carbuncle on the ass of this town. No more spoiled child ever grew up here. Pampered, given anything he wanted, and all it did for him was make him feel superior to everyone. I couldn't even let him ride to a tennis match in the school van. He was so arrogant and such a little shit toward the other players. That high and mighty mother of his would have her driver deliver him to the tournaments." And Sam McGill, who had coached Jason for four years as the number one seed on the tennis team, certainly knew a few things about Jason Aldridge.

There were other opinions, some more generous toward Jason. Mollie O'Farrell, who for thirty years had presided over youth outreach for the First Methodist Church, and knew both Jason and Meagan, defended him saying, "A finer young gentleman I never had. He went out of his way to bring this little fatherless, Episcopalian girl to some of our meetings and picnics their senior year in high school. But Meagan, from the time she hit fifteen, she was always a little wild, I heard. She was our answer to Janis Joplin. And don't think I haven't heard that she smoked pot, drank, and went to a lot of wild parties in her last few years." Jason was haunted more than anything by what the fine citizens of Hamilton Hills might have whispered to one another that night about how the accident really happened. But worse than that, Jason seemed more concerned about his reputation than he was about Meagan's life being extinguished.

Jason Aldridge, in his many ruminative moments then and later, would remain wrapped in the barbed-wire guilt and redundant rage resulting from his involvement in Meagan Sewell's death. Although the facts of Meagan's death were rather elegantly delineated in the deputy's report, the report failed to capture certain related factors, especially about the conflicted years following their high school romance. Jason had always fancied himself to be a perfectionist and a conqueror of life's challenges. He regarded his stoic attitude as a gift from the father who mercilessly drove him to excel in everything he touched, whether tennis, golf, or his scholastic endeavors. Indeed, Jason had come to see any challenge as a small, usually insignificant, mathematical equation to be solved easily by "simply sticking to the facts and eliminating any unnecessary emotion" as his father would say repeatedly. The facts of Meagan's death and his ambivalence toward her for having loved him, doted upon him, and even dying in his arms remained a sticky, messy digression in the otherwise perfectly programmed and linear success of the twenty years of his young life.

Jason made a perfunctory visit at nine o'clock that night of the accident to Sarah, having called earlier to ask her if he might meet with her alone. She told him that Father Flaherty had driven her from the hospital and would be visiting, but that she would be glad to see him. When he arrived, Sarah greeted him with a formal handshake and introduced him to Father Flaherty, who had the unfortunate assignment to be the third priest assigned to the faltering St. Michael's Episcopal Church since Reverend Reid's departure. No one knew what to say, including Father Flaherty. But Sarah made everyone feel at home by preparing sausage biscuits and coffee. "I have to keep myself busy because they wouldn't let me see Meagan's whole body at the emergency room and her head was bandaged. They did let me kiss her cheek and hold her cold, lifeless hand. Jason, I know this is as hard on you as anyone except myself. I heard you were checked out at the hospital and were fine except for some scrapes and bruises and that fractured wrist. Is there anything you can tell me about the accident or help me understand why, why Meagan would have ever ridden without a helmet?" Sarah asked.

"Ms. Sewell, you know how guilty I feel letting Meagan ride without a helmet. She was always chomping at the bit to do it and the afternoon light was so beautiful, so I just gave up and let her," Jason said, unable to meet Sarah's benevolent gaze.

"Jason, nothing that happened is your fault. I always thought Meagan would push life to the limit. None of us really knew much about her father except that his wanderlust drove him, drove him to keep moving and drove me to distraction. But Meagan was a free spirit riding the wind though she had a heart of gold. You don't know this but she told me many times during the past three years that she had never quit loving you. That's why she would go out with you even after your disastrous break-up. She never got over you or the pain of your broken romance. She said that underneath that macho mask of yours was a hurt, lonely little boy," Sarah said as she reached for Jason's hand.

"I'm sorry I can't take any more of this, Ms Sewell," Jason said as his hands shook.

"Jason, I'm not meaning to intimidate you. I'm telling you what it's like when somebody loves another person more than herself. If you can't bear to hear this or can't let yourself be loved, you're going to miss out on what life is really about. And I guarantee that if you learned anything from my baby girl, it's that Meagan lived life with ferocity from her soul. She laid it all out there," Sarah concluded.

"Ms Sewell, I'm very dizzy and about to be sick. I believe you are completely sincere but I really must go. Father Flaherty, I'll be saying good night now," Jason said as he grabbed his jacket from the hat rack and bolted through the front door.

Jason fled the warm serenity of the Sewell home for the cold sterility of his parents' home and, ensconced in his room, he admired his trophies from tennis, golf and debate. He pulled the annual from his senior year at Hamilton Hills High from a shelf and looked at the picture of each classmate and then read the messages written by them inside the front and back covers and scattered among the pages of photographs. When he saw the page-long letter Meagan had written the week before graduation, he felt a balloon expanding in his chest and thought he would begin to weep. But instead he ran into the bathroom with sweat running down his head and neck and vomited. He showered and went to bed.

During the several days before Meagan's funeral, Jason retreated to the sanctity of his parents' home. Just as his mother had often talked to him in double entendres when he was a child, leaving him uncertain of what she had said or meant, so had Jason come to have a distorted if not slightly disturbed view of life. While Meagan's death seemed sudden and inexplicable on its surface, Jason felt strangely detached from her, her broken body, and her now stilled whimsical views and outrageous humor. In many ways, Jason felt that he didn't really know

Meagan, that by her staying in Hamilton Hills after high school, she had abandoned him. When, of course, the opposite was the reality, the truth. Somewhere between Jason's self-centered mother and his automaton of a father, Jason had matured into something other than the sweet little boy Ms. O'Farrell remembered from the Methodist picnics. It wasn't so much that he was born old as the aphorism has it, as it was that he had grown old at an early age.

That Saturday morning, Jason avoided his parents and refused to answer their knocks on his door. He then decided to ride into the countryside, drive his Corvette as fast as possible and see what fate would decree. But of course, he loved himself too much to kill himself. As he returned home, he slammed his Corvette into third gear, drove seventy in a thirty-five mile an hour zone, slid around the corner three blocks from his parents' home and ran over a neighbor's cherished tabby cat. He never slowed although he felt the sickening thump as the low front spoiler collected the bounding tabby. Two children on bikes saw the speeding car and one said, "That man has killed little Bennie." The other replied, "Yeah, it looked like that mean, stuck-up Aldridge boy. Can you believe he didn't even care enough to stop?"

Jason looked in his rearview mirror, saw the cat tumbling toward the gutter and murmured to no one, "How unfortunate, two deaths in two days."

Saffron Flags, Sugar Maples and Golden Gingkoes

Plans for the memorial service got off to a shaky start when Sarah, Meredith and Toni met on Friday. While Meagan might be described as a lapsed Episcopalian who more recently professed to be a follower of Buddha, her death divided Sarah, Toni, and Meredith. "I think we should use the service to suggest a return to our roots, to recognize the Lord Jesus Christ as our savior and that we are all fallen," Toni said. She had remained true to her religious roots and was unwavering in her quest as a teacher and as a volunteer at a local abuse center to save a small niche of her world. She attended mass regularly and was involved in many activities of the local Catholic Church. Meredith, not so different from Meagan, changed her views as often as she changed lovers. Meredith championed Meagan's recent dedication to Buddhism and her position regarding the memorial service was both vitriolic and implacable.

Meredith was visibly angry when she said to Toni and Sarah, "The last thing I will tolerate desecrating the memory of my godchild, the most adventurous of any of us, is some holy-roller priest coming in here with his misogynous homilies and Jesus-baited hooks hoping to snare a few more desperate souls. Sarah, you know how strongly Meagan felt about her search for enlightenment. And she truly believed that whole thing in Buddhism about how we inject so much suffering into our own lives. She listened, studied, and practiced what she was taught with a dedication I've never seen her show for anything else, especially this last year. And she was even more invigorated by her studies in Colorado. It gave her a different slant on how she could be the rebel she sort of always was but not be so self-destructive."

"There is no doubt to me that her meditation, her practice as she called it, provided her the strength to stay off drugs. She had even been volunteering at Manna House, seeing a side of life that did not center about her and her whims, not that I am one to be judging her as you both remind me so often. And her health spa for meditation and yoga was rocketing off the ground. With her energy and dedication there's no question it would have been a success. To be clear about it, I'm opposed to any priest or preacher of any kind. We four women, now three, have survived well without men telling us what to do or directing our lives. And Toni, I think what you and your husband have worked out is a good partnership. I mean it's not for me but you've made it work. I say we each remember Meagan in our own words. By that I mean our little eulogies can reflect how we saw her and how we see our messed up world. Then maybe read a poem from Eliot about impermanence and the strange nature of time, one of those sections from *The Four Quartets* sounds about right to me," Meredith concluded.

Sarah, who understood how different Toni and Meredith were and also knew how to navigate those differences better than anyone, calmly put an end to the discussion. "Somehow, we need to include all you've both said and at the same time make all of her friends and my customers feel included too. And that's why we've got to have some of our past in the ceremony. Toni, you are the only truly religious one of us, I mean in any respectable way. Meredith, you and I are about the same, just making our way along the old rocky road of life. And my baby girl, Meagan, wasn't really like any of us. She thought I was the explorer but like you said she was the real explorer. So, I want to respect her and I don't pretend to know anything about her Buddhist business, but we'll have some of that too."

Sarah paused, looked at both Meredith and Toni, then continued, "I think the most reasonable thing to do is to have a casual memorial service because Meagan hated anything too stuffy or formal. While we can honor her interest in those Buddha sayings, she and I owe a lifelong debt to Reverend Reid and Saint Michael's Church. He saved my life, three or four times I might add. Once when I came here, again when I was pregnant with Meagan, and of course when he loaned me the money to buy that first salon. If he is able to come, we would all cherish his words. Toni, we know how important your religion, your Catholicism, is to you so we'll also have a part for poor old Father Flaherty, who inherited Reverend Reid's church. I feel sorry for him because of all the turmoil he stepped into. After all, Episcopalians are just watered-down Catholics some people say. I want the two of you to do brief eulogies. As brave as I'm trying to be, I don't think I could make it through a remembrance of my baby girl."

The memorial ceremony on Sunday afternoon was held in Sarah Sewell's backyard. In front of the house, Meredith had arranged for two large saffron flags on bamboo poles. Among the deep crimson leaves of the sugar maples and the golden leaves of gingkoes, six more large saffron flags were interspersed at the periphery of the yard. The effect was far more celebratory than funereal, just the way Meagan would have wanted it, Sarah had said as the plans had congealed. Meredith had said that the saffron flags were an allusion to Meagan's interest in Buddhism because they resembled large Tibetan prayer flags. Meredith thought this might also lighten the mood of the ceremony. At the edge of the already yellowing grass was a small wooden podium with the urn containing Meagan's ashes and a white orchid reaching out over the urn. Reverend Reid was ill and could not attend, so Father Flaherty opened the ceremony with a prayer and mentioned the presence of friends of many varied faiths, beliefs and philosophies. This seemed to relieve the tension among the gathered group of almost three hundred and brought a smile to Meredith's pained face. Father Flaherty read the twenty-third psalm but then began a brief homily about the necessity of what he called "formal religion" in everyone's life before concluding with a brief prayer.

Almost shouldering the fine Father away from his place next to the podium and clearly agitated by the Father's emphasizing his faith when he had been requested to keep his comments more general, Meredith stood behind the small podium and looked over the crowd. She said, "Well, thank all of you for coming. As Sarah, Toni, and I planned our memorial for this beautiful day we wanted our messages to be balanced, to be what our dear soul sister Meagan would have wanted us to hear. Even ecumenical is too strong of a word because we all know how devoted Meagan was to her interest in Buddhism, but mainly to how each of us can save our own souls through perseverance and having a healthy body and awakened spirit. And that was really what her yoga and meditation spa was all about. Those of you who attended some of her classes know how her Buddhist practice changed her life and how much she wanted to help us improve our own lives."

Meredith then launched into her personal paean about Meagan's independence, her free and adventurous spirit, and how she was forever a fighter despite her challenges. She then segued into a brief history of the survival over adversity of both Meagan and Sarah, and how far women in society had progressed in the past several decades. Generally civil, Meredith could not help a slight dig when she nodded to Father Flaherty and said, "Despite what Father Flaherty suggested, I think it's far more important that each of us find a spiritual path that fits our individual needs and not simply his mandates. And one more thing, it is my hope that someday perhaps all formal religions will recognize the place of women in their hierarchies as the rest of the world has done. But I suspect the Father is far more human than we know," and she actually winked at him.

The crowd twittered as Father Flaherty smiled uncharacteristically and smoothed the lapels of his vestment that seemed oddly out of place, although its colors complemented the beauty of Sarah's backyard. Toni, attired in a prim black wool suit, rose timidly from her nearby chair and, seemingly unsteady, held the edge of the urn-centered podium. She began by reading not a poem from Eliot but from Frost that, as one might surmise, celebrated the path not taken, the same poem Reverend Reid had recited at his retirement. She began her personal remembrance, saying, "Meagan was one of us but not one of this earth, being one never bound by tradition. Although we, the three of us sitting here together, have always been best friends, I suspect Meagan thought me a little strange for my conventional ways. I read the Frost poem because my path has always been predictable, unexciting. Meagan never saw a path she wouldn't take. Sometimes she paid for it, I mean her exploring, her journeying to ports of call that could be trouble. But no matter the storm, she righted her ship, adjusted her compass and set a new course. You never had to worry about her energy. Our sweet girl always had the wind at her back and full-blast in her sails. Maybe she didn't truly like me or my conservative life style, or what I represented, maybe she, she, she. . . ." Toni began to weep, placing her hand over her eyes, unable to stop.

Finally, Father Flaherty stepped forward to guide her back to her chair as Meredith and Sarah comforted her. Father Flaherty then concluded with a brief blessing and assured the mourners that "Meagan has surely been borne up to God's beautiful heavens whose doors are adorned today with these fall leaves, these wreaths prepared by angels. Just as Meagan herself was a fierce warrior on earth, so shall she be borne up on eagles' wings to sing in the choir of a God all of us know or shall know by his grace and by the grace of Jesus Christ, our Lord and Savior."

After the ceremony, the crowd quickly divided itself into two discrete groups. The smaller group was rather morose, stoically quiet if not speaking in hushed tones. They sought, one by one, Father Flaherty's comforting touch and brief words of benevolence. And the other group was rather the antithesis. As they ambled about freely, their actual physical movement seemed more uninhibited and bordered on being too joyful. For while it is fine to celebrate this liberation from suffering as the Buddha would say, it is another to face the sorrow of death and the hole it leaves in one's heart. Jason wanted to be inconspicuous but found it hard to do so in his fine double-vented Harris Tweed jacket, maroon cashmere sweater, black slacks, and polished Edmonds loafers. It was an ensemble that seemed almost anachronistic if not slightly amusing for a memorial service. But it seemed strangely coherent on Jason, and certainly a brief flip of the middle finger to the formality his father would have decreed. As the service ended, he found himself uncertain where he should mingle. He thought that no matter which group he chose, he would be uncomfortable. And so, the lesser of the two evils he assumed, he edged his way into the periphery and anonymity of the larger group of Sarah's friends.

"Actually, I didn't think you would have the audacity to come, Jason," Meredith said quietly, speaking behind his right shoulder before disappearing into the crowd.

Jason turned to respond or at least to look at her since he found Meredith to be quite beautiful and especially provocative. He wasn't certain if that was because of her physical presence, something as simple as her perfect posture, or how she too always spoke her mind. In fact, he regarded her as one of the most aggressive women he had ever met. And there was something about her sexuality, something about her smell that was almost intimidating. But maybe part of that was her mouth, he thought, meaning not merely her full lips but how she never equivocated in expressing her opinions. He followed her into the crowd that seemed now even looser in conversation, their palates whetted but not slaked by the tilted flutes of Veuve Cliquot. This was Meredith's favorite champagne and, yes, was provided by her drug company. He worried that this faction of barely modulated mirth appeared on the edge of dance until he noticed that the more formal Christian contingent too was moving now among themselves with a renewed vigor, their hearts opened and tongues loosened by this fine champagne.

"Meredith, may I have a word with you," Jason said as he reached to touch her arm after he found her by the colors of her blouse and shawl.

"You may, Jason, but I have to tell you, you remind me of a character in a little French novel who went to his own mother's funeral and had no reaction, almost didn't know what he was doing there and damn sure didn't feel anything," Meredith said.

"I think I know the little French novel you're referring to. So appropriately titled I might add. And wouldn't that be Camus' *The Stranger*?" he asked.

"And well you do remember, which is so befitting Hamilton Hills' own star student and tennis stud wrapped all in one sweet little package. I have to admit you always were a cutie, even when you were just seventeen and started dating our Meagan," Meredith smiled and touched two fingers to her lips.

"Well, with all the rumors and gossip and even a few threats on the phone I've received, I wasn't sure whether to come or not. But, frankly, I know Meagan would have wanted me here. We have been through so much together, you know. And in some ways, we never left each other, even after high school," Jason said.

"I don't doubt that, but what offended all of us was your remoteness and your absence these last two days. You don't seem to have any sadness or remorse or anything we could even call affect, much less anything like pure old raw emotion. I'm not blaming you because we, Meagan's family, have a place for you in our hearts. While you've been at college, you clearly seemed to have forgotten her except when you blew into town and expected her to be conveniently available. Your detachment doesn't seem like a defense or facade, but more like a stratagem, something to make us all feel more uneasy about Meagan's death than we already do," Meredith concluded, pursing her mouth and appearing like a marionette stopped short by its ventriloquist.

"Maybe we can talk later, Meredith. I've always thought there was some unspoken bond between us," Jason said, knowing that, as the gamblers say, he had doubled down by being a bit too brazen.

"We'll see, Jason. I can't help that I'm passionate about how I live whether it's in my love life or business. That's just me. And I have all these mixed feelings because Meagan and I were so much alike. You know, eat, drink, and be merry for tomorrow you can do it again. Toni and I were always there for her because Sarah was always struggling to stay alive, staying ahead of the next catastrophe, until she really got it together and was successful beyond any of our dreams. I know she's still a woman from the hills of West Virginia in some ways but she reads, she works hard, and runs a damn good business. Anyway, what I can't get out of my mind is what in the hell was Meagan thinking when she jumped on that Harley like she was on some fucking trick pony. It's like she was warning you or challenging the fates or simply fucked-up on cocaine again and none of us knew it."

"But, Meredith, don't you see that her death has done this to all of us by creating guilt about what we might have done. How do you think I feel? I truly thought I could grab her and pull her back on the bike. That it would appear to have been a botched circus act at worst, even if she fell. What I don't understand is whether she wanted to punish each of us, because I'm certain she wasn't high and hadn't been for months, you know that. I could always tell when she was strung out on some really strong weed by that fixed and bizarre grin she wore. In fact, she was unusually calm when I picked her up after work. She even said she thought she had finally found some answers and one of them involved our relationship. So now we are all left with a mystery, haunted by questions we can't answer."

"By the way, Jason, why are you dressed like a fraternity kid or some old English professor, I'm not sure which. No dark suit, just unusually casual for a memorial service I'd say. Is it a little inside joke or just another slap at your father's conventionality? Oh, and where are your parents?" Meredith asked.

"I thought they should come but he — Dad — said no, that there would be too many people, mainly friends of Sarah's and her customers. He said he just didn't mix well with that class of citizens as he called them," Jason answered.

"Well, Jason, I tell you what. I may just devise a little entertainment that you can take home to that father of yours. You know, like when you're sitting on his knee receiving your allowance, you'll have a touching story to share with him."

"What's that supposed to mean?" Jason asked.

"Oh a surprise is not a surprise if you give away too many hints. We will simply have to see what develops, cutie, because I may not like you too much, but I've always had this strange almost satanic attraction to you," Meredith said with sarcasm dripping from each syllable.

The Machinations of Meredith

Jason watched Meredith move comfortably among this crowd of mostly women. He saw her approach Father Flaherty, who stood now apart from the crowd, alone, erect and unsmiling. She must have said something with just the right ring to it in that inimitable way Meredith had of making anyone feel at ease. For Father Flaherty appeared immediately engaged, his face, usually as implacable and fixed as one on the Rushmore monument, brightened. It was the face of an old and fatigued priest that over the years had become inured to pain and tears, tragedy and death, finding it hard to remember to smile even at a christening or wedding. It was this face, so dour, that became almost radiant, imbued with color. And it was this body, usually as lifeless as an old scarecrow, which was now suddenly awakened, alive.

Meredith reached to embrace him, her hands behind his neck, pulling his head close to her face, kissing first his celibate brow and then kissing each cheek, her lips lingering longer than decorum might dictate. It was as though she wanted to appear as one of his parishioners, obsequious and doting. When in fact she would say to anyone that she believed in almost nothing except herself, the sanctity of her work, and her ability to control men rather than be controlled. Jason, at a distance just beyond hearing, continued to watch in quiet and still amazement as they began to talk. He could see that the words, the sentences, their sentences, had an equally profound counterpoint in the movement of their bodies. And it was in watching this dance of words and bodies that he became aware again of Meredith's power, a force that seemed to compel even this aging if not decrepit priest to respond with an almost adolescent if not slightly ataxic fascination. He, a son of God, a servant of man, enraptured seemingly by the enchanting eyes of a temptress whose only sin (to this point) was that through guile and intrigue she had resurrected his entire being. Jason saw Father Flaherty reach repeatedly to touch her, politely on the arm, the shoulder, even once in the exaggerated arch of her back as he had when she had so warmly approached him, forcing him to respond not as a priest but as a man.

Jason noticed how Meredith's pale gray blouse, silhouetted against Father Flaherty's bright purple vestment, seemed to ripple against her skin like serpentine ribbons of smoke defining her flat abdomen and her breasts as the early fall breeze played upon her. He wondered if what Father Flaherty perceived as a blessing (the presence of this woman) may not be equally a curse, a temptation tossed to him by fate, teasing even his holy vows of celibacy. As everyone knew, Father Flaherty was one of the few Episcopalian priests who had taken his own personal vow of celibacy to exclude any expression of sexuality, reasoning that his thoughts and acts could then be more wholly devoted to his church, to his parishioners. Jason wondered if Meredith did not know of her power or whether this was simply another manipulation, especially after she had winked at the Father during the ceremony.

And did she herself not know it? Or do all women not know of this power over men indeed when they are even young? Yes, girls at play, running at recess with reckless abandon yet staring over one shoulder at the still innocent boys admiring the fluid stride, the carefree flip of ponytail or the perfect plait of corn row, yes girls at play but girls already calculating the trajectory of their subtle seductions, whether genetic or schooled, unleashed not randomly but with a delicate and deliberate specificity soon to be sealed with a kiss as the old love letters used to say. Although Jason saw Meredith gesturing to Father Flaherty as though directing him to go into the house, perhaps to await the dispersing crowd so that they might speak again, he thought nothing of it. As she was turning, he thought he could see her mouthing a simple parting message, "Wait for me there."

Indeed, at that moment, Meredith turned from her conversation with Father Flaherty, tightened the shawl that draped her forearms, breathed deeply and looked at Jason as though she sensed unconsciously his precise location, her eyes providing the invitation that he knew was already answered because of what he had been watching. As she walked toward him, Jason sensed that he would be her next prey, but still wanted her despite her earlier comments to him, wanted her to say anything to him that might assuage his feeling so alone in such a large crowd. He felt caught in a strange play in which he had no power to resist, propelled toward some fate he could not see or hear, and then he thought too of the novel they both had alluded to earlier.

"Jason, I didn't want us to end our conversation on a negative note especially since we are here to honor Meagan. Although I didn't always condone your behavior or especially your lack of loyalty toward her, she was a long link between all of us including you, and she alone chained you to this little town. I wish you would level with me about why you would keep coming back to her even in your sporadic way," Meredith said as she stepped closer to him and held his hand loosely.

Jason seemed uncomfortable despite being struck by Meredith's beauty and by witnessing how she had so adroitly flattered and entertained Father Flaherty. He moistened his lips and looked furtively toward a small group of young girls laughing. "Well, Meredith, I'm surprised you've approached me at all, but I don't know, have never known, if I can trust you. I mean if I respond to you, how do I know it's not going straight back to Sarah?" he asked.

"Come on, Jason, give it up. I'm not in some high school debate with you. And I know you've always been, shall we say, a little stiff and reserved. I'm asking you a simple question, one human being to another. I'm asking what drew you to Meagan, because you were like polar opposites in so many ways," Meredith reiterated.

Jason seemed to relax, his breathing calmed as he answered, "To be honest, Meagan had so many things about her that always intrigued me. I mean it is or was a given that she was attractive and personable. But what hooked me was that, just as I trusted and maybe even loved Miss Sarah when I was younger, I always thought I could trust Meagan in the same way. Trust or closeness in my family didn't exist. You're the one who mentioned the Camus novel, that sense of aloneness and being disconnected. But what I experienced was more like a combination of being abandoned by a heartless mother and being driven relentlessly by a controlling father. Like you could name our house the *Heart of Darkness* if you want to throw around a few book titles."

"Jason, you're getting way off target. Like we're back to you again. I'm asking for the third time, what was it about Meagan that drew you to her?"

"Yeah, yeah, I know. So, one thing was her honesty, how direct she was, and how she was sort of an anchor for me. And another was her sense of freedom, her thirst for life. Now I think it got her in trouble later because she got rather loose and wild. I always hated her smoking weed that she claimed calmed her down. Maybe the third big thing was a sort of subtle vulnerability. Like they say, she wore her emotions on her sleeve or maybe both sleeves in her case. Finally, I have to admit that although I haven't had that many lovers, we had a great sex life. She taught me far more than I did her," Jason concluded.

"Well, Jason, that's very forthright, especially for you. Now, one more question. When we were chatting earlier this afternoon, we both hinted at some kind of vague attraction between us despite our age difference. So now that we've both had three or four glasses of champagne, I wondered if we could go to the house. No one's there and maybe we could have a little privacy to finish this conversation," Meredith said as she again leaned against him and squeezed his hand hard enough to make him flinch.

As she walked with him, guiding him toward the house, the colors of this magical fall day turned about him in a vertiginous dance as though he was somehow no longer watching but was at the epicenter of some celestial kaleidoscope. How could it be that no one noticed them, as though they existed outside of time or even gravity? Lost in this hypnotic intoxication with this woman, Jason was uncertain how he and Meredith then found themselves in a bedroom of Sarah's house.

As he sat down on the bed, she turned her back to him. Then she pulled his hands around her back and placed them on her breasts, saying, "I know you must have noticed I never wear a bra, even to funerals or this memorial service. Now help me with these little buttons on the back of my blouse because I've got a nice surprise for you, Jason."

"Meredith, what in hell do you think you're doing?" Jason asked.

"I know exactly what I'm doing. Be a good boy and tease these buttons loose, cutie."

Jason found himself releasing the three small pearl buttons behind

Meredith's neck, then slipping both hands into the long slit in the back of her blouse, holding her hair with one hand while removing her blouse as she raised both arms in one effortless gesture with a balletic simplicity suggesting they, though strangers to each other physically, had practiced this for hours. Turning to face him, she saw the thin line of sweat above his lip. She pulled his mouth to her breast to gauge his willingness. She kissed him, her mouth hot and fervent against his still cool, uncertain, and dry lips.

"Yes, I want you to do this, now," she whispered, her hands wrestling with Jason's belt, not remembering, not even knowing, that he was left-handed, his belt reversed from what she anticipated, before unbuckling it and quickly slipping his zipper down.

"My God, Meredith, we're burying Meagan, your godchild, and the love of my life. You've lured me into Sarah's house with people milling around outside so that you can tease me or trap me. Are you absolutely crazy?" Jason protested.

"And you, my sweet Adonis, have been watching me like a hawk all afternoon. Now, you're going to be my prey, because I hate to admit it but I've always wanted to take you for a ride," Meredith said as she teased him, barely touching him, her fingers as light as the gossamer wings of a butterfly. Then she bent to take him into her mouth, muttering, "This will convince you of how serious I am, Jason."

Meredith pushed her skirt and panties to the floor without interrupting the rhythm of her mouth. Pausing, she reached to flip the loafers from his feet and pulled his pants down as she pushed him backwards onto the bed. "You may not like it, but I'm on top sweetie because I want to come first and then we'll take care of you however you want it."

"But you're insane, Meredith. There's a line between desire, even such crazy, drunken desire as this, and what's right," Jason protested weakly.

"What's right is what feels right. Shut up before you lose this beautiful erection. Oh, that's it, how I love that rough ridge. I think I can feel it when I come up on you. Here, I want my nipples in your mouth while I'm over you. Oh, you're being such a good boy, suck them as hard as you want to. It helps me to come faster like that. Oh, God, that's good, so good, so very good, my darling. Close your eyes, you stupid pig and here, put your hand here. I've waited so long for this. Oh yes, yes, and now we're almost there. How sweet it is."

As Meredith sank the nails of both her hands into the cheeks of Jason's muscular ass, she pulled him up into her with a renewed violence, barely muffling her scream. He did not feel her loosen her grip or understand that her scream was now, inexplicably, laughter and not just laughter but something as primordial as an ape's grunting. "Oh God, I'm still coming, my little Jason. Oh, sweetie, that's so fine for me, just touch me here a little more. Yes, like this, oh yes, oh now it's slowing. Oh the perfect fuck you are, you little shit."

He thought she would lie now upon him before he too would float upon this magical carpet. He had closed his eyes as she had rocked above him, so he did not see her raise her arm. Then she slapped him so hard that his left ear seemed to explode with what sounded like the simultaneous ringing of a thousand tiny bells. Startled, aghast, he opened his eyes to see the enraptured face of his lover, her eyes wild with a kind of rapacious fervor and unleashed fury he had never seen in a human.

As Meredith pulled herself off Jason, she looked at him with utter disgust and yelled, "You, you pompous little shit, are guilty of leading Meagan on for years after it should have been over, for using her as a convenience. And now you see what it's like to be used, yourself. If I could get away with it, I would kill you as you killed Meagan's heart. Don't ever forget that. So this blistering slap is from both of us. How can you live with yourself, you rotten piece of shit?"

And then Jason heard a bumping sound from the closet to his right, a kind of rhythmic knocking. Glancing to his right at the suddenly opening closet door, he saw the other half of that late afternoon's gray and purple silhouette when Father Flaherty had all but embraced Meredith. He saw the Father still wearing that vivid purple vestment tumble clumsily out of the closet onto the bedroom floor. Not only did Father Flaherty have his hand thrust inside his vestment, he seemed lost in the moment, genuflecting in tearful and ecstatic bemusement while groaning, whimpering like a hurt dog. He turned his head to look at Meredith and stupidly gaped at Jason, still naked on the bed, before muttering, "My God in heaven, we are all doomed to hell."

Meredith, already standing and dressing herself, looked down at him and said sneeringly, "And one more man so easily seduced. You're all like lost little animals and so very pathetic. You, most Holy Father of the floor, represent all that's wrong with religion, especially yours. You take advantage of the poor, the ignorant, and of little boys and girls I might add, purely for your own personal gain. As long as you keep the largesse flowing to your Episcopalian bishop and your Catholic brothers keep the cash coming to their precious Pope and Vatican, you think you are justified, free to do anything. You are a supposed beacon of strength but look at yourself now. You make me sick, both of you." As Meredith walked from the bedroom, Jason realized that this was a memorial service unlike any other he or Father Flaherty would ever attend.

A Shaken Jason Returns to Wharton

Jason Aldridge did not linger in his less-than-beloved hometown. His bag was already packed and his Corvette gassed, but he took time to stop by his bedroom at his parents' home. He tossed his trophies for the many tennis and golf victories that had spanned four years of his life in high school into three large cardboard boxes. He removed everything from his desk and ripped the photographs from his bulletin board. After deliberating for a few seconds—his only real indecision—he removed three large framed posters of James Dean, Steve McQueen, and Cher (photographed in a thong). Systematically he turned each with the glass facing away from him, shattered it on the edge of his desk and tossed the remnants into a large garbage can he had dragged up the stairs. He did not feel well. The hearing in his left ear vacillated between a high-pitched buzzing that sounded like a dentist's drill and a hollow nothingness as though he had cupped a small drinking glass over his ear. Sitting briefly at his desk, he looked around his room, then removed a piece of paper from a box of Crane stationery. His note was simple:

Dear Mother and Father,

I do not plan to return to this house or to this bedroom because both hold mostly bad memories for me. It is also doubtful that I will return to this town and its provincial ways. Please arrange for someone to dispose of these boxes filled with the shards of my past. I appreciate your financial support and I look forward to my graduation from Wharton in December. With the AP courses from high school and overloads each semester, college has been more than challenging but I'm delighted to be finishing early.

For those of us graduating in December, there will not be a formal ceremony, so I suppose we will have to postpone the family celebration until next spring.

Respectfully,
Jason

P.S.: The memorial service for Meagan was quite lovely and the champagne fine, but with everyone drinking a bit too much, the service rather deteriorated at the end.

Jason expected a call from his parents when he arrived at his twenty-first floor condominium in Philadelphia around eight that night. Indeed, the answering machine was beckoning when he walked into the living room that had a stunning view of the Schuylkill River. He considered not returning their calls that numbered seven over the past hour and a half. Instead, he poured a generous tumbler of an inexpensive merlot, and played his favorite Miles Davis CD. An hour later, he decided to call his parents so that he could sleep, knowing that the confrontation he surmised was waiting would then be over.

"Mom, sorry I'm late calling. Got into Sunday night's returning traffic. Oh, and about that mess in my room, just hire someone to haul it away."

"Why, Jason, what about the trophies? You were so disciplined, so devoted to your sports not to mention your father's financial investment and encouragement," Mrs. Aldridge exclaimed in a plaintive almost pitiful voice.

"Forget the crap, Mother. Why did you call?"

"Oh, Jason, for God's sake don't be so blunt. You know I didn't call. I wouldn't want to disturb you. Anyway, I had two couples over for dinner — the Goldsteins and the McMillans. Diversity, you know. Their wives are just infinitely boring. They talk on and on about their golf games, and how a little group of their girlfriends play the stock market. They don't use real money but, instead, use monopoly money. Can you believe that? Oh, but anyway, it's your father who's been calling. He's quite upset. I could see him tensing those funny little jaw muscles all during dinner. Here, here he is now. Bye, honey. You do know I love you, don't you, and in such a special way."

In the background, Jason could hear his father yelling, "Give me that goddamn phone. You sound like one of those women on 'The Young and the Restless.' Jesus Christ, just go on to bed will you?"

"Hello, Father. Mother said you had called before I arrived back in Philly. I've got a lot of reading to do before classes at ten in the morning, especially since I've been away for a lot of last week, so could we make it quick?"

"Jason Aldridge, you just listen to me. First of all, you left your room in the most despicable wreck I've ever seen. We don't live like that in my house. It looks like a tornado blew through it. But secondly and most importantly, is this ridiculous bullshit about not returning to Hamilton Hills. I agreed you could take off a year to work before getting your M.B.A., but the intention all along was for it to be a year of apprenticeship at the bank. I was planning for you to work under Tim McLaughlin, Vice President for loans. You'll get to know the community better, both the elite and the, well, what I call the commoners. Not to their faces of course. At our interest rates and return on equity, hell, I'll loan to anyone who qualifies."

"Excuse me, Father, what precisely is the point of this diatribe?" Jason interrupted.

"Don't you 'diatribe' me, young man. I've made you what you are up to this point. My money, my tutoring, my pushing you to exercise your genetic talents, although I'll concede they're mostly from me. Anyway, December is barely two months away, and I've got to finalize our plans about where to fit you in at the bank."

"Father, there are no so-called 'our plans' to consider. From here forward, I'm taking over the reins of my life and you can have the shackles."

"What the hell does that mean, son?"

"It means I've been interviewing since September with three financial groups in Boston. With my grades, several honors in economics you are not even aware of, not to mention accomplishing four years of course work in three years, well, all three firms are seriously recruiting me. I do thank you for what you've done. You may be an aloof father and a shrewd banker, but I'm one fool you won't be controlling any longer."

"Jason, I don't want to have to drive up there. Well, actually I can't this week. We're opening another branch office. But I'll conclude by saying that I expect you to live up to your side of our bargain. I don't like to lose, so we'll talk later in the week."

"Good night, Father. I don't think we have anything else to say."

A week later, Jason accepted a position with DeLouche and Trotter, a firm specializing in analysis of business plans and in mergers and acquisitions of mid-size companies valued at ten to fifty million dollars. Although their offices were scattered along the Eastern seaboard, Jason knew the new recruits were all funneled to the Boston headquarters. The day he received his letter of offer, he faxed it to his father with a note on its border: "Now maybe you'll believe me and be able to live with it. My accepting this position doesn't preclude a change of venue (like joining the bank) sometime in the future. Once again, thanks for everything you've done for me."

Returning to Wharton, Jason knew his objective, his only real concern, was to complete the semester in fine form, because DeLouche and Trotter had stated his signing of a final contract in December was dependent upon completing his courses with 'A' or 'B' grades. As usual, he was carrying twenty-five hours instead of fifteen or eighteen. Except for a double course in third-world politics and failed economic policies in Africa, he had found the senior-level courses more interesting and less demanding than the first two years at Wharton. Although he had continued his readings during his week in Hamilton Hills, he knew he was in danger of making a "C" in this ten-hour course. What was more confusing was that the two professors, one teaching the political ramifications and the other focusing upon the failed economic policies, rarely coordinated their lectures. From his return on October tenth until mid-November, he performed poorly on two tests in this double course, making a "B" by only two points.

Because of the nightmares that plagued him, Jason decided to resume his visits to a local health club, where he would swim and lift weights, primarily to distract himself from the rigors of school and his ruminations about Meagan. He also began to again date a senior student at Penn majoring in art history. Morgan was the daughter and only child of a local lawyer and his wife, who were both fifth-generation Philadelphia. She was attractive and tall like her father and also had his red hair but not his temper. Her pale porcelain skin appeared to be a gift of her mother along with a population of freckles so tiny they appeared to be mosquito bites. And yes, she had been featured in the *Philadelphia Inquirer*'s Society Section as a debutante of the most exclusive cotillion. But what distinguished her most was her whining, defeatist attitude. She saw her fate as being thwarted at any and every effort to make her mark, any mark. So it was that her major in art history was a default position from having failed and having been asked to leave The Pennsylvania Academy of Fine Arts across town after only a year of study. And it was very likely only an endowment gift from her father's law firm along with at best a modicum of talent that had led to her admission to The Academy out of high school. "Dismissed, deflated, doomed and knew it," seemed to be her motto despite her beauty.

So why would Jason have dated her for almost six months after meeting her in the school cafeteria over a year ago during his second year at Wharton? He was fascinated by her beauty and delighted by her garrulous nature despite its doomsday tone. As he had told a friend at the time, "With Morgan, I really don't have to commit to anything except listening to her rants. One day, it's about how she is majoring in art history so that she will be in a position to establish a new travel agency with European jaunts led by her. The next month, she is describing a new Manhattan art gallery that she and a friend are going to open. She expects her darling father to fund whichever venture she selects. She's so dense that she ignores the competition, not to mention the emergence of the internet in the world of travel and even art. But mainly, she's just good, cheap entertainment and, if she has any talent at all, it's in bed." Jason's friend had if that was all he wanted in a woman, to which Jason had said, "Damn right and even that may be too much."

Morgan was open to their dating again when Jason called her the week before Thanksgiving. Despite his studies, he found the relief of the gym and the frivolity of his consort as welcome respites. Indeed, he spent the brief four-day Thanksgiving holiday with her and her family. December, though, was his final push and he knew that his grades would be dependent upon his final exams for his last semester. Yet, before the last week of classes, Morgan proposed that they go out for dinner and then to an early showing of her cult favorite, "The Rocky Horror Picture Show," a movie that Jason detested. But he relented. After the movie, Jason was eager to return to his condo so that he could get a full night's sleep before a Saturday of feverish study. Morgan was demurely dressed in black and white while trying to resemble Magenta, the domestic servant in "Rocky Horror." She demanded that they go instead to her apartment. Jason agreed reluctantly to share a bottle of champagne and was startled when she opened a magnum of Veuve Cliquot, the same champagne Meredith had provided for Meagan's memorial.

"Jason, I got this champagne so that we could celebrate our first month back together and also because you seem to be content with having me only as a friend and that's not enough for me," Morgan said.

"Well, Jesus, I've been under a lot of stress. You know quite well that I have been studying constantly except for our weekend dates. The other thing I haven't really mentioned is that a dear friend died suddenly while I was visiting my parents in Hamilton Hills earlier this fall. That's also been something of a plague on my psyche."

"Was this just a friend from your high school days or someone you were really close to?" Morgan asked.

Not wanting to divulge the convoluted history of his and Meagan's relationship and especially the circumstances of her death, Jason said merely, "Well, I would call her an acquaintance but also someone I respected. Her athletic abilities were exceptional and her wit stimulating. She was very popular until she sort of went off the deep end," Jason chuckled as he finished his first glass of champagne.

They drank the entire magnum in an hour, glass after glass, until Morgan said, "Wait here so I can get a surprise for you, something that will help you relax before you have to study and concentrate in the week ahead," as she left the room.

She returned five minutes later wearing Western boots, a wide-brim hat with a sheriff's badge, a silver-studded black leather belt with twin toy pistols, handcuffs and a small whip but her clothing was limited to black, lacy panties. She walked straight to where Jason was reclining on the sofa, leaned down into his face and said, "Jason Aldridge, I'm the new sheriff in town. Now let me see your hands, you're under arrest."

Jason, laughingly complied, reached for her and said, "Well, well, well, from Magenta the Maid to Shirley the Sheriff in five minutes and how fetchingly sweet you are. You can arrest me only if I can feel those beautiful breasts first," his voice slightly slurred as he reached and delicately teased her tensing nipples.

"Sure, Jason, but consider that your last taste of freedom. What I'm arresting you for is that for the entire month we've been dating, you've kept it on a totally sophomoric, casual level. You haven't once made love to me, even touched me, and I find that very strange, especially in view of how we used to love to fuck," Morgan said as she adroitly snapped her handcuffs around both of his wrists. "And now you're mine to manipulate, just as you always seem to be in control of our friendship I'll call it. It's damn sure not a relationship. You don't talk to me, you don't respect me, and don't even want to fuck. So now I'm going to fuck you, sweetie."

She reached for his belt, quickly unbuckled it and slid his pants and underwear down around his ankles. As she did so, Jason began to swear at her, calling her "Bitch," and "Whore." He resisted her efforts to excite him. He thought of Meredith, how she had lured him into Sarah's bedroom to seduce him. Then, yes, had seduced him and humiliated him. And, finally, left him stunned and in the surreal company of a blathering and confused Father Flaherty. He panicked, grabbed Morgan by the throat with both hands even though handcuffed and rolled with her onto the floor.

She screamed, "Stop it, Jason, this is only a game. I just wanted to do it a different way. I thought maybe it would turn you on, because you've been so cold and remote. Now get off me."

Jason did not hear her. He saw Meredith's face. He imagined in those few seconds that he had somehow rolled Meredith from their bed in Sarah's bedroom onto the floor, landing on top of her before she had seduced him and slapped him, temporarily deafening him in her fierce delivery of justice. He could see Meredith laughing at him. With his hands still around Morgan's throat, he lifted her head and banged it hard against the floor.

She screamed, "Jason, stop it, stop it, don't do this, you're going to hurt me. Stop it this second. The key to the handcuffs is on my belt."

He stopped, and with barely enough slack in the handcuffs, removed the key from her belt, unlocked one side then the other. He rolled off her and then lay next to her, panting as she began to cry. Finally she stuttered, “Oh, Jason, this went so horribly wrong. All I wanted was for you to just hold me like you once did. I just don’t understand you at all, even if you are stressed out over final exams. You don’t talk, you don’t laugh, you can’t have fun. When you do listen to me, it’s like a zombie. I was simply trying to get to you in the only way I knew. Thank God, you didn’t panic enough to seriously hurt me. But what is it with you?” Morgan implored.

“I don’t know, I just lost it for a second. I didn’t mean to hit your head. It was just some primitive reaction to being captured, handcuffed by you. I can’t explain it except I just lost it. I’m not like that and you know it.”

“Then leave and don’t ever call me again, or I’ll have you arrested. You may not respect me, may think I’m stupid, but my father has clout in this city that can make your head roll, not to mention ruining whatever chance you have at a career in business. Get your warped ass out of here before I call him right now,” Morgan said as she got to her feet then fell backwards onto the sofa.

Jason Takes a New Job in Boston

The promised land for Wharton graduates who did not remain in Philadelphia was thought to be Boston, Manhattan, or Washington D.C. unless, by some aberrant finger of fate, you had been pointed west to L.A. or San Francisco. It was unusual for a top graduate to stop short of a M.B.A. but the B.S. in economics from Wharton still carried more than a few grams of gravitas. Jason had secured his position with DeLouche and Trotter because he had graduated third in his class. He had assured his new employer that he would return after a year for his M.B.A. And the firm was aware of Jason's father's major gift to Wharton for the new computer lab. When his parents had visited him for dinner in Philadelphia before his move to Boston, his father had given Jason $5,000 and a new Mercedes C-class coupe for Christmas.

As they were concluding their dinner, Mr. Aldridge said, "I fully expect you to ultimately join our bank, so I'm going to extend my wager on you although we may have had our differences. You also need to always refurbish and enhance your image. That is one's primary asset in the world of business along with how well you network. A young man driving a Corvette is simply a young vagabond. So I'm paying the difference on your trade for the C-class coupe, a conservative statement with the right brand. Now make us all proud, son."

It was well known that there was a rigid structure regarding how the Boston office of DeLouche and Trotter functioned. A sacrosanct rule for first-year recruits was the requirement of wearing a dark suit and subdued tie daily, while the few women recruits were required to wear non-provocative black suits of various styles. Jason's peerage of ten top recruits from primarily Ivy League business schools, soon joked that "D & T" were the initials for "a douche and the trots all in one," referring to both constant pressure and their less than esteemed status on the promotional abacus of the firm. They were like colonels at the Pentagon, meaning that half would be gone after a year and never heard from again.

Mondays at 10 a.m. were known unofficially as "Full Dress Parade Day." Two senior vice presidents typically reviewed all on-going projects and assigned new projects. Potential conflicts of interest were discussed, and then the projects were stratified by variables such as cost, client relationship, legal issues, and probability of success. It was at one of these meetings that Jason had presented after being at the firm for only three weeks. Robert Starling, the CEO and founder, had unexpectedly dropped by the meeting that Monday and heard Jason's presentation. The following Tuesday afternoon, Jason received what the junior members referred to as a "Stalin Memo from Hell." Memoranda from Mr. Starling (aka Stalin) were usually caustic, sarcastic, acerbic or some combination of the three. But Jason's was highly laudatory and concluded with "Your immediate supervisor, Mark Almann, has referred to you as energetic, very analytical, and more polished that most of our junior members. I must say that I heartily agree with him. Welcome aboard, Mr. Aldridge."

Jason bounded up the steps of the DeLouche and Trotter Building early the next Wednesday morning and failed to speak to the administrative assistant assigned to him. "Good morning, Jason, hope your evening was as rapturous as mine," Amelia said as he entered his cubicle on the fourth floor. Amelia McAfee was about twenty pounds overweight on an unfortunately squat, five-foot-two-inch frame. The luck of the Irish was missing the day she was born, or more accurately the day she was conceived. It wasn't that she was simply pear-shaped but that she, defying gravity, was almost eggplant-shaped with the large end up. Jason was especially amused when she would wear a certain colorful, horizontally striped dress. He would imagine her spinning, full of bands of color melting into each other, like one of those old spinning tops from the fifties he had seen in an antique shop. But Jason was actually quite fond of Amelia.

Jason knew from their past conversations that what she wanted was for Jason to engage her, to question her about her evening and what "rapturous" meant. At times, he imagined her tap dancing in a diamond-studded leotard under stage lights, her red flowing hair aflame and her teeth bleached to a point of jeweled radiance. And her feet in mad terpsichorean flight, rivaled only by a dancing elephant at the circus. Oh, the world at her fingertips or painted toe tips more precisely, but finally at the end of her "rapturous" performance, she could not bend over to retrieve the roses tossed from the gallery. But in less cynical moments, Jason reluctantly admitted that there was something nurturing about her solicitous manner, and he could not help speculating about how she might be in bed.

On this cold morning in January, he thought Amelia was just a bit too friendly and excitable. He returned to her desk to ask if something was happening in the office that he was not aware of. She simply winked at him and shrugged her shoulders. At doughnuts and coffee, the buzz was neither muted nor suppressed. One of the other first-year "rising stars" came up and slapped Jason on the back, just a fraction too forcefully, and said, "Well, well, our Wharton wonder-boy, out to make the rest of us look bad and a bit diminished in the old man's eyes, huh?"

Jason flinched when slapped but, still stirring his coffee, said, "Right, Allen, what's with the old coach's slap?. Are you sending me into the big game to catch the winning touchdown pass?"

"Come on, Jason. Don't act so innocent. Certainly by now you know we've all seen a copy of the Stalin Memo, only this one was inviting you into the politburo instead of sentencing you to the frigid steppes of Siberian hell, if you'll forgive me extending the metaphor, old chap," Allen concluded sarcastically.

"Frankly, Allen, I do not know what you are referring to," Jason retorted, puzzled.

Allen leaned backward and sneered in apparent disbelief, saying, "Amelia leaked the memo and when it got back to the old man late yesterday, he simply laughed and said, 'Good news travels fast especially when bad news is the expectation.' So, yeah, I'm a little pissed but most people are pleased for you, making your mark so soon, dude. And to think you've been here only a little over a month, while most of us have been here approaching seven months. Some are saying that you've joined Samantha and me as the rising stars among our first-year group."

"Allen, I assure you I was going to say nothing about the memo. Frankly, I was somewhat embarrassed because now I've got to figure out how to stay on my game without offending anyone. But hey, we're all in it together. So let's just go at it like that old Scottish Black Watch Regiment, one for all, all for one. I hope you get the next gold star, man," Jason said, smiling.

Despite their ambivalent camaraderie and jousting, Allen and Jason, in part because of their "rising star" status, remained friends. Along with several other junior staff and certain favored administrative assistants, they would spend Saturday nights at the trendy bars for young professionals. Since Allen liked Jason, he refrained from telling him that his nickname among some of the women of "D&T" was Bambi. It was well known that Jason would visit a local gym four times a week where he no longer swam but continued to lift weights and bike. What was not known was whether he dated, despite repeated casual entreaties from several of these women. And it was one of these women who nicknamed him Bambi for three reasons. One, his precise manners and calm, gentlemanly nature were a constant. Two, he had rather soft and delicate hands that did not seem to fit his muscular and chiseled body so admired on "dress-down" Fridays when he would wear a tight black turtleneck and non-pleated slacks. And three, because of his private nature, his unknown social life, several of the women thought there was something vaguely "ambiguous" about his sexuality leading them to place a "B" in front of "ambi." In fact, the only woman besides Amelia with whom Jason would at times have lunch was Samantha Kreel, who had a M.B.A. from Harvard and was the third "rising star." But their friendship seemed to center primarily around light debates about economic theory and editorials in *The Boston Globe*.

Unknown to anyone except Amelia was Jason's view that office politics was mundane and boring and that the machinations and stratagems of "D&T" in catalyzing mergers seemed often to be malicious and bordering on impropriety. So he was not happy, all appearances aside. Especially on weekends when he could divorce himself from the frenetic tenor of work and his compulsion to excel, he would notice a certain malaise. He did not know what to call it but it was a disquieting hint of something awry, something missing, or something alienating. He did not think he was depressed, and except for the recurrent nightmares about Meagan, he slept well and had no trouble concentrating at work.

Still, he was haunted by a number of skeletons rattling around in his psyche's closet. Not the least of these was Meagan's death and his as yet unresolved role in her death. He hated to admit it even to himself, but his estrangement from his parents to whom he never spoke after moving to Boston also bothered him. This was despite his absolute awareness that his mother had never cared for him (by her own admission) and that his father cared for him primarily as his accomplishments reflected favorably upon the family. Against the notion that he should and would someday return to Hamilton Hills to assume leadership of the bank in which they were majority shareholders, was the angst that it would be the end of him, a capitulation to his father's control unless, of course, his father were to die.

There was one other small reverberation of the closeted skeletons, one of which had recently slipped under the doorsill, so to speak. Jason had played with the notion of viewing bondage sites on the Internet in his last few months at Wharton. During the past month in Boston, that burgeoning interest had become something of a compulsion. What began one gray Sunday afternoon during this cold January in as random web surfing at home had culminated around 11 p.m. with an encounter with a certain "Miss Nadia Mystic." Miss Mystic's website featured a rather provocative pose of her appearing to be astride a gigantic Komodo lizard. Her stiletto heels were dug into its sides with some sort of green blood or bile trickling out of its perforated rib cage. Beneath the obviously computer-doctored photograph was a simple message: "Role Play, Role Reversal, Conflict Resolution, Guilt Exorcism, and Examination of Fantasy Frustrations." In Miss Mystic's right hand rested the requisite whip, presumably to keep the Komodo in line should it take offense at the angle of her stiletto heels. Her attire was strange because she wore a knee-length blue gingham dress with a pattern of small yellow ducks at play. The bodice was unbuttoned tastefully to give only a hint of her small but perfectly shaped breasts. But what shocked Jason was that he remembered a picture of his mother when as a child she wore a dress almost exactly the same as Miss Mystic's.

Jason emailed Nadia Mystic at 11:15 that Sunday night: "Just met you (meaning, just discovered your website) after attending a play with a friend, followed by a glass of wine. You took my breath away, and since I have to say something to get your attention, how about this: The Komodo dragon's smile was sweet but he was missing three teeth. I wondered if you had ever kicked him in the mouth? By the way, my teeth are perfect and I intend to keep them that way. I would like to know when your services are available, although I must admit I would be quite new to this scene."

Surprisingly, barely five minutes later he received a reply: "It takes a lot to touch my heart, but Kiki's smile (and already missing three teeth) did it for me so I took him under my wing a year ago. We have grown very close. He is not for sale for any price, but my consultative services are available. I am rather expensive but let me know if you are interested. I do have a time slot open early tomorrow evening and on Thursday evening." Excited but exhausted, Jason went to bed.

The next morning at work, Jason retreated to the relative quiet of his office that was really nothing more than a cubicle with a large desk for displaying spreadsheets and a smaller desk for two computers and a few personal items. After checking the stock market's open and the five-day weather forecast, he hesitantly began an email to Miss Mystic: "I am at work but unable to get you off my mind. I guess that means, like a cow, I keep chewing over your last message to me. In my so-called relationships, I am always the one in control, total control I guess. I sense that would not be the case with you. Not that I would have to give it up (the control) but that you would assume it, demand it. In some ways, sending this email to you from work already represents my relinquishing control. I mean I could be fired. Now you know my email address at work as well. I don't care. What I do want is a consultation with you sooner rather than later. Please label your email back to me as Project X-217."

Jason checked his emails compulsively every thirty minutes. At 3:30 p.m., he noticed a Project X-217 response: "You seem too eager, like a puppy dog lapping warm milk. What if my milk is poison? What if your tongue is furrowed with glass? What if my nipples already bleed for you, my sweet, mean-tongued puppy? So many questions, so little time to answer them. I have an opening at 7 P.M. tonight (my working hours are usually 3 P.M. until 11 P.M.). A two-hour session (which is usually the minimum to get any real work done) is $750 cash or money order. I consider that cheap for what you get, ferreting out the truth you might say. Go to 1411 North Avenue, ring 12A, and identify yourself. You will need a legitimate driver's license photo or passport as, in this business, I must know with whom I'm working. After I know, I no longer remember. The only real remembering is with my clients, most of whom are trying to forget what they can't stop remembering. My effect is like shock therapy because I make my clients forget everything, at least for the time they're with me. Of course some sessions are longer, and occasionally I travel with clients who have what I call special needs."

Meeting Miss Mystic

As Jason showered after work, he thought of the old standard, *Singing in the Rain.* He began singing then the few lyrics he remembered until he recalled Malcolm McDowell singing the same song in one of the more violent scenes in the movie, "A Clockwork Orange." His greatest concern, though, was what he should wear for his initial meeting with Miss Mystic. He wondered whether he was dressing for an interview, a date, or some kind of introduction to the paraphernalia of Miss Mystic's profession. He displayed on his bed three possibilities: a gray herringbone blazer with black slacks and black turtleneck sweater, a Polo green velour warm-up suit, and black Guess jeans with a yellow Lycra shirt and a leather vest. After much deliberation and considering how what he wore might affect Miss Mystic's first impression, he opted for comfort, or at least for something to sartorially soothe his anxiety, namely the warm-up suit.

1411 North Avenue was a four-story brownstone in a neighborhood known as an area once fallen but now gentrified. It had become an area favored by the more adventurous, up-and-coming young professionals. When he rang 12A, a flat voice answered, "You must have the wrong address." A thin line of sweat graced Jason's upper lip and beaded his forehead despite the cool winter night. He reached into his pocket to retrieve the yellow note with Miss Mystic's address.

"No, I'm certain this is the address in my email. I also called and confirmed around five o'clock today. My name is Jason Aldridge,"

Jason spoke into the polished aluminum box.

"Just a little test, Jason," the voice retorted. "Do come in at the buzz, take the elevator to the fourth floor, then the first door on your right. You should expect to see no one on my floor. My living quarters occupy the suite across the hall from my work studio."

As Jason entered apartment 12A, he noticed two ceramic masks representing comedy and tragedy, then the muted violin of a Vivaldi concerto, and finally Miss Mystic herself. He was impressed by her height and the strength of her handshake. Since he was now an inch over six feet, he guessed she was probably five feet, nine or ten. Except for Sarah Sewell, Cathy Eubanks, and Morgan, he had rarely been around a woman this tall. He was surprised by her large, cat-like eyes that seemed to fix him in her sight and were unblinking. Her copper-brown hair was cut short, but in small discrete ringlets and there was a hint of a mustache. He was struck by the symmetry of her eyebrows, ears, cheekbones and dimpled chin as though she were carved from stone. She wore a dark purple sweater, gray slacks, and black flats with a small silver Gucci emblem. Her lips were full and she wore no makeup of any kind. He wondered whether she felt the cool damp creases of his palm or noticed the sweat on his brow and above his lip that he had already wiped once before.

"Have a seat, Jason, and welcome to my studio that will also be our laboratory. But be forewarned that you may suggest the topic but I design the experiment. That's my cardinal rule because ultimately everything between any two people is about who is in control. I suffer no fools before me and you young stud-muffins can be recalcitrant, if you know what I mean. In general, I don't work with men under thirty because they're so narcissistic that they simply aren't aware of other people. And they don't learn because their imaginations are clogged like a sewer with images mainly of themselves. The only world they see is a world in which they reign supreme. It's sad, really. But first, let me take a quick look at your license, a small formality in my line of work."

Jason settled into a white leather armchair and found the unusual color of the walls, something between a pale lavender and a persimmon blue, to be strangely soothing despite his sweating hands and the uncomfortable staccato of his racing heartbeat. The long wall behind Miss Mystic, who sat in one of a pair of black leather Barcelona chairs, was populated by portraits of ten men Jason wondered if he should have remembered from the heady intellectual days of college.

"I notice you seem entranced by my collection of men and I wonder if you realize you haven't uttered a word since walking in," Miss Mystic said with a soft, comforting voice.

"Well, I feel somewhat like I did when I was sixteen and while visiting a Penn State summer program, I hooked up with an older grad student from Quebec. She taught me all I would ever need to know about sex but scared the hell out of me at the same time," Jason stammered as he avoided looking directly at Miss Mystic's constant gaze.

"Oh, a Penn State graduate, I've had several of those before and what class were you?" Miss Mystic queried.

"Well, actually, no. I decided, or it might be more accurate to say that my father decided, I would go to the University of Pennsylvania, specifically Wharton which is their business school. By December, I was fed up with the rigors of study so I opted out after getting my B.S. in economics. But that wasn't my point. The point I was trying to make was about my anxiety in that first sexual encounter," Jason said.

"Yes Jason, I know what your point was. Your point was that as a sexual novitiate that summer you were intimidated, scared, and now, five or six years later, you're in a similar situation. Fear of the unknown, as most would say. You're not here to pass any tests, you know, so just relax. In fact, that may be part of the problem. Maybe you aren't sure why you are here if you've never done this kind of thing before. And you don't have to call me Miss Mystic. By the way, the 'Miss' is a gross anachronism. I only use it because most of my clients are over fifty, and on my web site it doesn't scare them as much as a conventional 'Ms.' might. You may call me simply by my Christian name, Nadia. Actually, I get called all kinds of names: names of hated wives, imagined mistresses, animals, you name it. It's also sort of common for me to be called Nurse Nadia because of some of the things I do. But it ranges from something as dismissive as Connie Cockroach to Monsignor Mystic. Jason, you may find that you have the name of someone else you would like to project or tease me with, most of you do," Nadia suggested as she smiled for the first time.

"What do you mean by 'most of you'?" Jason asked.

"Well, men, of course. You come to me generally because you

want to discover or rediscover or uncover the bad boy in yourselves. You come as tyrants, traitors, priests, hedge fund managers, alpha males above all else. And you come with some story you want to tell but haven't been able to. Usually it's because you've been trapped within some image you've lived with for so long that even you have come to believe it. But in your hearts, those small organs you abhor, you all still know that something is slightly sour in your soul, as an old black lady said to one of my clients while telling his fortune. Now in your case, you're rather young to have any kind of fixed self image," Nadia said in a slightly provocative manner.

"I don't know what you're talking about," Jason said.

"I suspect you do know what I'm talking about, Jason, so just breathe deeply and let's slow down a bit. Just a few very deep breaths, there, that's called relaxing. Do you know how to do that? To give you a break, let's focus not on you for a few minutes but on what I call my collection of mystery men, meaning those portraits on the wall behind me. During my almost fifteen years of teaching here, I call myself a teacher, only one man has identified all ten of them. Unfortunately, he committed suicide and selfishly took all that knowledge with him. Do you recognize any of them? Almost everyone gets two or three and it's strange, now that I think about it, these men on the wall, except for maybe two, had trouble with women. Either they wanted to dominate women or were totally dominated by women. Well, maybe in several cases, they weren't sure whether they were the male or the female," Nadia said as she turned slightly in her chair to invite Jason's answer.

"I think I know three of your rogues' gallery. James Dean is pretty obvious, especially standing next to his Porsche, the same car that would destroy him. Then, I think the bearded guy on the left, my left, is Freud, Sigmund Freud, our classic shrink. And the young but totally bald guy, although almost no one has seen him without one of his hairpieces in place and his trademark, overstated glasses, certainly looks like Elton John. How am I doing so far? And how did you select this group?" Jason asked with pride.

"You're doing pretty well, Jason. But like most of you young, preppie types, you only get the easy ones. Basically, it's a reflection of your lack of experience. Or to put it another way, you don't know enough about life yet," Nadia said.

Jason looked at Miss Mystic with a sort of smirking incredulity, sensing that he had lost control, not only in his first email from the office but now, at the moment that he had stepped across the threshold of Nadia Mystic's apartment. Even earlier in the evening when his moist finger had slipped on the elevator button, he had gone to the third floor rather than the fourth floor. Embarrassed by the presence of an elderly couple, he got off the elevator and walked up a flight of stairs on the service steps. Though, in retrospect, he thought that seemed a good strategy for avoiding detection during future visits. Jason leaned forward, frowned and said, "Miss Mystic, Nadia, whatever, I admit that I am really anxious about being here. In fact, it's hard to focus on you or any of these portraits. I'm not trying to get into a control-thing with you. I feel like I did in a piano recital in the sixth grade when I made several mistakes and barely made it off the stage to the bathroom before throwing up my lunch."

Without looking up, Nadia reached for a Baccarat paperweight of a woman apparently at prayer. While holding the paperweight, she said quietly, "You, you were a vulnerable child, Jason. That's what I can work with and that gives us a direction to explore. Namely, what child hides behind a facade of assurance that you seem to want to project? You know how all the men on the soap operas have that same look: chiseled jaw line, a chin like DeNiro, the sullen mouth of Brando, sunken cheeks, bedroom eyes, all so faux macho, so perfect you could just puke? Well, I'm certain you've been told often how handsome you are and presumably bright or you wouldn't have been accepted at Wharton."

Placing the paperweight back on the table, Nadia Mystic rose from her seat, raised her arms toward the ceiling then leaned as far backward as possible like a long, lithe, drawn bow. "Excuse me, but when I'm a little tense, a sort of half sun-salute loosens me up. That and slow, deep breathing tends to do the trick." She walked slowly around the room, stopping in front of each photograph. She then addressed Jason without looking at him, "Yes, you're handsome and bright and from that fine sartorial flair, somebody's got a little money. So, we know all of that. What we don't know is what secret or secrets are hidden in your heart. I will be introducing you to a jungle whose paths you also won't know at all. You might even call it something like our little journey into your big unknown. The real question is whether you think you're ready for this?"

"I don't know if I'm ready or not, but I do know I've been miserable and basically alone most of my life. And for the past four months, I've had these recurrent nightmares and headaches that have nothing to do with school or the stress of my new job here in Boston with DeLouche and Trotter. You've probably heard of my firm. They hire only graduates, primarily Ivy League, who were at the top of their graduating classes. But first, I'm really curious who the other seven men are, the portraits I mean."

"It's funny you ask because I thought we were past that and were about to learn a little more about you. But I'll indulge you. Sometimes I think of them as a kind of Rorschach test. As I've said, all of my clients are men and all of the portraits are obviously men. So I find it curious to see whom each of you recognizes, identifies with, or projects himself onto. In some cases, like if they're homophobic, they'll say how much they despise Elton John or even James Dean. God only knows who James Dean really was although he was a genius and to think he was in his mid-twenties when he died. Obviously, everyone in the world knows Elton John is gay, fine with me, but you wouldn't believe some of the reactions I get to him," Nadia said, still facing the portraits.

"And what about the guy who identified all ten of them, was he some genius?"

"Well, yes, he was extremely bright, actually a famous actor who was also an accomplished, published writer. Even though he got all ten correct, it was in a way an insight into his personality. He had such a fluid, amorphous personality that I was never certain who would be walking through that door. Biggest challenge I've ever had, trying to work with him. His whole life was like a gigantic spider web, sort of like those big ones an orb dweller constructs. And he had all these strange relationships, like he would have different people trapped in various parts of his spider web. Of course, the irony of it was that he would be running all across his web like a madman. So he was the one really trapped by his own web. His frenetic spinning of silk so to speak, his elaborate schemes, subterfuges, caveats of capture, delicacies entombed for future feasts, those were just some of the things he would talk about. He had something we call a borderline personality disorder," Nadia concluded.

"What's his name? I mean would I know him from the movies or from his books?" Jason asked naively.

"Jason, I told you that little story, that anecdote, to suggest to you how we are all trapped in the little webs of our own making. The story may or may not be completely true but it's simply an illustration. Now, as for names, let me remind you that nothing is more important than confidentiality in this work. Whether it is Sigmund Freud up there, a clinical psychologist over at Harvard, or me, we never discuss one client with another. You'll never hear me talk about anyone I see or have seen over these last fifteen years. There may be times when I sort of abstractly pull from an earlier experience to make a point. I admit the kind of work I do is different from most therapists, but my kind of work seems to meet the needs of a particular kind of man. I think of my therapy as a medium to the message. In this case, the medium comprises my techniques and the message is what we need or you need to get out of you. That's the reason my sessions are two hours. And I also schedule ten minutes in between sessions so that no one encounters another client."

"Well thanks, Nadia, now I actually feel a little more comfortable because of what you've said. So, about the other seven portraits?" Jason asked.

"I'll only name one of them because I want you to study them as I'm speaking. For the remaining six, I want you to do a bit of homework to see if you can improve your performance. So, over there, third from the end, is Beethoven, born in the late eighteenth century. He was one of the great Baroque composers, one who was not necessarily a rascal but was definitely irascible. He was short and stocky, not very attractive, but an absolute genius. I love his music although I don't pretend to know a lot about classical music. He's famous for those nine symphonies and the little crowd-pleasing *Moonlight Sonata*. But if you want to hear something so sublime, so ethereal, it doesn't seem of this earth, then you should listen to his late quartets. God, they are truly out of this world, and of course he was totally deaf the last ten years of his life. He just turns me on for some reason," Nadia laughed as she touched her fingers to her lips and blew old Ludwig Van a kiss.

"Well, you don't go to business school and get that kind of exposure. So at least I've got an excuse for not knowing him. I do read other books, mainly science fiction and biographies. I probably read more in high school than now though. So where do we go from here?"

"Before we go on a tour of my studio, I want you to suggest a few reasons why you've decided to seek my help. While you may be attracted by the provocative nature of my website, I'm assuming you do know you're here for a form of therapy. This is not about sex or sensationalism."

Jason leaned forward, looked directly at Miss Mystic, and then took a deep breath. "I have to admit that the sort of erotic nature of your work intrigues me although I've never really been into pornography. But the other aspect is that I really do struggle with some issues. Maybe like everyone my age, I regard my parents as having always been my nemesis and as contributing to the ways I have trouble relating to people. He, my father, is so controlling, almost tyrannical, in how he wants to engineer my life. And of course he is determined that I will return to that small town in southeastern Pennsylvania and be heir to his banks. I just don't want to end up being like him."

"Well, could you give me an example of how he has tried to control or manipulate you, Jason?"

"Sure. I could give you hundreds. One is how he determined at the last minute that I would go to Wharton rather than Penn State. Actually, all my life he has called the shots even in having me drilled in sports before I was physically ready. He tells my mother what kind of preppie clothes I must buy. He doesn't talk to me as a son, but he lectures me. And everything I do is a direct reflection upon him, he says."

"What about your mother? How does she fit into this equation? And make it succinct because I want you to be aware of what happens here beyond talking," Nadia said, smiling as she leaned forward.

"Mother, oh my mother, my darling, remote, detached, impersonal mother. She's programmed like a robot to worship my father first and herself second. I think the way she froze me out as a young boy was more wounding than anything. It was always about her trips, her clothes, her social engagements, her friends, and never any consideration about what a scared, lonely little boy might need. But beyond these obvious things, I think she was cold and truly manipulative. I think it was she who caused my breakup with my high school girlfriend, Meagan, at the end of our senior year. Before, I had always blamed it on my father's ambitions for me. Then, after Meagan died in an accident last October, I've had these almost constant nightmares," Jason concluded as he slumped back into his chair.

"Well, young man, if you decide to pursue this journey, we're going to have plenty of caves to explore. Spelunking through the psyche, you might say. Before we are out of time, though, I want to show you my studio so that you'll have some notion of the kind of radical therapy we practice here. Now if you'll join me, please."

Nadia stood and motioned for Jason to follow her into an adjoining suite of rooms. A large metal cage was centered in the first room while on the walls were masks similar to some Jason had seen once in a shop in south Philadelphia. There were beautiful, hand-made masks of animals, sequined saints, and distorted demonic figures that seemed about to emit rabid cries from another world. Hanging from a separate rack were studded leather masks and a variety of muzzles, some braided and others more confining but with intricate stenciled patterns on the leather. On another side of the room were two saddles, one ornate and Western, the other simple and English, each attached to a wooden sawhorse. Another wall held racks of whips of various colors and weaves, made of both leather and long strands of hair.

"You will notice that the rather large cage can serve as either a containment chamber, you know like wild and angry animals might need, or it could be a platform for various interventions. Now, come along to the second chamber, which I call the tutorial center for my graduate students," Nadia said as she led Jason into a larger room, perhaps four hundred square feet, with a large mirrored ceiling. Without acknowledging his hesitancy to enter, Nadia guided him by the elbow and explained the essentials, saying, "Notice the coffin, the chains, the large wooden crucifix, the rack, the two meat hooks, the hooding masks, and over in the corner, the trapeze. It is here that my clients sometimes have spiritual experiences, because they act out the same play they've perpetrated on others so often and then they see how it feels to be the pawn in that play. Another way of saying that is that most of you come seeking some kind of relief, some kind of salvation, through humiliation. You can call it something trite like getting in touch with your hurt self that hurts others, if you like. Do I think you already know what you need? Hell no, but that is the beauty and the nature of our journey, our game for which there are no rules. I even had a rabbi who tried to hang himself from that cross. I mean the irony of it all. And, yes, I've had my share of moments that came close to being calls to 911. Thankfully, never a serious injury or death, or we would be out of business to say the least," Nadia sighed.

"But where do I fit into all of this?" Jason asked.

"That's what we don't know yet," Nadia answered.

"But what I mean is where do we start?" Jason reiterated.

"Well, let's go back to the first room and I want you to give me that thin buggy whip against the wall behind you. It will be a good starting point. It's rather innocuous and by that I mean it has the bite of a mosquito compared to some of the other whips." Nadia motioned to a small rack of straight, thin whips. Jason did as he was told, then sat on the edge of the metal cage at the center of the chamber.

"There are two things you need to learn immediately," Nadia explained. "One, I am always in charge and this generates endless questions about trust. And secondly, you must learn to assume an appropriate position whenever you anticipate a punishment, realizing that the so-called punishment is not really a punishment but a reward. Think of it as a step towards your enlightenment," Nadia said as she gestured for Jason to bend forward across the edge of the metal cage.

"Now, one little whisper of the whip for each of the portraits you failed to identify," Nadia said as she raised the whip.

Jason looked at her somewhat startled, then said, "Well, I guess I'll go along with this as some kind of initiation or at least out of curiosity. But I didn't know you would have all those portraits, and you said it wasn't a test and I thought...."

"Shut the fuck up and pull up the legs of your pants, young man," Nadia said as the first lash immediately stung the calves of both legs. Each lash of the whip's tail drew a thin line of blood across the back of Jason's calves. After the fourth lash, he began to sweat though the room, the chamber, was cool. By the fifth lash, he felt nauseous and confused the sound of the whip's tail striking his calves with the shrill scream of a diving hawk. With the seventh and last lash, Nadia placed the whip on the floor, and whispered to Jason, "Each instrument we use is always cleaned with a disinfectant. It's a dangerous, diseased world we live in, Jason. Now I want you to excuse yourself from this lesson and when you've done your homework, can identify at least one more portrait, you may call me for another appointment if you think you're man enough for this adventure. Leave, just walk through those two doors. You make me sick, you pious little prick."

"But I thought I was being a good novitiate to use your word," Jason protested.

"That's precisely what I mean. There's something about you that's just a little too good, too good to be true. But we're going to dig it out, the truth I mean. I want you to call for another session only if you are serious about this work, young man. Now get out," Nadia hissed as she stood by the door with her arms on her hips forcing Jason to have to squeeze between her and the doorframe.

"Bitch," he murmured as he passed her.

"What did you say, Jason Aldridge? Now step back here and apologize to Miss Mystic," Nadia said.

"Yes ma'am. I'm sorry, honestly I am," Jason said with tears in his eyes.

"If you think you are old enough for this and that you want to commit to our journey, then call or email me because we will need to establish a weekly schedule. Good night, Jason."

Discovering New Emotions

Arriving in Boston after securing a position with DeLouche and Trotter, Jason had assumed the distance, psychological and geographic, from Hamilton Hills would free him from the nightmares that plagued him. No parents nearby, no casual or accidental encounters with Sarah or her friends to remind him of Meagan's death, and even an escape from several women at Wharton, one of whom would appear at his apartment after a night of bar-hopping. These were some of the demons that chased him. Still, Meagan, dreams of Meagan, had never left him for more than a week. But now something was changing. He thought of his adventure with Miss Mystic as something dangerously challenging. He hoped that she might show him a new way to understand himself, his world, and to release the pain of the past. He observed in the mirror the now barely visible lines from his whipping with a sort of pulsating pride, a delight that he could feel anything at all albeit something as simple as pain. He had even talked to a friend at the gym about a new relationship with a woman who, as he said, "provokes my curiosity about what really makes me tick." Of course, he was evasive about the nature of the relationship. He thought of Nadia Mystic as a sort of combination of a Medea dabbling in witchcraft and a Mother Superior offering some secret path to salvation.

A week after his initial visit to Miss Mystic, Jason emailed her that a follow-up appointment seemed indicated, that he had researched his homework assignment and was eager to pursue their unique relationship. Nadia responded with a non-committal response of having an opening at 7 p.m. and for him to follow the usual procedure.

As Jason rang Miss Mystic's doorbell, he realized that he was far less anxious than when he had first arrived on her doorstep a week ago. He was also curious about how the sessions might evolve and whether he could continue to give up so much control to a woman, to anyone, but especially a woman. He considered that he should try to sound more intimate, less formal, as though they were new friends. "Maybe that will give me a little leverage in the sessions as well," Jason murmured to himself as he entered Nadia's studio.

"Well, here we are and I'm ready to identify at least one more of the portraits," Jason said as he again chose the white leather chair with the wide supple arms which seemed both inviting and secure. He leaned forward and gave her a money order of $750 for the two-hour session.

"Jason, I'm not interested in your research. I assigned it only to determine whether you were involved with your work here. I hope you are serious about our work. Although I get paid either way what makes my work rewarding is when I see my clients gradually awakening to a new reality. It's like therapy obviously. As they get their demons out, identify them, play with them, have them appropriately punished for their sins, my clients seem freer, more liberated. They even sometimes walk with a new bounce to their strides."

"Well, it took me about four days to walk with any bounce at all. But what I like is the secretive pretense. All week, I went to work smiling like when you fall in love, and I awaken each morning to certain favorite songs on the radio so that going to work makes me feel alive. I mean those songs have been there all along. I just didn't listen to the words. So all week, I go into work and Amelia, our somewhat corpulent greeter, actually accuses me of, as she says, 'looking like you have just inherited a million dollars or met a new woman'."

"Jason, you were talking about pretense, but now you are off on falling in love. Exactly what are you talking about?" Nadia asked, sipping from a glass of what appeared to be grape juice.

"What is that stuff, some kind of exotic drink?" Jason asked.

"No, its pomegranate juice, if you would like some. I hope you know I would never consider any alcoholic drink while I am working," Nadia said, grimacing as she stared at Jason.

"No thanks on the juice. So, let's see, pretense. Well, you gave me the nastiest six lashes I've ever had in my life and while I think I didn't deserve it, having the pain for those first four days made me actually joyful. I felt alive but in some strange body-mind disconnect. Like having you humiliate me made me stronger. I even asked Amelia out for dinner two nights ago, not because I felt sorry for her, my usual reaction to her, but because I could sort of sympathize with her struggle, the way she tries to be so cordial, so warm to everyone. She's like all obese people, as sweet as the marzipan they covet. But, you know it's simple because all they probably want is to be respected. Maybe it's simpler than that. Maybe they just want someone to look at them instead of looking through them as though they didn't exist."

"Jason, did you have sex with her?" Nadia asked.

"No, I did not and I resent your saying that. We did have a bottle of wine at dinner and another at her apartment, so we rolled around on the floor when I never would have imagined myself touching her. I've never made love to a fat woman before. I actually alluded to you, referring to you as a consultant for a new project. I don't think she had any idea what I meant. What would happen if I brought her to visit you sometime in the future?" Jason asked.

"Well, that's up to you because I'm here to learn and teach. I would need to know that she would treat coming with total confidence. If you've just started dating her, don't really know her, it would seem grossly inappropriate. It is true that some men will bring a mistress to display her or as a sort of bizarre gift. Occasionally, one will even bring his wife to watch, to learn the ropes, so to speak, or to acquire a few take-home techniques. Those are really long-term clients who have been coming for many months or even years. I just see all of that as a further testimonial to my good work, to be very humble about it. But I would discourage anything like that for now. And of course with your rules at work, I'm surprised you can date Amelia."

"Yeah, DeLouche and Trotter is known for its structure and rules, but as long as she is not connected to me in any supervisory manner, it's sort of tolerated. And the nice thing is that Amelia is well read and a great conversationalist. I really enjoyed her the other night and her kisses were ravenous. It's like she's hungry for any attention, whether just talking or something physical."

"This is all very interesting but I wonder if you're not sort of avoiding why you've returned for another session. What do you see as your biggest unresolved issues? Like, what awakens you in the middle of the night when you are having those nightmares, Jason?"

"It's something we haven't talked about, not that we've talked that much anyway. But in a nutshell, I would say what comes closest to driving me just totally insane is something that happened to me about four or five months ago. And while that may be long enough to forget anything, for me it is like every day still has echoes of that day. It is never far from my mind. I guess they call it a closed-loop tape that is constantly replaying itself."

"So, I suppose it has something to do with your mother, your father, sex, a former girlfriend, or something else traumatic."

"It relates to only one of the above, and that would be a girlfriend. Meagan, whom I've talked a little about, was her name. We don't have to get bogged down in details because it was the classic high school romance. The richest kid in town meets and falls in love with the cutest, smartest girl in school whose mother is a beautician and wasn't even married when Meagan was born. And we were truly in love, I mean if you can call it falling in love when you're only seventeen. That senior year was pure bliss but somehow my parents, and me too to a certain extent if I'm honest about it, didn't see her as fitting into my life once I was leaving for college although we continued to date at intervals. Then she got wilder, weirder, and not even her mother could rein her in. Finally, she decided she was a Buddhist of all things and went to some Buddhist school in Colorado. I admit that the last year or so, doing all that meditating and chanting I guess, she seemed to settle down, find some peace and direction. And the last few months of her life, she had opened a yoga and meditation center that was becoming very popular from what I heard."

"Jason, I'm getting a clear picture of this Meagan, but I'm not sure where you fit into all this, and why it creates such an ongoing dilemma for you," Nadia said, purposefully looking somewhat bored.

"If you weren't so impatient, you would soon understand. You fancy yourself to be a real therapist, but I'm sure that you don't have any formal education," Jason retorted.

"Well, actually I do have a degree with a double major in psychology and English from Bowdoin, a small school you've probably never heard of. And then I got a masters degree in psychology, followed by a year's internship as a marriage counselor. And I do have a counseling license. But that's not where I learned anything of consequence. I've learned what I know in this highly specialized field of therapy after working with another woman for two years, and now I have almost fifteen years of experience with my rather unusual techniques. But let's get back to you. What is it you are trying to tell me?"

"She, I mean Meagan, killed herself using me as her foil, her fool. A fall afternoon ride with me on my motorcycle ended as a catastrophe when she caused us to crash. Then she slid into a tree, spilling her brains and my reputation at the same time. I had been close to her mother since I was very young. Hell, she and the beauticians in her salon were my mothers! Now, Sarah Sewell, Meagan's mother, and others in that little jerk-water town of Hamilton Hills, Pennsylvania, would treat me like a pariah if I were to return. Half of it may be my imagination but it all contributes to why I would never return there, even to manage my father's bank. But all that is just small town background music. The real tragedy is how Meagan and I grew apart and then when I would occasionally return, I couldn't resist calling her. What haunts me most is the accident and her death. I may even tell you some day about the weird crap that happened to me at her memorial service," Jason concluded, his voice now subdued, his face ashen.

"Jason, in telling all of that, you appear to have aged ten years in ten minutes, like your lifeblood has been drained from you," Nadia commented. "And I'm wondering, who have you talked to about all of this? And more, what do you feel about it? Your words flow easily, your body seems relaxed, and your voice is calm, and yet something comes over you. The only thing that betrays you is your color. Those sweet, rosy cheeks become a pale yellowish chalk like you've seen some ghost or demonic creature."

"That's just it, goddamn it, she could have killed me too when she killed herself," Jason exclaimed.

"And now here you are, with me I mean. You've sort of set me up the same way she set you up, saddled you with the guilt from that fateful ride that ended in a fatal tragedy, for her, for you, for her mother, maybe the entire town. And by that, what I'm saying is that you've put me in a position of caring for you, feeling sorry for you, wanting to protect you. It's called a projection. Or in the older analytic terms, it was called projective identification. You've made me be you, feel the feelings you won't or can't feel or won't let yourself confront. Does this make any sense to you?"

"I guess so. I was trying to listen to what you said and not get lost. And no, I've never wanted to see a real therapist or psychiatrist. I don't trust them and don't believe in them. I haven't even talked to a friend about this, not that I have any close friends anyway. But there was something about your website that triggered my desire to talk to you, like maybe you could squeeze the truth out of me," Jason said.

"We've used most of our time talking instead of working tonight. But I want you to come with me. I think we need to try one simple intervention," Nadia said as she led Jason into the first room of her chambers. "And don't forget that in this tango only one can lead and that's me, young man. So I want you to take off that coat, that ridiculous tie and those slacks. In the future, if there is a future for you and me, don't come here from work dressed in business attire. It raises suspicions. Wear casual clothes or one of your gym outfits. Now, take them off and strip down to your underwear."

Jason dutifully placed his clothes across the nearby English saddle and asked, "Are you going to punish me for opening up to you, or is it that you're thinking about seducing me?"

"I'm going to do what I get paid to do and what I think you are ready for. You need to remember that I've been at this for a long time. Now, lie down on the cage, face down with your arms stretched forward and your feet at the two rear corners, please. And, one more thing, I'm going to place this blindfold across your eyes so that you will concentrate on your body and your feelings."

Jason, wearing only his Hilfiger briefs, stretched himself across the top of the cage while Nadia attached the leather cuffs to his wrists and ankles, tightening them so that his feet and hands could not slip through them. She then stood to the side of the cage and with two rotating levers began to slowly increase the tension on both his arms and his legs.

"Am I supposed to tell you when it starts to hurt so that you'll stop?" Jason asked.

Nadia Mystic did not respond to Jason's question but continued to wind the tensioning belts slowly, slowly until she saw Jason begin to sweat, first his face, his arms, then back and legs, his body now maximally stressed, just short of dislocating his shoulders. Jason suddenly screamed, "Jesus Christ, woman, you're at the limits. I mean this is like a fucking torture chamber, more than I bargained for. Listen, crank down the tension and let me up. I've had enough of this bullshit. I mean now or I'll have my father sue you."

Admiring her work, Nadia leaned down near his ear and whispered, "I have to leave for a few minutes, Jason," in a voice so cold and detached that it could have been generated by a computer.

"Please don't leave me, don't leave me like this, I'm begging you," Jason pleaded. Then he screamed as he heard Nadia open the door to leave and yelled, "Miss Mystic, don't do this to me. You're going to kill me leaving me alone like this. I'm afraid that I'm going to panic. Please, please, don't do this to me."

Nadia Mystic could hear neither the muffled screams nor the wailing cries of what sounded like a young child because all of the chambers were sound-proof, sealed, protective of the demons that dared dance within those chambers. After twenty minutes, Nadia opened the door and could then hear Jason's childlike whimpering. She leaned down near his face and very quietly said, "How is my little stud-muffin now? Are we feeling a little relief?"

"Let me up from here, you sorceress. You've almost killed me."

"You have to be polite, Jason, and when I do remove the leather cuffs, you have to respect your teacher and tell her what you learned. Agreed?"

"Yes, yes, whatever you say, just let me up," Jason begged.

As Jason began to dress, Nadia said, "I don't want to do too much processing, but the intervention was not to physically hurt you as much as it was to stress you to the point that you would get in touch with your emotions. But what one thing did you get out of this experience?"

"Well, it's the first time I've cried since I was eight years old. That's the time I remember that my mother humiliated me when I cried about being left by her, something she did all the time. And she looked at me with such disdain, like some sadistic German prison guard, and said, I'll never forget it, she said, 'You remind me of the daughter I never had but always wanted, the greatest disappointment of my life besides having to care for you.' I swear those were her words, if you can believe it."

"I could see how that would hurt you or any child. It makes me really sad to hear it. Beyond being a violation of trust, it's downright cruel. And I can see why you've so efficiently learned to contain your feelings. We might even think that you never really mourned Meagan's death at all, that you resolve problems with your head and keep your heart out of it. So, in the coming week, I want you to think about tonight's experience. But I especially want you to reflect on Meagan, how you loved her, if you did, and how she loved you. Finally, what did her death really mean to you, how did you deal with that death. Well, good night, Jason, that's all for now."

As Jason struggled to get his strained left shoulder and his sore arm into the sleeve of his coat, he turned sheepishly toward Nadia. "You know, I had no idea what to expect when I first came here and, actually, I still don't. But somehow I think what we are doing, even if it's painful, may help me. Well, goodnight, Nadia. I know this sounds really weird but in some strange way, I feel like I'm beginning to really care about you."

"We can talk about what is called transference later, Jason. But it's a little early for you to be either hating or falling in love with your therapist. Maybe just beginning to have any feelings at all has stirred things up for you. And that's a good thing. Now, good night, Jason Aldridge," Nadia Mystic said as she opened the door to the hallway.

A Dutiful Son, a Reluctant Friend

Mondays for Jason became a ritual, a day of frenetic activity at work followed by his seven o'clock appointment with Nadia Mystic. Nadia was surprised by Jason's willingness to talk, his malleability, but most of all by his tolerance of her interventions. As she said to him, "Behind that Samurai warrior, behind that control-freak façade, is a little boy who wants to be loved or at least recognized and touched."

Their sessions during February and into March assumed many avenues along what Nadia had said to Jason were "the bizarre and circuitous paths through the jungle we will explore." Of course, when Jason would step into her studio, the jungle and its relative quiet were fractured by the searing light of his revelations along with the screams and sobs elicited by Nadia's interventions. Nadia was especially surprised that Jason so readily acquiesced to her demand for power and control, total control. And yes, the crack of the dominatrix's whip like a lightning strike in that jungle came to echo in Jason's mind not only during their sessions but also at the office, the gym, and even as he and Amelia lounged together on her couch with a glass of wine.

Nadia encouraged Jason to explore his feelings toward his mother and father. He discussed how between the ages of six and ten, his father had sent him to summer camps for six weeks each summer and, to foster his independence, had decreed that Jason should not call or correspond with his parents. Of course, the fact that all the other kids were called or shared letters from home or were visited by their parents on weekends, made Jason's loneliness more profound. Jason often picked fights and several times each summer would leave his cottage in the middle of the night and wander the streets of the nearby village until the police returned him. He told Nadia how his father also decided that he should go to tennis and golf summer camps from the age of ten and then to daily private lessons at the local country club after school despite practicing with his team so that he would learn the techniques and strategies he would soon need to defeat almost any opponent. But Jason's anger and resentment toward his mother was equally vicious.

"Probably the most painful part of being around my mother was this strange dance she would do with me. I don't mean a real dance. I mean a dance like Japanese actors do when the actors and the action move from one side of the stage suddenly to the other. I wouldn't know anything about that but in high school Meagan and I went to what they called Noh plays at the local university. I've mentioned Meredith a few times during our talks and it was her father who taught drama at the university. So one semester he insisted they perform three of these weird Noh plays."

"Jason, what could Noh plays possibly have to do with your mother?" Nadia asked twisting in her chair.

"So, I'm trying to give you a feel for how she operated, how she treated her only child. She was extremely remote and impersonal because she saw herself as regal, the prima donna of that little town. She even used a chauffeur at times and my stupid father tolerated it while the remainder of the town laughed at it. But let's get back to my mother and me. She was either really remote or she feigned this bizarre intimacy. In elementary school, she loved to dress me in a suit and tie and then take me to the country club for Saturday luncheons attended only by middle-aged and older women. She would introduce me as her 'little man' and then say something like, 'better to have him learning some manners here than sulking alone in his room.' I felt like an idiot."

"Go ahead, Jason. Just stay with this to see where it will go," Nadia suggested.

"She had this way of ridiculously talking to me in double entendres, not sexual but using puns and stuff. I didn't know what she meant half the time. It even got to the point that I hated hearing her voice. She also liked to say things at the dinner table that were deliberately insulting. I remember one thing she said to my father, and I'll use her voice just so you'll get the full effect. It was something like,

'Harold, I was considering having a friend of Jason's for dinner but then I knew we might have to call his teacher to nominate one of his classmates since he seems to actually have no real friends.' That really stung and although it may have been true, why didn't they try to help me make friends? Or when we would go to Meagan's mother's salon, she would have me open the door for her then look at me with this sadistic grin and say, 'Well, aren't we someone's perfectly trained little doorman, and so loved I'm sure.' From the time I was around six, she would take me shopping to department stores in Pittsburgh and leave me for as long as an hour with some stranger like the salesperson at the cosmetics counter. Oh, and she had another favorite, unnerving threat. She would say, 'If your father didn't dote upon you and want to groom you for the bank, we could put you up for adoption for a month and go to Paris for April.' That should give you a taste of her perverted, malicious sense of humor," Jason concluded.

Nadia would listen to these stories and anecdotes that he related in exquisite detail until finally, bored to distraction, she would stop him. One evening she said, "Jason, it seems you have this encyclopedia of wrongs and frustrations along with a seething cauldron of absolute hatred for your mother and father, but there is almost never any emotion attached to the stories. It's time we retreated to our work-out studio to see if we can find any feelings lurking underneath those stories."

On one occasion, she had Jason change into faded gray pajamas before she shackled his hands to a ring on the wall. She returned to the room dressed as a German Nazi officer with "SS" insignia. Except for the officer's hat her uniform was black leather and was obviously tailored for her judging by its perfect fit. She carried a low-voltage cattle prod and a small leather whip. She spoke in a strange voice, deep, angry, and authoritative. She yelled at Jason as she twirled to face him, saying, "Do not ever look at me, my face, and by that I mean to keep your eyes on the floor. You are to march in place while saying, 'I am animal, I am pig, I am trash.' After every ten repetitions, I will either shock your ass or whip your legs. A single, rather benign lash of the whip on your legs is what you'll receive if you're good, dutiful. If you are slovenly, resistant, or not compliant with my orders, then you'll get a nice little jolt on your ass from my cattle prod. Now start!"

"And where is this supposed to get us, Nadia?" Jason asked,

looking at her, trying to see her eyes beneath the lowered brim of the black officer's hat.

"Shut up, you fool. I am Captain Himmler of the Fatherland, the Deutschland," she screamed as she flailed the front of his leg with a sudden snap of the leather whip. "And one more thing, if you disobey an order so crudely again, the consequences will be far more severe than a whip or a prod."

"Jesus Christ, I get it, I get it," Jason said as he began to recite repeatedly "I am animal, I am pig, I am trash."

"Louder, you swine, and start marching in place as you chant."

After a hundred repetitions that earned him seven quick lashes and three shocks from the cattle prod, Nadia ordered him to cease his chanting, but he continued until she stood again directly in front of him and yelled, "Stop, you fool. Stop stamping your feet, and now you're drooling. Didn't you hear me order you to halt your actions?"

"I just didn't know what to do because it's confusing when it's happening at once, and I'm so dizzy that I feel like I'm on a roller coaster. It's like I'm caught between a rock and a hard place, either be whipped or shocked. I've always tried to follow the rules, to do everything expected of me whether I wanted to or not," Jason said meekly as he leaned against the wall with sweat dripping from his head.

Nadia released his shackled hands that were raw at the wrists where he had strained against the metal cuffs. He never looked up at his tormentor as he slumped to the floor and rested his head on his knees. He then began to cry, first barely audible cat murmurs of soft whimpering, but finally a wracking, hoarse sobbing like that of someone innocent who had been incarcerated for months but was suddenly, unexpectedly exonerated and released from the hell of prison. He cried this way for fifteen minutes, neither humiliated nor afraid as the tears and snot ran down his chin onto his pajama top.

Finally, Nadia removed her hat and said in her native voice, measured and calm, "I understand your sadness but I want you to sit now on that stool and try to connect this specifically to your father. Connect it to the predicament, the paradox, he presented to you growing up. Here, dry your face with this towel."

"I guess you could say he had all the power over me like you did just now. I had to obey his orders, follow his suggestions about sports, and learn his attitude about winning at any cost. For him, it was wealth through the banks and power through his positions in the community. For me, it was ruthlessness on the tennis court or the golf course. Win, destroy, and demolish your opponent even if he appeared overmatched from the first serve or the first hole. But when I would get home, it was the unbearable loneliness of my room, the absence of any friends, having no one to talk to or share anything with."

"And what did that get you, Jason?" Nadia asked.

"Well, to make it worse, I knew whatever I accomplished would never be enough. With my mother at least I understood that she loved herself so much that she had no love left for me. But with him, it was worse. He simply didn't like me. Hell, he rarely came to my sports events. When I went to the state finals and won the class A singles in tennis, I thought I would look up in the stands and see him. But no, he never came. When I was second my last year at the state finals, he said, 'It's disgraceful to be slipping, playing second fiddle, when you are only seventeen. Maybe it's ominous enough to suggest your life is going to be a failure and what kind of son would that be to represent me?' I can hear his words as clearly now as I did four years ago," Jason concluded.

"That's even painful for me to listen to, and I've heard a lot of heavy stuff in my day and in my work. Now when I asked you about the predicament you were constantly presented with, I also asked how it seemed like a paradox as well. Maybe you don't quite get what I mean, but what I'm aiming at is for you to describe your life to this point as you sit here at twenty-one or twenty-two years old. Like how does Jason Aldridge, and I'm emphasizing the last name, how does he relate to people? Why is it that you really don't have any true friendships or that you don't trust your own feelings?"

"Oh, I get it. You mean despite how I described my father, how much I detested his strategies for shaping me, there is this great fear that I am going in the same direction. This fear that I have maybe already become as cold and calculating as he is. Is that what you mean?"

"Precisely, my prince of bad tidings. You do indeed get it. And do you remember the humiliating session we had two weeks ago? Do you remember what provoked me to show you how your ruthless, maniacal behavior on the tennis court may have defeated your opponents but also defeated you in another way? And what about that poor kid who looked up to you, wanted you to help him with his serve, and tried to befriend you?"

"Yeah, sure I do. So I told you about when Meagan and I double-dated with Peter Dexstrom and his girlfriend. Peter was on the tennis team with me, played number two singles and teamed with me as the first-seeded doubles team. Not a bad guy really except a little on the nerdy side and always kissing coach's ass. Well, he sort of worshipped me, and one day he says, 'Jason, old buddy, you know how much I respect you and I want you to help me develop a first serve, a power serve, similar to yours. I'm no threat to you in singles and it may help us win more of our doubles matches.' Nadia, you don't know it, but I was really good. Like I said, I won state and I could have played varsity on any Ivy League team."

"And why didn't you if you were so highly regarded and I would assume also recruited?"

"One simple reason and that was that he, my father I mean, had always said that when it came time for college, there would be no sports. What he really said was I should take off my jock, study my ass off, and go straight through my courses until I got my M.B.A. As you know, I'm very good at following orders, so that's what I did. But I got lost because I was talking about Peter Dexstrom. So Peter wants to not only learn how I hit my power serve, but he also wants to be my new and best friend, comes by the house, wants to hang out, tells people be basically worships me. Finally I decide to lay a little trap for him. I had been dating Meagan for several months and I suggested to Peter that we double date and use his car. The three of them smoked some weed and had a few beers after the movie. Since I didn't either drink or smoke, I'm the designated driver. When the girls went into this club to use the restroom while we waited in the car I pulled out this small plastic Ziploc bag of dog shit. Then I slipped on a latex glove, reached in the back seat and smeared it on old Peter boy's pants just as the girls are coming back. Well, he's screaming and cursing. I tell the girls that he's drunker that we think and that he's shit his pants. So home we go and the next day, the scent of his shame is spread all over school. He never forgave me but I definitely succeeded in getting rid of him. I honestly don't think he ever understood why I did it."

Nadia leaned toward Jason who was still sitting on the stool and said, "So, just to backtrack a few more minutes, what do you remember about how you processed that incident in our session two weeks ago. And yes, this is a little test."

"Listen, I've just been through hell, your Gestapo torture chamber, so give me a break. Sure I remember how you pointed out that whenever I had a chance to have a friend, in high school or college, I would do something to alienate or humiliate them. And finally they would give up trying to befriend me. It's the story of my life. Of course, because of how insulting I was to Peter, you devised something equally nasty for me. You had me wear bathing trunks and cuffed my wrists to my ankles in a terrible stressful position. Then you proceeded to paint my trunks and legs with that concoction you made of emulsified fish fertilizer and buttermilk. You left me in that position, basically smelling that shit, for an hour. I've never smelled anything so foul in my life and I can't imagine how you got the idea for it. And here I am again. Sometimes I don't know why I keep coming back to you on this little search for the true me."

"Of course you do, Jason. It's because you're beginning to feel alive, like a real person. That's why I subjected you to that smelly scene so that you would have some idea how this Peter fellow felt although it didn't come close to capturing his humiliation at school the next day. Gradually, you've begun to mention some things from work about how you can see the other side of an argument you are having with one of your peers at D & T. The way you have begun to talk about Amelia in more flattering terms and feeling closer to her the evenings you two are together is far different from the sarcastic things you used to say. You used to joke about her weight and laugh about the fact that she had only an associate degree from that on-line DeVerity College. She was more an entertainment for you than anything else. Maybe you are changing a little bit, we'll see. Listen, we've gone over our time by an hour, so next week add another hour to my usual fee. We need to stop for now."

"I understand. Although you see me in all kinds of positions, I don't like you watching me dress so I'll be out in a minute. There is one last thing I want to say. You know my mother collects Meissen porcelains and that's about what she resembles. I mean she uses too much makeup and wears these outrageous, expensive ensembles even to the grocery store. And my father is always reminding me to, as he says, 'have muscles of titanium, a steel-trap mind, and a heart of

Carrara marble, son, and you'll go far in life.' And that describes him perfectly. So when I've been caught between a Meissen mother and a fanatical Carrara father, what can you expect?" Jason asked plaintively.

"That's all for tonight, Jason. You know each of us carries a lot of baggage. It may be about parents, traumas, lost loves, death, whatever. But ultimately your life is yours to claim and to live. You'll know things are better when you stop blaming everyone else and assume ownership of yourself. Sort of like that time you cleared your room at home of all your memories, threw away your trophies, ripped down your posters, and then when your parents called that night, you basically told them to go fuck themselves. That was very strong. Now, goodnight."

"And thank you Miss Mystic, my messiah, my messenger of sanity, my mistress of mysteries. Jesus, you drive me nuts. One moment you hate me and the next moment you are cheering me on. Sometimes I don't know whose side you are on. Anyway, see you in a week."

Coming Clean in the Cage

After his tenth visit to Miss Mystic, Jason was emboldened by what he regarded as his new knowledge. The first daffodils had forced their faces into the late winter sunlight of April, signaling the promise of an early spring. In a more concrete than romantic way, Jason saw the blooming of the daffodils as symbolic of his own awakening. To celebrate not the daffodils but another over-the-hump Wednesday, Jason and Amelia had decided to share a pizza. During the past several months, their friendship had evolved so that Jason seemed to trust her more than anyone except for how he had once confided in Sarah Sewell and, of course, Meagan. Because they worked together on a daily basis, they had mutually arrived at the view that any sexual relationship seemed both foolhardy and fraught with potentially damaging repercussions for both of them. Besides talking with Amelia about how alone he had felt in both high school and college, he had not hesitated to tell her about what he talked about in his therapy with Nadia Mystic. He had not mentioned Nadia by name and had avoided discussing the humiliating nature of her sadistic interventions. He hoped that he had not given Amelia so much information that she might be able to locate Miss Mystic's website.

As they were eating and having a glass of wine, Jason said, "You know I've sort of waited all of my life to start living, obsessed with grades in high school and at Wharton and, more recently, with climbing the ladder at D & T. But it seems that now I'm learning who I really am."

"Jason, I have noticed what I'll call something of a softening, a calming, but you still have times when you pull away from me, when you're very remote. And at work you will often avoid people, even Allen and Samantha, and they really do care about you," Amelia responded.

"Well, I'm sure you're right but, except for what I've told you, you can't quite envision how I grew up, the coldness, the loneliness of it. On the surface, to everyone else, and especially with my father's money, I'm sure everyone thought I had the perfect family and the perfect life."

"Do you talk about all that with the therapist you finally admitted to me a few weeks ago that you are seeing, Jason?"

"I mean I don't want to get into more of that right now because it's rather complicated, and you and I have talked already about some of it. But yes, I talk to her about anything I want to, and sometimes she brings things up even when I don't want to. In fact, I've got another appointment at seven tonight. Although I've been seeing her for only three months, it seems like an eternity, like I've known her all my life. I guess that's because I don't mind sharing my most hidden feelings with her. We've been getting close to some really serious stuff. The reason I gave you that letter several weeks ago is that if anything ever happens to me, I want you to be certain to mail it."

"Jason, when you talk like that it sort of worries me. I've never thought of you as depressed or as wanting to harm yourself. I mean of the new recruits, you, Allen and Samantha have more energy than all the others together."

"No, I'm not trying to alarm you and I'm not depressed, never have been. If there is one single thing that I obsess over, it's the Meagan business. At times, I feel truly remorseful. Then at other times, sort of like my manipulative father, I think she deserved to die, that she wanted to trap me. So, yeah, there is some guilt about her death. But then I sense I may just be another cruel chip off the marble statue of my father. It's just that so much has come up in therapy so fast and in such a brief time that sometimes I do think about just saying, 'fuck it' and taking a year off to roam around Europe or somewhere."

"Well, even that would look bad on your resume especially with the meteoric start to your career with D & T. So, if you get too antsy, maybe we could just sneak away for a long weekend. And yes, I know, nothing serious until and unless we make, shall I say, a firm decision to ratchet things up."

"Oh, you funny girl, I do love you in some strange way. You really do understand me and it's so easy to talk to you. Now I've got to run."

As Jason rang 12A for entry, he felt strangely uneasy. He remembered how anxious he had been about his first visit to Miss Mystic but also knew that he looked forward to his later sessions. And now, again, he felt agitated, almost angry. He had recently completed a major project at work and had been recognized again the previous Monday by Mr. Starling. With two congratulatory memos now from "the old man," he was virtually assured of a permanent position with the D & T firm. And his relationship with Amelia had evolved into a companionship founded upon friendship, trust, and still a subtle physical attraction.

"Greetings to you, Jason. I'm almost surprised you emailed me for another visit after the last two rather rough sessions," Nadia said as Jason entered her studio.

"Why would you say that?" Jason asked.

"Well, just have a seat and we will talk about it. And how interesting that you've chosen a new chair, the black Barcelona that matches mine. So now you're going to avoid looking directly at me sort of like last week if I remember correctly."

"Please, I've had a long day at work and, as you said, I'm not even sure I want to be here tonight. So the last thing I want is a little lecture on that projection crap or how I avoid intimacy even with you."

"So, we are a tad on the sensitive side tonight," Nadia responded.

"One thing that I'm upset about is this long letter I got from Meagan's mother, Sarah. I guess she got my address from my parents although I'm not really in touch with them. I brought the letter with me and I'm going to read you a few parts of it. She starts off by summarizing how close Meagan and I seemed in high school until our breakup. So, here, I'll read it. She says 'Jason, you evaporated like a cloud of contaminated air and that left my Meagan so sad, so lost, that then she really did get lost in drugs and drinking and just erratic behavior. The way you never called or wrote simply devastated her,' is the way she ends that part."

"So go ahead, what else does she say?"

"So she rambles on about some of Meagan's troubles before she gets to the heavy part. She writes, 'I have never fully understood what or why you wanted to reunite with my Meagan those last few months when she was finally getting her act together and breaking away from you. It was almost like you enjoyed luring her back into your life in some cruel way. And the whole business about that last motorcycle ride and her not wearing a helmet just puzzles me. So, I want to sit down with you and rehash exactly how the accident happened, how my Meagan died. Now you know I'm dedicated to my work and I'm doing fine. It's just this stuff is unresolved. I've even called your parents because I know your mother as one of my long-time customers, but they won't really talk to me. So that's it for now. I hope you are distinguishing yourself in your new job and I know you are.' And she ends it there," Jason concluded.

"Well, Jason, I frankly don't see anything so unusual about a mother, especially one so dedicated to her daughter as you've described her before, about a mother wanting to get closure on a catastrophe like she suffered. You, yourself, keep alluding to it and to how you have such mixed feelings about Meagan even though she's dead," Nadia said.

"Look, whose side are you on? And what right does she have to come after me? I've got enough problems, not to mention the nightmares and everything else."

"Jason, all I know is that I don't remember seeing you ever so agitated. I don't know if you realize it but your speech is sort of disjointed and you're sweating like you do when you get really uptight about something."

"I don't give a fuck what you think or say. My life is all about me and what I want out of it for me. I owe nobody anything. And Miss Sarah, as sweet and caring as she always was toward me, well she can stuff her curiosity up her ass," Jason screamed as he leaned toward Nadia, almost threatening her.

"Well, Jason, let's avoid the bullshit and go in and get to work."

"Sure, whatever you say, Nadia Mystic," Jason said sarcastically, enunciating "Nadia Mystic" as though they were foreign words or objects of derision.

"Jason, in all of our sessions, we've avoided the cage but I think tonight is a good time to introduce the cage to you or, I should say, introduce you to the cage."

"What do you want me to do?"

"First, I will dim the lights and I want you take off all your clothes, everything including your underwear."

"So, you're finally going to try to seduce me," Jason said.

"Actually, it may shock you to learn that I am not the least interested in you sexually. But I am interested in this conflicted, confused mood you're in tonight. Are you with me in this or not? If I'm going to direct your therapy, as we agreed, then I don't want any trouble from you."

"Fine, I'll do it. For one reason, I'll show you I'm not afraid of your little games. And when you say everything, you don't mean my underwear do you?"

"Yes, that's what I have already said. I want you nude so that you get the full effect. In the cage now, Jason, be a good doggie. And of course one thing we are trying to do is to locate the more primitive or animal part of you, because you are always so controlling and so in control. I mean of yourself as well as those around you."

The only way Jason could enter the cage, which was seven feet long but only three feet tall, was to lower himself to the floor and crawl into the end where Nadia Mystic had opened the fortified wire mesh door. The steel cage was made of a plastic-coated steel mesh with five-inch square openings and was bolted securely to the floor at the corners and along the sides with heavy metal plates. Nadia did not simply close the door to the steel cage, she slammed it and secured it with a large padlock. The padlock was for effect, but it served as a sort of exclamation mark, reminding Jason that he was essentially captured and now at the mercy of Miss Mystic.

"What are you going to do now?" Jason asked. "I suppose you're going to poke me with a broom or tease me with that cattle prod again. Well, I'm not sure I want to get into any of that stuff tonight. Sure, you're in control as usual. I know you'll want to humiliate me in some manner. Or, is it your objective to bring forth that animal in me you mentioned? Or maybe you want to see how violent I can become under the controlled conditions of your cage? You know I may be outgrowing my interest in your disturbing little schemes. What you peddle is a sort of pop psychology fad for sick old men. Suck on that, Little Miss Misfit."

"Sweetie, do you know how crazy you are tonight? And it's not

Miss Misfit, it is Miss Mystic, or Nadia if you must, but don't make that mistake again."

"Shut the fuck up, you bitch. You've been running the show from the first day, actually the minute I stepped into your so-called studio, which is more like a whorehouse for masochistic, perverted old men. Or maybe we should call it a spa for wretched souls searching for hell on earth just because they feel a little guilty about something. You preside like the queen in her lair when you're nothing more than a streetwise dominatrix. You remind me of my darling mother in so many ways. And that's not one of those projections you talk about all the time. That is simply the truth. I hate her fucking guts, and I hate your fucking guts. Do you hear me? I said I hate you," Jason screamed, saliva spraying from his mouth as he continued to yell, now sweating, almost panting, his hands griping the wire cage as he stared out at Nadia Mystic who also was now down on the floor, facing Jason through the cage door.

"What is it, Jason? What's bothering you? The party has hardly begun and you're already misbehaving. You're a very disturbed little boy tonight and you're forgetting all of your manners. Miss Mystic may have to punish you more than she had planned."

Jason, sweating, his muscles tight, cringing with rage, shoved the cage door repeatedly, trying to tear the door from its steel hinges. Then, suddenly, he spit on Nadia, hitting her across her mouth, chin and neck. "You bitch, if I could get out of here, I'd like to kill you. That's how furious I am with you and your shenanigans."

"Listen to me, Jason," Nadia said as she wiped her face and chin with a towel. "And listen to me very carefully. Something is bothering you and I don't think it has anything to do with me. I think it relates in some way to Amelia. I think that you may be falling in love with her even though until recently you described her in such unflattering terms and were always harping on her weight. You know it's rather strange that although she's not your type at all, you've dated for almost three months now and still no sex from mister stud-muffin, no less."

"Yeah, so maybe you're right. I don't know what to do about her. I'm afraid she would want to trap me, just another fat woman having her dreams come true. Actually, what I'm really afraid of is that she might get pregnant which is why I haven't screwed her."

"Jason, that's ridiculous, no one accidentally gets pregnant these days."

"Well, Meagan did!" Jason screamed.

"What are you talking about?"

"I'm talking about the truth. I'm talking about somebody I know called me about seven months ago from a hospital lab on a sunny fall afternoon in October when I was about to go home to Hamilton Hills from Wharton for the weekend. He told me Meagan had a urine test that was positive for pregnancy. He called me because he thought she had been dating someone else in town and that I needed to know so I would avoid her. But I knew she had not been dating anyone else. And I knew that when we had last made love two months before, she had begged me not to because she was off the pill, but I made her anyway. So, of course, that afternoon in October, when I later went to take her for a ride on my motorcycle, she said she had a nice present for me, what she called a secret that would change our lives forever," Jason said.

"But, Jason, even though that may have happened, your life went on. It's Meagan who couldn't face the music. She's the one who was always so spontaneous and impulsive from all you've said about her. She's also the one who didn't wear a helmet when you knew she should have when you talked about her death last month. It's her lack of control and idiocy that have haunted you these last few months. Although I do understand why you would feel guilty about your part in the accident."

"You just don't quite get it, you fucking bitch. Meagan Sewell did not slide, jump or catapult herself into that tree. I did it. I could see my entire life ending in the absurd abyss of my father's office at that stuffy, confining bank except it would be my feet on the president's desk and not my old man's. And, yes, Meagan would be at home with our kids. Me, I'd be tethered to the boardroom of that bank and to the boredom of that shit town and all I hate about it."

"What are you saying, Jason?"

"I'm saying I set it up so that she wouldn't survive a little craftily engineered accident. When we were about to get on the bike, I'm the one who encouraged her not to wear a helmet. And it was easy to convince her because she had always wanted to ride without one. I just decided it on the spur of the moment. Let's just call it the perfect plan to be rid of her. And when we got to a dangerous curve lined with trees,

I knew I could lay the bike down. Meagan, suspecting nothing, would be catapulted into one of the trees. Even at forty miles an hour, you're going to get pretty broken up. Twice before I had to lay the bike down in a controlled skid to avoid hitting a car so I wasn't worried about myself. Sure, I was skinned up a bit and had a fractured wrist, but that made it look even more like an accident. My only concern was that Meagan might be seriously injured but not killed. But, hey, it worked perfectly. She didn't suffer and I was free!" Jason added, chuckling, still crouched on all fours.

The openings in the steel cage mesh were barely large enough for Nadia's hand to breach and she had never before reached into the cage with other clients but now she did, grabbing a forelock of Jason's thick hair. Jerking his head forward and upward, she said, "Look at me, you bastard!"

"I don't have to."

"Look at me, Jason. If this is true, if you have killed someone, someone who loved you and someone you probably loved but obviously not as much as yourself, then we've got a big problem," Nadia said.

"Yeah, I guess we do."

"Well, what are you going to do about it? The real question is whether you can live with yourself and face your God. And the second question is whether you are dangerous. How do I know whether it's safe to even let you out of this cage?"

"I think you know me well enough to know that I don't have anything against you. You, Nadia Mystic, brought me to this point, this realization, this confession, if you will. I always said, both to myself and to Amelia, that you offered me some kind of salvation. I just wasn't sure how it would be delivered to me. Now, open the door, Nadia."

Nadia stood and paced back and forth in front of the cage, controlling her breathing, letting her feet glide in small steps, collecting her thoughts, before she said, "Jason, why should I trust you?"

"You've always trusted me, Nadia. Even when you've tortured me, you knew that when you released me, I would always respect you. And you know how strong I am. I could have rebelled against you at any time and didn't."

"But this time is different. Now, somehow, you've got to get square with the world, your conscience, and especially Meagan's mother. This is not about me. And it's also about your finding some kind of peace with yourself. Why do you think you have nightmares? Why do you think it's so hard to relate to people?"

"You know how attached I've become to Amelia and actually to you. I think there are ways I can atone for my deeds. And I promise you that I will do that. You've probably had other clients who had more blood and blood money on their hands, more victims, than me. Now kindly unlock the cage door. I'll call you tomorrow to let you know how I'm going to proceed. My little nasty secret has been destroying me more than anyone else, just as you mentioned. Obviously, I can hardly live with it, the guilt. It colors my days and even my nights with those recurrent dreams that I've talked about."

Nadia spoke slowly, carefully, her words measured, "Jason, I'm going to unlock the door. I want you to dress and I want you to see an attorney tomorrow. Then call me and let me know what you're going to do. You do owe some kind of confession to Meagan's mother, however you may couch it. You've put us both in a terrible and awkward situation. No one knows you are here with me or that you've ever been here. So my own safety is at stake and I'm not sure I can trust you, but I'm going to let you out. When I do, I want you to get dressed and leave immediately. But you must call me tomorrow to let me know what you're going to do about all of this. There is no salvation without repentance."

Nadia took the key from a lariat hanging on the horn of the Western saddle. She leaned to look at Jason who seemed unusually calm, his breathing slow and rhythmic. She unlocked the padlock and slowly pulled it from its hasp. In that instant, Jason pushed against the cage door, rammed it open, stood, and with his forearm caught Nadia Mystic on the left temple, knocking her backward into the rack of whips with such force that the whips themselves seemed to sing, to vibrate. Nadia fell to the floor, slumped against the rack of whips, only barely conscious. Jason grabbed her by her hair, leaned down and whispered to her, "Now we will see who's in control, miss queen of freaks. I hate you for pushing me to this point."

Five minutes later, the sirens on North Avenue, as they approached the 1400 block, screamed in eerie cacophony, each slightly dissonant from the other. The two police cars were harmonious, but the EMT truck, the fire truck, and the detective's unmarked car were all discordant, each with a different resonance and cadence. North Avenue, this pleasant street of brownstones and cafes, was usually a calm oasis in the city, especially at nine at night, but this night was different. For on the street lay a broken, disfigured body over which someone had draped a white sheet, though blood seeping from the irregular outline of the head underneath it created the effect of a shroud. And on the fourth floor of 1411 North Avenue, as on several other floors now, there was an open window with the edge of a drape casually wafting in the light breeze of an almost spring evening.

A Late-night Phone Call

Miss Mystic: Sheila, you don't know how glad I am that you answered. I've just had the biggest shock of my life except for that time that crazy rabbi tried to hang himself on the cross.

Sheila: Listen, I can be right over. You don't even sound like yourself.

Miss Mystic: Yeah, I don't doubt it. I'll relate the entire story when I see you tomorrow. Anyway, you remember my telling you about that narcissistic kid I've been trying to work with during the past three months. Well, everything spun out of control tonight in a session. I truly thought he was going to kill me when I let him out of the cage. He did knock me down, almost out cold, and then he bolted, ran into the street, and I think he killed himself. At least there's a body out there in the street with a sheet over it.

Sheila: Jesus Christ, girl, you are lucky to be alive. What's the scene over there?

Miss Mystic: Sirens on top of sirens, and more red lights than at Christmas. I finally closed the hallway window and drape. I've retreated to my bedroom, no lights, just a candle. At least I can breathe now. It's almost like watching a horror movie except I'm one of the characters involved. I've never consciously thought about it, but maybe that's how some of our clients feel when things get a little chaotic. At least we're in charge or think we are. We've just got to hope this disaster with the kid doesn't create problems. The good thing is that I'm almost certain no one knew he was coming here to see me, and I know for a fact that no one in this building ever saw him. He was a very secretive, very cautious dude.

Miss Mystic: The Lord works in strange ways, Sheila.

Sheila: You know, we're probably lucky that we don't have more trouble than we do. But what do you mean about the Lord, like in getting revenge?

Miss Mystic: No, not necessarily. Maybe it's more like avenging some injustice or, as they say, a wrong being righted. Until I tell you the whole story, you can never imagine what this guy pulled off.

Sheila: And you are the agent, the black angel getting the job done.

Miss Mystic: Well, maybe he's not dead. But then I don't know why someone would put a sheet over the body if he were not dead. And there was this distraught taxi driver standing in the street before the police arrived. Half the building had their windows open what with all the sirens. Probably the first time some of them had even looked out those windows. So, anyway, the cabbie kept screaming, "I didn't mean to hit him, he just came out of the dark, like lowered his head so the front of the car would catch him square on. It looked like the dude slipped out from between two cars and then charged me like a bull. It was sickening, sounded like a watermelon exploding." So, Sheila, after I saw what had happened, I closed my window and turned off all the lights. You know I had never had that window open, and I actually think he opened it and thought about pushing my old limp body out the window. The last thing I need is for someone to speculate about what goes on up here. I will say that I've got two politically strong friends in city hall, if we ever need to call on them.

Sheila: So I think we've got to assume he's dead, Nadia, and in the morning on the news or even tonight at eleven, we'll know for sure.

Miss Mystic: Maybe I'll go on vacation or maybe it's time to retire, but the money is good and most of my clients love me. I really mean that, and the reality of it is that I care about most of them. Hell, I've got some who have been coming to me for ten years, especially my little rotund workaholic babies who need to be spanked and changed almost every week.

Sheila: So why not sleep on it, tonight. Then, if you want to take a week off, do that. I'll cover for you like we did two years ago when you got sick. Anyway, there are bills to be paid and lives to be liberated.

Miss Mystic: Yeah, all those poor souls we corral, offering them some kind of salvation, some kind of relief from their sins, when everyone else is so sick and tired of their tyranny, their tirades, their self-serving righteousness.

Sheila: It's like we are a court of last resort except we don't pass judgment on them. We're more like advocates for the truth. Then they become their own juries. And what do we do? We just provide the punishment that each knows in his heart he deserves and needs.

Miss Mystic: Yeah, that's about how it works, girl.

Sheila: You feeling better now?

Miss Mystic: Sure I am except for that knot on my head. Right before I blacked out, I thought the dude was going to kill me for sure. And you know, I think he was going to off me but something sparked at the last second in whatever little hint of a conscience he had. Maybe he thought carrying around the guilt of two murders would be one too many.

Sheila: Call me if you need me. Good night, Nadia.

Miss Mystic: Night, Sheila. Sometimes I don't know what I would do without you as my best friend and confidant. You're a real doll.

Sheila: And you're a real angel, Nadia. Don't ever let anyone convince you otherwise. If you do take a week off, where will you go?

Miss Mystic: I don't know, maybe New Orleans. Listen to the Neville Brothers and Doctor John, just chill out to some blues and jazz. Then maybe I'll get a massage and visit that crazy Cajun voodoo woman we met down there three years ago. What was her name? It was some sort of a French name like Monique. Anyway, I'll say goodbye now, love.

The Viewing

On this last Saturday of April, the jonquil and daffodil have forced their faces through winter's still burnt blanket of grass in the backyard of Sarah's cherished Victorian house. Against this green canvas of newly leafed elm, sycamore, and ginkgo, the fruit trees Mrs. Willingham planted over forty years ago have now bloomed. The subtle pink whispers of cherry and the white puffs of flowering pear are silhouetted in stark relief against this green blanket of trees that sweep down to the muffled babble of the creek. And it is to view this first and florid blush of spring that Sarah has invited Meredith and Toni. Of course, it was here too only six months ago that they had mourned the death and celebrated the life of Meagan.

"I have asked you both to be with me this afternoon because you are all I have left in my life. I never had much, actually had nothing as a child until I moved here, and of course I'm not talking about material things. This beautiful house is beyond all my dreams. What I think I'm talking about is some place or something firm and with meaning on this earth. You know, some kind of anchor because I've always had to be my own anchor and now I'm, what is that ship term, unmoored. And maybe what I'm trying to describe is the struggle to find love here on Earth or whatever God there may be out there. To be honest, I have felt really deep love only with Meagan. That was mainly when she was a baby and then only until she was eight or nine. Toni, you know what I mean. You and I both called it the purest of all loves. After she became about ten, I thought she had gotten so independent so fast that she didn't really need much of my love. She seemed to want mainly my support, like that phrase young women use now when they say, 'I just need somebody to cover my back'."

Meredith looked at Toni and rolled her eyes, but Sarah continued, "Yes, Meredith, I know you're ready for a glass of wine, but try to hold on another minute or two and I'll be finished. But then there was Sam, and I know all too well what both of you thought of him. I admit I was a dumb, naïve girl and simply infatuated, but he really did leave with a small piece of my heart. Maybe I simply wanted to save him. Even though I was only seventeen, I thought I was really strong, invincible, could do anything because I had already survived so much. I'm sure it looked to both of you, and certainly to Reverend Reid, like I was seduced by a con artist and maybe I was. It's just that whenever I think I've got it all together, my life starts falling apart and everything evaporates. Like right now we couldn't be in a more beautiful place, but I'm wondering when will the next axe fall, the next spear be launched. Thank God, I've got the two of you."

Meredith interrupted, waving her hand in front of Sarah's face before saying, "Whoa, get off your horse for a minute. I feel like I'm at one of our company's pharmaceutical promotion dinners for doctors where the guest speaker gets on a roll and monopolizes the conversation. That's when the doctors either start drinking more wine or looking for the fastest way out of the restaurant. Just slow down or at least dumb it down. We're not on some mission here to save the world or even you. Listen, Sarah, you always land on your feet."

Toni seemed startled at their exchange, and said, "Look, I thought we were here to have a glass of wine and admire the new blooms of these cherry trees and pear trees. They're simply brilliant out here with the sun on them and even brighter set against all those old, ancient trees down toward the creek. Unlike both of you, I've been hauling kids around all week. I'm also teaching probably the worst group we've ever had at Evergreen Middle since I moved up to the seventh grade. If that's not enough, I usually end the day cooking two or three dinners during the week. My only relief is if we head out for the pizza parlor. So, it may look like I'm living the great American dream, but at this moment I'm ready to let go of a little tension, girls. Am I missing something here?"

Meredith and Sarah looked at one another as though each might be nominating the other to speak. Finally, Meredith said, "Toni, as much as I love you, I do think yes, you are missing something and always have been. Even in high school and college, you were the idealist. I mean you always said no sex, no weed, watch the booze, don't waste money. And you had this holier-than-thou attitude about how God will save all of us if we give him a chance. I won't even bring up that virgin vow business you and your Christian sisters were so proud of. So, yeah, you see only what you think is good and righteous and steel yourself to hear no evil, see no evil, like two of those three monkeys."

"And am I supposed to be condemned for that, for having a sense of morality that gives me something firm to stand on with God and my family as my daily bedrock? Something that Sarah is talking about and trying to find, I might add. I'm sure you haven't discovered the Holy Grail either, unless for you it's money and if not that, then sex just about any way you can get it," Toni retaliated.

"Hey, I don't pretend to have all the answers. It just seems you could use a strong dose of reality to clear your vision and maybe your gastrointestinal track as well," Meredith retorted.

"Oh, so like you, I'm coming up short. I admit I haven't slept with half of the Phi Delts at Carleton, had an abortion, two failed marriages, and no children, I might add. That's not to mention your outrageous salary. Like your drug company's not ripping off everybody so you can wear those couture outfits that we can't even afford copies of. You spend more on clothes in a weekend than either Sarah or I do in an entire year. Admit it, you're a greedy pig and you always want your way. Although you can have anything you want, you had better watch out when you're older. You may end up with nothing, sister. And since Sarah brought up Meagan, don't you remember at her memorial service which one of us had to have the last word? You, of course! And you almost knocked Father Flaherty and me out of the way to have it. Speaking of your big mouth, I've heard again that you might have had not only the last word but also the last blowjob on poor old Father Flaherty. The rumor was that you got him in a pretty compromised situation, seduced the oldest living virgin in Hamilton Hills. Did you know that was still circulating around town?"

"Not true, not true, my sister. I might have let the good father be a voyeur to a little escapade I've never mentioned to anyone on this earth including both of you. But I would never give him a blowjob because I don't want him dying on me like one of those famous politicians we heard about on television. I want to . . . ."

Sarah interrupted, her voice calm, soothing, "You know what is so strange about this is that it reminds me also of when we were planning the memorial service for Meagan. No one agreeing, each of you fighting for what you thought Meagan would want or maybe what you wanted for yourself. It was like a series of skirmishes."

"Yes, we both remember, don't we Toni? And Sarah, I don't know what's on your mind this afternoon. I've never heard you even talk about love or whatever you mean by some special space, something firm. We've always said you were the least romantic or idealistic of any of us. I mean you're mainly a workaholic who's overcome about any obstacle fate has thrown in your face. Now you sound so reflective, almost maudlin. So let's chill out with this special chardonnay I brought from the city. I just love it. It's made by Cakebread Cellars and it's the smoothest white wine I've ever tasted. But what I want to know, Sarah, is whether we are here only for this spring spectacle or is something else up?" Meredith asked.

Sarah reached for Aunt Sallie's music box on the table between them. Then she leaned forward and wound the key that triggered the movement of the ballerina still delicately balanced and pirouetting after all these years. At the same time the old brass cylinder inside began to turn with that perfectly synchronized German precision, gracing the fine spring afternoon with the melody of that *Dance of the Sugar Plum Fairy.*

Sarah paused to pour each of them a glass of wine before saying, "Both of you know how this old music box has always been my comfort in times of stress since my sweet Aunt Sallie gave it to me. My little ballerina's lost an arm but she still turns and bows just as if she were on some stage in Germany. She's always been my protector, my balm in Gilead, as my dear old Aunt Sallie used to say. Through all the years, all the stresses and disappointments, even Meagan's death, I knew I could always turn to my little ballerina and her music box late at night. It truly soothed my wounds and salvaged my soul."

"Speak, speak to us, Sarah, you gorgeous doll, and I love the way you've finally cut your hair and styled it differently after all these years. Anyway, tell us what this is all about, although I admit I love the suspense. And Meredith, you and I can argue and disagree but you know I love you. The three of us are like sisters indeed. I mean, how many women do we know from our high school class who've made it this far as best friends. What is it? Is it twenty-four years and counting? And sure, we're all three totally different but I'm not giving us up for anything. What we have is right up there with my love for my husband and two kids. You can laugh at me, but what we have is truly an amazing, enduring love," Toni concluded.

"Well, girls, I found these cards at Hallmark and I thought how perfect they are. So I got one for each of us to keep as a little way to remember this afternoon. They're all the same and the photograph on the front is this real old Japanese woman with two other women having tea. You can see in the background cherry trees in full bloom just like ours. The title under it is 'The Viewing.' It seems that a tradition among some of the older ladies in Japan is to invite a few friends to tea when the cherry trees are at their peak. So there they sit quietly while sipping their tea. There's such a serenity to the whole scene."

"I guess that would be us except we're drinking wine not tea. Thank God, we're still young, healthy, and vibrant with a lot of good years before us," Meredith chimed in.

"Hush, Meredith. I think Sarah's serious about this because it's rare to see her get misty eyed," Toni said.

"You two are something else. So yes, here we are like you said, twenty-four years after we met when I was a gangly mountain girl speaking what sounded like a foreign language. You two didn't mind that I talked that way, sounded different and still do. I won't say that I trusted you at first, but pretty soon I did. Then, when I needed you, you stuck by me as best you could through that masquerade of a marriage. You know, I was really struggling during that first year with my little salon. Not to mention that baby at home and trying to support Cathy Eubanks too. It was those Saturday night suppers with you once a month that sustained me. You both thought it was nothing special, and you were both caught up in the newness of college, but it truly meant everything to me. I mean beyond Reverend Reid or Momma Reid's brigade of mothers, it was having us to hold onto that let me sleep at night."

"But where are you going with all this, Sarah? You don't think we would ever forsake you, do you? I hope you aren't about to tell us you've got cancer or that, even worse, you've met another Sam Braxley," Meredith interrupted.

"No, honey, it's not that. I'm sure you both heard about the mysterious circumstances of Jason Aldridge's death a week ago. Some people think he was on drugs and some say it was an accident because like a fool he was jogging in the dark. I've even heard several of the ladies at the salon say it looked strangely like a suicide. After the funeral, Toni and I visited Mr. and Mrs. Aldridge but because of Meagan's death and how they both reacted then, something seemed so strange and out of place. As Toni knows, they basically ignored us when their other friends showed up. The other thing was that Jason's death brought up all the pain of Meagan's accident, the great sorrow of my life. If I have survived that, well I guess I have, then I can survive anything that'll come down the pike."

Meredith was now squirming and downed the last sip of her second glass of wine before saying, "Well, I'm certain you both must know why I was a no-show at that punk's funeral. I never trusted him and I thought he used Meagan, toyed with her, kept her involved just enough to poison her efforts to escape him. I always said that to both of you and I said it to Meagan. I saw him as a pompous, spoiled, egocentric little shit. And Toni, I know you won't approve, but I could care less if he's six feet under and burning in hell. I could tell you about how I got a small measure of revenge but I won't. He's not worth it. But go ahead, Sarah."

"Well, the other reason I wanted the two of you here with me is so we can read this letter I received two days ago addressed to me with Jason's name as the return address. My guess is that a friend of his found it in his apartment and mailed it to me. Otherwise, it makes no sense at all. It's sort of like the viewing this afternoon is both a viewing of these pear and cherry trees and of his letter at the same time."

"Jesus, I can't believe this is happening. It's sort of macabre or as my father would say, it's like one of those film noir movies from the forties and fifties. At least we've got this backyard in living color and those films were in black and white. He loves them and still watches them," Meredith said, smiling.

Sarah poured each of them another glass of wine from the already-uncorked second bottle. "All right, sisters, drum roll please while I open this envelope. Hmm, it's typed instead of written, which is about what I would expect from him," Sarah said as she began to read aloud.

April 4, 1999
Dear Ms. Sewell,

I am writing you because we are now about six months beyond the unfortunate passing and the disturbing accident that befell Meagan. As you know, she and I had a long romance, were extremely close, and remained so until her death. I am sorry for any heartache that she (and her lifestyle) may have caused you or, for that matter, your dear friends, Toni and Meredith, and the ladies at your salon. At least none of you ever abandoned her. And in my mind, I never abandoned her either. Indeed, I tried always to be a gentleman, to respect her and honor her.

Not long ago, I entered a kind of psychotherapy and perhaps should have done so in high school, because I always felt about a half wavelength different from everyone else. Your Meagan was in many ways my angel, my savior, because (as you can imagine, knowing my mother) I had a sterile emotional environment at home and many of the kids at school envied my position of privilege in our town. So I really had no close friends.

Be that as it may, what I have to tell you is neither pleasant nor a true reflection of the kind of person I am deep inside. It may be that I will destroy this letter, or I may realign my priorities so that I don't feel the compulsion or necessity to relay this information to you (or anyone). In that regard and in the event that something should befall me, I have instructed the only person I trust here to mail this letter. Perhaps this is a sort of reluctant dragon syndrome. But I digress.

What I wish to tell you, Ms. Sewell, is that Meagan lived with a take-no-prisoners attitude but met her untimely death in a fashion that was unfair to her, to you, and to all of your friends and acquaintances. When one has an intolerable toothache, it results in either an abscess or somehow heals itself. I have had one of those toothaches since last October, but mine seems never to go away. It is like riding a roller coaster of temporary relief (and sanity) between peaks of pain. That pain is hard to describe so I won't try. But the abscess that needs to be incised, lanced, is this: Meagan did not die in that motorcycle accident because of her carelessness (not wearing a helmet) or her carefree attitude (being reckless on the bike). She died because I made a terrible mistake of judgment. I knew that if I went into a controlled slide with that motorcycle I would very likely imperil her life, but I did so anyway.

So I made a grievous, unconscionable maneuver that sacrificed your daughter. You lost her in that millisecond of my miscalculation and that is a loss for which I can never compensate you. The supreme irony is that I also lost the only person in my life who truly loved me and, unsuccessfully, tried to teach me how to love. There is a sort of perverse if not cruel logic in that but perhaps you can parse it for both of us.

To bring this to a conclusion, let me say very simply that this letter constitutes a mea culpa *of sorts. What I did was wrong, irresponsible, and caused grievous harm (i.e., death) to your daughter. I know you cannot forgive me for what is an unpardonable sin, and I don't really expect you to, but I need to confess it anyhow. I remember how Meagan would speak of your blue eyes (and hers were just like yours). She said some distant aunt of yours told you they had a luminous, unworldly color like a blue diamond (which I've never seen). Meagan said that when she was a child you would awaken her and she would look into your eyes and see God or a hint of heaven. If I were to look into the depth of a gem like that (or, for that matter, into a mirror in a brightly lit room), I would not see beauty or the hand of God. I would see the devil. And I would see me.*

Sincerely yours,
Jason Aldridge

CPSIA information can be obtained at www.ICGtesting.com
Printed in the USA
LVOW12s0042300415

436679LV00003B/3/P